People are raving about

THE
CALLER

'Be warned, this book will give you nightmares ...'

CRIME FICTION LOVER

'Another **killer of a book** by Chris Carter' **KATHRYN F.**

'Chris Carter is **outstanding** at making you feel part of the story ... an excellent read' **BEST CRIME BOOKS**

'If anything will stop you from using your mobile phone, this will'

AIMEE L.

'I absolutely **loved** *The Caller*' **JULIE O.**

'An **intriguing and scary** thriller' **BETTER READING**

'Chris Carter **has created a modern-day masterpiece**'

MICHAEL C.

'**Superb chiller** ... you won't be able to put this one down!'

BOOKS MONTHLY

'*The Caller* had me gripped from the word go. It's **truly terrifying**'

JADE H.

'Carter has delivered another **hit** ... I couldn't put it down'

CRIMESQUAD

'**Absorbing and unsettling** in equal measure'

BREAKAWAY REVIEWERS

'**Gripping and gruesome in equal measures**, *The Caller* is certainly not for the faint hearted!' **FIONA C.**

THE
CALLER

CHRISCARTER

**SIMON &
SCHUSTER**

London · New York · Sydney · Toronto · New Delhi

A CBS COMPANY

First published in Great Britain by Simon & Schuster UK Ltd, 2017
This paperback edition published 2017
A CBS COMPANY

1 3 5 7 9 10 8 6 4 2

Simon & Schuster UK Ltd
1st Floor
222 Gray's Inn Road
London WC1X 8HB

www.simonandschuster.co.uk

Simon & Schuster Australia, Sydney
Simon & Schuster India, New Delhi

A CIP catalogue record for this book
is available from the British Library

B format paperback ISBN: 978-1-4711-5632-8
A format paperback ISBN: 978-1-4711-5638-0
eBook ISBN: 978-1-4711-5633-5

Printed and bound by CPI Group (UK) Ltd, Croydon, CR0 4YY

Simon & Schuster UK Ltd are committed to sourcing paper
that is made from wood grown in sustainable forests and support the Forest
Stewardship Council, the leading international forest certification organisation.
Our books displaying the FSC logo are printed on FSC certified paper.

THE
CALLER

One

Tanya Kaitlin shut off the water, stepped out of the shower and slowly dried herself before putting on her favorite black and white bathrobe. That done, she reached for the matching towel that hung from one of the small hooks behind her bathroom door and wrapped it around her beach-blonde hair, turban-style. Despite being only lukewarm, her shower had produced more than enough steam to completely mist up the large mirror on the wall just above the black granite counter basin. Tanya stepped up to it and used her hand to clear a circular patch on the mirror. Leaning forward, she carefully studied her reflection. It took her only a couple of seconds to notice it.

'Oh, hell, no,' she said, turning her face so she could better see her right profile and using both of her index fingers to stretch a patch of skin by her chin. 'No fucking way, Mr. Zit. I see you coming.'

Tanya fought the urge to squeeze the small pimple. Instead, she opened the left drawer under the basin and began roaming through its contents like a woman on a mission. It was packed full of bottles, tubes and vials containing oils, creams, lotions, and whatever else new 'miracle' skin treatment had been recently advertised in any of the many fashion magazines she bought religiously.

'No, not you ... not you ...' she murmured as she moved items around. 'Where the hell is it? I have it, I know I have it.' The roaming became a little more frantic. 'Oh, here we go.' She breathed out a sigh of relief.

From deep inside the drawer she retrieved a small white tube with a roll-on tip at the top. She had never used that particular product before, but an article she'd read just days ago had rated it one of the best five acne-fighting 'potions' on the market at the moment. Not that Tanya had a problem with acne. In fact, she had incredibly healthy skin for a twenty-three-year-old, but she sure as hell was a 'just in case' girl. The amount of beauty products she had purchased over the past two years 'just in case' was staggering.

Tanya unscrewed the cap, rechecked her reflection in the mirror, and gently used the roll-on tip on the small pimple that was threatening to break out on her chin.

'That's right, Mr. Zit, you're zapped,' she said, looking triumphant. 'Now fuck off my chin. And you better do it before the weekend.'

Tanya was just about to start her body and face moisturizing ritual, when she heard a sound coming from her bedroom, or at least she thought she did. She opened the bathroom door, readjusted her turban to uncover her right ear, stuck her head outside, and listened for a brief moment. The quirky melody she heard told her that she was getting a video-call request from one of her three closest friends.

'Coming ... coming,' Tanya said, rushing out of the bathroom and into her bedroom. She found her smartphone vibrating on her bedside table. It was moving unevenly from side to side, as if it was dancing to the song itself. She snatched it up and checked the display screen – incoming video-call from her best friend, Karen Ward. The time read 10:39 p.m.

Holding the phone in front of her face, Tanya accepted the call. She and Karen video-called a lot.

'Hey, babe,' she said as she sat down at the edge of her bed. 'I just had to zap a zit on my chin, can you believe it?'

As the image materialized on her smartphone screen, Tanya frowned. Instead of seeing her best friend's face in full like every previous video-call they'd made to each other in the past, all Tanya could see was a close-up of Karen's deep-set blue eyes, nothing more. And they were full of tears.

'Karen, is everything OK?'

Karen didn't reply.

'Babe, what's going on?' This time, Tanya's voice was leaden with concern.

At last, and very slowly, the image began to zoom out, and as it did Tanya felt fear clothe her like an ill-fitting coat.

Karen's fair hair seemed drenched in sweat. It stuck to her clammy forehead and the sides of her face like moist paper. Heavy tears had caused her eye makeup to smudge and run down her cheeks, creating a crazy pathway of dark lines.

Tanya brought her phone closer to her face. 'Karen, what the fuck is going on? Are you all right?'

Again, no reply, but as the image continued to zoom out, Tanya finally realized why. A thick leather gag had been tied around Karen's mouth so tight it had skewed her face out of shape and dug into the corners of her lips. Blood had already begun to trickle down her chin.

'What the hell?' Tanya breathed out the words in a wavering voice. 'Karen, is this a fucking joke?'

'I'm afraid Karen isn't able to speak at the moment.'

The voice Tanya heard through her tiny smartphone speakers had somehow been digitally altered. Its pitch had been turned down several notches, making it sound scarily deep. Too deep for a human voice. A time delay had also been added to it, causing it to drag inconsistently. The result was a voice that could easily fit the image of a demon in a Hollywood movie. Tanya couldn't really tell if the voice was male or female.

'What . . .?' She frowned at her screen again. She could see no one else. 'Who is this?'

'Who I am is not important,' the demonic voice replied in a steady monotone. 'What's important is that you listen carefully, Tanya, and that you do not hang up the phone. You can't see me, but I can see you. If you hang up, the consequences will be severe . . . for Karen . . . and yourself.'

Tanya shook her head, as if trying to shake away a bad dream.

'What?'

Confusion turned into perplexity.

As the image zoomed out a little more on Tanya's screen, she was able to notice that a thick rope had been used to tie Karen up to a dining chair. Tanya narrowed her eyes at what she saw. She recognized the chair and the large poster on the wall just behind Karen. The images were being broadcasted from Karen's own living room.

Tanya paused, considered the situation for a quick second then tilted her head to one side skeptically. *This has to be a joke,* she thought. And then it dawned on her.

'Pete, are you back? Is that you with the fucking devil's voice?' Tanya's tone was now a little steadier. 'Are you guys fucking with me?' She undid the towel from around her head, allowing her damp hair to drop down to her shoulders.

No reply.

'Ha-ha-ha, you guys. C'mon Pete, Karen, quit it. This ain't funny, you know? It's quite freaky, actually. I nearly peed myself.'

Still no reply.

'C'mon, you guys. Stop it or I'll hang up.'

'I wouldn't do that if I were you,' the devilish voice finally answered, maintaining the same monotone as before. 'I'm not sure who Pete is, but maybe I should find out. Who knows, he could be next on my list.'

Still Tanya could see no one else on her screen other than Karen. Whoever the person with the demonic voice was, he or she was probably the one doing all the filming, though the phone had probably been placed on some sort of tripod, as the footage seemed rather steady for a handheld device.

This is nuts, she thought, keeping her gaze locked on to her best friend's eyes.

On the screen, Karen sucked in a deep breath and the air seemed to have entered her nose in thick lumps, because her entire head shook with the effort. New tears welled up in her eyes before overflowing them and running down her cheeks, creating even more dark-tear pathways.

Tanya knew Karen well enough to know that those tears weren't fake. Whatever it was that was happening, she now knew it was no prank.

'Though I'd love to chat some more,' the fiendish voice continued. 'Time is of the essence here, Tanya. At least for your friend, Karen. So let me tell you how this is going to work.'

Tanya tensed.

'I have placed a bet.'

Tanya wasn't sure if she'd heard right. 'What? A bet?'

'That's right,' the demon confirmed. 'I placed a bet with Karen here. If I lose, she will be set free and neither of you will ever hear from me again. I promise you that.'

There was a deliberate long pause.

'But if I win ...' The person at the other end of the line allowed those words to simply hang in the air ominously.

Tanya shook her head as she exhaled. 'I ... I don't understand.'

'It's a very simple game, Tanya. I call it, surprisingly enough, two questions.'

'Huh?'

'All you have to do is correctly answer two questions for me,' the inhuman voice explained. 'I'll ask them one at a time. You can give me as many answers as you like per question, but we can only move to the next question, or if we're talking about the second question, end the game, once you are able to give me a correct answer. If you take longer than five seconds to answer a question, it counts as a wrong answer. For your friend, Karen, to be set free, all I need is two correct answers.' There was a millisecond of a pause. 'I know, I know. It doesn't really sound like an exciting game, does it? But ... I guess we shall see.'

'Questions? What kind of questions?'

'Oh, don't worry. They're all directly related to you. You'll see.'

Tanya had to draw in a deep breath before she was able to speak again. 'And what happens every time I give you a wrong answer?'

Tanya's question caused Karen to shake her head ever so slightly. Her eyes widened, this time full of fear and terror.

'That's a very good question, Tanya,' the voice replied. 'I get the feeling that you're a smart woman. That's a good sign.'

There was silence for a moment, as if the line had gone dead. This was a product of the pitch shifter and time delay being used by the caller.

'What I can tell you is that, for Karen's sake, let's hope you don't.'

All of a sudden, Tanya's breathing became labored. She didn't want to play this game. And she didn't have to. All she had to do was hang up.

'If you hang up the phone,' the person at the other end of the line said, as if able to read Tanya's thoughts, 'Karen dies and I'll come after you next. If you disappear from the screen and I can't see you through your phone's camera anymore, Karen dies and I'll come after you next. If you try to call the police, Karen dies and I'll come after you next. But let me assure you that that would be a futile exercise, Tanya. It would take them nearly ten minutes to get here. It would take me only one to rip your friend's heart out of her chest and leave it on the table for them to find it. The blood inside her veins would still be warm by the time they got here.'

Those words sent bolts of fear down Karen and Tanya's spines. Karen immediately began screaming behind her leather gag and hysterically wiggling her body from side to side, trying to fight her restraints, but to no avail.

'Who are you?' Tanya asked, her voice beginning to falter. 'Why are you doing this to Karen?'

'I suggest that you concentrate on the problem at hand, Tanya. Think of Karen.'

It was then that Tanya saw new movement on the screen. Someone dressed all in black had positioned him or herself just behind the chair her best friend had been tied to, but Tanya couldn't really see past the person's torso.

'Jesus, what kind of sick prank is this?' she yelled at her phone, now fighting tears herself.

'No, Tanya,' the demon replied. 'This is no prank. This is as real as it gets. Shall we start?'

'No, wait . . .' Tanya pleaded, her heart now beating twice as fast as a few minutes ago.

But the person with the demonic voice wasn't listening anymore. 'Question one, Tanya: How many Facebook friends do you have?'

'What?' Confusion masked Tanya's face.

'How many Facebook friends do you have?' the voice repeated, this time a fraction slower than before.

OK, now this has to be a joke, Tanya thought. *What kind of silly question is that? Is this shit for real?*

'Five seconds, Tanya.'

Tanya's puzzled stare searched Karen's face. There was nothing there but fear.

The evil voice began counting down. 'Four ... three ... two ...'

Tanya barely had to think about it. She had checked her profile just before jumping in the shower. 'One thousand, one hundred and thirty-three,' she finally replied.

Silence.

The air inside Tanya's bedroom seemed to thicken like heavy smoke.

Finally, the person standing behind Karen's chair began applauding.

'That is one hundred percent correct, Tanya. You've got a

good memory. And that answer just got your friend one step closer to freedom. All you need to do now is answer one more question correctly and this will all be over.'

Another deliberate long pause.

Without realizing it, Tanya held her breath.

'Since Karen is your best friend, this next question should be a walk in the park for you.'

Tanya waited.

'What's Karen's cellphone number?'

Tanya's brow creased with doubt. 'Her number?'

This time the demon didn't repeat the question. It simply started the countdown. 'Five ... four ... three ...'

'But ... I don't know it by heart.'

'Two ...'

A choking knot came to Tanya's throat.

'One ...'

'This is stupid,' Tanya said with a jittery giggle. 'Give me a second and I'll get it for you.'

'I gave you five, and those five seconds are up. You haven't answered me.'

This time, there was a new tone underlying the demon's voice. A tone Tanya couldn't properly identify but, whatever it was, it filled her heart with terrorizing fear.

'You wanted to know what happens when you give me a wrong answer ... watch this.'

Two

Detective Robert Hunter of the LAPD Robbery Homicide Division noticed the redhead woman as soon as he entered the 24-hour reading room on the first floor of the historic Powell Library Building, which was part of the UCLA campus in Westwood. She was partially hidden behind a pile of leather-bound books, a coffee mug on the table in front of her. She was sitting alone, busy typing something on her laptop computer. As Hunter walked past her table on his way towards the one at the far corner of the large room, she met his gaze. There was nothing in it. No intrigue, no invitation, no flirt. Just a casual unconcerned look. A second later, her stare returned to her computer screen and the moment was over.

This was the third time Hunter had seen her in the library, always sitting behind a pile of books, always with a coffee mug in front of her, always by herself.

Hunter loved reading and consequently he loved the 24-hour reading room at the Powell Library, especially in the early hours of the morning on the nights his insomnia got the better of him.

In the USA, one in five people suffer from chronic insomnia, mostly brought on by a combination of work, financial and family-related stress. But in Hunter's case, the condition had grabbed hold of him way before he had to deal with the pressures of having a stressful job.

It all started just after his mother lost her battle with cancer. Hunter was only seven years old at the time. Back then, he would sit alone in his room at night, missing her, too sad to fall asleep, too scared to close his eyes, too proud to cry. The nightmares that followed his mother's death were so devastating to the young Robert Hunter that as a self-defense mechanism, his brain did all it could to keep him awake at night. Sleep became a luxury and a torment in equal measures and to keep his brain occupied during those endless sleepless hours, Hunter read ferociously, devouring books as if they empowered him. They became his sanctuary. His fortress. A safe place where the ghastly nightmares couldn't reach him.

As the years went by, Hunter's insomnia and nightmares subsided considerably, but just a couple of weeks after receiving his Ph.D. in Criminal Behavior Analyses and Biopsychology from Stanford University, his world crumbled before him for the second time. His father, who had never remarried and at the time was working as a security guard for a branch of the Bank of America in downtown Los Angeles, was gunned down during a robbery gone badly wrong. Hunter spent twelve weeks by his side in a hospital room while he lay in a coma. Hunter read him stories, told him jokes, held his hand for hours on end, but once again, love and hope proved not to be enough. When his father finally passed away, Hunter's insomnia and nightmares came back with a vengeance, and they had never left him since. On a good night, Hunter could probably manage to find three, maybe four hours of sleep. Tonight wasn't one of the good nights.

Hunter reached the last table at the end of the hall and checked his watch – 12:48 a.m. Like always, despite the late hour, the place was relatively busy, with a very steady flux of students all throughout the night.

He had a seat, making sure that he was facing the room, and flipped open the book he had with him. He read for about fifteen minutes before deciding that he too needed a cup of coffee. The closest vending machines were just outside the reading room, by the elevators. As Hunter crossed the library hall once again, he caught another glimpse of the redheaded woman. Though her stare reverted back to her laptop, it didn't do it quickly enough. She had been looking at him again but, despite being caught out, her body language gave no signs of her being embarrassed; on the contrary, it showed confidence.

The brand new coffee machine outside offered fifteen different types of coffee, nine of them flavored. The most extravagant one, which came loaded with whipped cream, caramel sauce and chocolate sprinkles, was served in a cup that held twenty fluid ounces. It was priced at $9.95. That made Hunter chuckle. Student prices and measures had come a long way since his college days.

'Unless you like your coffee sickly sweet, I'd stay clear of that one.'

The advice, which came from the person standing a few feet behind Hunter, caught him by surprise. As he turned, he found himself face to face with the redhead.

Her beauty was evident and intriguing at the same time. Her bright red hair, which fell just past her shoulders, was naturally wavy, with her fringe looping above her forehead and slightly to the right, creating a charming victory roll – pin-up style. She wore old-fashioned, black-framed cat-eye glasses that perfectly suited her heart-shaped face and gently called attention to her green eyes. Centered just under her bottom lip, she had a labret piercing, with a dainty black stone stud. Her septum was also pierced, showing a delicate silver ring. She was dressed in a black and red 1950s-inspired rockabilly dress, which exposed her arms in full. They were both covered from shoulder to wrist in colorful tattoos. Her Mary-Jane shoes matched the colors on her dress.

'The option you were looking at,' she clarified, sensing Hunter's confusion and pointing at the machine with her empty coffee mug. 'The Caramel Frappuccino Deluxe? That one's excessively sweet, so unless that's your thing, I wouldn't go there.'

Hunter hadn't realized that he'd been checking the selection so attentively.

'I'd say that sweet isn't the only thing it excels at then,' he replied, quickly peeking over his shoulder. 'Ten bucks for a cup of coffee?'

Her lips parted into an agreeing smile that was both charming and shy.

'I've seen you here in the library before,' she said, moving the subject away from 'sweet and expensive coffees'. 'Are you a student here at UCLA?'

Hunter regarded the woman in front of him for an extra moment. Age-wise, it was hard to place her. She carried herself with the pride and authority of a head-of-state, but her delicate features could belong to a college senior. Her voice also gave little away, bearing a gentle, girlish tone combined with enough self-assurance to disarm the most confident of guesses.

'No,' Hunter replied, honestly amused by her question. He knew that he looked nothing like a college student anymore. 'My student days are well and truly over. I just ...' His eyes moved past her and on to the reading room. 'Like coming here at night. I like the serenity of this place.'

His answer brought a new smile to the woman's lips.

'I guess I know what you mean,' she said, as she turned and allowed her gaze to follow Hunter's through the doors and into the large reading room, transitioning from the checkered wooden floor to the dark mahogany tables, and finally to the large, gothic-styled windows. 'Plus,' she added, 'I also like the smell of this place.'

Hunter frowned at her.

Her head tilted sideways slightly as she explained. 'I always thought that if you could put a scent to knowledge, this would be it, don't you think? A combination of paper, both old and new, leather, mahogany ...' Her quick pause was shadowed by a shrug. 'Overpriced coffees, and students' stale sweat.'

This time Hunter returned her smile. He liked her sense of humor.

'I'm Tracy,' she said, offering her hand. 'Tracy Adams.'

'Robert Hunter. Pleasure to meet you.'

Despite her delicate hands, her handshake was firm and strong.

'Please,' Hunter said, taking a step to his right as he nodded, first at Tracy's empty coffee mug then at the vending machine. 'Be my guest.'

'Oh no, you were here first,' Tracy replied. 'I'm in no rush.'

'It's OK, really, I'm still deciding,' Hunter lied. He only drank black, unsweetened coffee.

'Oh, OK. In that case, thank you.' Tracy stepped up to the machine, placed her mug on the designated spot, slotted some coins into it and made her selection – regular black. No sugar.

'So, how are the classes going so far?' Hunter asked.

'Oh no,' Tracy replied, collecting her mug and turning to face him. 'I'm not a student here either.'

Hunter nodded. 'I know. You're a professor, right?'

Tracy looked at him curiously and with an intense, searching gaze, but his expression revealed nothing at all. That just served to intrigue her further.

'That's right, I am, but how did you know?'

Hunter tried to shrug it off. 'Oh, just a guess, really.'

Tracy didn't buy it.

'No way.'

She quickly thought back to the leather-bound volumes she had on her table. None of their titles really hinted at her occupation, and even if they did, Hunter would've needed super-human vision to be able to read them from where he'd been sitting, or as he walked past her table.

'That was too confident a statement for it to be a guess. Somehow you already knew. How?' The look in her eyes was now very skeptical.

'Just simple observation,' Hunter replied, but before he could develop his answer any further, he felt his cellphone vibrate inside his jacket pocket. He reached for it and checked the display screen.

'Excuse me for a moment,' he said, bringing the phone to his ear. 'Detective Hunter, Homicide Special.'

Tracy's eyebrows arched. She wasn't expecting that. A few seconds later she saw his whole expression change.

'OK,' Hunter said into his cellphone, checking his watch – 1:14 a.m. 'I'm on my way.' He disconnected and looked back at Tracy. 'It really was a pleasure to meet you. Enjoy your coffee.'

Tracy hesitated for an instant.

'You forgot your book,' she called out after him, but Hunter was already halfway down the stairs.

Three

The LAPD's Homicide Special Section (HSS) was an elite branch of its Robbery Homicide Division. It had been created to deal solely with serial and high-profile homicide cases, and cases requiring extensive investigative time and expertise. Due to Hunter's criminal behavior psychology background and the fact that Los Angeles seemed to attract a particular breed of sociopaths, he was placed in an even more specialized entity within the HSS. All homicides where overwhelming brutality and/or sadism had been used by the perpetrator were tagged by the department as UVC – Ultra Violent Crimes. Robert Hunter and his partner, Carlos Garcia, were the HSS UVC Unit.

The address Hunter was given took him to Long Beach, more specifically, to a three-story, terracotta building that was sandwiched between a drugstore and a corner house. Even at that time in the morning, and taking the fastest route possible, it took him nearly an hour to cover the thirty-five miles from the UCLA Campus in Westwood to the Harbor.

He saw the concentration of black and white units as soon as he exited Redondo Avenue and turned left on to East

Broadway. A section of the Broadway had already been cordoned off by Long Beach PD. Garcia's metallic-blue Honda
Civic was parked just across the road from the three-story
building, by a white forensics-unit van.

Hunter had to slow down to an almost crawl as he
approached the cordoned-off area. In a city that barely slept,
it was no surprise that a small crowd of curious onlookers
had already gathered by the police tape. Most of them had
their arms extended above their heads, filming away on their
cellphones or tablet devices, as if they were at some sort of
musical concert, all of them hoping for at least a glimpse of
something. And the more gruesome the better.

Once he finally cleared the crowd, Hunter displayed his
credentials to the two uniformed officers by the black and
yellow crime-scene tape and parked just next to his partner's car. As he stepped out of his beat-up Buick LeSabre, he
stretched his six-foot frame against the cold early-morning
wind. Menacing, dense clouds had covered the sky, hiding
the stars and adding a new layer of darkness to the night.
Hunter clipped his badge on to his belt and looked around
slowly. The road segment that had been cordoned off by the
police was about one hundred yards long, running from the
intersection with Newport Avenue, all the way to Loma, the
next avenue along.

The first thought that came to Hunter was that the location provided a wide selection of escape routes, with a major
freeway less than a mile and a half away. But it really didn't
matter if the perpetrator was driving or not, anonymously
disappearing down any of those roads wouldn't have been a
problem for anyone.

Garcia, who had been standing by a black and white unit,

talking to an officer from the Long Beach Police Department, had spotted Hunter's car as it cleared the crime-scene tape.

'Robert,' he called as he crossed the road.

Hunter turned to face his partner.

Garcia's longish brown hair was pulled back into a sleek ponytail. He wore dark trousers with a crisp light-blue shirt underneath a black jacket. Though he seemed wide-awake and his attire could've come straight out of a dry cleaner's, his eyes looked tired and bloodshot. Unlike Hunter, Garcia usually slept well at night. Tonight, though, he'd been asleep for only two hours before he was dragged out of bed by an LAPD phone call.

'Carlos,' Hunter said, greeting his partner with a head gesture. 'Sorry about the early call, buddy. So what have we got?'

'I'm not sure yet,' Garcia replied with a subtle headshake. 'I got here a couple of minutes before you did. I was just trying to find out who the officer in change was when I saw you clear the police line.'

Hunter's gaze moved from his partner and refocused on the person approaching them from behind Garcia. He was coming from the terracotta building.

'I guess he found us,' Hunter said.

Garcia turned on the balls of his feet.

'You guys from Ultra Violent Crimes?' the man asked in a voice clearly battered by years of cigarette smoking. The embroidered chevrons on the upper sleeves of his jacket told Hunter and Garcia that he was a second-level sergeant with the Long Beach Police Department. He looked to be in his late forties or early fifties. His thick peppery hair was brushed back off his high forehead, revealing a small jagged scar just above his left eyebrow. He spoke with a light Mexican accent.

'That's correct,' Hunter replied as he and Garcia stepped forward to meet him. They all introduced themselves with firm handshakes. The sergeant's name was Manuel Velasquez.

'So what have we got here, Sergeant?' Garcia asked.

Sergeant Velasquez chuckled at the question, but it was a nervous, full-of-hesitation chuckle.

'I'm not really sure I could describe what's in there in words,' he replied, turning to face the building behind him. 'I'm not sure anyone can. You guys are going to have to go see it for yourselves.'

Four

Guided by a gust of autumn wind, which had strengthened considerably in the past couple of minutes, the cluster of heavy clouds above them had thickened, and as Hunter, Garcia and Velasquez began walking towards the terracotta building, the first drops of rain splashed against their heads and the dry asphalt.

'The victim's name was Karen Ward,' Sergeant Velasquez announced, picking up the pace to escape the rain and leading Hunter and Garcia up the few concrete steps that led to the building's entrance door. Instead of relying on memory, he reached for his notepad and flipped it open. 'She was twenty-four years old, single and worked as a cosmetologist in a beauty spa on East Second Street.' Instinctively he indicated east. 'Not that far from here, actually. She'd been living in this building for only four months.'

'Rented?' Garcia asked as they entered the building.

'That's right. The owner and landlady is one ...' He flipped a page on his notepad. 'Nancy Rogers, resident of Torrance, in South Bay.'

'Burglary?' Hunter this time.

An uneasy shake of the head from Velasquez.

'Nope, and the perpetrator didn't even try to make it look like one. No apparent sign of a break-in or a struggle either. Her handbag was found on the sofa in the living room. Her purse was inside it with two credit cards and eighty-seven dollars in cash. Her car keys were also inside her bag. Her laptop was in her bedroom, where we also found a few pieces of jewelry on top of a dresser. Wardrobes, drawers, cabinets . . . nothing seems to have been touched.'

At the building's front door, the only security the place seemed to offer its residents came in the shape of an old intercom entry system. There were no CCTV cameras.

'Did she live alone?'

'That's correct,' the sergeant replied with nod.

With the building offering no elevator, Hunter and Garcia followed Velasquez up a second set of stairs and then a third to the top floor.

'I've had cops on every floor doing a door-to-door,' Sergeant Velasquez informed them. 'Nothing.' He made a not very surprised face. 'Nobody saw or heard anything.'

'Not even her next-door neighbor?' Hunter asked.

The sergeant shook his head. 'Her next-door neighbors are a middle-aged couple,' Velasquez explained. 'Mr. and Mrs. Santiago. They both have hearing problems. I talked to them myself, but even with the loud knocks, it took Mr. Santiago almost an hour to answer the door, and he only did it because he got up in the middle of the night to take a leak, that was when he heard us knocking.'

The stairs led them to a long and narrow corridor, now brightly lit by powerful forensics spotlights. Karen Ward's apartment was number 305, the last one on the right. Nicholas Holden, one of the CSI team's fingerprint experts, was kneeling outside her front door, busy dusting it for latent prints.

'You mentioned that she was single,' Garcia said as they made their way down the corridor.

'She was,' Velasquez confirmed.

'Do you know if she was seeing anyone? Had a boyfriend?'

The sergeant knew exactly why Garcia had asked that question – a young woman is brutally murdered inside her own apartment without any apparent motive and no signs of a break-in, and the names that will comprise the initial 'person of interest list' will belong mainly to the people with whom the victim might've had any sort of romantic involvement in the past few years. In the USA, so called 'crimes of passion' account for over half of violent homicides committed against women.

'Sorry, Detective, but we didn't have time to gather that sort of information.' The sergeant clarified, glancing at his watch. 'The truth is, we were able to find out very little about the victim and what happened in her apartment before it was confirmed that this investigation was to be passed on to the LAPD's UVC Unit.' He paused and turned to face both detectives. 'Frankly, those kind of decisions usually piss me off. This is our jurisdiction, so this should be our investigation, *comprendes*? We're not "little league" over here. But this case had Violent Crimes Unit written all over it from the get-go, so we were all expecting it anyway.' He showed Hunter and Garcia his palms in a surrender gesture. 'And in this case, you'll get no complaints from me, or any of my men. You want that evil in there ... you won't have to ask twice. It's all yours.'

Hunter and Garcia were now frowning at Velasquez.

'Hold on a sec,' Garcia said. 'What do you mean – "this case had Violent Crimes Unit written all over it from the get-go"?'

The sergeant's stare moved from Garcia to Hunter and then back to Garcia. 'You weren't told about the phone call?'

The reply from both detectives came in the form of inquisitive silence.

'Oh, man!' Sergeant Velasquez looked down at the floor while shaking his head. 'OK,' he began. 'Nine-one-one received a call from a semi-hysterical woman at around eleven-twenty last night. The woman was making very little sense, but she was screaming the word "murder". As we all know, that's a "red flag". The call was transferred to our precinct and then to my desk.'

'So you talked to her yourself?' Garcia asked.

The sergeant nodded. 'And she was indeed hysterical, claiming that someone had murdered her best friend right in front of her eyes.' He paused, lifting his right index finger as he clarified. 'Well, not exactly right in front of her eyes, but she was allowed to . . . or better yet, forced to watch it via a video-call.'

'I'm sorry?' Garcia's unsure look had quickly turned into a confused one.

'You heard right, Detective. The woman was yelling down the phone, claiming that some psycho had called her *from* Miss Ward's cellphone, and forced her to play some sort of game, in which her friend's life depended on it.'

'A game?' Hunter this time.

'That's what she said, yes. Look, I don't know the specifics because, as I've said, the woman was going hysterical. The first thing I needed to do was follow protocol and send a black-and-white unit down here to check on the alleged murder victim, a Miss Karen Ward. A couple of uniforms drove by just before midnight and guess what? The door was unlocked. They walked in to check on her and ... you guys being here is the result.'

'You said that this hysterical woman claimed to be the victim's best friend?' Garcia asked.

Velasquez nodded. 'Her name is Tanya Kaitlin. I have her details back in my vehicle. I'll get them all to you before you go.'

As Hunter, Garcia and Velasquez finally reached apartment 305, Hunter greeted the CSI fingerprint expert. 'Hey, Nick.'

'Hey guys,' the agent replied robotically.

After signing the crime-scene manifesto, Hunter, Garcia and Velasquez were handed a disposable white Tyvek jumpsuit each, together with a pair of latex gloves. As they began suiting up, Hunter noticed the fire exit door at the end of the corridor, past Karen Ward's apartment.

'Where does that lead to, do you know?'

'Metal stairs that will take you down to an alleyway at the back of the building,' Velasquez explained. 'Go left and you'll come out on Newport Avenue. Go right and you're on Loma Avenue.'

Before zipping up his jumpsuit, Hunter walked over to the exit door to have a better look at it. The internal push bar on the fire resistant door indicated that it could only be opened from his side. It would offer no access into the building, but coming from apartment 305 it would've provided a much faster exit route than tracking back down the corridor all the way to the concrete staircase at the other end.

Hunter pushed the bar down, unlocking the door. Not a sound. The door wasn't alarmed. As he turned to face the door to apartment 305 again, he noticed the CSI agent tilting his head to one side first, staring at the door, then tilting it to the other side and staring at it again.

'Find something, Nick?'

'Just checking against the light,' Holden replied without deviating his attention from his work, his nose mask bobbing up and down as he spoke. 'But I'd say that so far we've got about three different sets of prints here, and I've just got started.'

Hunter nodded his understanding. 'Could you do us a favor and also dust the fire exit door when you're done there? I'd like to run a comparison test between the fingerprints found on both doors.'

Holden glanced at the fire exit. 'Sure. No problem.'

Both detectives finished suiting up and pulled the hoods of their coveralls over their heads; a second later they stepped into apartment 305.

Five

Karen Ward's front door opened into a small entrance hall with a couple of large flower prints hanging from its white walls. A warm-red anti-slip rug greeted everyone as they walked through the door. Separation between the hall and the rest of the apartment came via a makeshift chimed beaded-curtain that dropped from the ceiling in uneven strands.

Hunter hadn't seen one of those since he was a young kid. His grandmother used to have one in her kitchen.

The chimes rang noisily as he pulled the curtain to one side and he and Garcia stepped through into the apartment's living room. Before following them inside, Sergeant Velasquez crossed himself, murmuring a few Spanish words as he did so.

The living room was relatively spacious and it had been pleasantly decorated with just a few well-chosen pieces of modern furniture, but its main feature was no doubt the large, glass sliding doors behind another beaded-curtain at the far end of the room, leading out into a corner balcony. A compact open-plan kitchen sat against the north wall. Strategically positioned to separate the kitchen from the living room area was a dark pinewood, four-seater dining table. On the other side of the table, by a dark wood display cabinet, there was a full length mirror. Both detectives paused as they entered the room, their attention immediately drawn to the chair at the head of the table and to the horribly mutilated body sitting on it.

Hunter's eyes narrowed as his brain picked up the pace to try to understand the savagery he was looking at.

The victim had been stripped naked. Her arms had been pinned down to the sides of her body by a thin nylon rope, which tightly looped several times around her torso, just under her breasts, and around the back of the chair. Two separate pieces of rope had been used to securely restrain her ankles to the legs of the chair. She was sitting upright, with her head slightly slumped forward, as if she had fallen asleep, bringing her chin to less than an inch from her chest. But what made Hunter doubt his eyes were the many shards of thick, mirrored glass that had been violently rammed into the woman's face, disfiguring it into an unrecognizable mess of skin, glass and flesh. Blood had cascaded from her facial wounds in heavy sheets, covering her entire torso and thighs in crimson red before dripping down on to the wooden floor and pooling up under the chair. Part of the tabletop, just by where the victim had been sitting, had also been sprinkled by blood.

From where Hunter and Garcia were standing, what once was her face now looked like a grotesque human pincushion, with numerous glass spikes protruding from it in all different directions.

'I'm guessing you two are with the UVC Unit.'

Those words came from the forensics agent who had been carefully collecting hairs and fibers from the large rug in the main living room area, just past the dining table.

A couple of silent seconds went by before Hunter and Garcia finally managed to drag their attention away from the body.

'I'm Dr. Susan Slater,' the agent said, getting up from her kneeling position. 'I'm the lead forensics agent assigned to this scene.'

Neither Hunter nor Garcia had ever worked with Dr. Slater before. She was about five-foot seven and looked to be in her early thirties, with a slim body, high cheekbones and a delicate nose. Her head was covered by the hood of her Tyvek jumpsuit, but a thin sliver of blonde hair could still be seen cutting across the top of her forehead. Her makeup was subtle and work-like, but effective enough to keep her attractiveness and femininity even under the unappealing white coverall. Her voice had an odd tone to it – soft and jovial, but at the same time giving the impression of being full of experience and knowledge.

'Detective Robert Hunter, LAPD UVC Unit. This is Detective Carlos Garcia.' They both greeted the doctor with a simple head nod before reverting their attention back to the victim.

'It boggles the mind, doesn't it?' Dr. Slater commented. 'How can anyone do something like that to another human being?'

'The killer stabbed her in the face with glass shanks?' Garcia asked, his expression clearly revealing his disbelief in his own words.

'Might've done, Detective,' Dr. Slater replied. 'That's impossible to tell without a proper autopsy examination but, if that's the case, that's only part of the story.'

'So what's the other part?' Garcia asked.

She took a couple of steps towards the victim. 'Let me show you.'

Hunter and Garcia followed her. Sergeant Velasquez stayed by the chimed curtains.

Being careful to avoid the pool of blood on the floor, Dr. Slater squatted down by the side of the chair and beckoned Hunter and Garcia to do the same. Up close, the injuries to Karen Ward's face were even more disturbing.

Several different-sized shards of mirrored glass had sliced through her skin and muscle tissue, practically tearing her face from its skeleton structure. Slabs of skin and flesh dangled loosely from her cheeks, her forehead, and her chin, where bone had also been exposed.

'You see,' Dr. Slater began, 'if you look only at the large shards of glass ...' She indicated the ones protruding from the victim's right and left cheek, left eye socket, and the one that had completely traversed the victim's under-chin soft tissue, pinning her tongue to the lower part of her mouth. 'The impression that you get is that the perpetrator violently stabbed the victim with improvised glass shanks, leaving each and every one embedded in her face as he did. Some were rammed into her face so hard, they have either fractured bone, or implanted themselves into it.' She called their attention to two other pieces of glass – one sticking out of the victim's lower jawbone, the other from her forehead. 'But that's not all we have here, Detectives. There's an even larger number of smaller pieces of glass entrenched in her flesh.' She indicated a few of them as she spoke. Some were as small as a pea. 'These pieces are small enough to make it physically impossible for anyone to be able to use them as some sort of stabbing weapon. They are impact residue. Broken pieces from larger ones.'

Hunter tilted his head left then right as he studied the victim's face. Despite all his experience, he still couldn't help but cringe at the ferocity of her wounds. Each one would've brought with it a whole new dimension of pain. What that young woman must've suffered was almost unimaginable.

Dried blood covered most of her body, making it hard to be certain, but the impression Hunter got was that she carried no other wounds or bruises anywhere else. The killer's rage had been exclusively directed at her face.

After several seconds, Hunter stood up and repositioned himself behind the chair to have a better look at the back of the victim's head.

'So what are you saying, doc?' Garcia asked. 'That the killer tied her to this chair and then slammed glass sheets into her face?'

'No,' Hunter was the one who replied, turning to look at the floor behind the victim's chair – no glass residue. 'The inverted motion, Carlos,' he explained. 'The killer rammed her face into glass.'

Six

A few hours earlier

'This is stupid,' Tanya Kaitlin said with a jittery giggle. 'Give me a second and I'll get her number for you.'

'I gave you five,' the demonic voice replied. 'And those five seconds are up.

'You wanted to know what happens when you give me a wrong answer ... watch this.'

All of a sudden and to Tanya's surprise, the person standing behind Karen's chair grabbed hold of the leather gag around Karen's mouth and, in one violent movement, yanked it down and off her lips so hard, it tore a gash to the right side of her bottom lip. Speckles of blood flew up into the air.

Tanya's eyes were filled with shock as she struggled to understand what was really going on.

Before Karen could let go of a scream that must've been locked inside her throat for God-knows-how-long, Tanya saw her assailant place a gloved hand on the back of her head. A split second later, she heard a crushing noise as Karen's head and face were firmly pushed forward and slammed down against something that had been previously placed in front of her.

Tanya couldn't quite see what it was.

'Oh my God!' she screamed, her own head jerking back in horror. Despite how spooked she was, she never let go of her phone. 'What are you doing? What the hell are you doing?' Her tone lifted with a mixture of anxiety and fear.

The same gloved hand grabbed Karen by the hair and brought her head back up to its starting position. As her face filled the small screen on Tanya's phone again, Tanya felt vomit travel up from her stomach and stand fast at the base of her throat.

Three large shards of glass had embedded themselves on to Karen's face. The first one, about three inches long, had sliced through Karen's left cheek. Its tip, which was now sitting inside Karen's mouth, had also severed a small section of her tongue. The second piece of glass, this one much smaller than the one in her left cheek, had penetrated Karen's right nostril, ripping a whole at the top of her nose. The third and last piece, which was about one and a half inches long, was protruding from her bloody forehead.

Tanya was no expert, but she was sure that the glass had hit bone. 'Oh, my God, no ... what the hell are you doing?' Tanya's words were drowning on tears. 'Karen ... no ...'

'Look ...' the demonic voice said threateningly, moving Karen's face from left to right ever so slightly to better display the extent of her injuries. 'Look ...'

Tanya was staring straight at the camera in her phone.

'Look ...' the demon said again.

'I *am* looking ...' Tanya's voice squealed with agony, as if she could physically feel her friend's pain. 'Oh, my God,

Karen . . .' With her left hand, she desperately began wiping tears from her eyes and cheeks.

'She's your best friend, Tanya,' the demonic voice came back. 'She has been so for many years. You should know her number by heart. What kind of friend are you, really?'

'I know . . . I know . . .' Tanya could do nothing but sob. 'I'm so sorry.'

'You don't need to be sorry. What you need to do is answer me. You have five seconds.'

'No . . . ple- . . . please don't do that.'

'Five . . . four . . . three . . .'

Tanya sobbed as her fingers ferociously attacked her touch-screen. 'I'll get it. Just give me a moment. I'll get it.' Tears blurred her vision. Fear made her hands unsteady.

'Two . . .'

'Please . . . Don't.'

'One . . .'

In her panic, Tanya dropped her phone. It fell down on to her bed with the screen facing down.

'Oh no, no, no.'

'Time's up.'

SLAM.

As she fumbled for her phone, Tanya heard the same crushing noise as before, only louder. She flipped the phone over just in time to see the gloved hand bring Karen's head back up again.

Tanya froze.

Karen's face was utterly unrecognizable. The new head-smash had caused several new shards of glass, big and small, to lodge themselves into her flesh, shredding her face into a horror mask. But what brought Tanya to a hair away from fainting was the new piece of glass that had punctured Karen's left eye, eviscerating her ocular globe. A viscous substance had begun oozing from it, but the glass piece hadn't traveled deep enough to reach her brain. Tanya could tell that Karen was still conscious.

'Her number,' the demon demanded yet again, but Tanya's nerves had turned to mush. Her fingers were trembling uncontrollably. Her vision was blurred by a barrage of never-ending tears. Her breathing had become labored and erratic. She tried to speak but her voice got caught somewhere between her throat and her lips.

The countdown began again. Tanya didn't even hear it get from five to one. All she heard was – 'time's up' – then ...

SLAM.

SLAM.

SLAM.

Three times in quick succession, each harder than the previous one. The last crunch noise was followed by a faint gasp from Karen.

The gloved hand brought Karen's head back up, and everything went silent for a while. Her lips had been so severely sliced they were hanging off to one side awkwardly. Her nose had been slashed from the bottom up, rupturing most of its cartilage. Its tip was now held in place only by a thin piece of skin. Her right eye had now also been punctured. Blood seeped out of it in wide sheets. The three head slams had driven the piece of glass that had penetrated Karen's left eye deeper into her eye socket.

Though Tanya felt faint, she found herself unable to look away, her eyes paralyzed by the grotesque images.

On the screen, Karen convulsed twice. With the second

one, her head went completely limp. The gloved hand held it in place for another twenty seconds before finally letting go of her hair.

Her lifeless body slumped forward one final time.

'I guess this game was exciting after all,' the demon said. 'And just look at what you've done, Tanya. You've killed your friend. Congratulations.'

'Nooooooo!' Tanya's scream came out as an undecipherable shriek.

'You can now go back to your pathetic life.'

The demon moved from behind the chair and reached for Karen's smartphone to end the call, but as he grabbed it, the phone panned upwards just enough.

Tanya's body went rigid.

For a second, she was given a glimpse of the demon's face, and what she saw made vomit explode from her mouth.

Seven

Garcia's gaze first moved to the pool of blood under the chair then to the sprinkles on the tabletop. He'd been so taken aback by the ferocity of the victim's wounds that until then he had failed to notice that except from the ones projecting out of the victim's face, there were no pieces of glass anywhere else.

'That's the exact same conclusion I came to,' Dr. Slater agreed, as she joined Hunter behind the victim's chair. 'The way in which she'd been tied up, with the rope looping around the mid-section of her abdomen, would've easily allowed the perpetrator to grab her head and slam her face forward and downward.' She pretended to grip the victim by the hair on the back of her head and simulated the movement. 'The slam-down would've been fast and hard.'

Garcia walked around the table to the other side, his eyes still searching the floor. 'So the speculation is that the killer placed some sort of container filled with glass pieces in front of her, maybe on the table, maybe on her lap, grabbed her by the hair and slammed her face into it?'

Sergeant Velasquez, who was still standing by the beaded curtain, grinded his teeth as he readjusted his weight, shifting from one foot to another.

'As absurd and sadistic as that might sound, Detective,' Dr. Slater replied, 'that theory is right at the top of the list at the moment.'

'Have you found this ... container?' Garcia asked.

'No, not yet,' the doctor admitted. 'But I can certainly tell you where the glass came from.'

Eight

Hunter, Garcia and Sergeant Velasquez followed Dr. Slater through the short hallway that led deeper into apartment 305. The corridor offered three new doors – one on the left, one on the right, and one at the far end of it. She guided them into the door on the left.

The apartment's only bathroom was of a comfortable size and tiled all in white. A beige ceramic bathtub hugged the south wall, with a showerhead directly above it on the right-hand side. A see-through shower curtain, which had been pushed to one side, dropped down from a metal rail. No explanation was needed. As soon as they entered the bathroom they immediately understood what Dr. Slater had meant when she'd said that she knew where the glass had come from. The entire south wall, spanning all the way from the ceiling down to the edge of the bathtub, was a huge wall-to-wall mirror. It had been completely smashed. Most of it was now gone. All that was left were a few shattered pieces still stuck to a couple of corners.

'The supply was vast and plenty,' the doctor said. 'The killer didn't have to look far.'

From the bathroom door, Hunter and Garcia regarded

what was left of the mirror before stepping forward to have a look inside the bathtub. Nothing. It was completely clean. Not even minor splinters of mirrored glass had been left behind. The killer had either been very meticulous while collecting the pieces of broken mirror that had surely fallen into the bathtub, or had very carefully lined it with some sort of protective sheet.

Garcia took a step back and studied the rest of the bathroom. The washbasin was positioned to the right of the door, the toilet to the left. A six-shelf unit, which held a multitude of toiletry items and perfume bottles, sat between the bathtub and the toilet. A digital scale was propped against the unit. A pink bathrobe hung from the single hook behind the door.

'Any guesses as to the time of death?' Hunter asked.

'The first signs of rigor mortis are just beginning to set in,' Dr. Slater answered. 'So I'd say more than two and a half hours ago, but less than four.'

Hunter consulted his timepiece – 2:42 a.m. 'Has her cellphone been found?' he asked.

'Yes,' Doctor Slater replied. 'Inside the microwave, nuked to high heaven.'

'How about a computer, or a laptop?'

'Her laptop was found on the sofa in the living room. We'll take it to IT forensics when we're done here.'

Hunter acknowledged it, but he suspected that IT Forensics wouldn't really find anything. Why would the killer destroy the victim's phone, but leave her laptop intact? He walked over to the washbasin and pulled open the cupboard mirror above it. Inside it he found all the usual suspects – toothbrush, toothpaste, mouthwash, Band-Aids, eye drops, and a couple of boxes of strong headache pills. There was also a full bottle of sleeping tablets. The trashcan to the left of the toilet was empty. With the exception of the broken wall mirror, nothing else inside the bathroom seemed to have been touched.

Hunter stepped back into the corridor and tried the door on the right-hand side. Just a small storage room where the victim kept several miscellaneous items, together with various house-cleaning products. He closed the door and moved on to the one at the far end of the hall – Karen Ward's bedroom.

The room was spacious enough, with a low queen bed, a black fabric armchair, a four-drawer dresser, and an eight-shelf wooden shoe rack. Instead of a wardrobe, Karen Ward had preferred to have her clothes hanging from an extra-wide chrome clothes rack. Despite one of the room's two west-facing windows being partially covered by the clothes rack, the room would still get enough sunlight during the day.

As Hunter's eyes carefully circled the room, something began bothering him. He walked over to the bed, which had been positioned against the east wall, stopped and turned to face the clothes rack all the way across the room from it.

This doesn't feel right, he thought.

The clothes rack was flanked on one side by the armchair and on the other by the dresser. The shoe rack was to the right of the door, against the north wall, every inch of space on it taken. There was only one bedside table, on the near side of the bed. On it Hunter found a reading lamp, a digital alarm clock, and a dog-eared paperback. He pulled open the bedside table's only drawer and paused.

'Carlos, come have a look at this.'

Garcia walked over to where his partner was standing.

From inside the drawer, Hunter retrieved a thirty-eight caliber, Colt 1911, Special Combat pistol.

'Whoa,' Garcia said, lifting both hands in surprise. 'That's one hell of a gun to have by your bed.'

'She's got a permit for it,' Hunter announced, indicating the official document inside the open drawer. On the pistol, he thumbed the catch to release the magazine. If the gun had surprised them, its ammunition took it a step further. The clip was full to capacity with nine thirty-eight Special, Flex Tip bullets.

Hunter and Garcia exchanged a concerned look.

The Flex Tip bullet was a patented design by Hornady Ammunition, and it was part of its Critical Defense range. Both detectives were very familiar with it. It was an extremely destructive round; upon entering soft tissue, its flexible tip would swell up, distributing equal pressure across the entire circumference of the bullet cavity. The result was total bullet expansion and maximum damage. Flex Tip bullets weren't the type of round used for target practice.

Hunter slotted the magazine back into the pistol and returned it to the drawer. Other than the gun permit, there was nothing else inside it.

'You mentioned that the victim's handbag was found on the sofa in the living room,' Hunter said, addressing Sergeant Velasquez.

'Yes, that's correct.'

'Anything interesting inside it?'

'No.'

Hunter scratched the underside of his chin and took a slow stroll around the room, his eyes roaming everywhere. He paused momentarily as he reached the space between the clothes rack and the dresser before returning to the side of the bed. His attention went back to the bedside table.

'This feels all wrong.'

'What does?' Garcia asked. 'The gun?'

'That too,' Hunter confirmed. 'But I'm talking about this room.'

With an unsure look, Garcia looked around the space.

Hunter saw Dr. Slater and Sergeant Velasquez do the same.

'What do you mean, Robert?' Garcia queried.

'If this was your room,' Hunter said, 'and these were your things, would you arrange it this way?'

Garcia took a moment, allowing his gaze to pause over each furniture item for a few seconds. 'Well, I ... probably wouldn't need the shoe rack, or the dresser with all the makeup paraphernalia.'

'No, that's not what I mean, Carlos. I'm talking about the position of the bed, the clothes rack ... everything you see in here. If this was your room and this was your furniture, would you *arrange* it like this?'

Once again, Garcia regarded the room and its contents, this time paying more attention to their positioning. 'Well, it does feel a little too crammed in here.'

'Exactly,' Hunter agreed.

'But it's not because of lack of space,' Dr. Slater cut in, her gaze moving from floor to ceiling then from wall to wall. 'This is a large enough room. The problem here really is the furniture placement. If you just move a few things around, the room would feel much bigger.'

'OK,' Hunter went with it. 'So what would you change? What would you move around?'

Everyone looked like they were thinking about it for a short moment.

'I'd probably swop the bed with the clothes rack for starters.' Garcia was the first to reply.

Dr. Slater nodded. 'For sure. Just look at this. The bed's footboard is just a few feet from the door, practically blocking your path as you enter the room. Take your attention away from it for just a second, and you'd bang your leg against it every time. There's also no real need to block half of that window,' she added, gesturing towards it. 'If you just swop the bed and the clothes rack around, the room wouldn't only feel a lot more spacious, it would also become much brighter during the day.'

'Maybe it's an energy thing,' Sergeant Velasquez proposed from the door. 'You know . . . like that feng something.'

'Feng shui,' Garcia said.

'That's it. Maybe she was going for that kind of feel.'

Hunter shook his head. 'No. The principle of feng shui is that energy should flow unrestricted and uninterrupted. In this case, the energy from the door would cut across the bed and the energy from the window would be blocked by the clothes rack. There's nothing feng shui about this room.'

Dr. Slater and Sergeant Velasquez looked at Hunter curiously.

'I read a lot,' Hunter explained with a shrug. 'Could you do me a favor?' he addressed Sergeant Velasquez, taking a step closer to the bed. 'Could you stay right outside the door and close it for me, please? Just for a second. I want to have a look at something.'

The sergeant frowned at the request, but complied.

Hunter's eyes moved from the door, to the bed, and then the windows.

'It's OK, Sergeant,' he called out after a couple of seconds. 'You can open the door again.'

'Pardon my curiosity,' Velasquez said as he re-entered the room. 'But what does how the victim arranged the furniture in her bedroom have to do with her murder?'

'Maybe nothing,' Hunter conceded, getting down on his knees to check under the bed. He found nothing. 'But there're too many things in this apartment that just don't feel right, like this entire room, and I don't think that that's just a coincidence. There must be a specific reason why.'

'OK, and what do you think that reason would be?' Velasquez asked.

Hunter got back on to his feet. 'I think it was because she was scared.'

The sergeant hesitated for a moment. 'Scared? Scared of what?'

'Not of what?' Hunter replied. 'Of who.' He indicated as he clarified. 'By placing the bed right here, she could sleep facing the door. That's why she slept on the left side of the bed, and we know that because of the bedside table. If she left the hallway lights on, which I'm sure she did every night, she'd be able to see shadows under the door – footsteps of anyone approaching her room. Just like I saw yours while you were standing outside.'

Instinctively Velasquez looked down at his shoes.

'There's also a reasonably new sliding lock on the inside of the bedroom door,' Hunter continued. 'I bet it wasn't there four months ago when she moved in. She put it there herself, and the scratch marks on both, the lock and catch, suggest that she used it regularly.'

Sergeant Velasquez checked the lock. He had to agree that it did look fairly new.

'Then there're all the other telltale signs around the apartment that tell me that she was definitely scared of someone.'

'And which signs are those?' Velasquez asked.

'Well, we've got a thirty-eight Special Combat pistol in her bedside table, loaded with "extreme prejudice" rounds.' He drew everyone's attention back to the bed. 'We also have a low platform bed, close to the floor, so no one could hide under it. A clothes rack, not a wardrobe, so no one could hide inside it.' He made his way back to the door. 'In the bathroom there's a clear, see-through shower curtain, so no one could hide behind it. She had trouble sleeping but she refused to take her sleeping tablets. There's a full prescription inside the mirrored cabinet in the bathroom from nine months ago. In the hallway, inside the storage room, there's a dark-red curtain packed away. I'm guessing the curtain belonged to the sliding balcony doors in the living room. She took those down, replacing them with a somewhat unattractive chimed beaded curtain. Similar to the one at the front door. I don't think she did it because she liked the way they looked.'

'The noise,' Sergeant Velasquez said, picking up on Hunter's line of thought.

Hunter agreed again. 'If any uninvited guest gained entry to this apartment, either through the front door or the balcony, she'd get a warning.'

'The balcony?' the sergeant questioned. 'She's three floors up.'

Hunter nodded. 'And still, for some reason, she didn't feel safe. Not even in her own home.'

Nine

With nothing more to be done but wait for Dr. Slater's forensics team to finish what they were there to do, Garcia left
the crime scene at around 3:20 a.m. He wanted to try to get
at least a couple of hours sleep before sunrise.

Hunter, knowing that sleep would be an impossibility,
chose to stay behind and wait until Karen Ward's body had
been cut loose from her restraints and then transported to the
Los Angeles County Coroner. They would need the official
autopsy examination results to be sure, and that would take a
day, maybe two, but with no other visible wounds or bruises
to the victim's body, Hunter was fairly certain that Dr. Slater
had been correct in her assessment – death had come as the
consequence of severe brain trauma, caused by perforation
of the temporal lobe, which was achieved through the left
ocular globe cavity. In other words, Karen Ward lost her life
after she was violently stabbed through the left eye with a
glass shank long enough to reach her brain, but not before
her face had been savagely ripped to shreds by mirrored glass.

By the time Hunter left apartment 305 in Long Beach, the
first rays of sunlight had begun erasing the night. The rain,
which kept on coming and going all throughout the early

hours of that Thursday morning, also seemed to have grown tired of its own ordeal, receding completely by daybreak.

Hunter opened the door to his one-bedroom apartment in Huntington Park, southeastern Los Angeles, and stepped inside. The place was small, but clean and comfortable, though any visitor would be forgiven for thinking that most of his furniture had been donated by Goodwill. And they wouldn't have been far off the mark. The black leatherette sofa, the mismatched armchairs, the bookcase that looked like it was about to buckle under the weight of its over-crowded shelves, and the scratched wooden breakfast table that doubled as a computer desk, all of it had come from different yard sales around the neighborhood.

Hunter closed the door behind him, but stood right where he was, permitting the silence and darkness of his apartment to slowly envelop him for an instant. His eyes circled his living room, resting on shadows, and he tried to imagine what it would be like for a woman who lived alone to feel afraid and unsafe every time she stepped into her own home. What it would feel like to be scared every time she went to bed, or walked into her kitchen. He tried to imagine how quickly anxiety and paranoia would take over her life.

Not long at all, he decided.

In the bathroom, Hunter turned on the shower and stepped under the strong jet of hot water, allowing it to massage the stiff muscles on the back of his neck and shoulders. He closed his eyes and managed to relax for nearly ten seconds before images of the crime scene began playing on the inside of his eyelids like a horror film. He hadn't even filled in the investigation's opening report yet, and already a multitude of thoughts were colliding with each other inside his head.

Was Karen Ward being stalked?

So much of what Hunter had seen inside her apartment certainly hinted at it. He had worked on enough cases where the perpetrator had turned out to be a stalker to be able to recognize the behavior pattern of a person who lived in constant fear of someone else. And he knew that the statistics were staggering, scarily so.

Over six million people were stalked every year in the USA. In Los Angeles alone that number transposed to one in every six women and one in every fourteen men. One in every eleven women was stalked more than once and these numbers weren't taking into consideration Internet and social media stalking, where the issue had already run out of control. The problem in the City of Angels had become so severe that a unit dedicated to deal solely with harassment and/or stalking had been created by the LAPD in 1990 – the Threat Management Unit (TMU). A few celebrity cases had made the news over the years, but they accounted for a negligible percentage of the problem. The truth was that most of us didn't really consider being watched. Most of us didn't see ourselves as the object of someone else's obsession and so we were less careful, less private with our actions, and our attention to the problem was usually low or non-existent. What would also come as a surprise to so many was that female stalkers were a lot more common than people would allow themselves to imagine and they could be just as violent and deadly as their male counterpart – obsession didn't discern between gender, skin color, social class, religion, or anything else for that matter.

But if Hunter was really right about Karen Ward's behavior pattern, then the killer's MO was all wrong.

The brutality of repeatedly slamming someone's face against a container filled with shards of broken glass exceeded the violence in any stalker case Hunter knew of, but the uncharacteristic excessive use of violence wasn't all. Apparently, as part of some sordid game, her killer had also used the victim's cellphone to contact her best friend, forcing her to watch everything over a video-call.

Why? What was the logic in that?

Essentially, stalking was the unwanted or obsessive attention paid by one person to another, usually driven by rejection, jealousy, revenge, envy, insecurity, or simple maniac compulsion. It's a *person-to-person* thing, never a group one, Hunter knew that better than most, so why the sadism of the video-call? Why bring someone else into one of the most individual of compulsions? Why publicize the anger, the savagery? It didn't make any sense. And that was what scared Hunter the most.

Ten

After a quick breakfast, Hunter liaised with Garcia and they met up in South Vermont Avenue in West Carson, one of the thirteen neighborhoods that made up the Harbor Region in southern Los Angeles. The address had come from Sergeant Velasquez, and it belonged to the person they wanted to talk to the most: Tanya Kaitlin, Karen Ward's best friend.

Vermont Avenue is one of the longest-running north/south streets in Los Angeles, with its overall length exceeding twenty-three miles, twenty-two of which travel in an almost perfect straight line. The address they were given took them to the lower tip of South Vermont Avenue, just past West Torrance Boulevard. The building, a tired-looking blue and white rectangular structure in visible need of some care, sat opposite a row of shops.

'Have you been waiting long?' Hunter asked as he stepped out of his car.

Garcia, who was leaning against the driver's door of his Honda Civic, consulted his watch – 8:16 a.m.

'Not even a couple of minutes.' His words were followed by a half-curbed yawn.

'Did you manage to get any sleep at all?'

'Very little.' Garcia's reply came with an awkward head-tilt. 'I decided to sleep in the living room so I wouldn't wake Anna up for the second time in the same night. Bad move. My couch just wasn't made for sleeping. At least, not for someone who is six-foot two.'

Hunter could perfectly relate.

'By six o'clock I had enough of the tossing and turning, so I thought that I might as well get some work done.' Garcia's eyes dropped to the blue file in his right hand. 'How about you? What time did you get out of there?'

'About an hour or so after you, once the body was taken to the coroner's, just before dawn.'

'So asking if you got any sleep would be a silly question, right?'

Hunter looked back at his partner.

'Yep,' Garcia agreed with himself. 'Silly question.'

'So what's in the folder?'

'Victim's basic profile.' Garcia shrugged. 'Well, some of it, at least. Operations is still working on it. This is all the info they managed to gather on her in such short notice.'

'OK, so what have we got?' Hunter asked, as they crossed the road in the direction of the blue and white apartment building.

Garcia flipped open the folder. 'Karen Ward, twenty-four years old, born March seventeenth in the city of Campbell, Santa Clara County, where her parents still live. No criminal record. No substantial debts. Clean driver's license. She came to Los Angeles four years ago to study esthetics and makeup at the Academy of Beauty LA.'

They paused as they reached the building. 'And where's that?'

'Culver City.'

Hunter acknowledged it and Garcia carried on.

'She was a dedicated student, graduating a year later in the top five percent of her class. The Academy has a placement program, helping graduates find work. They got her an internship in a beauty spa called ...' Garcia turned to the next page. 'Trilogy Day Spa, in Manhattan Beach.'

'Where did she live then?'

'Umm ...' Garcia quickly searched through the file. 'She shared a house in South Bay with ...' His eyebrows bobbed up and down once. 'None other than the person we're here to see – Tanya Kaitlin.'

'OK.'

'Karen Ward was with Trilogy Day Spa for a year before taking a new job with a different beauty salon – Glique, located in Monterey Park.'

Hunter looked a little surprised. 'Monterey Park? That's quite a way from South Bay.'

'No doubt,' Garcia agreed, 'but she didn't commute. She relocated to Alhambra.'

'Sharing again?'

Another quick scan of the file. 'It doesn't say, but I guess Tanya Kaitlin will be able to clear that for us.'

'True.'

'She spent another year with Glique, before changing jobs once again.' Garcia locked eyes with Hunter. 'You guessed it. New job. New part of town. New address.'

'Where this time?'

'Back to the Westside – Santa Monica. The new job was with a high-class beauty salon called ... Burke Williams, on Third Street Promenade.'

'And her new address?'

'Appleton Way in Mar Vista.'

Garcia read on in silence for a moment before frowning.

'What?' Hunter asked.

'Very fast change. She stayed with Burke Williams for only four months before moving on to a new spa, a place called True Beauty in Long Beach, on East Second Street.'

'Her last job before she was murdered,' Hunter said. He remembered Sergeant Velasquez mentioning the address.

'That's right,' Garcia confirmed.

'Anything about any relationships?' Hunter asked. 'Anybody she was seeing?'

Garcia leafed through the file pages. 'Nothing.'

'How about her reasons for any of the employment changes, does it say? Has any of the spas she worked at shut down? Was she laid off?'

More page flipping. 'Nope. I've got nothing here, but I'd also be very interested to know. She'd been in LA for four years. One of those she spent studying, and in the next three she changed employment three times. OK,' Garcia admitted, 'not really unheard of, but she wasn't skipping from odd job to odd job. She was trying to establish a career, and in the case of a cosmetologist, I'm sure that she would've been working hard to try to secure a regular clientele. Hard to do that when you're moving around as much as she was and in a city as big as LA.'

Hunter agreed. 'Same job, different employers, which indicates that she probably wasn't being let go. If she were, she wouldn't have found a new job so quickly because she'd lack references.'

Garcia agreed. 'The decision to leave came from her,

not her employers.' He pressed his lips together in thought. 'Looking at her employment history, I'd say that her first two job changes look pretty normal. First job – fresh out of the academy and an intern at Trilogy Day Spa. Internship over, it's natural to go looking for growth, more money, better opportunities, whatever ... cue her next employer, Glique. Location-wise – not great, but when you're trying to kick-start a career you tend to make sacrifices. She spends a year in her new job before securing a position with a high-class beauty parlor in Santa Monica. Probably what she'd been striving for since qualifying as a cosmetologist.'

'Nevertheless,' Hunter added. 'She stays with them for only four and a half months before moving on again.'

'Barely a probation period,' Garcia admitted. 'But this time it doesn't look like a step up the ladder. Why would she do that?'

Hunter made a 'who knows' face. 'Running from something or someone?'

'Could be.'

Hunter faced the building. 'Maybe Tanya Kaitlin will be able to shed a light on more than just this crazy video-call thing.'

Eleven

Similar to what Hunter and Garcia had encountered at the front door to Karen Ward's apartment block, security to Tanya Kaitlin's building was also provided exclusively by a dated intercom entry system.

Hunter pressed the button to apartment 202 and was greeted by total silence. No clicking sound. No hiss. No beep. Nothing.

'Is that thing working?' Garcia asked.

'Not sure, but I wouldn't be surprised if it isn't.'

Hunter moved a little closer, bringing his right ear to a couple of inches from the intercom speaker, and tried it again. Still he heard nothing to suggest that the system was working properly. As he took a step back and regarded the locking mechanism on the door, they both heard a static click come through the tiny speaker. It was followed by a barely audible female voice.

'Yes?'

'Ms. Kaitlin?' Hunter asked. 'Tanya Kaitlin?'

'Yes.'

'I'm Detective Robert Hunter with the LAPD, we spoke earlier over the phone?'

A couple of silent, memory-searching seconds went by.

'Yes, yes, of course.' Her voice sounded tired and defeated. 'Please come in.'

A strident buzz rattled the heavy door before unlocking it with an even louder click. As they pushed it open, it screeched at the hinges.

'Damn,' Garcia commented. 'It sounds like the door is being tortured. Somebody should put some oil on that.'

Once inside, access to all three floors was gained solely via a concrete stairwell that led to long, narrow, and poorly lit corridors.

'Do we have anything on her?' Hunter asked, his chin jerking upwards as they took the steps going up to the second floor.

'Very little,' Garcia replied, flipping over to the last page inside the blue file. 'Tanya Kaitlin, twenty-three years old, born and raised right here in Los Angeles – Lakewood. The younger of two children. Father, deceased. Mother, suffers from Alzheimer's and lives with her son in San Diego. Just like our victim – no criminal record. Ms. Kaitlin works as a cosmetologist at DuBunne Spa Club in Torrance. She attended the Academy of Beauty LA at the same time as Karen Ward. They graduated together and, as you know, shared a house in South Bay during their internship.'

'Did they both do their internship at the same place?'

'Nope. As I've told you, Karen Ward did hers at Trilogy Day Spa, while the academy arranged for Ms. Kaitlin to go to a place called Six Degrees, also in Manhattan Beach. Both of their internships lasted twelve months, but Tanya Kaitlin's employment history after that is a lot more compact.' Garcia lifted his left index finger. 'Only one job, and that was – still is – with DuBunne Spa Club.'

'How long has she been living here?'

'Just over three years,' Garcia confirmed. 'This is where she moved to after leaving the house she shared with our victim.'

There were ten apartments per floor. Tanya Kaitlin's flat was the first door on the right as they exited the well-worn staircase. A brown doormat just outside number 202 met all visitors with the words – THE NEIGHBORS HAVE BETTER STUFF.

Hunter and Garcia positioned themselves to the right and left of the door respectively. It was just one of those LAPD force-of-habits that they now did without even realizing they were doing it. There was no doorbell, so Garcia gave the door a couple of firm knocks. Ten still seconds elapsed before they heard slow and heavy footsteps approaching from inside, but as the footsteps neared the door, they stopped and everything went back to complete silence.

Outside, Hunter and Garcia exchanged a couple of curious looks.

Garcia shrugged and was about to knock again when the door finally unlocked with two loud rotations of the key. It was then pulled back slowly, up to the allowance of the security chain.

Both detectives were forced to reposition themselves to be able to partially see the woman who had appeared through the sliver of open door. She kept the immediate lights switched off, cloaking most of her figure under shadows. All Hunter and Garcia could tell was that she looked to be about five-foot five.

'Ms. Kaitlin?' Hunter asked, tilting his head to one side, looking for a better angle. He didn't find one.

Instead of uttering a vocal reply, Tanya Kaitlin sucked in a difficult breath through a clogged nose, following it with a subdued nod.

'I'm Detective Hunter with the LAPD Robbery Homicide Division.' Up came the credentials. 'This is my partner, Detective Garcia.'

Her tired gaze moved from their faces to their identifications, and then back to them. She nodded once, releasing the security chain.

'Please, come in,' she said as she fully opened the door and took a step to her right. Light from the corridor outside fell over her, finally banishing her shadow coat.

Hunter's eyes lingered on Tanya Kaitlin for only a couple of seconds. She looked like a human definition of distress. Deep dark circles framed a pair of puffed eyes that normally would've been pale blue but, due to total lack of sleep and countless hours of crying, looked a light shade of cherry-red. Her blonde hair had been tied back into a disheveled ponytail, from which wild strands fell by the sides of her face. Her sore-looking nose mimicked the redness in her eyes, and the skin on her forehead and cheeks looked just as dry as her lips. She wore a black and white bathrobe and no shoes. Her entire being smelled heavily of cigarettes.

'Please come in,' she repeated, guiding them into a living room that had been decorated on a budget, but with a lot of taste.

The flowery curtains that covered the balcony doors were drawn shut to almost completion, allowing only a weak breath of light through, just enough to keep the room from dying in darkness. Tanya indicated the sitting area by the east wall, where a blue sofa was accompanied by a couple of matching armchairs. A nearly empty pack of cigarettes sat on the glass coffee table that centered the seating suite. Next to it, an improvised pickle jar ashtray. The cigarette butts inside it had been smoked all the way to their filter. A couple of large scented candles burned at opposite ends of the room, their delicate aroma of vanilla and berries completely overpowered by the smell of cigarette smoke.

Hunter and Garcia followed Tanya inside, but waited for her to have a seat first. She took one of the armchairs, the one closest to the balcony. They took the sofa, which placed them directly in front of her.

As she sat down, Tanya pulled her bathrobe tighter around her, as if all of a sudden she had been disturbed by a cold gust of wind. Within seconds she seemed to have grown uncomfortable of her initial position, which saw her at the very edge of her seat. She shifted left then right before scooting back a few inches, all the while keeping her eyes low, aiming at her knees. She finally settled for sitting halfway up the cushion, with her back tense and away from the backrest, her shoulders hunched forward, her fingers interlaced together, and her hands thrown down between her knees.

'Ms. Kaitlin,' Hunter began, 'we know how difficult this must be for you, and we'd like to thank you for seeing us and for your time. We'll be as brief as we can.'

Tanya didn't say anything. She didn't look up either.

'We understand that you and Karen Ward were best friends.'

A subtle head nod.

Another deep breath.

And then Tanya exploded into tears.

Hunter and Garcia had been through this same situation

more times than they were able to remember. It never got easier. The best they could do was give her a moment.

Hunter got to his feet and disappeared into the kitchen. A couple of seconds later he resurfaced with a glass of sugary water.

'Here,' he said, coming up to Tanya. 'Have some of this. It will make you feel a little better.'

Her hands had moved to her face; in a matter of seconds, crying had escalated into sobbing.

Both detectives waited.

'I don't understand . . . I just don't . . .' she said in between deep sobs.

'Here, Ms. Kaitlin,' Hunter tried again. 'Just a couple of sips. It really will make you feel better.'

After a new series of deep breaths, Tanya finally let go of her face. Her gaze found Hunter and she reached for the water.

'Thank you.'

Hunter gave her a sympathetic smile.

She had the tiniest of sips and motioned to place the glass down on the coffee table. Garcia moved forward on his seat.

'Just a little bit more, Ms. Kaitlin,' he urged her. 'It will help, I promise you.'

She hesitated for a long moment before giving in and bringing the glass back to her lips. This time she had three human-sized sips.

'Please, call me Tanya,' she said as she placed the glass down. 'And, yes – Karen and I were best friends.'

Before returning to his seat, Hunter handed Tanya a paper tissue.

She thanked him again and dabbed one of its ends against the corner of her eyes. Her gaze moved to the pack of cigarettes on the table and, maybe due to her grief, she felt the need to explain.

'It's been over two years since I lit up one of those.' She chuckled apprehensively. 'That was my emergency pack.' The corners of her lips arched up a little, but not enough to produce a smile. 'Do you smoke?' she asked.

'No.' The reply from both detectives came in unison.

'Have you ever?'

Garcia shook his head.

'A very long time ago,' Hunter replied.

'A lot of ex-smokers I know keep an emergency pack hidden somewhere, just in case the nerves really get out of hand for one reason or another. I came close to cracking the seal on that pack a few times in the past couple of years, but I did good ... until last night.' She looked away for a moment. 'I'm not really supposed to smoke in here, and if I could handle the brightness outside I would've smoked out on the balcony, but ...' She let the sentence hang in the air as she shook her head. 'Funny how everything that tastes good or makes you feel good, turns out to be really bad for you, isn't it?'

Hunter smiled at her again. The sugary water was starting to take effect. She ran her tongue across her dried lips and looked back at the detectives as if saying, 'I'm ready'.

'Tanya,' Hunter said in a calm and steady voice, establishing eye contact, 'I know this will be hard, so please take as long as you need, but could you tell us about this video-call you received last night, in as much detail as you can remember?'

Tanya's stare returned to the coffee table and she reached for the glass again. Two more large sips were followed by a heavy pause, and then her stare became distant, focusing on nothing at all.

'OK,' she finally said.

Hunter and Garcia readied their notepads.

Tanya began her story from the time she stepped out of the shower.

Twelve

Hunter and Garcia listened to Tanya's account of events in almost complete silence. They only interrupted her a couple of times, either to clarify a point, or to try to calm her down during the moments when the memory had become so vivid in her mind she had come close to becoming hysterical.

As she told them about how the call had ended, Tanya once again found herself fighting the urge to be sick. She reached for the cigarette pack on the table, and with a trembling hand brought its very last one to her lips, but even with the combined calming effect of sugary water and nicotine, Tanya's nerves managed to get the best of her and she once again broke down into a fit of tears.

Hunter handed her a new paper tissue.

Throughout the nearly twenty minutes that it took Tanya to recount the details of the video-call she'd received, Hunter had been paying close attention not only to her words, but also to her body and eye movements, together with her facial expressions. Yes, she did have tell signs: the nervous hand up to her face every so often, tucking a loose strand of hair behind her ear; the uneasy shake of the head every time she related something that she found hard to believe – and there were many of those – and the picking of the fingernails; but those weren't lie tale signs, they were fear ones. What she had experienced had truly petrified her.

Garcia brought Tanya a new glass of sugary water, and this time she needed no incentive, finishing the whole glass in three large gulps.

When she looked like she had calmed down enough, Garcia asked the first question.

'You told us that when the caller reached for Ms. Ward's phone to end the call, the phone panned upwards intentionally, and you got to see the caller's face, is that right?'

Tanya sucked in another lumpy breath.

'Yes, but it wasn't a face.'

Garcia frowned.

'I'm sorry?'

'It was a mask. Some sort of sick horror mask.'

Garcia quickly glanced at Hunter before scooting up to the edge of his seat. 'I know this is going to be hard for you, Tanya, and I apologize for having to ask you to try and bring those images back into your mind, but do you remember any of its details? Could you try to describe this mask to us?'

Tanya locked eyes with Garcia. 'Remember it? I'll never be able to forget it for as long as I live.' She brought her right index finger up to the right corner of her mouth. 'There was this large open cut on the side of his face, going from here to here.' She dragged her finger from her mouth, across her cheek and all the way up to her right ear. 'Like a lopsided, horror-clown smile, and you could see his teeth through it, but they weren't like human teeth. They were these enormous, sharp, pointy teeth, with blood smeared all over them. It was smeared all over his mouth and chin too.'

She paused for breath, clearly struggling with the images her memory was throwing at her.

'The other corner of his mouth wasn't cut, but it was all droopy and deformed out of shape.'

Hunter noticed that Tanya's hands were trembling again.

'He had no nose either,' Tanya added. 'Just a stump, as if it had been bitten off, or ripped off his face, or something. And his eyes were like a devil's.'

'Like a devil's?' Garcia asked. 'What do you mean?'

'Their color.'

'What about their color?'

'They were red. And I don't mean just the iris.' She pointed at one of her own eyes. 'I mean everything. There was no white to them at all. They looked just like two blood-filled holes.'

Her breathing had once again become labored. It took her a moment to get it back to normal.

'The rest of the skin on his face, including his head ...' Tanya gestured as she explained, '... was lumpy and leathery, as if his face had been burned.' Another nervous shake of the head. 'Look, I know it was just a mask, but it was the most evil-looking thing I've ever seen. I've never been so scared in my life.'

Hunter wasn't surprised. After hearing Tanya's story, he was sure that she felt exactly the way the killer wanted her to feel – vulnerable and terrified.

'So it was a full-head, rubber-type mask?' Garcia asked. 'Not one of those with an elastic band or a ribbon that you fix or tie around the back of your head?'

'Oh no, it was definitely a full-head mask. I'm sure of it.'

'Do you mind if we ask one of our sketch artists to get in

contact with you?' Hunter enquired, grabbing Tanya's attention again. 'A composite drawing of this mask could help us.'

Tanya breathed out while pulling her robe tight around her body again. A typical sign that she was feeling vulnerable.

'Yes. Of course.'

Hunter thanked her with a smile before continuing. 'You also referred to the caller as "him". But you said that the voice had been electronically altered to sound like a demon's voice in a horror film, right?'

Tanya agreed.

'Was there anything that gave you a clear indication that the caller was male?'

She took a second. 'The mask was one thing. As horrific as it was, it was of a male's face, not a female one, but there was also the shoulders and the body type. Too wide. Too strong for a woman's. Whoever that maniac was, he was dressed all in black, and the clothes were tight-fitting. I couldn't see all of him, but what I saw was definitely too muscular for a woman.' For a moment Tanya looked a little confused. 'Are women even capable of doing something like that? Of that sort of violence?'

'Some are,' Hunter replied.

Confusion mutated to shock.

'How long have you and Ms. Ward been friends for?' Garcia took over.

'Umm ... about three and a half years. We met during our cosmetology course at the Academy of Beauty and instantly became best friends.'

'Was Pete Ms. Ward's boyfriend?'

Tanya's left eyebrow lifted slightly as she looked back at Garcia.

'You said that for a moment during the call, you thought that Karen and someone called Pete were playing a joke on you. Who's Pete? Was he Karen's boyfriend?'

'Oh, no.' Tanya smiled as she shook her head. 'That would be Pete Harris. He's not into women at all. He's a makeup artist and a very good friend of ours. He does a lot of "on location" makeup for film studios, so he's always traveling. The last I heard he was in Europe working on-set with Tom Cruise or some big name. I thought that maybe he was back and he and Karen had decided to punk me with some sick joke. Pete's got a very weird sense of humor, if you know what I mean.'

Garcia wrote something down on his notebook.

'OK . . . do you know if Ms. Ward was romantically seeing anyone?'

'Pfff, not even close,' Tanya replied in a tone that suggested the implication was bordering on the ridiculous. 'Not with all the . . .'

All of a sudden she paused, holding her breath.

'Oh, my God.' Her eyes widened, but they seemed to be focusing on nothing at all again. 'I never thought of that.' She blinked once. 'I had completely forgotten about that.'

Hunter and Garcia eyeballed each other for a split second.

'Forgot about that, what?' Garcia asked.

Tanya's gaze slowly crawled back to the detectives sitting in front of her.

'Karen's stalker.'

Thirteen

Though Mr. J (that was how the man preferred to be called) had had the same infuriating melody programmed into his 'waking-up' alarm for the past year and a half, that morning it took him more than a moment to shake off the fog of sleep that enclosed him, and for his ears and brain to recognize and decode the sound he was hearing. Fog finally cleared, Mr. J sprang into action, reaching for his cellphone on the bedside table and quickly switching off his alarm.

Carefully, he rolled over and looked at the woman lying in bed next to him. Cassandra, his wife of twenty-one years, was facing the other way, seemingly still fast asleep.

Mr. J breathed out a sigh of relief, glad that he had gotten to the alarm before it had a chance to wake her up. He lay there for a couple of beats, staring at the way Cassandra's wavy fair hair caressed her naked shoulders. He thought about sliding over towards her and gently kissing the back of her neck – once, twice . . . a thousand times – but he knew that if he woke her up then and in that particular manner, they would both end up late for work . . . and that had already happened twice that week.

When Mr. J had first met Cassandra all those years ago, her temper and impulsiveness were among the many things that had attracted him to her. She was the most understanding and supportive woman he had ever met. Her opinions on whatever subject they discussed were always intelligent and thoughtful. She was stimulating. She was inspiring. She was fun, and not a moment they spent together could ever seem dull. They had gotten married only three months after they'd started dating and, back then, their lust for each other seemed to know no end. They spend most of their time together in bed, and no one was surprised when they announced her pregnancy so soon after the wedding. If it'd been up to Mr. J, he would've had more children, at least one more, but Cassandra told him that for the time being, one was enough.

'Maybe a little later, honey,' she had said, but that 'later' had never materialized. Instead, their relationship took a nosedive.

Every couple, no matter how in love they are or once were, will inevitably reach a rough patch in their relationship, especially when it comes to their lovemaking. In Mr. J and Cassandra's case, that rough patch began with the birth of their son, Patrick. At first, although still relatively regular, sex had become a lot less fervent, and a lot more calculated and careful. The almost total withdraw came years later, when little Patrick reached his teens. For Mr. J, those had been the worst years of his marriage.

Virtually every time he tried approaching his wife, Cassandra would politely but unequivocally reject his advances. Only occasionally would she allow him to make love to her, and even then the act was quick and felt highly mechanical; yet, on some very rare nights, *she* would be the one reaching for him, and on those nights it would be just like the old days, better even.

Cassandra would wait for Mr. J to turn off the lights and climb into bed before pulling him towards her. First she would kiss his entire body until she could taste his goose bumps, then she would tease him even more with little passionate bites to his neck and shoulders before taking him into her mouth and bringing him to the verge of explosion, but never quite. She would give him a moment to catch his breath and then make him lie on his back and climb on top of him. She would dig her nails into his chest so wildly that most times she would draw blood, but Mr. J didn't care. In fact, he loved everything about it. He loved how Cassandra would shiver while she was on top of him. He loved when he heard her pleasured moans, and, most of all, he loved seeing her close her eyes and gasp in such an intoxicating way, it would virtually transport him into another dimension.

Yes, there was no doubt that Cassandra had quieted down considerably after the birth of their son, particularly during his teen years, but now that he had gone off to college, she had started behaving more and more like her early self. The impulsiveness was back. The unpredictability was back and her passion and lust for her husband was back, albeit not with the same intensity as when they first met, which was understandable and, in Mr. J's eyes, a blessing of sorts. He was now long past his early twenties and, in reality, he wasn't sure he'd be able to handle Cassandra if her desire for him had reverted back to the way it was all those years ago.

But one thing was for sure: despite all the hurdles their marriage had been through, despite all the little problems they still had, Mr. J had never stopped loving his wife. If there really was such a thing as a soul mate, he had no doubt found his.

Fourteen

Despite Hunter and Garcia's suspicions based on all the clues they had found inside Karen Ward's apartment, the word 'stalker' still resonated in their ears like a bomb going off inside an echo chamber.

'Karen Ward was being stalked?' Garcia asked, sending a skeptical look Hunter's way.

'Oh, my God,' Tanya whispered under her breath, bringing a hand to her mouth. She didn't seem to have heard Garcia's question. 'I can't believe it. I can't believe I didn't even think of it.'

'Tanya?' Garcia called, dropping his head a little to his left to try to recatch her eye. It didn't work. Her stare had refocused on a random spot on the rug.

'Tanya?' He tried again.

Nothing.

'Ms. Kaitlin?' Firmer this time.

She finally broke away from her mini-trance and looked back at Garcia.

'Sorry. What was that?'

'Did Karen Ward ever tell you about her being stalked?'

'Umm ... yeah.' Tanya still looked a little dumbfounded.

'Yes, of course she told me. We were best friends. I just can't believe I didn't even . . .'

'Could you tell us about it?' Garcia interrupted her.

Tanya let go of a laden breath. 'I can tell you what I know.' She readjusted herself on her seat, this time finally scooting deeper into it and resting her back against the backrest. 'I think it all started less than a year ago, after Karen got her job with Burke Williams, a very prestigious beauty spa in Santa Monica. You see, Karen was an awesome cosmetologist. Very knowledgeable. Very attentive to detail. Very good at what she did, and a sweet, sweet person. All of her clients loved her, so it was no surprise that she managed to land such a desired job so quickly.'

'And that was when she moved from Alhambra to Mar Vista,' Hunter said, remembering the information Garcia had read from his file.

'Yes, that's right,' Tanya replied. 'Very nice little apartment too.'

'Was she sharing it with anyone?'

'No, she lived alone.'

'OK,' Garcia said. 'So what happened once Ms. Ward started working at Burke Williams?'

Tanya crossed her legs and scratched her left knee. 'Well, I think it was about two months after she joined BW, she started getting these creepy notes.'

'Notes?'

A head nod. 'Yes. Paper notes – not text messages, not emails, not voice messages. Just a note on a regular piece of paper – no name, no signature, no address, no nothing.'

'Did she recognize the handwriting at all?' Garcia asked.

'Oh no, I forgot to say, they weren't handwritten either.'

Tanya's gaze moved to the now empty pack of cigarettes on the coffee table and she breathed out in disappointment. 'They were put together from letters and words cut out from magazines and newspapers. Just like those freaky ransom notes you used to see in old movies.'

Hunter found that odd and particularly unsettling. 'You said "notes", so there was more than one?'

'Yes. I think she got maybe two or three of them in the few months she was working at BW, but they were enough to scare her.'

'Was that the reason why she decided to leave Burke Williams so soon?' Hunter asked.

A new, emphatic head nod. 'Karen was really shaken by those notes. She didn't know what else to do.'

'Didn't she take them to the police?' Garcia this time. 'Filed a complaint? Started an enquiry? Got them investigated?'

Tanya uncrossed her legs. 'That's what I told her to do. I even offered to go with her.'

'And did she? I mean, did you go to the police with her?'

'No, she didn't want to.'

Garcia's surprise was palpable. 'And why not?'

Tanya shrugged. 'She didn't think the police would be able to do much since the notes were completely anonymous. She was afraid that they would just ask her a few questions and then push everything on to the backburner. She couldn't see how that would stop her being scared, or any subsequent notes that could've followed. The notes really frightened her. She wasn't sleeping well. She believed that if she simply moved away and changed her job, everything would be OK again. The notes would stop.'

'Did she believe that the notes could've come from one

of her clients at Burke Williams?' Hunter asked, scribbling something down on to his notepad.

'I did ask her that,' Tanya confirmed. 'But the truth was that she didn't know what to think. She couldn't understand why she was getting them at all. Karen had just started working at BW back then. She didn't have that many regular clients. She also told me that at the time, all of her clients were women. Plus, as I've said before, Karen was the sweetest person you could ever meet. Everyone loved her, why would a client want to do something like that to someone like Karen?'

'You said before that Ms. Ward wasn't seeing anyone romantically?' Garcia asked.

'No, she wasn't.'

'When was the last time she was involved with anyone?' Garcia insisted. 'Do you know?'

Tanya looked away for an instant, thinking back. 'Way over a year ago,' she replied. 'She was just finishing her internship at Trilogy, but it wasn't anything serious.'

'How so?'

Tanya shrugged. 'Karen went on a few dates with this guy she met back then. He wasn't American. He was from somewhere in Europe – Sweden or Switzerland or something like that, but neither of them was looking for anything serious. Karen's priority was to get as much experience as she could from Trilogy so she could get a good first job. The guy, I think his name was ... Liam, or something like that, he was studying music somewhere. Anyway, he finished his studies and went back to Europe just before Karen finished her internship.'

Garcia nodded. 'No one else in recent months? Ms. Ward

was a very attractive young woman. I'm sure she got asked out often.'

'No one else I know about,' Tanya replied. 'Yeah, you're right. When we went out together to bars or lounges or whatever, usually someone would try his luck, but she never really looked interested. I never saw her take anyone's number, or give hers away.'

'Did Karen ever show you any of these notes?'

Hunter saw Tanya's jaw tense.

'Yes . . .' she replied. 'She showed me one of them, once.'

'Do you remember what it said?'

Tanya eyed the empty pack of cigarettes on the coffee table one more time. She was getting anxious again. She rested her elbows on the chair's arms as she thought back. The memory brought with it an uncomfortable shiver.

'It said something about touching her, about making her scream and about tasting her fear. I . . . can't remember the exact words, but I remember that the note did creep me out, especially because of the cut-out letters and all. That was why I told her that she should take it to the police.'

Hunter was still observing Tanya attentively. The jittery edge had returned to her.

'You said that Ms. Ward believed that if she moved away and changed her job everything would be OK again. The notes would stop.'

'Yes, that's right.'

'Did they?'

As she began shaking her head, tears came back to Tanya's eyes. 'No. At first she thought they had. She'd been in her new place in Long Beach for over a month and everything seemed great. Her new job at True Beauty was also going well. Karen was beginning to relax again, but then one night, a few weeks back, she called me in a panic, saying that she'd gotten another note.'

'Did Ms. Ward show you this new note?' Garcia asked. 'The one she received after she moved to Long Beach?'

'No, she just told me about it over the phone.'

'Did she tell you what it said? Do you remember it?'

'No, she never told me. I asked her, but she never told me. She just said it was just like the others.'

'Did she ever tell you how she got the notes?' Hunter pushed. 'Were they left in her postbox ... or under her door?'

Tanya nodded at Hunter, but this time it was a nervous, almost fearful movement. 'The previous notes were all left under her door, not in her postbox, but not the one she got once she moved to Long Beach.'

She paused, as if she needed time to wrap her head around what she was about to tell them.

'The note she got in Long Beach ... she found it on her bed. It was left under her pillow.'

Fifteen

'We need to call Operations,' Hunter said as soon as they stepped out of Tanya Kaitlin's apartment.

'Sure,' Garcia replied. 'What do you need?'

'We need to ask them to run a check against all logged nine-one-one calls for Karen Ward's residential area for the past . . . I'd say three months.'

'Nine-one-one calls? Why?'

'Because the guy we're after is cautious,' Hunter answered. 'And he likes to plan ahead.'

Garcia flicked his palms up while giving Hunter an inquisitive look. 'What does that mean?'

'Do you remember what Tanya Kaitlin told us about the call she received?'

They reached the stairwell, and as they took the first steps down to the floor below they encountered a tall and well-built individual in black jeans and a red hooded sweatshirt tucked under a dark baseball jacket. He wore a faded pair of black All Stars. His hands were buried deep inside his pockets, his head low; with his hood pulled well past his forehead, Hunter and Garcia were unable to see his face. As they crossed each other, Hunter had to twist his body to one side to allow the man to go past him.

'What part?' Garcia asked.

'When the caller told her not to call the police,' Hunter clarified. 'He told her that it would be a pointless thing to do because it would take them around ten minutes to get to Karen Ward's apartment, while it would take him only one to rip her heart from her chest.'

Garcia nodded. 'Yeah, I remember.'

They got to the first floor.

'OK,' Hunter said. 'Right now I'm willing to bet that the average response time from Long Beach PD to Karen Ward's apartment after a nine-one-one call is somewhere between eight and ten minutes.'

Garcia paused and looked back at his partner.

'Something tells me that he didn't just guess that time frame,' Hunter added.

'He clocked the response time.'

'That's what I would've done,' Hunter conceded. 'And to be absolutely sure, I would've done it at least three times, probably more.'

Garcia allowed that thought to run free inside his mind for a few seconds.

'But that would still give him no guarantees, Robert,' he said. 'Police cruisers aren't fire trucks. They don't sit at the station's parking lot waiting for a call. They cruise the streets. A black and white could've been just around the corner when dispatch sent out the call. That eight-to-ten-minute response-time could've easily been reduced to one, less even.'

Hunter agreed with a head nod. 'And I'm sure he knew that too. But as I've said, this guy seems to be very cautious, calculating, and he likes to plan ahead. Someone like that would've wanted to know the actual average police response time so he could factor it into his plan. The risk of a cruiser being just around the corner was something he could do nothing about, that's just the law of probability, so he tackled it from a different angle.'

The inquisitive look was back on Garcia's face.

'And what angle is that?'

'By making sure Tanya wouldn't even contemplate calling the cops. With no call, it didn't matter if twenty cop cars were parked right in front of the building. No one would've disturbed him.'

'OK,' Garcia agreed. 'But to do that he didn't actually need to know the correct response time. He could've just made one up. Isn't that a known psychological principal? Say something with enough conviction and most people will believe you, even if it isn't true. He could've thrown any number at Tanya and I'm sure she would've bought it.'

'Yes, you're right, and that would've worked for a lot of people, but not for someone who seems to be very method-ical, someone who looks to have been planning this for some time, because this sure as hell wasn't a spur of the moment murder.' Hunter shook his head. 'No, people like this are usually either OCD or bordering it. For his own peace of mind, this guy would've dug for the correct answer.'

'OK,' Garcia said. 'So what do we need?'

'Tell Operations that we're looking for bogus calls. Wild-goose chases, but logged as high-priority ones – gunshots heard, life-threatening violence, something along those lines – where the address given would've been either Karen Ward's apartment block or immediately surrounding areas.

The time of the call would've also been fairly close to the time of the murder, give or take a couple of hours. There's a chance that he would've used his real voice while making the calls.'

'And depending where the call originated from,' Garcia offered, 'and if it was made from a pay phone or not, we might get lucky with CCTV footage.'

Hunter agreed once again.

'We should also get started on a warrant to retrieve whatever we can from either Tanya or Karen's cellphone network about this video-call,' Garcia suggested. He knew that Tanya had done her best to remember and recount the call with as much accuracy as she could, but even a person in a clear state of mind wouldn't have been able to remember every word, every detail, never mind someone as shaken and as traumatized as Tanya was.

'There's no point,' Hunter said. 'The networks won't have the data.'

'How come?'

'No network in US territory is allowed to keep video-call logs in the same way they do regular call ones,' Hunter explained. 'They're already struggling with all these new privacy laws as it is. Retaining people's personal images or videos without their consent would mean a whole new dimension of war for them. One I'm sure they're not keen to fight.'

They finally exited the building.

'How about the audio or a transcript of it?' Garcia asked.

A new headshake from Hunter. 'They still won't have it because the audio doesn't get split from the video when the call is made.'

'So if they can't store one,' Garcia concluded, 'they can't store the other.'

'Exactly.'

'Are you sure? How do you know all of this?'

Hunter gave his partner a shrug. 'I read a lot.'

Sixteen

'So how long do you think you'll be this time?' Cassandra asked, as Mr. J finished his last piece of toast.

'Not long. Two, three days at the most.'

'That's exactly what you said last time.' Cassandra had a sip of some dark-green drink she'd just blended. 'And yet, you were away for almost a week.'

'Yes, and I'm sorry about that,' Mr. J conceded. 'But sometimes things get delayed, people get delayed, and business takes a little longer than expected.' He used a fabric napkin to dab the corners of his mouth. 'But I don't think there will be any misfortunes this time. I'll call you and let you know if anything changes. If not, I shall be back on Sunday at the latest.' He looked at his wife and frowned. 'Cass, what the hell are you drinking? It looks ... revolting.'

'Trust me,' she replied, finishing the rest of her juice, 'you don't want to know. But it tastes a lot better than it looks.'

'I sure hope so, because it looks like you just drank a glass of ... baby's diarrhea.'

'You are so disgusting sometimes, do you know that?'

Mr. J laughed. 'Me? I'm not the one drinking it. You look beautiful, by the way.'

Cassandra was charmingly dressed in a dark pencil skirt with a plum blouse and shiny black shoes. Her hair was loose, falling past her shoulders, but the sides were held back over her ears by a couple of dainty hair clips in the shape of butterflies. Her makeup, though she'd applied it herself, looked professionally done.

Mr. J checked his timepiece – 8:17 a.m. 'OK. I've got to go.' He got up, drank the rest of his coffee in one gulp, collected his plate and cutlery, and took everything to the sink.

'You can leave it there,' Cassandra said, before he had a chance to switch on the faucet. 'I'll wash it up later.'

'Are you sure? I can quickly do it. It's not a problem.'

'No, it's all right. I'll do it later. You get going.' She walked over to him and gave him a peck on the lips. 'Where are you going again?'

'Frisco,' he lied.

'Oh yeah, that's right,' she lied back. She didn't really remember him telling her before. She placed her empty glass in the sink together with the rest of the dishes. 'Well, drive carefully, and call me once you get there, OK?'

'Yes, of course.'

Mr. J gave his wife another kiss and grabbed his suit jacket, which was resting on the back of his chair. His dummy briefcase, the one he had packed in front of Cassandra the night before and which contained a change of clothes and a small bag of toiletries, was waiting for him by the door. His real briefcase, the one which contained what he really needed, he would pick up on his way to his hotel, from a storage unit he had rented years ago under a different name.

Seventeen

With mid-morning traffic in full flow, it took Hunter and Garcia over forty-five minutes to cover the almost fifteen miles between Tanya Kaitlin's apartment in West Carson and Karen Ward's one in Long Beach. They both wanted to have a second, undisturbed look at the crime scene before it was handed over to the CTS Decon team – crime and trauma scene decontamination – the team responsible for cleaning up and disinfecting the aftermath of crime and accident scenes.

With the exception of the victim's body and several forensics agents walking around in white coveralls, the apartment was exactly how they encountered it in the early hours of the morning. The pool of blood that covered part of the living room floor was still there, but it had by then dried up and clotted, which exacerbated the strong metallic smell that blood acquired once it came into contact with oxygen. With every window shut and locked to avoid the influx of insects that pooled human blood inevitably attracted, and with the temperature outside already getting up to seventy degrees, the eye-watering, rusty-like smell that lingered in the air had intensified considerably and spread into every corner of every room in the apartment.

As they cleared the beaded curtain at the front door, Garcia slipped on the nose mask he had brought with him.

Hunter did the same.

'I'd say that it'd be easier if we divided the workload, don't you think?' Garcia said, bringing up a hand to cover his nose, despite the mask. 'So how about you take the living room and kitchen, and I'll take the bedroom, the corridor and the bathroom. Sounds good?' Without waiting for a reply, Garcia crossed the living room towards the entrance to the hallway on the other side.

Hunter couldn't blame him. Not surprisingly, the intoxicating smell was much stronger in the living room. In spite of all their experience, neither Hunter nor Garcia had ever gotten used to the smell of blood from a crime scene, or, more precisely, the psychological smell of blood from a crime scene, something that most LAPD homicide detectives understood very well. To them, there was a distinct difference between the smell of blood from a crime scene and the smell of blood from anywhere else, including accidents, hospitals and morgues. They found that at specific crime scenes, especially the ones shrouded by overwhelming violence, the sickly sweet, copper-like smell of blood was always complemented by something else. A scent no one could really explain or agree on, but they could all smell it. They could all sense it. They could all feel it crawling up their skin, as if it were alive and had somehow gotten trapped in the scene. A smell that saturated the walls and soaked the air with its presence.

Some thought of it as the smell left behind by fear.

Some thought of it as the smell left behind by pain.

Some thought of it as the smell left behind by violence.

Hunter thought of it as the smell left behind by evil.

Before he could nod his agreement at his partner, Garcia had already disappeared down the short hallway and into the bathroom. Once he was gone, Hunter turned and faced the dining table and the chair in which Karen Ward's body had been found. He pulled down his nose mask, letting it hang loosely around his neck, and then stood there, immobile, just staring at the chair. He blanked out every distraction in his mind, and allowed the strong and violating smell of blood, evil, and death to suffocate his senses. A minute later, Tanya Kaitlin's sequence of accounts began playing in his ears again and, as if a film was being projected before him, his mind began visualizing scenes.

He pictured the killer's anger as he slammed Karen's face down into a container full of broken glass, over and over again. He saw the ugly and deformed mask covering the assailant's face, just like Tanya had described it. He imagined the killer's satisfaction as Tanya failed to answer his question correctly. He pictured Karen's desperation. Her fear. Her powerless struggle. But the images Hunter saw in his mind were broken and incomplete. Too many frames were still missing. Something wasn't right.

He finally snapped out of his daze and walked over to the open-plan kitchen. It was small but well equipped, with a modern microwave and fan oven all rolled up into one, an induction cooker, and a fridge/freezer with an external water and ice dispenser. Hunter pulled its door open and looked inside. It was practically empty, with the exception of a half-full carton of orange juice, and one of milk. A tub of ice cream – chocolate brownie flavor – sat alone at the very back of the large freezer compartment. Hunter shut the door, turned from the fridge, and tried the cupboards on the wall behind him. A few canned goods but no spices or condiments. It didn't take a detective to figure out that Karen Ward barely, if at all, cooked at home, and something told Hunter that it wasn't because she didn't know how, or didn't like to, but because she wanted to be home as little as possible.

In the living room, Hunter avoided the pool of dried blood and moved over to the sitting area, where a three-seater, dark-brown sofa was flanked by a matching armchair on one side, and by a round acrylic coffee table on the other. The weaved, brown and beige rug in front of the sofa looked new, and so did the TV stand and the dark wood display cabinet that were pushed up against one of the walls.

Hunter walked over to the TV stand and opened the drawer on the left; inside it he found a power extension flex, a couple of paperbacks, and the instruction manuals for the TV, the cable box, and all the kitchen appliances. He tried the drawer on the right – spare light bulbs, a set of screwdrivers, and two plastic folders containing house bills. The display cabinet, to the right of the TV stand, held a few well-arranged and colorful decorative items – pots, bowls, jars, wooden flowers, a square tin box, and a couple of cat figurines. He reached for the tin box and pulled its lid open – empty.

A loud noise, which came from deep inside the apartment, startled Hunter.

'Carlos, are you all right in there?' he called out, returning the tin box to the display cabinet.

'Yep,' the reply came from the bedroom. 'All good. Just bumped into the shoe tower in here by accident and half of them came crashing down on me like a shoe rain. Man, do you think she had enough shoes?'

Hunter smiled. He would never be so pretentious to claim he understood the way a woman's mind worked, but there was one thing he knew for sure, when it came to women's shoes, in their minds there was no such thing as 'enough shoes'.

He turned on the balls of his feet and his gaze circumnavigated the crime scene for the nth time. And that was when realization finally hit him.

Earlier that morning, something inside Karen Ward's room had bothered him. Something other than how unnecessarily crammed the space looked, but he couldn't really figure out what it was, until now.

Adrenalin shot through his body like a bullet, causing the hair on his arms and on the back of his neck to stand on end. He took two steps forward and paused, looking straight at something.

'You sick sonofabitch!'

Eighteen

In the bathroom, Garcia pulled open the cupboard mirror above the washbasin and once again rummaged through the contents inside it. As he did, he felt like one of those people who needed to open the fridge door every time they stepped into the kitchen.

'Yup,' he said. 'Just like I thought. Nothing new has magically materialized in here since this morning.'

He closed the mirror and moved over to the shelf unit to the right of the bathtub. The top three shelves held an astounding number of beauty creams, lotions, and oils, all perfectly arranged in separate groups. Garcia reached for one of the bottles on the top shelf and silently read the description on its label.

Facial cream with high UV protection.

He looked thoughtful for a moment. He was sure that his wife, Anna, had bought that exact same product not that long ago. He placed the bottle back and reached for another one.

Facial cream with low UV protection.

And another.

Facial cream with cucumber extract.

He carried on.

Facial cream with avocado extract.

Facial cream with olive oil.

Facial cream with almond oil.

Garcia shook his head, a little amused. 'I feel like I'm shopping for salad here,' he said under his breath. He returned the bottle to the shelf and tried a different group. This time he frowned at the bottle. 'What? Strawberry cheesecake scented body lotion? Really?'

His lips parted with a smile but, despite finding it funny, he was also quite intrigued and couldn't resist. He pulled his mask down, flicked the bottle cap open and brought it to his nose. To his surprise, it smelled so much like freshly baked strawberry cheesecake, he heard his stomach rumble. The question bouncing around in his head though, was why would anyone want to smell like strawberry cheesecake?

Garcia readjusted his mask back over his nose before going through a couple more bottles.

Coconut.

Vanilla.

'I guess this must be the dessert group.'

He decided to move on to the next shelf.

Eye cream.

Eye cream.

Eye cream.

Hand cream.

Foot cream.

Neck cream.

Once again he paused. 'There are creams developed specifically for your neck?' he asked the empty bathroom.

The next shelf was full of hair and skin hydrating oils and

lotions. The one after that held several expensive-looking perfume bottles. The fifth and sixth shelves were where Karen Ward kept all her towels.

Garcia exited the bathroom and moved on to the bedroom. Instead of switching on the lights, he walked over to the unobstructed window on the west wall and pulled open the curtains, allowing sunlight to finally bathe the room. From where he was standing, he looked around the crammed space for a long moment before deciding that he would start with the bed.

First he checked under the pillows, the bed cover, and the bed sheet – nothing. He pulled his sleeves up and lifted the mattress to check the bed frame – nothing. He crossed the room to the dresser and tried the first drawer. It was full of lingerie, stockings, and socks; all of it neatly packed away in straight rows. He moved on to the next drawer – T-shirts, blouses, and spaghetti strap tops, again, perfectly arranged to maximize the drawer space. The third drawer was a repeat of the first two, only with sweaters and hot pants. The fourth and last drawer was packed full with a variety of accessories – belts, hair ornaments, necklaces, bracelets, sunglasses and so on.

When Garcia was done looking through the drawers, he dropped to his knees and looked under the dresser. There was nothing there other than some dust.

This is silly, he thought. *If there was anything to be found in here, forensics would've done it already.*

As Garcia swung his body around on his way back up, his right knee slammed into the shoe rack to the right of the dresser. A downpour of shoes came down on top of him.

'Crap!' he said, bringing both arms up to protect his head. 'I'll be goddamned.'

'Carlos, are you all right in there?' Garcia heard Hunter call from the living room.

'Yep,' Garcia replied, finally getting back on to his feet. 'All good. Just bumped into the shoe tower in here by accident and half of them came crashing down on me like a shoe rain.' He paused, scratching his forehead. 'Man, do you think she had enough shoes?' he called out, turning to look at the mess on the floor. Shoes of all different colors and styles were absolutely everywhere. His next words came out as a murmur. 'Why would anyone need this many shoes?' He thought about his wife again, then nodded to himself before answering his own question. 'Because she was a woman, that's why.'

Garcia began picking them up and placing them back on the rack. Judging by how well organized Karen Ward's shelves and drawers were, he was sure that every pair had its specific place, probably arranged either by color or style.

Out of sheer respect, he started grouping them as best as he could, and he wasn't at all surprised to find that most of them looked like they'd never even been worn. And now probably never would be.

Garcia was about halfway through the large pile when something that must've come down with the shoes caught his eye.

He reached for it and paused.

'Oh, shit!'

Nineteen

Fall in the City of Angels was a very elusive thing. There was no sting to the air, no characteristic cold bite at night, no typical shiver early in the mornings; on the contrary, autumn could bring with it some of the warmest days and nights, easily matching the temperatures reached at the height of summer, and today certainly was one of those days.

Hunter had all four of his windows rolled down on his way to the Police Administration Building on West First Street, downtown Los Angeles, but in stop-start traffic he could barely reach enough speed to produce any sort of breeze. The still and stale air inside the cabin, combined with over 70 percent air humidity, made his car feel like a sauna and a steam room at the same time. As he and Garcia finally stepped into their office on the fifth floor of the PAB, the first thing Hunter did was blast the AC unit to full power. Garcia stifled a smile. He could see the long and thin wet mark running all the way down the back of Hunter's shirt.

'In this heat,' Garcia said, as he fired up his computer, 'having a car with no aircon is a bitch, isn't it?'

Hunter looked back at him sideways. 'Don't you start.'

'I'm not starting anything, but you do understand that

your car doesn't even belong to this century, right? You really need to take that thing to a scrap yard, my friend.'

'Why? It's a great car?'

'That's not a car, Robert. That's a rusty twenty-year-old bathtub with wheels. I know you like to call it a classic, but ...'

'No,' Hunter interrupted him. 'I just call it a car. It does its job, which is to get me from A to B, and it's very reliable. What else could I ask for?'

'Aircon,' Garcia said, throwing more salt into the wound. 'You could ask for aircon.'

Without anyone knocking, the door to their office was pushed open and Captain Barbara Blake stepped inside.

Captain Blake had taken over the LAPD Robbery Homicide Division's leadership a few years back, after the retirement of one of its longest-standing and most decorated captains, William Bolter. She had been hand-picked by Bolter himself, which angered a long list of candidates, but angering people was something that simply came with the captain's job, and Barbara Blake had absolutely no problems with it.

She was indeed an intriguing woman – strong and resilient, but at the same time attractive and elegant, with long black hair and suspenseful dark eyes that never gave anything away. Despite being greeted by some hostility when she took over, she had quickly gained a reputation for being a tough-as-nails, no-nonsense captain. She wasn't easily intimidated, took no crap from anyone – including her superiors in the police department – and had no reservations about upsetting high-powered politicians or government officials if it meant sticking to what she believed was right.

Within a few months of her stepping into her new shoes, the initial hostility began to dissipate, and slowly but surely she earned the trust and respect of every single detective under her command.

'OK,' Captain Blake said, closing the door behind her. 'What's the story on this case that came in overnight? The report I read from Long Beach PD is as loose as a clown's pocket, but it mentions something about the killer making a video-call to the victim's best friend? What the hell is all that about?'

'As crazy as it sounds, Captain,' Garcia replied, stirring a single cube of brown sugar into the cup of coffee he'd just poured, 'that's exactly what happened. We just got back from talking to Tanya Kaitlin. That's the victim's friend who the perp called.'

The captain leaned back against the door. 'OK, I'm listening.' Her inquiring eyes moved from Garcia to Hunter.

They quickly summarized what Tanya Kaitlin had told them about the call she'd received from the killer.

'Wait a second,' the captain said, lifting a hand to interrupt them when they told her about the killer's MO. 'The killer called her to play a game?'

'That's right,' Hunter replied. 'Two questions, get them right and your friend lives. Get them wrong and ...' On his computer screen, he double-clicked the photo file he'd received from the forensics team. 'Come see for yourself.'

As Captain Blake positioned herself behind his chair, Hunter began clicking through the photographs.

'Jesus!' she exclaimed, unable to disguise her shock, but at the same time transfixed by the brutal images. The eighth picture in the sequence was a close-up of the injury to Karen Ward's left eye. The one believed to have been the fatal one, with a long shard of mirrored glass protruding out of her eye socket. This time, Captain Blake looked away in disgust.

'OK,' she said, stepping back and away from Hunter's desk. 'I don't need to see any more. What the hell is wrong with this world?' She shook her head, trying to blink away the images. 'That goes way beyond sadistic. Way beyond psychopathic.'

Hunter understood the captain's frustration well. He knew that, unlike what most people might think, killing wasn't such a hard a task to achieve. Every human was capable of doing it.

In the USA, a great number of homicides happened as a consequence of an error of misjudgment. All it really took was a moment of insanity. A second of someone losing his or her temper and it was done – a quick squeeze of the trigger, a push, a direct knock to the temple, a swing of a bat to the head, a sharp instrument to the right part of the body – there were hundreds of different ways to end a life in just a second. What took a specific type of individual – cold, calculated, sadistic, devoid of emotions – was preceding the murder with torture. Being able to deliberately inflict tremendous physical pain on another human being and getting a kick from it was something that not many on this earth were able to do.

'It gets worse,' Hunter said. 'He forced her to look.'

'Yes, I know,' Captain Blake replied. 'You just told me.'

'No.' Garcia this time. 'Not her best friend, Captain. The victim.'

A look of confusion came over Captain Blake.

'The killer forced Karen Ward to look at her reflection after each head slam. He forced her to watch her own disfiguration.'

'What?'

'In our first visit to the crime scene,' Hunter said, taking over, 'something in Karen Ward's living room bothered me, but I couldn't really pinpoint it. I should've realized what it was when I checked her bedroom for the first time, but there was so much wrong with it that it escaped me, pure and simple.'

'And what was it?' Captain Blake asked.

'The mirror.'

'What mirror?'

Hunter pulled his chair closer to his desk and clicked his mouse a few times until he found what he was looking for.

'These are the crime scene pictures of Karen Ward's living room.' Once again he pointed at his computer screen.

Captain Blake returned to Hunter's side.

'See this?' He indicated the full length mirror positioned between the dining table and the sitting area. 'What's a dressing mirror doing in the living room?'

The captain shrugged. 'That's not that uncommon, Robert. Maybe she lacked space in her bedroom. Plus, a lot of women like to have one last quick look at their outfit just before walking out the door.'

Hunter nodded, acknowledging the captain's point. 'The problem is: the space is there, Captain.' A few more clicks. 'This is a picture of her bedroom. See the space between the clothes rack and the dresser? I checked the floor. There were four small rubber marks, which exactly matched the rubber feet on the dressing mirror. It was moved, Captain.'

'Tanya Kaitlin also told us that the killer kept on telling her to look,' Garcia offered, 'and she couldn't understand why, because she *was* looking, and she kept on telling him so.'

'That's because the killer wasn't really telling her to look,' Hunter again. 'He was telling Karen.'

Captain Blake pressed her lips tightly together. One of her 'worried' telltale signs.

'He wanted to torture her in every possible way,' Hunter said. 'Physically and psychologically.'

No one said anything for a long while.

'How about this mask the killer was wearing?' Captain Blake finally broke the silence. 'Was the witness able to give you some sort of description of it?'

'She was,' Garcia replied. 'We're getting a sketch artist to her by this afternoon. If the killer hasn't created this mask himself, there's a slim chance that we might be able to identify the supplier.'

Captain Blake nodded to herself. 'And how did the killer get access to the building? To her apartment? Does anyone know?'

'Security at the victim's building was pretty basic and easily breachable,' Garcia told her. 'Just a dated intercom entry system with a door buzzer, nothing more. An earth magnet against the door's weak locking mechanism and, boom, you're in.'

'How about her apartment?'

Garcia sipped his coffee. 'There were no signs of a struggle ... no signs of a break-in, so the speculation is that the victim could've buzzed the killer in herself, either because she knew him, or because he came up with a believable enough story when he rang her apartment. Either way, she would've opened her front door for him herself.'

'There's also the possibility that he was waiting for her inside when she got home,' Hunter added.

Captain Blake's forehead creased. 'How would he have gotten in?'

'That we're not sure yet, but we know that he's done it before.'

The captain's interest visibly grew. 'What? He's been inside her apartment before? How do you know?'

Hunter leaned back on his chair. 'When we first attended the scene,' he explained. 'We found several tell signs that hinted that Karen Ward lived in fear. Our suspicions were confirmed earlier this morning by her best friend.' Hunter proceeded to tell Captain Blake what Tanya Kaitlin had told them about the stalker-type notes Karen Ward had received.

'And she told you that one of these notes was left on the victim's bed?' Captain Blake asked.

'That's correct,' Garcia confirmed, taking over again. 'But it doesn't end there. After we left Ms. Kaitlin's apartment, we decided to drive back to the crime scene to have another look.'

'And ...?'

'And while checking her bedroom, I bumped into the victim's shoe rack by accident. Half of her shoe collection rained down on me and, let me tell you, Captain, there were enough shoes there to open up a shop.'

'There's no such thing as enough shoes,' the captain shot back. 'But go on.'

'Well, after the shoe rain stopped, I found this. It had slipped out from inside one of them.'

Garcia pointed to a see-through evidence bag that was sitting on his desk. Inside it was a white, eight-by-five-inch sheet of paper. Captain Blake hadn't noticed the evidence bag until then. She stepped closer to have a better look and her eyes instantly widened. The scrap of paper was actually a collage of letters and words that had been cut out from a magazine to form a note.

A stalker's note.

Twenty

Cassandra left her cul-de-sac house in Granada Hills, San Fernando Valley, about an hour after Mr. J. It was Thursday morning, and every Thursday she volunteered at one of the several charity shops for 'WomenHeart' – the national coalition for women with heart disease.

Her mother, Janette, with whom she had been very close, had passed away eight years ago, victim of coronary thrombosis, caused by a severe spasm of the left coronary artery. Her father wasn't home at the time, and Janette, who was outside, attending to her garden, didn't manage to get to her phone in time. She died in her backyard, surrounded by roses and sunflowers, but the real shock was that no one saw it coming. Cassandra's mother had never showed any symptoms related to heart disease – no upper-body discomfort, no chest pains, no shortness of breath, no dizziness, no nausea, no sleeping problems – nothing. In fact, she was a fairly fit sixty-one-year-old woman, who exercised regularly and ate a well-balanced diet. The reason for the coronary artery spasm was never identified.

After her mother's death, Cassandra decided to dedicate

some of her time to helping people with heart problems. At different times she volunteered at different heart disease organizations. WomenHeart was her favorite one.

Cassandra checked her watch as she locked her house's front door behind her. There was no need to rush. She had plenty of time to get to the shop before it opened at 11:00 a.m. She jumped into her silver Cadillac SRX, which was parked on her driveway instead of on the road, and switched on its engine. She shifted the transmission into reverse and checked her mirrors.

'Huh?' she murmured to herself, narrowing her eyes at the interior mirror before turning around to check her rear window. There was something caught between the window and the rear wiper. It looked like a white piece of paper. *More rubbish advertisement,* she thought.

Cassandra flicked on the wiper to get rid of it, but instead of disposing of the piece of paper, it simply dragged it along from left to right a couple of times.

'Oh, for crying out loud!'

Cassandra undid her seatbelt and opened her car door. As she got to her rear window she realized that it wasn't a piece of paper, but an envelope. She reached for it. There was no stamp and no recipient or sender's address. All she could see was the name – Cassandra – across the front of the envelope, but it hadn't been handwritten or typed. Someone had cut out each individual letter from a magazine page and glued them together to form her name.

'You've got to be fucking kidding me,' she said out loud, her tone of voice immediately breaching the threshold into 'anger' level. She quickly swung around, throwing her gaze up and down her street. There was no one there, and the only cars she could see she recognized as belonging to her neighbors.

She kept her eyes on the street a moment longer, before bouncing them back to the envelope in her hands. She knew that inside it she would find another note.

This one made it three in total. The first two had been left on the counter in the Women's Heart shop where she had been volunteering for the past seven weeks. Just a white envelope with nothing more than her name across its front, formed by a collage of individual cut-out letters.

'I think you have an admirer, Cass,' Debora, a senior fellow volunteer worker, had told her as she handed Cassandra the first envelope almost two months ago. But the note inside it was no admiring one. The clear intention of the message was to frighten her; but it actually made Cassandra chuckle.

Cassandra asked Debora if she had seen who had left the note on the counter, but Debora said that she had no idea. She said that the note had been left by the cash register, and she only saw it when she rang in an item.

The second note, delivered four weeks later, was pretty much a repeat of the first one, also left by the cash register. This time the message it carried didn't make Cassandra chuckle, it made her angry. In her mind, the notes had clearly been the handiwork of some 'idiot' trying to be funny and maybe scare her, but failing miserably at it ... but who?

Unfortunately the charity shop she volunteered at had no CCTV camera, or else Cassandra would've worked her way through the footage until she had identified the culprit, and the next time he or she stepped into the shop, she would have given the person a piece of her mind.

Despite everything, Cassandra didn't give the notes much

importance, so much so that she had completely forgotten about them. In fact, she had never even mentioned any of it to Mr. J, or anyone else.

OK, Cassandra thought, her eyes going back to the note in her hand, *now this has gone too far.*

Whoever this person was, he or she had come to her home to place the note on her car, and she wasn't about to just let that one slide.

Cassandra thought about tearing up the whole thing right there and throwing it all in the trash, but, in a burst of anger, she ripped open the envelope and pulled out the piece of paper from inside it. It looked just like the previous two notes – a white, eight-by-five sheet of paper, where someone had glued together letters and words that had been cut out from a magazine to create a message.

Her eyes scanned the short note and she paused. This time the message didn't make her chuckle. It didn't make her angry either. It finally made her scared.

Twenty-One

The cut-out letters and words that formed the note Garcia had found in Karen Ward's bedroom had all come from article and advertisement headlines, varying in color, size, and shape.

Captain Blake repositioned herself by Garcia's side and silently read the short note on his desk twice over:

A friend once told me that to really know what it's like to be someone else, one has to step into that someone else's shoes. Maybe walk in them a little. Well, I've just stepped into yours, Karen.

Captain Blake's gaze ping-ponged from Garcia, to Hunter, and then back to Garcia. 'This slipped out from inside one of her shoes?'

Garcia nodded and reached for a second evidence bag, which was on the floor by his chair.

'This one,' he said, placing the bag on his desk, next to the note. It contained a pair of shiny, black and red, five-inch-stiletto shoes. 'I was just about to take it all to forensics for analysis.'

The captain tilted her head slightly to the right as she studied the shoes.

'OK,' she said at last, indicating the items on Garcia's desk. 'So what the hell does this all mean? That the killer tried on her shoes?'

'Right now we're not discarding any possibilities, Captain,' Garcia replied. 'We'll ask forensics to check the insoles and the inside of the shoes for DNA or what-have-you, but if that's the case, the killer is either a woman posing as a man, or he's got tiny, tiny feet. Those are four and a half sized shoes.'

'What it does mean, Captain,' Hunter offered, 'is that it confirms what Tanya Kaitlin had told us earlier today – that whoever put that note together, whoever was stalking Karen Ward, had once again gained access to her apartment without her knowledge.'

'Have you found any other notes?'

'No, and we checked everywhere,' Garcia replied. 'Inside every shoe, pocket, drawer, cupboard, under the furniture – you name it, it's been checked.'

'But her friend told you that she had received more than one note, right?'

Both detectives nodded.

'So where are the others?'

Garcia shrugged. 'We don't know; chances are, she threw them away.'

A moment of surprised silence.

'Why would she do that?'

'Because they scared her, Captain,' Hunter responded. 'Why would she keep something that scared her in her house? Most people wouldn't.'

'Because they constituted physical proof, Robert, and they could've carried forensic evidence. Didn't she take them to TMU? Register a complaint? Start a process?'

'I understand, but according to her best friend, that's not how she saw it,' Hunter clarified. 'What she believed was that because the notes were completely anonymous, the police wouldn't be able to do much for her. She was afraid that they would just ask her some routine questions and push her case to the back of the queue. She was scared. She wasn't sleeping well and all she wanted was for the notes to stop. The solution she came up with was to move.'

Captain Blake chewed on that thought for a moment. 'OK, so why do you think she kept this particular one?' She nodded at the note on Garcia's desk.

'That is the problem, Captain,' Hunter said. 'We don't think she did.'

It took the captain just a second to pick up on what Hunter was suggesting. 'She never actually found it.'

'That's what we think,' Garcia agreed. 'Which, to be honest, isn't that surprising.'

Captain Blake injected a little inquisition into the look she gave him.

'I'm telling you, Captain,' he said in reply, 'there were over sixty pairs of shoes on that rack. If she was anything like Anna, it doesn't matter how many pairs of shoes she had, she'd mainly stick to wearing three, maybe four pairs. The comfortable ones. The rest are just the consequence of some innate female obsession with shoes. It doesn't matter that they'll only wear them once, if that. They just have to have them.'

Captain Blake couldn't argue with Garcia's logic. Despite

owning a staggering number of pairs of shoes herself, she did mainly stick to a handful of them. The rest she would wear sporadically, maybe once or twice a year, depending on the occasion. She took a step back from Garcia's desk, while mulling over a couple of thoughts.

'So do you think this means that the perp wasn't that familiar with the victim after all?' she asked both detectives.

'Because he placed the note inside a shoe which she didn't wear very often? It could,' Hunter agreed with a nod, then followed it with a sideways head-tilt. 'But not necessarily.'

'What do you mean, Robert? A stalker would've noticed her shoes. He would've noticed her earrings, her handbag, her lipstick ... everything about her. Isn't stalking the product of an unwanted and obsessive attention from one person to another?'

Hunter nodded once.

'So if he was obsessed with her, he would've noticed her shoes. He would've known which ones she wore more often.'

Hunter agreed again, then explained. 'The problem we have is that people driven by uncontrollable obsessions can very easily become delusional, Captain, and stalkers are very high on that list. They desperately want to be part of their "victims'" world.' He used his fingers to draw quotation marks in the air because he knew that most stalkers didn't see the source of their obsession as victims. 'To achieve that, many will break into their victims' homes while they are gone and sleep in their beds, eat their food, watch their TVs, wear their clothes, their shoes, anything, just to make them feel like they belong. Like they have a connection. Some, and Karen Ward's stalker seems to fall into this category, like to push the boundaries and leave little clues behind so their victims would know that they'd been in their home. Sometimes those clues come in the shape of notes.' Hunter once again indicated the note on Garcia's desk. 'But it could be something a lot more subtle. Something that would fill the victim's head with doubts, like an object out of place, a door left ajar, or a light left on.'

Captain Blake considered the scenario. Nothing would scare a single woman living alone more than knowing that someone had been in her house, because if he got in when she was out, he could get in when she was in, or even worse – he could still be in there.

'So the reason why they would leave any of these sort of clues behind,' she said, 'is scaremongering – to simply bring fear to the victim.'

'For some of them, yes,' Hunter agreed. 'But not all, and here's where the delusional part kicks in. It's called erotomania, a fairly common trait in stalkers. It's a type of delusion where they believe that the object of their affection, usually a total stranger or somebody famous, is in love with them.'

'Well, this is the perfect city for that, isn't it?' Captain Blake commented.

'So,' Hunter continued, 'breaking into their victim's home, sleeping in their bed, using their toothbrush, or whatever it is that they do while they're in there, *makes* them believe that they are indeed part of their victim's world. It makes them believe that they belong. In their fantasy the hiding of notes is nothing more than a fun game that two people in love would play.' Hunter paused, giving Captain Blake a moment to absorb his words.

'Because if he believes that she's in love with him,' she said in conclusion, 'then he'd also believe that she enjoys playing the game just as much as he does.'

'Exactly.'

'So you're saying that he could've placed the note inside a shoe she didn't wear very often on purpose, just to make the Easter egg hunt a little more fun.'

'It's possible,' Hunter admitted.

Captain Blake walked back to the center of the room; as she did, she noticed the look on Hunter's face. A concerned look that she'd seen many times before. 'OK, what is it, Robert?'

Hunter looked back at her and his eyebrows arched.

'C'mon, don't give me that "what are you talking about?" look. Something is clearly bothering you. What is it?'

'Everything about this case bothers me, Captain.'

'Well, it bothers me too, but I know you well enough to see that there's something that's already frying your egg, so what is it?'

Hunter walked over to the coffee machine and poured himself a large cup. 'Coffee?' he offered.

Captain Blake declined with a hand signal.

'This stalker business,' he finally said. 'The way I see it, it blows hot and cold.'

'How so?'

Hunter returned to his desk but didn't take a seat, instead he leaned against its edge. 'His actions. From the little we have so far, some of them are very consistent with the behavior pattern of a stalker, but some don't come even close.'

'Could you clarify, please?' the captain asked.

Hunter sipped his coffee. 'As we've just discussed, breaking into the victim's house when she wasn't there, leaving clues or notes behind, even murder as a consequence, all of that can easily be associated with stalking. The fact that all of the killer's rage was directed exclusively towards Karen Ward's face – its injuries, its complete disfiguration – indicates a fixation with the way she looked, which again is very consistent with the behavior of someone who was obsessed with her beauty. Someone who could very easily become delusional. But the phone call to Tanya Kaitlin, the question game he made her play, the way he forced her to watch her best friend being murdered, and the brutality and the self-indulgence of the whole act, all of that falls way beyond the realm of stalking, Captain.'

Captain Blake's eyes narrowed as she clearly began pondering something else.

'Let me ask you something,' she said. Her gaze slowly moved from Garcia to Hunter. 'Do you think he was bluffing? If Tanya Kaitlin had answered both questions correctly, do you think that he would've allowed Karen Ward to live?'

Silence ruled the room for several seconds, and as Hunter considered the captain's question, something new suddenly fired inside his head and he paused. His eyes moved down to the floor while he tried to organize his thoughts.

'Clever sonofabitch,' he finally whispered to himself, but not soft enough to escape Garcia and Captain Blake's ears. 'He knew she wouldn't.'

'He knew she wouldn't what, Robert?' the captain asked.

Hunter's stare moved to her.

'He knew she wouldn't get it right,' Hunter replied. 'That's the only reason why he forced Tanya to play the game.'

Intrigued looks from both, Captain Blake and Garcia.

'Think about it, Captain,' Hunter said. 'Who would've

gone through that much trouble, that much preparation, that much risk, to play a simple game where he could've lost?'

No replies, but the intrigued looks mutated to thoughtful ones.

'What would he have done if Tanya had given him a second correct answer?' Hunter continued. '"OK, you win. Well played. Give me a minute to untie your friend and I'll be out of here in no time. By the way, sorry about the wall mirror in the bathroom, I'll send you a check in the post."'

Several more silent seconds went by while Captain Blake and Garcia chewed on Hunter's words.

'But you said that both questions the killer asked her,' Captain Blake said, 'were directly linked to her.'

'That's right,' Hunter confirmed. 'He first asked her for the correct number of friends she had on Facebook then for Karen Ward's cellphone number. Very simple questions, designed to make the game seem fair.' Hunter paused, lifting a finger. 'Actually, more than fair. Designed to make the game seem easy, winnable, but most of all, to inflict a tremendous sense of guilt.' He looked at his partner. 'Carlos, how many times in this morning's interview did Tanya bury her face in her hands, crying and saying that it was all her fault, that she should've known Karen's number by heart?'

Garcia made a face. 'Pff, countless.'

'Exactly. And that's the clever part. The illusion. A simple, easy question, but one he knew for sure she wouldn't get right.'

'How could the killer have known that, Robert?' Captain Blake asked.

Hunter reached for his cellphone. 'Because he asked her before.'

Twenty-Two

Once Hunter and Garcia left her apartment, Tanya Kaitlin returned to the sofa in her living room. As she sat down, she once again pulled her bathrobe tightly around her, crossing her arms over her stomach. Her eyes aimlessly circled the room a couple of times before, for no specific reason, focusing on the tip of her toes. Right then nothing made sense and something inside her head was telling her that it probably never would.

'Why couldn't I know her number?' she whispered softly to herself. Her body began rocking back and forth ever so slightly, but her eyes never left her toes. 'I should've known her number.'

There was a long, shivering pause before her voice was reduced to a whispering breath.

'Three, two, three, nine, five . . . no. That's not it.'

The body-rocking stepped up a notch.

'Three, two, three, five, five . . . no. That's not it either.'

Tanya had thought that she had cried all the tears she had to cry, but she was wrong. Without even noticing them, new tears glassed over her eyes and began zigzagging their way down her cheeks.

'Three, two, three, five, nine, four ... no. That's wrong too.' The rocking, the shivering, her breathing, all of it were becoming a lot more emphatic.

'I ...' Her voice caught on her throat. 'I don't know. I can't remember. I should remember, but I can't.' Her quivering hands jetted to her face and she began sobbing again. 'Karen ... It's all my fault. I'm so, so sorry.'

Tanya had no idea how long she kept her face buried in her hands for, but by the time she lifted her head up again, her fingertips were starting to prune up. Her eyes found the empty pack of cigarettes on the coffee table and reflexes made her reach for them.

'Fuck,' she said, full of disappointment.

She had, understandably, forgotten that she had run out of cigarettes.

'I need a smoke. I need a cigarette.' The fact that she had given up a few years back didn't seem to bother her anymore. She dropped the pack back on the coffee table and got to her feet. 'I really need a smoke.'

Tanya began searching the living room, the words 'I need a cigarette' spilling out of her lips every time she opened a new drawer. A new cupboard. A new box.

Nothing.

'Goddamn it.' She slammed another drawer shut. 'I need to go get some more cigarettes.' She looked around for her purse. Found it on top of the dining table.

In normal circumstances, Tanya would never leave her apartment without having put on at least a touch of foundation, a little eyeliner, and some lipstick; after all, makeup was what she did for a living. She would also never dream of stepping outside her front door in her bathrobe, or with her hair in the state it was in, but these were far from normal circumstances.

If people can go to Walmart in bikinis and underwear, she thought. *I can run across the road to the nearest grocery store in my bathrobe.*

Maybe people around her neighborhood were more used to Walmart oddities than what she thought, because no one, not even the cashier, gave her a second look.

By the time she made it back to her apartment, Tanya was already lighting up her second cigarette. Her tears had ceased and the shivering had subsided considerably. She returned to the sofa and this time she was even able to lie down. It didn't matter that she felt so exhausted, or that she hadn't slept a wink overnight, because she was sure that she still wouldn't be able to fall asleep then, not without the help of some sleeping pills.

Tanya considered that thought.

She knew that she still had a box of Aventyl at the bottom of her medicine drawer, but she had already gone back to one bad habit in the last few hours, she didn't really want to go back to a second one.

Tanya dismissed the idea and rested her head against a couple of cushions. Seconds later, her eyelids fluttered heavily and she found it impossible to keep them open.

The calming effect of her menthol cigarettes was a lot stronger than what she had anticipated, because almost as soon as she shut out the light, she was transported into a half-awake, half-asleep world. Dream and reality danced in front of her in a carnival of images that caressed and slapped her face at the same time, but what really bothered her was the noise. Piercing. Disturbing. Irritating. And it was getting louder.

What the hell was it?

It sounded like an electric knife.

Louder still.

No. A chainsaw.

Where is it coming from?

Too loud.

Finally, Tanya opened her eyes.

The room was silent.

'What a fucking crazy dream,' she said in a half-chuckle, rubbing her eyes with the palms of her hands.

Then she heard it again. Or at least she thought she did.

'What?' She pulled herself up into a sitting position quick enough to cause blood to rush to her head too fast. The effort made the room spin around her.

Tanya took a deep breath and grabbed on to the sofa to steady herself. She still wasn't sure if her mind was playing tricks on her or not.

Slowly the room stopped spinning, but the noise didn't go away.

Tanya looked left then right, but with the curtains shut, the low light, and the stupor of sleep, she could make sense of very little.

The noise came at her again, but not nearly as loud as moments ago. It had somehow lost its strength as it moved from dream into reality.

Then a memory came to her and it petrified her soul.

'Oh, my God.' Tanya cupped her mouth with her hands as she twisted her neck around to look behind her. Her front door was unlocked. The security chain undone. She had forgotten to lock it after she came back from the grocery store.

Her body stiffened with fear.

'Someone is in here. Someone is in my apartment.'

Tanya's breathing went from resting to 'marathon finishing line' in a fraction of a second. The lethargy of sleep was now completely gone, but then, just like that, so was the noise.

'What the hell. Am I going crazy?'

She focused on listening and waited.

Nothing.

She concentrated harder and waited some more.

Still nothing.

'Damn! I probably *am* going crazy,' she whispered, laughing at herself before finally getting to her feet and walking over to her front door to lock it. Just to be certain, she stood there for a moment, ears pricked like an animal's.

Silence.

Tanya coughed to clear her throat and that made her realize how thirsty she was. She walked over to the fridge and poured herself a large glass of cold water, but as she brought the glass to her lips, the noise echoed throughout her living room one more time, sending fear cascading down her spine and the glass plummeting from her hand. As it smashed against the kitchen floor, Tanya heard it again – muffled, subdued, but very real – and it had come from somewhere to her right. Immediately her body swung in that direction. This time it took her eyes less than two seconds to finally zoom in on the source of the noise.

Her cellphone.

It was vibrating on top of a paperback book on her dining table.

Tanya let out an almost hysterical laugh.

'You silly bitch,' she said to herself, stepping over the broken glass and snatching the phone from the table. She was about to answer the call when it finally dawned on her.

A phone call.

Her throat constricted as if she was being choked by strong fingers.

The phone vibrated in her hand.

Tanya checked the display screen – unknown number.

'Oh my God! It's him again. It's that fucking psycho.' Once again her eyes were flooded by tears of desperation. 'No. I'm not answering this. I'm not.'

The phone finally stopped ringing.

Tanya looked back at its display screen with a terrified look on her face – four missed calls.

'Why? Why is this happening again?'

Buzz, buzz.

The phone vibrated twice in quick short bursts. Not a call, but a text message. The message preview appeared on her screen.

Tanya, this is Detective Robert Hunter of the LAPD. If you're screening your calls, please pick it up. If not ...

The fog of confusion thickened inside her head.

Tanya was about to unlock the phone and read the rest of the message when it began vibrating again – incoming call. She hesitated for a couple of rings while the gears inside her brain slowly got back to normal speed. As they finally did, she brought the phone to her ear.

'Hello?' Her voice wavered.

'Tanya, this is Detective Robert Hunter. We spoke earlier this morning?'

Tanya immediately recognized Hunter's voice. There was

something about the way he spoke, a certain confidence in his tone of voice that somehow calmed her.

'Oh! Hello, Detective.' She felt her drumming heart begin to slow down.

'I'm very sorry if I've woken you.' Hunter sounded sincere.

'No, not at all. I still can't fall sleep, even though I've been trying.' Tanya turned to look at the clock on her wall and her eyes widened in total surprise. She truly believed that she'd been lying on her sofa for no more than fifteen or twenty minutes, when in reality it'd been nearly three hours since her head had touched those cushions. 'Oh God!' she exclaimed.

'Is there something wrong?'

'No. No. I just . . . lost track of time. Didn't notice it go by so fast.'

'Given the circumstances, Tanya,' Hunter said, 'that's not actually a bad thing.'

'No,' Tanya admitted. 'You're right. I guess it isn't.' She laughed again. Not hysterically, but still hard enough for Hunter to pick up on it.

'Are you sure everything is OK?'

'Yes, I'm positive.' She looked back at the broken glass and the spilled water on her kitchen floor.

Hunter gave her a few more seconds before he spoke. 'I'm truly sorry for bothering you again so soon, Tanya, but I just thought of something I need to ask you.'

Tanya took a deep breath. She didn't want to think about what had happened anymore, but she knew she had no choice.

'OK. Sure.' Her voice was back to being timid.

'What I'm going to ask you to do is to think back, but

unfortunately, I can't tell you how far back. It could be a few days, a few weeks, a few months, or even longer.'

'OK,' she replied, with no conviction at all.

'I need you to try to remember if anyone has ever asked you the same question you were asked yesterday, or something very similar. And by anyone I really mean "anyone", Tanya – friends, acquaintances, strangers, beauty clients, whoever.'

Tanya sat back down on her sofa. 'I'm not sure I understand, Detective.'

Hunter had a feeling he had worded it too much.

'OK.' He tried to make it simpler this time. 'I guess that since the advent of the smartphone, we have all become a little ... lazy when it comes to memorizing phone numbers. Go back ten, fifteen years maybe, and most of us knew at least five numbers by heart.'

Tanya was still young, but she knew Hunter was right. When she was only ten years old, she did have quite a few numbers memorized – her home number, at least two or three of her school friends, her father's work number and so on.

'Yes, that's true,' she agreed.

'Great. So my question is – have you ever found yourself caught in a similar conversation with anyone, talking about how we used to memorize several phone numbers before, but now we don't anymore?'

Tanya squinted her eyes at nothing while she thought about it for a moment. 'Yes,' she replied at last. 'Actually, Cynthia and I were talking about how we used to know so many numbers by heart only last week.'

'OK, who's Cynthia?'

'Oh, she's another cosmetologist at DuBunne, the spa I work at.'

Hunter jotted down the name on a piece of paper. 'Was anyone else taking part in that conversation?'

A couple more thoughtful seconds.

'No. Not really. It was only Cynthia and I.'

'Anyone standing close enough to be able to eavesdrop on the two of you? Can you remember?'

Tanya began chewing on her bottom lip. 'No. I remember it well, we were at the back, sorting out the supplies room.'

'OK,' Hunter acknowledged. 'Can you remember having a similar conversation with anyone else? Maybe a client, or on a night out with a date ... anyone, really. Maybe a conversation where someone dropped a more specific question?'

'Like if I could remember my best friend's cellphone number?' Tanya's voice lowered, sadness punctuating every word.

'Yes. But it might've not been so direct.'

Tanya took her time. Her left hand moved to her mouth and she began pinching her lips with her thumb and index finger.

Hunter waited patiently.

'I ... I can't be sure right now, Detective. My mind is still a bit of a mess.'

'That's not a problem, Tanya. Thank you for trying. Could you do me a favor and think about it for a while. It might suddenly just come back to you.'

'Yeah. Sure. Of course I can.'

'If you remember anything, anything at all, however small it might seem to you, please give me a call. No matter what time, OK?'

'Yes, of course. If I remember anything I will.'

Tanya disconnected and reached for the card Hunter had left by the ashtray on her coffee table. She studied it for a long moment before paranoia began whispering in her ear. Right then she decided that she would not put that card down until she had memorized both numbers on it.

Twenty-Three

It took another whole day for Karen Ward's autopsy results to finally come through on Saturday morning. The details of the brutality with which she was murdered were just as shocking on paper as they were visually.

In total, there were twenty-nine severe lacerations to her face. Three of those had breached through to the inside of her mouth. In consequence, her tongue had been almost completely severed. Her killer had used so much force in the head-slammings that chunks of glass had embedded themselves into six out of Karen's fourteen facial bones, including her nose, cheeks, forehead and chin. The force of the impacts also caused both of her cheekbones to fracture, together with her nose and jaw. Death had indeed come as the result of extensive brain trauma, where the hypothalamus and the optic tract were ruptured by a five-inch long shard of mirrored glass that had been introduced via the victim's left ocular globe cavity.

Toxicology came back negative on all counts. The killer had not sedated Karen, not even as he subdued her prior to her murder, which meant that Karen Ward was one hundred percent lucid throughout her entire ordeal.

CSI had also come back with several test results. Only one

set of fingerprints had been found inside the victim's apartment, and they belonged to the victim herself. The prints that were found on the outside of Karen Ward's front door also gave them very little to go on. One of the sets belonged to Karen herself, the other three got no matches against AFIT – Advanced Fingerprint Identification Technology – which meant that whoever they belonged to had no previous records, but the result that had really surprised everybody had been the fingerprint test that the CSI fingerprint expert had run against the fire escape door by Karen Ward's apartment. He hadn't found a single print, as if the door had been completely wiped clean that same night.

Forensics was still analyzing fibers, hairs and specks of dust that had been collected at the crime scene. So far, nothing had flagged up as unusual. The container the killer had used to hold the glass pieces he had obtained from the bathroom mirror was never found, nor were the remaining shards of glass. The speculation was that maybe the killer had kept them as trophies.

IT Forensics had also managed to breach the password security on the laptop found in Karen Ward's living room. Hunter and Garcia's team were already searching through text files, images, email messages, and everything else they could find, but just like Hunter had expected, they still hadn't come across anything they thought could be of any interest to the investigation.

'Any luck?' Garcia asked as Hunter finally got back to the office. He had spent the entire morning in Santa Monica, where he had visited Burke Williams, the beauty spa Karen Ward was working at when she started receiving the notes Tanya Kaitlin had told them about.

'Not sure yet,' Hunter replied, taking off his jacket and placing it on the back of his chair.

Garcia made a face at Hunter while waiting for his partner to clarify.

'I managed to get a list of all the clients who were attended to by Karen Ward during her short time at Burke Williams.'

'All right. How many?'

'Sixty-two names.'

'Wow.'

'It's not as bad as it sounds,' Hunter explained. 'From his body frame, Tanya Kaitlin was very sure that the killer was male, remember?'

'OK,' Garcia conceded. 'So how many out of the sixty-two are male?'

'Five.'

'That's a pretty good reduction.'

'Operations is already working on their profiles,' Hunter said. 'So let's wait and see what they can come up with and we'll take it from there.'

'How about the stalker notes Karen received? Did you ask the people at the spa about them?'

'I did, and no one had a clue what I was talking about.'

'What?' Garcia found that positively odd. 'What do you mean?'

'It seems like Karen didn't tell anyone at Burke Williams about the notes she was getting or about being stalked,' Hunter clarified. 'I spoke not only with the spa manager, but with everyone else who worked there, including the receptionist. They all echoed Tanya's words – Karen was a great cosmetologist and the sweetest person you could ever meet, but none of them knew anything about any notes. She never told a soul.'

'So what reason did she give them for leaving?' Garcia leaned forward, placing both elbows on his desktop. 'She must've told them something.'

'She did. She told them that she was going back to Campbell due to family problems. That was all.' Hunter had a seat behind his desk. 'She'd been there for less than four months, so no one felt that they were close enough to her to ask for any more details.'

'Well,' Garcia said. 'LA *is* such a mega-metropolis that moving neighborhoods could be just like moving cities. People could easily get away with a white lie like that.'

'After Burke Williams,' Hunter continued. 'I took a drive down to Long Beach to talk to the people at True Beauty.'

'Let me guess,' Garcia said. 'Exactly the same thing. Karen never told anyone about the notes she was receiving or about being stalked.'

Hunter nodded as he woke up his computer. 'Lastly, I dropped by DuBunne spa in South Torrance.'

'DuBunne? Isn't that where Tanya Kaitlin works?'

'That's right. I wanted to have a quick chat with that Cynthia woman Tanya mentioned.'

'The one who she had the conversation about remembering phone numbers with?'

'Exactly.'

'And?'

'She's a nineteen-year-old girl,' Hunter explained. 'Fresh out of beauty school. She's doing her apprenticeship at DuBunne. Still lives with her parents in Gardena.' He shook his head. 'Whatever conversation she had with Tanya about not remembering phone numbers by heart anymore was inoffensive. I did ask her if she remembered having that conversation with anyone else. She didn't. I don't think this killer acquired that information through her.'

'Talking about Tanya,' Garcia said. 'Any word from her? Has she recalled any other conversations about not remembering phone numbers and all?'

'No, nothing. My hope was that she would've remembered something when I asked her the question for the first time yesterday. That would've caught her brain by surprise. Now that she's had time to think about it, she probably won't.'

'OK, I don't follow,' Garcia said. 'Surely the more you think about something, the more you search your memory, the more chances you have of your brain remembering something, no?'

'In most cases, yes.'

'But not in hers? Why?'

'Because the guilt that she has placed on herself would've triggered a toxic defense mechanism response that would've pushed her brain into selective post-traumatic amnesia.'

Garcia kept his eyes on Hunter for a couple of silent seconds. 'OK,' he finally said. 'So just for a moment, let's pretend that I don't have a Ph.D. in psychology like you do, Robert, and tell me all that again.'

Hunter smiled before clarifying. 'Tanya feels guilty for Karen's death because she believes that she should've known her number. She thinks it's her fault her best friend is dead. Because of that, as a defense mechanism to lessen her pain, there's a chance that her brain will choose to let go of any memory that it somehow associates with that guilt. The more she thinks about it, the more her brain will push the memories away because remembering will make her feel even more guilty.'

'OK, now I get it and that's not good.'

'I'm still keeping my fingers crossed, though,' Hunter added. 'Everyone reacts differently to traumas, so you never know. I'll give her another call later tonight.'

Garcia reached for his notepad. 'By the way, I got off the phone with forensics just minutes before you got here.'

'Anything new?'

'They just finished analyzing the collage note we found inside Karen's bedroom,' Garcia said, sitting back on his chair. 'As we were expecting, they drew a blank. It's completely clear from fingerprints or DNA.' He looked up from his notes. 'Who goes through the trouble of cutting out letter by letter from a magazine to hide his handwriting, only to forget to wear gloves while piecing the note together, right?'

Hunter said nothing because, as crazy as it might sound, he'd seen it happen before. Most killers out there had a below-average IQ and were categorized as 'disorganized murderers'. Movies and books sometimes portrayed some of them as cunning masterminds, but in reality, most of them would struggle with a fourth-grade math exam. They were labeled 'disorganized' because they didn't really set out to kill their victims. They usually did it out of an uncontrollable violent impulse, which could have been initially triggered by a number of factors – shame, insecurity, anger, jealousy, low self-esteem, under the influence of mind-altering substances – the list was long and very personal. The problem was, the reverse of the coin, the killers who were categorized as 'organized murderers', tended to be highly intelligent, organized, and very, very disciplined.

'The piece of paper used as a backdrop for the note,' Garcia continued, 'came out of a common white-paper pad, nothing special about it either. Easily found in any supermarket or stationery store.'

'How about the shoes?' Hunter asked.

Garcia shook his head. 'They've been cleaned ... bleached, actually. Forensics found absolutely nothing inside them. No skin cells whatsoever. Not even from Karen herself.'

That didn't surprise Hunter. 'How about the mask, any luck with it?'

The sketch Tanya Kaitlin had worked on with the police artist had already been sent to every costume and party shop in the greater Los Angeles area.

Garcia breathed out. 'So far, no matches. Apparently no one has ever seen anything like it. No score over the Internet either. This mask wasn't bought from a shop, Robert. He created it himself.'

Hunter had no doubt that that had been the case, but they still had to try.

'But it's not all bad,' Garcia announced. 'We've got one positive result. One you were one hundred percent right about.'

'And what is that?'

'The nine-one-one calls.'

On his screen, Garcia clicked and scrolled a couple of times until he found what he was looking for.

'In the past three months there were four bogus, high-priority, nine-one-one calls made, concerning the general area of Karen Ward's home address. Two of the addresses given by the caller were to the same apartment block, the other two to neighboring ones.'

'Any luck when it comes to CCTV camera locations?' Hunter asked.

Garcia laughed. 'You would hope so, wouldn't you? You called it right, Robert – this guy is anything but dumb. He stayed away from payphones, choosing to use four different pre-paid cellphones – no chance of a trace.'

'Do we have the audio files for the calls?'

Garcia sat back on his chair and gave Hunter a quirky smile. 'We do now. I just got the email.'

Twenty-Four

Hunter got to his feet and walked over to Garcia's desk. The email showing on his screen had four different audio file attachments. The first one dated back three months, almost to the date. The last one was dated nine days ago.

'Let's go through them chronologically,' Hunter suggested.

Garcia nodded and double-clicked the first audio file. The time logged for the 911 call had been 10:55 p.m.

DISPATCHER [female voice]: 'Nine-one-one, what's your emergency?'

MALE VOICE: 'Well . . . I think I just heard gunshots coming from one of the apartments down the corridor from me.'

The voice carried a somewhat pronounced Southern accent, but what caused both detectives to exchange a worried look was the youth of its tone. The voice sounded like it belonged to someone in his early twenties.

Keyboard clicks.

DISPATCHER: 'Gunshots? Are you certain, sir? Could it have been just a loud bang, maybe?'

MALE VOICE: 'No, I don't think so.'

A short pause.

DISPATCHER: 'OK, could you describe exactly what you heard?'

MALE VOICE: 'One thing is for sure, they were arguing again. They argue a hell of a lot, you know. Always at night. Always screaming at each other. But tonight it sounded like they were going mad. I'm quite sure the whole building could hear it. Then suddenly – bang, bang, bang – three loud pops. And now everything has gone church quiet in there. I'm telling you, something isn't right in that apartment.'

DISPATCHER: 'OK, sir, what's the address?'

The address the caller gave the dispatcher would've taken the police to the apartment directly below Karen Ward's.

More keyboard clicks.

DISPATCHER: 'A unit is on its way now, sir. Could I have your—'

The caller put the phone down.
'It took around eleven minutes for a black and white unit

to respond,' Garcia said, reading from the email he had received. 'Their report says that they were quite surprised when a woman, apparently in her mid-twenties, answered the door holding a baby in her arms. The woman, Donna Farrell, shared the apartment with her boyfriend, who works as a night security guard, so he wasn't in. The officers asked her about any loud bangs or any neighbors who seemed to argue frequently, but she told them that she hadn't heard any loud noises, or voices, or anything. She also told them that she had never heard any arguments coming from any of the neighboring apartments. Before logging it in as a bogus call, the officers knocked on several other doors. The reply was always the same. No loud bangs. No known arguing neighbors.' Garcia scrolled down on the email. 'The call was made from a pre-paid cellphone. Untraceable.'

'Did they get a location?' Hunter asked.

Garcia scrolled down a little more. 'Yeah. The call came from the general location of Karen Ward's apartment building. He was probably standing right in front of it when he made the call.'

'Probably.' Hunter agreed. 'He had to be close by to be able to clock the response time. OK, let's check the next call.'

Garcia double-clicked it. The call had come in at 11:08 p.m., fourteen days after the call they'd just heard.

DISPATCHER [male voice]: 'Nine-one-one, how can I direct your call?'

MALE VOICE: 'Yes. I live on the corner of East Broadway and Loma Avenue in Long Beach. From my window I have a clear view of the balcony and

the windows belonging to the building across the
road from me.'

This time Hunter and Garcia exchanged an even more confused look. There was due urgency to the caller's voice, but
it sounded nothing like the one they'd heard in the previous
call. Gone was the pronounced Southern accent, replaced by
a typical Angelino inflection. The youth of the voice was also
gone. The person making the call sounded like he was in his
mid-thirties, with a much deeper and darker voice.

DISPATCHER: 'OK, sir, and what seems to be the
problem?'

MALE VOICE: 'I'm standing at my window right
now, and I can clearly see into one of the apartments
on the top floor. The curtains are wide open and
the lights are all on. There's a man walking back
and forth in there, waving his arms around like a
lunatic. The problem is, he's carrying either a sword,
or a machete, or something very similar. Whatever it
is, it's one hell of a menacing-looking weapon, I can
tell you that.'

DISPATCHER [now sounding a little more urgent]:
'Is there anyone else in the apartment with him?
Can you see?'

MALE VOICE: 'That's why I'm calling. I've been
watching this guy for the past five or ten minutes,
and all he's been doing, as I've said, is walking back

and forth in the living room, waving his weapon in the air and shouting at the walls, or so it seemed. But just now I saw this little girl appear at the other window, not in the same room as him, but in the next room along. She must be around twelve or thirteen. She looked terrified. I can't really see any details because of the distance, but I think she is crying.'

DISPATCHER: 'A little girl, you said?'

MALE VOICE: 'That's right.'

DISPATCHER: 'OK, sir. Do you have the address of this building?'

The caller gave the address to the dispatcher. Once again, it was the address to Karen Ward's building.

MALE VOICE: 'The apartment I'm talking about is the last apartment down the corridor on the top floor.'

DISPATCHER: 'And you said that you can see the apartment from your window, could you give me your—'

The caller had already disconnected.
'That would be Karen Ward's apartment,' Garcia said. 'He sent the cops to her apartment?'
Hunter nodded. 'What was the response time?'

Garcia checked the email. 'Around ten minutes this time.'

'Pre-paid cellphone again?' Hunter asked.

'You got it.'

Hunter leaned against the edge of Garcia's desk. 'OK, let's try the next call.'

Garcia opened the file. The third call in their list had been logged in twenty-eight days after the second one. It had come in at 11:13 p.m.

DISPATCHER [female voice]: 'Nine-one-one, what's your emergency?'

MALE VOICE: 'Umm ... She's not breathing. I don't know what to do. She's not breathing and it's all my fault.'

The nervous voice was full of trepidation and strangled on tears. Once again, its tone differed greatly from the previous two calls. This time it was low and husky, as if the caller were on the last stages of a bad sore throat. The accent had also changed completely, moving from a typical Angelino to a very distinctive Southern Texan twang.

DISPATCHER: 'Can you tell me your name, sir?'

MALE VOICE: 'Todd. Todd Phillips.'

Keyboard clicks.

DISPATCHER: 'And who is the person we're talking about here, Todd? Who did you say isn't breathing?'

MALE VOICE: 'My girlfriend. Her name is Kelly Dixon. You have to help us. Please.'

DISPATCHER: 'That's what I'm here for, Todd, but for me to be able to do that I have to ask you a few questions, OK? You said Kelly isn't breathing. Are you sure? Can you feel a pulse at all?'

MALE VOICE: 'No, no I can't.'

More keyboard clicks.

MALE VOICE: 'You have to send someone to help us. Please, send help.'

DISPATCHER: 'Help will be on its way very soon, Todd. Now what you need to do is stay calm and give me a few more details, OK? Can you quickly tell me what happened?'

MALE VOICE: 'I didn't mean to hurt her. I didn't. I swear it. I love her.'

DISPATCHER: 'That's fine, Todd, I believe you, but you need to tell me what happened, OK?'

MALE VOICE: 'I don't know. We had an argument about something silly and I lost my head. I held her. I squeezed, and now she's not moving. She's not breathing. You must send help. Please. You must.'

DISPATCHER *(she typed as she spoke)*: 'OK, Todd. What's your location?'

As soon as the caller gave the dispatcher the address, he put the phone down.

'Nine-one-one tried calling the number back,' Garcia read from the email. 'But "surprise, surprise" – no reply. Nevertheless they have to follow protocol, so a black and white unit, together with a paramedic team, was dispatched to the location, which took them to one of the buildings across the road from Karen's. Needless to say that they found no one by the name of Todd Phillips or Kelly Dixon. The apartment in question belonged to an elderly couple, who had lived there for over twenty-five years.'

'What was the response time for this call?' Hunter asked.

'Just under ten minutes.'

Hunter wrote the time down on his notebook.

'The GPS location recorded for the call,' Garcia added, 'matched the address given by the caller, so once again he was probably standing right in front of the building when he made the call.'

'Because he knew the call would be traced,' Hunter confirmed. 'And if he'd made the call from a payphone down the road or from anywhere else, the location wouldn't match his story. He was supposed to be with his girlfriend, who wasn't breathing, remember?' Hunter scratched his chin. 'No slip-ups.'

Garcia place the cursor over the last attached file. 'Shall I?'

Hunter gave his partner a single nod.

'I wonder what kind of bullshit we'll get now.'

Twenty-Five

The fourth and last call was received exactly five weeks after the third call, and a week before Karen Ward's murder. It was time-stamped – 11:19 p.m.

DISPATCHER [female voice]: 'Nine-one-one, what's the location of your emergency?'

FEMALE VOICE: 'Two-three-one Loma Avenue – Long Beach.'

Garcia looked at Hunter with wide eyes. 'It's a female voice,' he said. 'What the fuck is going on?'
Hunter was also caught off guard, but he decided to reserve his comments until he'd heard the entire recording.

FEMALE VOICE: 'Could you send someone to my house, please?'

The voice sounded scared and filled with emotion.

DISPATCHER: 'What's the problem there, ma'am?'

FEMALE VOICE: 'My ex-husband has just broken into my house. He's screaming and raving like a lunatic. He's out of his mind, and he's a violent man.'

DISPATCHER: 'OK, and where is he now?'

FEMALE VOICE: 'Right outside my door. Please, send somebody.'

DISPATCHER: 'Outside your door? Where are you, ma'am?'

FEMALE VOICE: 'I've locked myself inside my bedroom.'

Bang. Bang. Bang.

Hunter and Garcia heard what sounded like three loud knocks to a door.

DISPATCHER: 'OK. Has he been drinking? Do you know?'

FEMALE VOICE: 'Probably. That's what he always does.'

DISPATCHER: 'Has he hit you?'

FEMALE VOICE: 'No. He hasn't had the chance yet. As soon as he broke through the front door,

I ran and locked myself in here. But if he gets in here ...'

DISPATCHER: 'OK, ma'am, what's your name?'

FEMALE VOICE: 'Rose Landry.'

DISPATCHER: 'And your address is 231 Loma Avenue – Long Beach?'

FEMALE VOICE: 'Yes, that's right.'

Hurried keyboard clicks.

DISPATCHER: 'OK, a unit is on its way to you now. They won't be long. Can you stay on the phone with me, Rose?'

FEMALE VOICE *(sounding desperate)*: 'No, I can't. I can't. I've got to go.'

The call ended.

Garcia sat back on his chair and ran a hand over his mouth and chin, as if smoothing down an imaginary goatee.

'This time the address given was to a house just around the corner from Karen's apartment building,' he said. 'Less than thirty seconds away. It belonged to a retired schoolteacher and his wife – John and Judith Marble.'

'Response time?' Hunter asked.

Another scroll down on the email. 'Eight minutes. The fastest time of them all.

Hunter wrote the time down.

'Now, let me repeat myself here.' Garcia said. 'What the fuck is going on? It's a female voice. Is he working with someone, or was this just a coincidence?'

'No, not a coincidence, Carlos,' Hunter said, checking his notes. 'All four bogus calls were made inside the same thirty-minute interval – between ten-fifty-five p.m. and eleven-twenty-five. Do you remember what was the time logged for Tanya Kaitlin's nine-one-one call?'

'Not from the top of my head,' Garcia replied. 'But I'm guessing somewhere inside that half-hour bracket.'

'Eleven-nineteen p.m.,' Hunter confirmed. 'All four bogus calls were also made on a Wednesday evening. Karen Ward was murdered two nights ago, on a Wednesday evening.'

Garcia's gaze jumped back to his computer screen. All four calls had been date-stamped in the usual format – month/day/year. He hadn't yet worked out that they had all fallen on a Wednesday.

'If you average the four response times,' Hunter continued. 'You come to nine and three-quarter minutes. Round it up, and that's exactly the average response time the caller told Tanya over the phone.' He shook his head. 'This was no coincidence, Carlos. Our killer made all four calls.'

Garcia thought about the last call for a moment.

'A voice modifier?' he half stated, half questioned.

'Audio forensics will confirm it,' Hunter replied. 'But with the right equipment, changing a male voice into a female one is just a question of sliding a few faders up and down, that's all.'

'He probably also thought that a female voice would be a nice touch,' Garcia accepted.

'Certainly less suspicious,' Hunter agreed. He knew that about 70 to 75 percent of all bogus 911 calls in the USA were made by men, not women. 'Remember, Carlos, he'd already made three fake calls prior to that one – all using a male voice, all directing Long Beach PD to the same exact area. This was the last call before the actual murder. He wouldn't want to risk it.'

'Well, he certainly knew how to fake these calls,' Garcia said. 'Because I'll tell you this, If I didn't know better, I would've thought that they were all legit – sometimes tense, sometimes frightened, sometimes anxious, and absolutely no hesitation in his voice. Every question he was asked by the dispatcher, he answered it in character. I wouldn't be surprised if this guy has trained as an actor.' Garcia rethought his words. 'Then again, half of this city has trained as an actor.'

Hunter said nothing, but right at the back of his mind, something else began bothering him.

Twenty-Six

Hunter and Garcia spent the next hour revising crime-scene photographs, going over various documents, and trying to obtain a more thorough profile on Karen Ward. Garcia had been searching the Internet for the past thirty-five minutes when he paused and frowned at his computer screen.

'Wait a second,' he whispered, leaning forward and placing both elbows on his desk.

Hunter looked at his partner over the top of his screen.

Garcia looked completely absorbed as he began scrolling down the webpage.

'Something wrong?' Hunter asked.

Garcia lifted his index finger. 'I'm not sure yet. Give me a minute.'

Hunter went back to the file he'd been reading, but his thoughts were still on the four 911 calls they'd heard. The more he tried, the less sense he could make of everything – the less sense he could make of everything, the more the stalker theory bothered him.

In general, stalkers were fragile people who were highly

impulsive and almost always enslaved to their own emotions, rarely being able to control them. Sure, some were known for being very well organized when it came to certain aspects of their obsession. They observed the object of their affection compulsively because they simply needed to know all there was to know about them. They followed them. They took pictures. They fed the fire of their obsession in any way they could because, the sad truth was, most of them led somewhat boring, unadventurous lives and, strangely, that obsession gave their lives a 'sense of purpose', something to live for, and that was the catch.

If the object of their affection were to die all of a sudden, then so would that 'sense of purpose', substituted by a void so deep that it could potentially tear them apart inside. So why kill them?

History has shown that in most cases, when that had actually happened, it hadn't been a planned action. They hadn't set out to kill the one they were stalking. What happened was a return to that volatile individual who struggled to control his/her emotions. In short – a thoughtless, impulsive act that resulted in the death of the one being stalked. And that was nothing like this killer had shown so far. No, this killer was well prepared, methodical, very clever, resourceful, and if he'd begun clocking the police response time three months before the actual murder, he no doubt planned well ahead. Impulsiveness ... thoughtlessness ... simply didn't come into his equation.

'Sonofabitch,' Garcia said, ripping Hunter away from his thoughts.

They locked eyes.

'Maybe there's a different reason why Tanya can't

remember having another one of those conversations with anyone else.'

'And what reason would that be?' Hunter asked.

Garcia pointed at his computer screen. 'You've got to come have a look at this.'

Twenty-Seven

Cassandra closed her living room door behind her, dropped her handbag by the dark-gray sofa and slowly made her way into the kitchen. In there she retrieved a glass vase from one of the cupboards, filled it with water and placed the colorful bouquet of flowers she had brought home with her inside it.

No, the flowers hadn't come from a secret admirer, nor had they been sent to her by Mr. J. Cassandra had bought that bouquet herself; truth be told, even after twenty-one years, her husband still surprised her every now and then with unannounced little gifts – sometimes flowers, sometimes chocolates, sometimes an invitation to a romantic dinner, or tickets to an opera, or a ballet, or even a Lakers game, since Cassandra was a big LA Lakers fan. No matter the occasion, though, the card attached to the bouquet, or whatever gift he had brought home with him, would always say the exact same thing: *You make me the happiest man on earth. With all my love, today and always. J.*

The memory brought a sparkling smile to Cassandra's lips, mainly because she considered herself to be a very lucky woman. Despite the years, Mr. J was still a very handsome man, tall and square-jawed, with a shaved head and dark eyes that were so full of expression, he could make himself understood with a simple look. Physically, unlike so many of her friends' husbands, Mr. J had never let himself go. His frame still showed signs of all the physical training he did when younger, with strong shoulders, a flat stomach, and lean, muscular arms. Cassandra had never failed to notice the playful looks that other women, including most of her friends, would give Mr. J every time they were out, but she had never seen her husband reciprocate any of it. He was always polite towards other women, but never flirtatious.

Once, and only once, after she had rejected his advances in bed years ago, Mr. J had calmly asked her if there was someone else. If she had fallen for another man. If she had stopped loving him.

'Please don't be silly, honey,' she had replied. 'Of course I haven't fallen for anyone else. Of course I haven't stopped loving you. I'm just not in a good mood tonight, OK?'

That had been true then, and it was still true today. Cassandra had never fallen for anyone else, and she had never stopped loving Mr. J, of that she was absolutely sure. How could she? He was a good, kind and loving husband and a terrific father to Patrick. He had always treated her with dignity and respect. He listened to what she had to say and he truly valued her opinion on every aspect of their family life. Yes, a lot had changed over the years, especially after her son had hit his teens. That had been when Cassandra had felt the lowest in her life. She had lost her mother just a year before that and, for some reason, once her little boy started looking more like a young man, she found herself struggling with depression, a condition she had always kept a secret from absolutely everyone. A condition that had distanced her not only from her husband, but from all of her friends as well. Cassandra wasn't sure if it had been coincidence or not, but just as Patrick entered his senior year in high school, she finally began to get a grip on her depression and was slowly but surely crawling out of that dark hole. With every passing day, she was becoming more and more like her old self.

Cassandra checked the wall clock in the kitchen – 7:24 p.m. She had thought about going out for dinner, maybe a nice Italian, or even the new Mediterranean place that had just opened a couple of blocks from her house, but she discarded the idea on the drive back home. She didn't feel like sitting in a restaurant by herself, and though she could invite one of her friends to go with her, tonight she was in a more 'homey' mood.

She walked back into her living room, placed the vase with the flowers at the center of her dining table and returned to the kitchen.

'OK, let's see what we have, shall we?' she said out loud, pulling open the fridge door. 'Umm.' Cassandra screwed up her face as her gaze moved from shelf to shelf. Her fridge was packed full, but nothing in there seemed to excite her too much.

'You know what?' she began a conversation with herself. 'I've had a tough week, and it's Saturday night, the international night of "no-home cooking". If I'm not going out, how about if I get it delivered?' She closed the fridge door and thought about it for all of two seconds. 'Yup, that sounds like a plan to me.'

Cassandra walked over to the kitchen counter and opened the last drawer on the left. From inside it, she retrieved a handful of to-go menus.

'Pizza? Nope. Mexican? Umm ... nope.'

As she discarded them, she returned them to the drawer.

'Italian? ... Possibly.'

She put that one to the side.

'Healthy salad? Umm ... not tonight. Burger and ribs? Nope. Japanese?'

This time the 'umm' came out with a singing intonation. Cassandra unfolded the menu and quickly scanned the offerings.

'Chicken teriyaki sounds nice. Maybe even some sashimi.' She pressed her lips together and felt her mouth salivating.

Decision made.

'But first things first,' she said as she returned all the other menus back to the drawer. 'What I really need right about now is a large glass of wine.'

This time Cassandra didn't need to think about it. She knew exactly which wine she would go for. To-go menu in hand, she walked back into her living room and from their large and well-stocked wine cabinet she chose a bottle of 2002, Hourglass Estate, Cabernet Sauvignon. As she pulled the cork from the bottle, she brought it to her nose and gently breathed in its aroma – spring flowers and berries.

'Oh yes, absolute heaven.'

Cassandra poured herself a glass, but didn't sip it straight away. First, to better define its tones, she wanted to let the wine breathe for a minute or two. Meanwhile, she could order her dinner. She walked over to the sofa and grabbed her handbag. As she searched inside it for her cellphone, she found the note that some creepy psycho had left stuck to the back window of her car. She hadn't really forgotten about it, but as her fingers brushed against the white piece of paper, the memory of the words inside it came back to her and the skin on her arms turned into gooseflesh.

Have you ever felt like you're being watched, Cassandra?

'Urgh,' Cassandra said, shaking her shoulders as if to dislodge the uneasy feeling. She quickly grabbed her cell-phone, dropping the bag back on to the floor. Instinctively, she looked around her living room before walking over to her front door. She knew she had locked it. She could see the security chain safely in place, but paranoia made her go check it. The key had been turned all the way inside the lock until it could rotate no more.

'Fuck! How can such a silly and stupid note make me feel so unsettled?' Cassandra asked herself, but the truth was, she knew exactly why – for the past three or four weeks, way before she'd got that note, the feeling that she was being watched had been shadowing her like a dark ghost. Almost everywhere she went – to work, out with friends, dinner with her husband, it didn't matter. Wherever she was, she would suddenly feel like someone had their eyes on her.

Cassandra knew that everyone, every once in a while, felt like they were being watched. She had felt that way a few times in the past, but this was nothing like anything she had ever experienced. This was a dark, soul-choking feeling, as if evil itself was doing the watching.

Cassandra rushed over to the dining table, picked up her glass of wine and had a healthy couple of sips. She knew that that was no way to appreciate such a beautiful wine, but right then she needed the alcohol a lot more than she needed the palate experience.

She returned the glass to the table and checked her cellphone. No messages. No missed calls. Mr. J had promised her that he would call if his return plans were to change. So far, nothing, which meant that he should be back home by tomorrow at the latest. That notion brought a lot of comfort to her.

Cassandra had discarded the two previous notes she had received while working at the WomenHeart charity shop as some silly prank. Because of that she had never mentioned anything to her husband, but this time, whatever this was, it had gone too far. She had already made up her mind that she would show Mr. J the note that was left on her car. That's why she had kept it in her handbag, so she wouldn't forget it.

Cassandra reached for the Japanese restaurant to-go menu and was about to dial its number when her doorbell rang. She paused and frowned at the door. She wasn't expecting anyone.

Ding-ding.

'Are you kidding me?' she said, putting down the menu and consulting her timepiece – 7:36 p.m.

Ding-ding.

Holding on to her phone, she approached the door and peeked through the peephole. Standing outside, staring straight at the door as if he could see through it, was a uniformed, LAPD officer.

Cassandra's frown intensified three-fold. 'Who is it?' she called, without unlocking the door.

'Ms. Jenkinson?' the officer asked. His voice was calm but firm.

'Yes?'

'I'm Officer Douglas with the LAPD Valley Bureau. I was wondering if I could have a word with you, ma'am.'

A couple of confused silent seconds went by.

'A word with me about what?'

The officer took a second, as if he needed it to steady himself.

'It's about your husband, ma'am. John Jenkinson.'

Something in the officer's tone of voice made Cassandra's heart skip a beat.

'What? What about John? Is everything OK?'

A new, quick, silent moment.

'If possible, ma'am, I think it would be better if we talked inside.'

Cassandra felt as if the room was closing in on her.

'Oh, my God!' she whispered as she quickly unlocked the door and pulled it open. 'What happened? Is John OK? Where is he?'

Cassandra couldn't see the officer's eyes, as they were hidden behind mirrored shades, but his facial expression was dark, solemn.

'It would be better if we could sit down, Ms. Jenkinson.'

She searched his face again, but again, all she found was a dark wall.

'Why? What happened?'

'Please, let's have a seat.'

'Yes, OK, come in,' she finally said, fully opening the door and indicating the dark-gray sofa in her living room. 'Please tell me, what's going on? Where's John? Is he OK? Is everything OK?'

The officer stepped into the house.

As Cassandra closed the door behind them, the officer turned to face her.

'Can I ask you something, Ms. Jenkinson?'

'Yes, of course.'

The officer took off his dark glasses.

'Have you ever felt like you're being watched?'

Twenty-Eight

Hunter got to his feet and moved around to Garcia's desk.

'What have you got?' he asked.

The expression on Garcia's face was still half confused, half surprised. He clearly wasn't expecting to find whatever it was that he had found. He extended his index finger and once again indicated his computer monitor.

'Have a look.'

Displaying on Garcia's screen was a social media network page. Hunter looked at it blank-faced.

'So what exactly am I looking at here?' he asked.

'This post right here.' Garcia pointed to it.

Hunter read the entry, paused, read it again then looked back at his partner. 'Whose page is this?'

'Pete Harris's,' Garcia replied.

Hunter took a second. 'Is that the friend Tanya mentioned? The makeup artist who's supposed to be in Europe somewhere?'

Garcia confirmed. 'That's him. And by the looks of it, he really is in Europe. He posted something this morning.' He scrolled all the way up to the top of the page to show Hunter. 'He's on set in Berlin. Been there for nearly a month now.'

Hunter acknowledged it and Garcia scrolled back down to where they originally were.

'Now,' Garcia said, 'have you noticed the first comment?'

Hunter had. It had come from Tanya Kaitlin, with replies from Karen Ward and Pete Harris. His gaze searched for the date at the top of the post.

'This was posted over six months ago,' he said in a quiet, pensive tone.

'That's right,' Garcia agreed. 'So even if Tanya wasn't going through this post-traumatic amnesia stuff you mentioned, I'm not sure she would've remembered this.'

Hunter's attention returned to Garcia's screen. Pete Harris had uploaded an image he had probably plucked from the Internet. It showed two women standing side by side. The one on the left looked to be in her early twenties, the one on the right in her mid-fifties. The younger of the two was smiling at her cellphone, while the other one was holding the receiver of an old-fashioned, disc-dial phone to her ear. Across the face of the image, in black letters, a challenge was followed by a grading scale:

You vs. your parents' generation. The phone number challenge. Is technology making you brainlazy?

How many phone numbers can you remember without having to look at your contacts?

0 = 100% brainlazy. You're a slave to your phone. Can you still remember your own name?

1 to 3 = Believe it or not, you're already better than 85% of people out there, but don't kid yourself, you're still brainlazy and far from what your parents' generation could do.

4 to 6 = Now you're getting close, and you deserve a pat on the back. You made it to the top 3% of your generation. Yeah, seriously.

7 to 10 = Congratulations, you just equaled the average person in your parents' generation, and you're now in the elite 1% of yours.

More than 10 = What, really? Impressive. Your memory banks are hyperactive and brainlaziness has missed you completely. Your parents' generation has nothing on you when it comes to remembering phone numbers, and in this day and age, you could possibly be THE ONLY ONE OF YOUR KIND.

Pete had introduced the post with the following words: 'Be honest, people.'

The first comment had come from Tanya Kaitlin: *Lol, not a single one for me. Shameful, I know. I've become completely brainlazy* ☹. *And I admit, I am a slave to my phone.*

Karen had added a reply to Tanya's comment: *Really? Not even mine? What a great best friend you are lol.*

Or mine? Pete had added his reply directly underneath Karen's.

Tanya had come back with: *Sorry, guys, my memory is shit when it comes to memorizing stuff. You know that. But how about you two? You're also my best friends. Do any of you know my phone number by heart? Don't cheat.*

To that, Karen had added one last reply: *Point taken, Tanya, lol.*

And Pete: *Yup, subject closed. Thank god for the wonders of technology lol* ☺.

'How many people commented on this post?' Hunter asked.

'There are fifty-two comments from forty-six different people,' Garcia replied. 'But the post was "liked" by ninety-one.' He indicated on the screen.

'Can I?' Hunter asked, nodding at Garcia's mouse.

'Sure.' Garcia rolled his chair a little to the left.

Hunter bent forward a little, used the mouse to completely expand the 'comment' section, and slowly read through all forty-six of them. Most of them were very similar to Tanya's first reply, stating that they couldn't really remember a single number by heart. None of them stood out.

'Who are you logged in as?' Hunter asked.

'Myself,' Garcia replied, making a face. He knew why the question. 'Which means that Pete's profile is public, and so was this post. Anyone could've seen this. There's no way of tracking who did and who didn't.' He looked back at Hunter. 'And I wouldn't be surprised if this post was what gave the killer the idea for his sick video-call game. Right here in one place, he would've had everything he needed – Karen telling him that Tanya was her best friend, and Tanya telling him that without looking at her phone, she couldn't remember Karen's number. You were right, Robert, he knew beforehand that she wouldn't know the answer to his question.'

Hunter took a step back from his partner's desk and breathed out. Karen was going to die, no matter what,

Hunter was sure of it, and he knew that so was the killer. The game was just a front, but a front for what? To pleasure the killer's innermost sadistic desires? Possible. To fill Tanya with guilt that would probably torment her for the rest of her life? Also possible, but right now Hunter could offer no answer to his own questions.

'How about Karen or Tanya's profile?' Hunter queried. 'Have you checked? Are they also public?'

'I've checked, yes,' Garcia replied. 'Karen's profile isn't. If she weren't friends with you in here, you would barely be able to see any information on her.'

'And Tanya's?'

Garcia laughed. 'The complete opposite. Open to absolutely everyone.'

The fact that in this day and age people would so freely splash all sorts of information about their lives and their day-to-day activities over the Internet in the way they did had always amazed Hunter. Images, names, locations, dates, likes, dislikes ... it was all out there, and it didn't take a genius to grab hold of it all.

'Are we absolutely certain that this Pete Harris character has really been in Europe for the past month?' he asked.

Garcia's head jerked slightly to the right. 'We haven't officially checked, but he has been posting entries from Berlin for over three weeks now. Most of them are like the one I just showed you, with him in the forefront of the picture and some very famous Berlin sites on the background, so unless this guy has been Photoshopping his life for the past month, he's in Germany, Robert.'

Hunter accepted it, but didn't give up. 'Let's get it checked anyway. For someone who has gone through the sort of preparation that this killer has gone through, Photoshopping photographs for an alibi would've been the easiest of all his tasks.'

'I'll get someone on it,' Garcia said, reaching for the phone on his desk. The call lasted less than two minutes.

Twenty-Nine

Mr. J stepped out of the elevator on the fifth floor of the hotel he was staying in and calmly walked down the brightly lit corridor in the direction of his room – 515. As he stepped through the door, he placed the 'do not disturb' sign outside it and locked it behind him. A subtle and very pleasant scent of jasmine and vanilla hung in the air, courtesy of the aromatherapy treatment the hotel provided.

Mr. J dropped his briefcase and his jacket on to the sumptuous queen-sized bed, kicked off his shoes, and made his way into the white-tiled bathroom. In there, he turned on the washbasin faucet, bent forward over it, and began splashing his face and the back of his neck with ice-cold water. Some of it splattered on to his shirt collar and trickled down on to his chest and back, but Mr. J didn't mind it. In fact, he welcomed the cooling sensation. A whole minute went by before he looked up again and faced his reflection in the mirror.

He looked so different.

Staring into his own eyes, Mr. J inhaled an overly deep breath and held it in his lungs. A few seconds later, with his lips pursed, he let go of it slowly.

'Just breathe,' he silently told himself. 'Just breathe.'

He repeated the process five more times before he finally turned off the water faucet.

Time to go back to normal.

Mr. J brought his left hand to his face and, with the tips of his fingers, pulled down on his right-eye bottom lid. Then, using his right thumb and index finger, he carefully pinched and collected the baby-blue contact lens he'd been wearing for the past twelve hours. After collecting the one from his left eye, he dumped them both into the toilet and flushed them away. Eyes back to their original color, Mr. J proceeded to rid his face of the fake moustache, the goatee, and the false teeth, securely placing them to one side. He spent the next sixty seconds opening and closing his mouth in a stretching exercise and rubbing his chin and upper lip to do away with the awkward sensation.

Mr. J was starting to look like Mr. J again.

The last step was to carefully detach the blond wig from his head. That done, he took another minute and massaged his scalp with his fingertips.

Boy, did that feel good?

At that particular moment, Mr. J could think of only one thing he needed more than a shower. He returned to the bedroom and from the small fridge he grabbed a couple of mini-bottles of whisky and emptied them into a tumbler – no ice, no water. As he sipped his drink, he closed his eyes and allowed the golden liquid to envelop his palate. It wasn't good-quality whisky, but the alcohol was strong enough. He had one more sip and placed the glass on the bedside table. As he reached for his briefcase, Mr. J heard his cellphone ring inside his jacket pocket. He identified the ring as coming from his personal phone, not his work one. He reached for it, checked the display screen and frowned. The call was coming from Cassandra, but it wasn't a regular call, it was a request for a video-call.

Mr. J had only video-called with his wife once before, eleven months ago, to test the feature in Cassandra's new phone. Neither of them liked it very much.

She's probably calling to find out when I'm coming home, he thought. *But why a video-call?* The next thought that came into Mr. J's head filled him with relief: *Good job I've got all that crap off my face.*

He held the phone in front of him and accepted the call, but as the image materialized on the small screen, Mr. J looked even more puzzled. All he could see was one of the walls in his living room. He knew it was his living room because he recognized the wall clock and framed Gauguin print his wife had bought a few years back.

'Hello? Cass?' he called in an unsure voice. 'Where are you? Everything OK?'

No reply.

'Cass?'

Silence.

'Honey, I don't know if you can hear me, but I'm not sure if this thing is working OK. I can't see or hear you.'

Still no reply, but the camera slowly panned right and Cassandra's face finally came into focus.

Mr. J felt an awkward chill grab hold of the back of his neck. Something was off. Something was really off.

Cassandra was sitting down on one of their dinner chairs, with her hair tied back into a ponytail. Her head was low, obscuring part of her face, but Mr. J could still see enough of it, and what he saw shook him. His wife had been crying, and judging by the redness of her nose and blotted eye makeup, which had run all the way down to her chin, she'd been doing so for a while.

Emotionally, Cassandra was the strongest woman he had ever met. It took a lot to make her cry. Mr. J had only seen it happen once, when her mother passed away eight years ago.

'Cassandra, honey, what's going on? Are you all right? Why are you crying?' There was real concern in his voice.

She sucked in a deep breath through a blocked nose, but said nothing in return.

'Cass, talk to me for Christ's sake. You're starting to scare me now.' Mr. J twisted his phone left then right as if checking on something. 'What the fuck? Is the sound on this thing on? I don't know if I'm doing this video-call-thing right, honey.'

'There's nothing wrong with the sound, John.'

The voice that came through Mr. J's tiny cellphone speakers made his entire body tense. It had been digitally altered to sound deep and full of gravel, way too deep to sound human.

'What? Who the fuck is this? And what's with the demon-like voice? What the hell is going on?'

'What's going on,' the voice replied, 'is that I have placed a little wager with your wife.'

Mr. J's confusion intensified. 'What? Is this a joke?'

'Oh! Definitely not. I can guarantee you that this is as real as it gets, John.'

'Who is this?'

'Who I am doesn't matter. But this does. Look up.'

The instruction was meant for Mr. J's wife.

Shivering, she obeyed.

Cassandra lifted her chin, and as her gaze met her husband's in the small screen, a new onslaught of tears began pouring down her cheeks. Mr. J's heart sank. He focused his attention on her eyes and in them he saw something he had never seen before, hopelessness together with tremendous fear. He knew then that whatever it was that was happening, it was no joke.

'Cassandra, what's going on? Who's in the house with you?'

Her lips quivered again, and all she could do was gently shake her head.

'She's not allowed to speak, John,' the voice announced. 'I have to give her permission to first.'

Despite what the voice said, through drowning tears, Cassandra called out, but all she could manage was a poor whisper.

'John, please.'

SLAP.

Cassandra was hit across her face so fast, Mr. J missed the movement completely. The strength of the slap made her whole head twist left awkwardly. The skin on her right cheek immediately reddened, and an agonizing pain-filled scream exploded out of her, followed by desperate sobbing.

For a second, and out of pure surprise, Mr. J's heart lost its rhythm. His eyes widened in total disbelief.

'What the fuck? You sonofabitch.'

'I told you not to speak until I give you permission, didn't I?' the voice said calmly. 'Don't do it again.'

Slowly Cassandra turned her head and once again looked at her cellphone screen. The powerful slap had also split the right corner of her bottom lip, causing a small blob of blood to trickle down her chin. In her eyes, fear had suddenly become terror.

Anger traveled through Mr. J's veins like a dark avalanche, spilling off in all directions until his entire body was shaking with it.

'Cassandra, honey,' he said. 'Please listen to me. Everything will be fine, OK. I promise you. For now, just do what he says. I'll get this figured out. I promise you, my love. I will die before I let anything happen to you.'

Cassandra swallowed dry, as more tears made their way down her cheeks. She blinked once and her head bobbed down a tiny fraction to signal not only that she had understood, but that she was also putting all of her trust in him.

Mr. J closed his eyes and took a deep breath. When he finally reopened them just a second later, it was like he had mutated into a complete different person. One Cassandra had never seen before.

Thirty

Mr. J's face was expressionless, his eyes stone cold but full of focus, and despite all that was happening, his next words came out chillingly calm, steady, and overflowing with determination.

'Now you listen to me, whoever you are. I know why you're doing what you're doing. I know you're angry. I know you're hurt, but your problem is with me and no one else. My wife isn't part of this. So deal with me.' Mr. J brought his face a fraction closer to his phone. 'You and I. No one else. All you have to do is name a time and a place and I'll be there to face you. You have my word on that. Then we can go about this in any way you like. Your terms. No questions asked. But right now you're going to leave my wife alone, and you're going to leave my house.'

'You know why I'm doing what I'm doing?' the demonic-sounding voice asked. Even through all its distortion, the sarcasm in its tone was unmistakable.

'Don't play dumb,' Mr. J replied, his tone still arctic. 'We both know why you want revenge on me. How you managed to find me is a different question altogether, but I have obviously been careless in one of my jobs and left some sort of trail behind, which has led you to me. Congratulations. Hell knows how long it must've taken you to track me down, but that's not important anymore. You've got me. Here I am. That was what you wanted, wasn't it? So *have me*. Let my wife go.'

On his screen, Mr. J saw Cassandra's eyes narrow slightly. Confusion, brought on by his words, was starting to collide with her fear.

'This has just become very interesting,' the voice said with amusement. 'And judging by the look on your wife's face, she's as intrigued as I am. So why don't you tell us, John? Why exactly do you think that I'm seeking revenge on you?'

'If you are after me, you know exactly what I'm capable of. Are you sure you want to play dumb?'

Mr. J's face remained completely void of expression, but somehow his eyes looked a lot more menacing than just a moment ago.

'So let me tell you again. Leave my wife alone. Get out of my house, and you and I can sort this out in whichever way you like.'

'I'm very sorry to disappoint you, John,' the demonic voice came back, 'but despite what you may think, which, I must admit, has now made me very curious, there's nothing for you and I to sort out. But whatever it is that you've done, it must've been something very bad if you think someone would come after your wife for revenge. But whatever that is, frankly, it's none of my concern. Anyway, this charade game is getting old ... and time is ticking away, especially for your wife. So, let *me* tell you how this is going to work, John. As I've said, I have placed a bet with your wife. Two questions. I'm going to ask you two questions. All you have to do to win this game is correctly answer both of them. If you do, she will be set free and neither of you will ever see or hear from me again. But if you don't ...' The unfinished sentence hung in the air menacingly for a couple of seconds. 'Now listen carefully, John, because I'm only going to go over the rules once ...'

'You're not listening to me.' Mr. J cut the demonic voice short. His tone remained steady but powerful and demanding. 'We're not playing a game. Not with my wife's life. You and I meet face to face, and we can play whatever psycho crazy game you li—'

'Shut the fuck up, John,' the voice slashed back. '*You* are the one who's refusing to listen. I'm giving you a chance to save your wife's life, and the only way you'll be able to do that is if you give me two correct answers. If you choose not to, you forfeit and she'll die right here, right now, right in front of your eyes.'

On the screen, Cassandra burst into a new fit of tears. Her head dropped down once again and she began shaking hysterically.

Could this really have been just a coincidence? Mr. J thought. *Could this idiot really have no idea of who he was dealing with?* Possibly. Mr. J knew that he was the best at what he did. He didn't make mistakes. He was extremely careful. So how did this guy find him?

'Cassandra, honey, listen to me.' Mr. J tried to calm her down. 'He will not touch you. He will not harm you. I promise you that, my love.' He paused for a second; when he spoke again, he was addressing the voice. 'If it's true that you have no idea of what I do or who I am, let me give you a chance to rethink your actions. I work for the most powerful syndicate in Los Angeles. The most powerful syndicate in the whole of California. A syndicate that doesn't abide by any laws. It makes its own. Do you understand what I'm telling you?' Mr. J didn't care for a reply. 'My role within this syndicate is very specific. I am what you might call "the last enforcer" of their rules – the last instance in their problem-solving chain. In fact, I'm "the end of the chain". If I come to see you, I will be the last person you will ever see. Are you getting the picture?'

Another deliberate pause.

'So what you're telling me, John,' the demon replied with an odd quirk to its distorted voice, as if struggling to hold in a laugh. 'Is that you're a . . . gun for hire. A killer. An assassin. And you work for some sort of . . . crime syndicate. And I am now supposed to be very scared of you.'

'What I'm telling you,' Mr. J came back, his voice unaltered. 'Is that if you harm one hair on my wife's head, there won't be a rock on this earth under which you can hide that I won't find you, and I will skin you alive. This is not a threat. It's a promise. I will rip your heart from your chest and feed it to rats. I'll make you suffer in a way you're not even able to imagine. Is this getting through to you?'

No reply.

'So now I'm the one giving you a chance to save *your* life. If you set my wife free now and walk away, I will not look for you. I will not hunt you down. I *will* leave you be. You have my word. Just walk away and I promise that I will forget all of this. Are you listening to me?'

A few silent seconds went by.

'Yes,' the voice finally replied. 'Are *you* listening to me, John? Because if you are, keep your eyes on the screen.'

Thirty-One

Psychotherapist, Dr. Gwen Barnes, had stayed behind in her practice after her last evening patient had left. She preferred to go over her notes while the day's sessions were still fresh in her mind. If at all possible, she'd also rather not take any work home, especially on a Saturday night.

Dr. Barnes' first patient of the day had been a middle-aged woman, who she'd seen a handful of times before, and who, so it appeared, had problems for the sake of having problems. Their sessions revolved around discussing and trying to understand a problem that was never a problem to begin with, but became a problem because it had been forged into one.

'Not that much to revise here,' Dr. Barnes said to herself.

Her next four patients had all been people with complicated marital problems, who she did her best to try to help, but she knew that, in the long run, their relationships were, for the lack of a better word, doomed. All four of them could barely stand the sight of their partners and Dr. Barnes got the impression that the main reason why they came to her practice wasn't really to seek any sort of help, but just so they could spend another ninety minutes away from the person who they hated with a feral intensity.

Her last patient of the day, a seventeen-year-old girl named Beverly Dawson, was indeed a human conundrum. Beverly suffered from Dissociative Identity Disorder and her case was as intriguing as it was sometimes terrifying. After eight sessions, Dr. Barnes had already encountered five different personalities, each bringing with it a whole new dimension of complexity. The most frightening of them all was the one Dr. Barnes secretly referred to as 'Severely Aggressive Beverly', or SAB.

As Dr. Barnes finished revising her notes, she reflexively placed her right hand over to her left wrist, something she did unconsciously every time she was either nervous or thinking, but as her fingers touched her bare skin, she looked down at her hands and a sad, almost painful, feeling came over her. She closed her eyes and pushed the feeling away. Seconds later she pulled her chair closer to her desk once again and powered down her computer.

After finally locking her office for the rest of the weekend, Dr. Barnes took the elevator down to the building's underground parking lot. It'd been a long day. A long week, in fact, and she couldn't wait to get home, have a hot shower and indulge herself with a nice bottle of red wine. Hell, maybe she would have a spliff too.

As she approached her pearl-white Toyota Camry, one of the last few cars still left in the lot, she noticed that someone had left something on her windshield, which wasn't at all surprising. Almost every day she would get at least one leaflet on her car, most of them advertising fast-food joints around the vicinity, or a happy-hour deal down at one of the many local bars and lounges.

Dr. Barnes got to her car and grabbed the leaflet, ready to throw it away. Only this time it wasn't a leaflet, it was an envelope. Across its front, large letters, which had all been cut out from some glossy magazine, had been glued together to spell her name.

'What the hell?' she whispered as she placed her briefcase on the floor and tore open the envelope.

Her surprise heightened. Inside it she found a single piece of paper folded in half, with yet more cut-out letters and words stuck together to create a short message. She unfolded it and was about to read it when she heard some sort of noise coming from her left, or at least she thought she did. Her eyes immediately shot in that direction. In the dim parking-lot light she saw nothing. There was no one there. Dr. Barnes dragged her gaze around the nearly empty lot. Still she saw nothing. No one. Her attention returned to the piece of paper in her hand and she finally was able to read the note.

'What?' she asked, frowning, before impulsively looking up again. The parking lot was as still as a moment ago.

Her eyes went back to the beginning of the note and she read it again. This time, as she got to the end of it, she let out a half-humorless laugh.

'What a silly, stupid prank. Does someone expect me to believe this?' she asked herself, ready to trash the whole thing; but that was when she noticed that there was something else right at the bottom of the envelope.

She tipped it on to the palm of her right hand.

A split second later, her heart froze.

Thirty-Two

Hunter had stayed behind in his office after Garcia had left. Even though he wasn't very prolific with Facebook, Twitter, or any other social media network, he wanted to dig a little deeper into the personal profiles of Karen Ward, Tanya Kaitlin and Pete Harris. He began by carefully rereading all forty-six comments under Pete Harris's Facebook post about 'brainlaziness'. Still none stood out, with the exception of Tanya Kaitlin's comment, explicitly admitting that she didn't know a single phone number by heart. Sure, Karen Ward's killer could've come across that same information through a number of different methods, making that whole post nothing more than just a coincidence, but Hunter had never really believed in coincidences, especially in this case, where Karen had asked Tanya a very direct question – *Really? Not even mine? What a great best friend you are lol.*

Hunter spent the next hour and a half click-jumping from one profile to another, reading posts and looking at photos and uploaded images. The more he read, the more images he looked at, the more surprised he became. In short, people were laying their lives bare over the Internet for anyone who cared to read about it, and even though most social media sites tended to offer quite extensive security settings, a lot of people still chose to ignore them.

By 9.30 p.m., Hunter's eyes were watering from squinting at his computer screen. He needed to get out of that office.

Hunter's biggest passion was single malt Scotch whisky. Back in his apartment, tucked in a corner of his living room, an old-fashioned drinks cabinet held a small but impressive collection of single malts that would probably satisfy the palate of most connoisseurs. Hunter would never consider himself an expert on whisky but, unlike so many, he at least knew how to appreciate its flavor and quality, instead of simply getting drunk on it, though sometimes getting drunk worked just fine.

He thought about going home, where he could indulge in as much single malt as he wished without breaking the bank, but he quickly debated if staying in tonight was such a good idea.

Hunter lived alone. No wife. No girlfriends. He'd never been married, and the relationships he had rarely lasted longer than just a few months, sometimes a lot less. The pressures that came with being a detective with the LAPD's UVC Unit, and the commitment the job demanded, always seemed too much for most to understand and cope with. He didn't mind being by himself. Living alone didn't bother him either, but he was still human and sometimes the loneliness of his small apartment was the last thing he needed. Tonight was one of those nights.

Los Angeles nightlife was arguably one of the liveliest, craziest, and most exciting in the world. The spectrum of choice was almost interminable, going from luxurious and trendy nightclubs, where the rich and famous mingled with Hollywood stars, to themed bars and dingy, sleazy underground lounges and parties, where the freaks came out to play. Whatever mood, crazy or not, you found yourself in, you were sure to find a place in LA to suit it. Tonight, Hunter was in the 'stiff but quiet drink' mood.

Thirty-Three

'Are *you* listening to me, John? Because if you are, keep your eyes on the screen.'

The unwavering determination in the digitally altered voice sent a sickening knot into Mr. J's stomach. His eyes, full of doubt and anger, forever locked with Cassandra's, full of fear. But in them, he also saw something else. Something he'd seen before many times, but never in his wife's eyes. He'd seen it in the eyes of the people he dealt with, the people he terminated – desperation brought on by the total loss of hope.

Cassandra still had no idea what was happening, and why it was happening to her, but she trusted her husband with the utmost devotion and until a second ago she had blindly believed his words.

'*Cassandra, honey, please listen to me. Everything will be fine, OK. I'll get this figured out. I promise you, my love. I will die before I let anything happen to you.*'

But now she realized that that just wasn't true. What could he really do? How could he stay true to his word? How could he stop harm from coming to her? How could he protect her when he was miles away?

Cassandra's confusion was immeasurable. She had never seen her husband look so emotionless. She had never heard him speak so coldly. That was not the Mr. J she knew. That was not the man she had married. The man she had married was a business consultant. He ran his own small firm, didn't he?

'*I work for the most powerful syndicate in Los Angeles. The most powerful syndicate in the whole of California. A syndicate that doesn't abide by any laws. It makes its own. My role within this syndicate is very specific. I am what you might call "the last enforcer" of their rules – the last instance in their problem-solving chain. In fact, I'm "the end of the chain". If I come to see you, I will be the last person you will ever see.*'

What in the world was he talking about? Was any of it true? If he was bluffing to try to scare away the man in her house, it certainly didn't seem to be working.

'Keep your eyes on the screen,' the demon said again.

All of a sudden, almost as fast as the slap Cassandra had received earlier, Mr. J saw a gloved hand come from his wife's right and stab her in the neck. Her entire body jerked heavily, first from the impact, then from the pain. Her mouth dropped open, ready for the inevitable scream, but all her petrified vocal cords were able to let out was a humble cry, barely loud enough for it to be picked up by her cellphone's microphone.

'NOOOOOOOOO!'

Instead, the defining scream came from Mr. J.

Still with his phone in hand, he jumped to his feet, lost his balance, but quickly regained it by grabbing hold of the bed. The knot in his stomach turned into a bottomless pit that threatened to swallow him whole.

Cassandra's eyes, still sealed with his, lost all their focus in a mere second. Life was fast giving way to numbness.

As the gloved hand pulled away, Mr. J realized what had really happened. From the angle of the stabbing, blood should've spurted out from Cassandra's jugular vein with enough pressure to project it across the room. He knew that well enough, but instead, all he saw was a tiny blob form where her skin was pricked by the syringe needle.

'Relax, John,' the demonic voice said in a calm and eerie tone. 'Your wife isn't dead. Not yet. I simply injected her with something that will numb most of her body, but it will not do the same to her brain, or her nervous system. Her hearing and visual cortex won't be impaired either. You know what that means, don't you?' This time, the person with Cassandra was the one who paused for effect. 'It means that though her body will be temporarily paralyzed, she will still be able to hear, see, and feel absolutely everything. Isn't that precious?'

On the small screen, Cassandra's eyes wavered aimlessly for a couple of seconds before finally settling down again. The confusion in them first morphed into struggle then to desolation and ultimately into complete terror as she finally realized that she had no physical control over her body anymore.

Mr. J read her eyes like a book and his heart sank for the second time.

'So, as I was trying to explain to you before you interrupted me, John, these are the rules.'

Mr. J's body shook with a combination of rage and something he hadn't felt in a very long time – fear. He had meant what he'd said. Given half a chance, he would give his life for his wife's any day and without any hesitation.

'Take me,' he said, holding all his anger inside and keeping his voice as steady as he could muster. 'I will come to you, hands tied, blindfolded ... whichever way you want. Just tell me where and I'll be there. We can swop. You let my wife go, and you can have me. Then you can do whatever you like. If that's what pleases you, you can hurt me to your heart's content before killing me. I will not put up a fight. I promise you. Just let her go.'

Total silence.

Only then, a whole new theory slapped Mr. J straight across the face.

'Is this about money?' he asked, doubting his own words. 'Is that what you're after?'

Still silence.

'I have close to four million dollars in an international bank account. If I pull some resources, I can probably gather together another million. That's *five* million dollars. All yours. I can transfer every last penny to you. All you need to—'

'You're not listening to me, John.' The demon cut him short again. 'There's only one way in which you can help your wife right now, and that's by answering both of my questions correctly. If you interrupt me again, I will take that as a wrong answer. Every time you give me a wrong answer, your wife gets punished. Do you understand what I'm telling you?'

Cassandra begged her husband with her eyes.

'Yes or no, John? No other answer will do. You give me any other answer other than "yes" or "no" and I'll start punishing her.'

Away from the camera's eye, Mr. J's fingers closed into

a tight fist and his core shook with indescribable anger. He had never felt so helpless in his entire life. He finally gave the answer the voice wanted to hear.

'Yes.'

'Now, we're finally on the right track.' It took the daemonic voice just a minute to explain the rules. 'Simple, isn't it? And don't even think about calling the police. I can assure you that they'll never make it here in time.'

Mr. J's mouth went desert-dry.

'So listen up, John, because your wife's life depends on it.'

An overly tense pause followed.

'Where was Cassandra born?'

Mr. J squinted at the small screen. Had he heard it right? Was this psycho for real? What sort of life-depending, dumbass question was that?

'Is this a fucking joke?' he asked, his blood boiling in his veins.

'You have five seconds.' There was no play in the digitally altered voice.

Though Cassandra wasn't able to move at all, including her facial expressions, the look in her eyes mutated just as much as the one in her husband's. First, from terror to confusion.

'*What? Is that the question? This can't be real. What the hell is going on? This has to be some sort of sick joke.*'

Then from confusion to hope. Mr. J had been to the city where she was born so many times its name was probably etched in his brain. There was no way he could get this wrong.

'... four ... three ...'

'Cassandra was born in Santa Ana,' Mr. J replied. 'Orange County, California ... what the *fuck* is this?'

The look in Cassandra's eyes softened as new tears welled up in them. This time, they were tears of joy.

'That is correct, John. Congratulations. See? Not that hard after all, was it? Now, all you need to do is give me just one more correct answer and you and your wife can go back to being a couple again, though I have a feeling that you'll have quite a lot of explaining to do.' A new short pause. 'But let's not jump to conclusions just yet. One more correct answer.'

All the while, Mr. J's eyes never broke away from Cassandra's. The hope in hers now joined by apprehension. The anger in his by disbelief.

'Your wedding anniversary, John,' the voice said. 'When is it?'

On hearing the question, the look in Cassandra's eyes mutated yet again. This time from apprehension to total panic.

Despite how much he adored her, for the last seven years, Mr. J had completely forgotten about their wedding anniversary. Cassandra had reminded him three times, but when he didn't remember it for the fourth year running, she didn't see the point in reminding him anymore. She never really blamed him, though. She knew that his memory lapse only began once she'd entered her depression phase, a phase he knew nothing about, as she had always gone to great lengths to keep it all from him and everyone else. As Cassandra, guided by her condition, distanced herself from Mr. J, he did the same, but in his own way. Forgetting their wedding anniversary had been a simple consequence of it.

The despair in Cassandra's stare was mirrored in Mr. J's entire demeanor. For the first time since his wife's face had filled the small screen on his cellphone, he broke eye contact with her. As if searching the air around him, he first looked left, then right.

'You have five seconds ... four ...'

Mr. J looked up at the ceiling. He knew the date. Of course he knew the date of his own wedding. He just had to search his memory.

'Three ...'

He breathed in a lot more anxiously than he thought he had.

'Two ...'

His eyes returned to the screen just in time to see that tears were once again cascading down his wife's face. There was no joy in them.

'One ...'

'Seventh of March,' Mr. J finally blurted out. 'We got married on the seventh of March. The year was nineteen ninety-six.'

Thirty-Four

Sitting inside interview room number two at Rampart Police Station on West Sixth Street, Dr. Gwen Barnes had the last of her stale coffee. As she swallowed the bitter liquid down, it made her stomach churn inside her.

'This is it,' she whispered, placing the now empty paper cup back on the large metal table in front of her and readily pushing it away. Even if it had been the most amazing gourmet coffee in the world, after five cups, there was no way she could stomach another one. What she really needed was a large glass of wine. No, scrap that. A whole bottle was a lot more like it.

'C'mon, this is way past ridiculous now,' she said, turning to look at the large, window-like mirror to her right. This wasn't the first time Dr. Barnes had been inside a police interrogation room. She knew very well that what she was looking at was in fact a two-way mirror, but this wasn't an interrogation. No one would be at the other side of it, observing her, though she wished someone were. Maybe someone was listening in.

'This has got to be a joke,' she said, loud enough for her voice to be picked up by the multidirectional microphone at the center of the table. 'A detective must've come back by now. C'mon.'

As she finished her sentence, she turned, looked at the heavy door a few feet behind her and waited, urging it to be pushed open.

Ten.

Twenty.

Thirty seconds went by.

No luck.

Dr. Barnes took a deep breath and sat back in the uncomfortable metal chair.

Laid out on the table in front of her she had her cellphone, her car keys, the envelope that had been left stuck to the windshield of her Toyota Camry, and the note she had found inside it. Every time she looked at it, her heart skipped a beat inside her chest.

After reading the note down at the underground parking lot of the building where she had her psychotherapy practice, Dr. Barnes had laughed out loud, quickly discarding it as a 'ridiculous, humorless joke'. But then she found what had been left inside the envelope for her, something that gave everything a lot more meaning, and the laughter immediately turned into desperate panic. Twenty-five minutes later, she had stormed into the police station on Venice Boulevard.

An officer had spoken to her and taken down all her details, but Dr. Barnes had demanded to speak with a detective. She didn't want this brushed under a carpet.

The officer had explained that no detectives were available at that time and that she had two options. One: She was more than welcome to wait for one if she really felt the need to.

Two: She could go home and a detective would either call her or drop by at a more convenient time.

The last thing Dr. Barnes wanted at that particular moment was to go home alone, so wait she did, for a very long time, but still, no detective came to meet her. After almost two hours, four horrible cups of coffee, and five increasingly angry trips to the reception window, the officer finally told her that he had managed to talk to one of their detectives over the phone, and he was on his way back. The officer, who could clearly understand Dr. Barnes' frustration, had asked her if she wouldn't prefer to wait in one of their interrogation rooms, away from the noise and the mess of the station's reception lobby. Dr. Barnes happily accepted it. She was getting a little freaked out by the looks she was getting from the tattoo-covered, burly man, sitting across the hall from her.

That had been almost an hour ago.

Thirty-Five

Mr. J blinked once ... twice.

Cassandra held her husband's stare for a split second longer before squeezing her eyes tight.

Seventh of March, he thought. *That's correct, isn't it? It's got to be. Why else would the date have popped into my head the way it did? Cassandra and I got married twenty-one years ago, on the seventh of March, at the Cathedral of Our Lady of Angels in downtown Los Angeles.*

Cassandra reopened her glassed eyes. In them now, only terror.

'I hope that you are looking straight into your wife's eyes, John,' the demon finally said. 'Because you have just let her down.'

'What? No, wait ...'

'That's not your wedding date,' the voice cut him short. 'And the rules are – you give me an incorrect answer and Cassandra gets punished.'

'No, please wait ...'

'Rules are rules, John. You just told me that you are an "enforcer of rules" of sorts, so I'm sure you understand that they need to be enforced.'

Still keeping Cassandra's face as its main subject, the camera panned up a few degrees. Seconds later, a figure dressed all in black took position directly behind her chair. All Mr. J could see were his wife's face and the person's strong torso standing just behind her head.

'You remember the rules of our little game, don't you, John?' the demon asked rhetorically. 'You have to keep watching. You close your eyes, she gets punished again. You look away, she gets punished again. If you move away from your phone's camera and I can't see you on the screen, she gets punished again.'

Mr. J's gaze stayed exactly where it was.

'Now, would you like to know the real reason why I paralyzed your wife?' The demon didn't wait for an answer. 'So she wouldn't spoil the fun by moving.'

Suddenly, the demon's gloved hands appeared above Cassandra's head. They weren't empty.

Thirty-Six

Dr. Barnes checked her watch one more time.

'Oh, screw this,' she said under her breath.

She had had enough. She collected her belongings and placed everything back into her briefcase. She still didn't want to go home, so she decided that she was going to do what she should've done a long, long time ago – drive herself to a different police station.

As she got up and turned to leave, the door to the interrogation room was finally pushed open by a tall and sturdy man. He looked to be in his mid-forties, with a rugged face that gave her the impression that he hadn't smiled in years. His clothes were clean, but scruffy, as if they had been slept in, and his hair was lank and uncombed.

'Ms. Barnes,' he said, offering his hand. His voice sounded as rough as his clothes looked. 'I'm Detective Julian Webb. Pleased to meet you.'

She shook his hand, properly introducing herself as a doctor.

'I'm terribly sorry for making you wait for such a long time, doctor. If I could've made it back here any earlier, I would've, but tonight, so far, I've attended two homicide scenes, and one gang rape.'

Dr. Barnes didn't disguise her surprise.

'Unfortunately,' Detective Webb explained, 'some nights, that's just how this city rolls. If this is the City of Angels, God forbid I ever come across the City of Devils.' He gestured towards the table. 'Please ...'

Dr. Barnes returned to the same seat she'd been occupying for the past hour. Detective Webb took the one across the table from her.

'So, how can I be of any assistance?' He interlaced his fingers together and placed his hands on the table in front of him.

The doctor studied the detective for a couple of seconds. He had the look of a man who was used to hard work and responsibility. She breathed in through her nose and slowly let it out through her mouth before beginning. She started with when she got to the underground parking lot.

'And do you have this note with you?' Detective Webb asked, reaching for his reading glasses, which were hanging from a cord around his neck.

Dr. Barnes placed the note on the table.

Detective Webb retrieved a pair of latex gloves from his pocket, gloved up and turned the envelope so it was facing him.

'And you've said that you've never received one of these before?' he asked.

'This is the first one,' she replied with a headshake.

'And has anyone else other than yourself handled it?'

'No.'

'So since you've found this note no one else has touched it?'

'No.'

Detective Webb opened the envelope and pulled out the note. The fact that whoever had created it had used cut-out letters and words didn't seem to surprise him. He read it silently.

I bet that you never even noticed me standing right behind you as you picked up your copy of the LA Times *from the newsstand, did you?*

...

I must say, your hair smells different when you are awake.

After reading the note twice, Detective Webb's eyes lifted in the direction of Dr. Barnes.

She was staring straight at him.

Webb pulled his reading glasses from his nose and let them fall loosely by his neck again.

'When was the last time you picked up a copy of the *LA Times* from a newsstand, Doctor?'

'This morning. I do it every morning just before getting to my office.'

'And where is that?'

'Downtown. West Ninth Street.'

The detective nodded. 'Busy street. And *did* you notice anyone standing right behind you as you picked up the paper? I mean, anyone close enough to be able to smell your hair?'

'No, I didn't.'

'Think about it carefully now, Doctor. This morning, yesterday, maybe the day before?'

'Believe me, Detective Webb, I've thought about it more carefully than you could imagine. I didn't notice anybody standing behind me – this morning, yesterday, the day before, or any other day.'

Webb sat back on his chair and regarded the doctor for an instant. She was an attractive woman. Her midnight-black hair was perfectly styled into a short shaggy bob, with face-framing layers. Her eyes, which were just as dark as her hair, had a certain serenity to them that seemed contagious. Her whole presence somehow seemed very calming. Webb didn't find it surprising that Gwen Barnes had chosen to become a psychotherapist.

'Have you ever had any trouble with stalkers, Doctor?'

'No,' she replied. 'I can't say I have.' Her turn to regard him. 'You don't seem convinced.'

Webb shrugged. 'We get tens of stalker complaints every year, Doc. I deal with several of them. The truth is – you check most of the boxes for the sort of target they go for.'

Dr. Barnes was quite surprised by the comment, but her expression showed nothing. 'And what boxes are those?'

'You're an unmarried, very attractive woman, Doctor. You seem to have a great career—'

'How do you know I'm unmarried?' she cut him short.

Webb pouted his lips and raised his eyebrows as if asking – 'Is that question for real?'

Dr. Barnes lifted her hands in surrender. For a moment she had forgotten where she was.

'OK,' Webb said. He knew that Dr. Barnes had had more than enough time to think about the scenarios surrounding that note. 'Let me ask you a few quick questions, Doc. Do you think that this note could maybe have come from an ex-anything – husband, boyfriend, lover – someone who you'd had some sort of relationship with in the past? Maybe someone with whom the relationship didn't end on very good terms?'

The doctor shook her head. 'No ex-husband, and no. That's all I've been thinking about since I found this note. And since I've been waiting here for several hours, I've thought about it hundreds of times. I can think of absolutely no one.'

'Once again, I'm sorry about all the waiting.' Webb's tone was plain and sincere. He moved on. 'Are you seeing anyone at the moment?'

'No, nobody.'

Webb nodded. 'How about an ex-patient,' he suggested. 'Or maybe even a current one.'

Another shake of the head. 'Nope. I thought about that too. I can think of no one who'd be capable of something like this.'

'People are capable of things you just wouldn't imagine, Doctor.' Webb fumbled with his glasses. 'Can you think of anyone at all that maybe would want to scare you, or ... harm you?'

Dr. Barnes shrugged. 'No, I can't really think of anyone.'

Webb leaned forward and rested his elbows on the table. 'Would you like my truthful opinion, Dr. Barnes?'

'No, not at all, just give me the bullshit, because that would be much more helpful.'

Webb just kept his eyes on her.

'I'm sorry,' the doctor said, showing him her palms once again. 'It's been a very stressful day.' She tilted her head to one side. 'And I'm hungry.'

'No need to apologize, Doc. I understand.'

'So what's your truthful opinion?'

Webb looked at the note on the table one more time before his stare glided back to Dr. Barnes. 'I think this is just a hoax, pure and simple. Someone pulling your leg. Maybe someone who you don't even know. A practical joker. Someone who knows you're a psychotherapist and could maybe overanalyze the note. Maybe this person works in the same building as you. Maybe he's seen you around as you pick up your paper in the morning, I'm not sure. But I'd say that this ...' He nodded once. 'You being here. You being scared. Is the exact reaction he wanted to get out of the joke. I'm very sorry to say, Dr. Barnes, but I think that you've wasted your time.'

To Detective Webb's surprise, Dr. Barnes agreed with him. 'That was exactly what I thought when I first read the note. I thought it was a joke and not a very good one, but then I noticed that there was something else inside the envelope.'

Webb frowned as his stare hopped back to the envelope on the table. 'What else?'

She reached for the envelope, tipped it, and allowed whatever else was inside it to slide out on to the tabletop.

Thirty-Seven

With an imposing, three-hundred-plus collection of bourbon, rye, blended and single malt Scotch whisky, the Seven Grand was one of the most accomplished bars in the whole of Los Angeles for whisky aficionados.

Hunter jumped out of the cab directly in front of number 542, on West Seventh Street. The wind blowing from the coast had picked up considerably, and the night air had acquired the slight smell of damp soil, announcing that rain was imminent. Hunter pulled the collar of his jacket tight against the nape of his neck, pushed open the door and took the steps to the second floor, where the whisky bar was located.

'Hello and good evening.' The five-foot-seven, brown-haired hostess greeted Hunter by the Seven Grand glass door with an encouraging smile. 'Will you be having dinner with us tonight, or only drinks?' She spoke with a very charming Scottish accent.

'Probably both.'

Being five inches shorter than Hunter, the hostess tilted her head to one side, trying to look behind him. There was no one else there.

'Party of one?'

'Story of my life,' Hunter joked, nodding.

Her smile brightened as she collected a couple of menus.

'Please follow me.'

She guided Hunter through the short entrance hall, which was decorated with plaid wallpaper and taxidermy, past the pool table room and bar on the right, and on to the busy restaurant floor. The sound of loud conversations mixed unevenly with the quickstep beat of electro swing playing from the ceiling speakers.

'Have you dined with us before?'

'Yes, I've been here a few times, mostly just at the bar. It's been a while since my last time, though.'

'I was about to say, I don't recall seeing you here before, and I've been working here for the past eight months.'

'Well, I don't blame you,' Hunter replied. 'I don't have a very memorable face.'

The hostess paused and turned to look at Hunter. 'I wouldn't say that.' She renewed her smile. 'On the contrary, you have a very ... striking face, with kind-looking eyes. People remember that.'

'Thank you.' Hunter reciprocated the smile.

They moved past a large table where eight young men in expensive-looking, tight-fitting suits seemed to be having a party.

'Hey there, sexy *lassie*,' one of them said, addressing the hostess in the worst Scottish accent Hunter had ever heard. For some reason, as the young man threw them into his sentences, he decided to stress the few Scottish terms he knew. He also sounded way past his limit. 'We need another *tipple* over here, but none of this Scottish nonsense. We need another bottle of good old American bourbon – Tennessee-style, you hear? The *lads* over here are thirsty.'

The rest of his friends all broke out in loud laughter.

'No problem, sir,' the hostess replied politely. 'I'll send a new bottle to your table straight away.'

'*Aye*,' the young man retorted, stepping in front of her and blocking her path. 'I think it would be better if you brought it over yourself, *lass*.' From his wallet, he produced three fifty-dollar bills and waved them in front of her nose.

'I'm sorry, sir,' she said, taking a step back, but still keeping a well-mannered tone. 'I can't take payment right now, and I'm just seating a customer. If you wait a moment I can either send a bill together with the bottle, or you can just pay it all at the end when the table gets the check.'

'Oh, I'm sure the customer can find his own table, can't you, *lad*?' The man placed a hand on Hunter's arm and left it there.

Hunter first looked at the hand resting on his right arm then back at the drunken young man. As the man caught the look in Hunter's eyes, his smile vanished and his hand quickly returned to the side of his body. The hostess saw it and bit her bottom lip, stiffening a smile. But the young man wasn't done yet. Turning his attention back to the hostess, he then placed his arm around her shoulders.

'You should come party with us, *lassie*. We can show you a reeeeeal good time, can't we, *blokes*?'

'Aye,' the other seven said in unison before, once again, breaking into loud laughter.

Hunter was about to intervene, when the hostess, stepping away from the man's embrace, put him back in his place herself.

'Three things,' she said calmly, showing the count on her fingers. 'One: "Bloke" is a term that's used mainly in England, Ireland, Australia and New Zealand. It's not that popular in Scotland.'

The first finger came down.

'Two: It's never used vocatively. "Can't we, *blokes*?" makes no sense, really, and frankly, it just displays your ignorance when it comes to English grammar. You should've stuck with "lads". And three: I don't party with little boys.'

The laughter and shouts got even louder, as the entire table began mocking their friend. None of them seemed to realize that the comment had been aimed at the entire group.

'I like your style,' Hunter said as they finally moved past the annoying, drunken table. 'But I don't think any of them really know what "vocatively" means.'

'Probably not,' the hostess replied with a laugh. 'They look dumb enough.'

'And drunk enough,' Hunter added.

'Financial district city boys,' she said, looking over her shoulder at Hunter. 'We get a least one group of them in here every night of the week, since the financial district is just around the corner. It's always the same – too rich, too young, and because they have more money than they know what to do with, they think that they can do whatever they fancy. We have plenty of those back in Glasgow as well. Back home we call them "dickheeds".'

Hunter smiled. 'Appropriate.'

'Wait ...' She stopped as they finally reached a small squared table at the back of the spacious and packed restaurant floor. 'You don't work in the finance sector, do you?' She looked truly embarrassed.

Instinctively, Hunter looked at what he was wearing – black jeans, black shoes, and a blue shirt under a thin black leather jacket. 'Do I come across as if I worked in the finance sector?' He sounded a little concerned.

'No, not at all,' the hostess came back. 'But if there's one thing I've learned about LA it's that appearances over here are almost always deceiving.'

'Yeah, that's very true,' Hunter agreed. 'And no, I don't work in the finance sector.'

'That's a relief,' the hostess said. 'Or else I would have to back-paddle like a pro.' She looked at the vacant table they were standing in front of. 'Here we are. At the moment this is the only table I have free. Unless you'd like to sit at the bar.'

'No. This is perfect. Thank you.'

'My pleasure.' The hostess waited for Hunter to have a seat before placing two menus on the table in front of him. 'A waiter shall be with you shortly. Meanwhile, since you've been here before, perhaps I can get you something from the bar?'

Usually, Hunter would take his time and look through the whisky list, which was more like a booklet than a list, but he already had a pretty good idea of what he would like.

'Yes, that would be great, thank you. Do you still serve Kilchoman here?'

The hostess nodded in a way that told Hunter that she approved of his choice.

Kilchoman were one of the few distilleries in the whole of Scotland that still carry out traditional floor malting, taking whisky back to its roots, and in turn creating some stunning expressions.

'Yes, of course we do. Do you have a specific one in mind? We stock a few different ones.'

'Yes, the single cask release, if you have it.'

Her left eyebrow twitched up slightly. 'We do indeed. On the rocks?'

'No.' Hunter shook his head. 'With just a little spring water, please.'

This time the hostess gave Hunter a whole-heartedly approving nod. 'An American who not only knows how to choose his Scotch, but how to drink it too. You don't see many of those around.'

Hunter frowned. 'Really? In a big whisky lounge like this one?'

She chuckled. 'You'd be surprised. To start with, you lot spell *whiskey* with an "e". It can only go downhill from there.' Her head tilted in the direction of the 'city boys' table. 'Do you know what I mean?'

Hunter smiled. 'Yes, I suppose you're right.'

'I'll be right back with your drink.'

While the hostess disappeared in the direction of the main bar, Hunter flipped through the food menu.

'Here you go,' she said, placing a whisky tumbler on Hunter's table just a minute later, together with a miniature jar of water. 'Kilchoman 2010, single quarter cask.'

'Thank you,' Hunter said, closing the menu.

'Have you made a decision already?'

Hunter nodded.

'Well, in that case, since I'm already here, I might as well take your order.'

Hunter ordered a cheeseburger and fries.

'I'll get that for you straight away,' the hostess said, paused, then extended her hand. 'My name is Linsey, by the way.'

'Robert,' Hunter replied, returning the gesture. 'Pleasure to meet you.'

'And you.' Those words were followed by a very subtle but charming wink.

As the hostess zigzagged back through the tables, being careful to avoid the "city boys" one, Hunter reached for his glass and brought it to his nose. The smoky and complex aroma of the golden liquid made him smile again. He picked up the water jar and poured just a little more than a few drops into the tumbler, before finally sipping his whisky. Smooth sweet vanilla, with sooty smoke coming to the fore and a long honeyed ember finish – perfection in a glass. Hunter closed his eyes and enjoyed the moment, maybe for longer than he should have, because he didn't notice the person now standing right in front of his table.

'You owe me an explanation.'

Thirty-Eight

As the object slid out of the envelope and on to the tabletop, Detective Webb pulled his chair a little closer to have a better look at it. His eyes ping-ponged between the object and Dr. Barnes for several seconds and he wondered if that was all he was going to get. Nothing else came out of the envelope.

'It's ... a silver bracelet,' he said at last, unimpressed, staring at a serpentine chain bracelet, with a delicate heart charm.

'It's a white-gold bracelet,' Dr. Barnes corrected him. 'Not a silver one.'

'OK. I apologize,' Webb said back, not really knowing what difference it made.

Dr. Barnes saw the look in Webb's face and explained. 'This bracelet was given to me by my mother on my thirteenth birthday. We were a very poor family, living in a rough and neglected neighborhood. My father left us when I was five, and we never saw him again after that. My mother had to work two jobs to keep us going, and she saved every penny she could for God knows how long, just so she'd be able to afford something like this.' All of a sudden, the doctor's voice saddened. 'She passed away just months after that.'

Only then Webb noticed the tiny inscription on the heart charm. Three words – one above the other – *Always. Be. Strong.*

'I'm sorry to hear that,' Webb offered in a sincere tone.

The doctor acknowledged his words with a head gesture before continuing. 'Since my thirteenth birthday, I've worn it every day without fail. I never forget to. I've never lost it. It's always with me. The only time I take it off, is when I go to sleep.'

Webb looked intrigued.

'I can't sleep with any sort of jewelry on me,' she clarified. 'No bracelets, no necklaces, no rings, nothing. For some reason it freaks the hell out of me if I do. It gives me nightmares.'

Webb found that interesting because he had a friend who also couldn't sleep with any jewelry on her. She had to take it all off before going to bed, including her wedding ring.

'Last night,' Dr. Barnes carried on with her story, 'I got home, took off my bracelet, my rings, and my necklace, and left them on my bedside table; just like I do every night. When I woke up this morning, everything was still there, except the bracelet. The bracelet was gone.'

Webb was about to say something, but Dr. Barnes got there before him.

'Yes,' she said.

He frowned at her.

'Yes. Yes. No. And yes.'

'I'm sorry?'

'I know what you're going to ask me, Detective. You're first going to ask me if I'm absolutely sure that I had the bracelet with me when I got home. The answer to that question is – yes. Then you're going to ask me if I'm absolutely sure that I took it off in my bedroom and left it on my bedside table, like I said I did. The answer to that question is also – yes. Then you're going to ask me if there isn't a chance that maybe the bracelet had come undone somewhere and fallen off my wrist, like maybe in the parking lot where I work, or just outside my house, or even by the newsstand, where I pick up my paper every morning.'

Webb's impressed face was certainly more pleasant than his unimpressed one, but not by much. And he was impressed. So far, Dr. Barnes had hit every nail on the head.

He nodded at her as he added, 'That was exactly what I was thinking, Doctor.' He admitted it. 'If the bracelet dropped from your wrist at the newsstand, someone could've seen it and, instead of doing the right thing, which would be handing it back to you, decided to turn the whole thing into a practical joke.' He tapped the note twice with his gloved index finger. 'That would certainly explain this.'

'It would,' the doctor agreed. 'But the answer to that question is "no". There's no chance that my bracelet fell from my wrist at the newsstand the morning before last, or anywhere else for that matter.'

Once again, Webb was about to ask Dr. Barnes a new question, when she lifted her hand, interrupting him.

'How can I be so sure?' she said.

Back came the impressed look. Webb decided that it was pointless trying to butt in, so he sat back on his chair and allowed her to continue in her own pace.

'Because there's no way I can go a whole day without this bracelet and not notice it, Detective. Every time I get nervous, or every time I'm thinking, pondering something, I twiddle with it.' Her right hand automatically moved to her left wrist. 'It's an unconscious movement. I've been doing it for years, and on any given day I repeat the movement tens of times. I wouldn't have gone half an hour without noticing that my bracelet was gone.'

Webb had noticed the movement at least a couple of times in the past few minutes and it hadn't surprised him. Everybody he knew had a nervous tic. His was running his tongue against his top lip.

'And last night,' Dr. Barnes carried on, 'as I was driving home, I specifically remember twiddling with it in the car, which brings us to my last "yes". Yes, Detective Webb, I'm certain that the bracelet didn't fall off my wrist inside my car. I had it on me when I got home last night. I had it on me when I went to bed, and I had it on my bedside table when I turned off the lights. I am one hundred percent sure of it. This morning, when I woke up, it wasn't there.'

After over twenty years as a policeman, Webb had acquired a knack for summing people up at a glance, even better after spending a few minutes with them. Dr. Gwen Barnes appeared to be a very stable, intelligent, and grounded woman. She never raised her voice, regardless of mood. She was eloquent and, so far, all her arguments seemed to be based on very plausible and possible facts.

'Not finding the bracelet this morning drove me insane,' she added. 'I looked for it everywhere, and I mean everywhere, Detective – under the bed, behind the bedside table, in the drawers, under rugs, in the living room, in the kitchen ... you name it. Even in my car. It wasn't there. It wasn't anywhere. I wracked my brain retracing my steps from last night, from the time I got home, to the time I went to bed, because I knew I had it on me when I opened my front door last night.'

Dr. Barnes paused for breath. Right about then, she could really do with a very large glass of wine.

'And this morning was the first ever time that I was late for my first session of the day. I'm a psychiatrist, Detective Webb, I understand how the human brain works better than most. I'm fully aware that because night after night I go through the exact same motions just before turning off my bedroom light, i.e. placing all my jewelry on my bedside table, it's very easy for my brain to be tricked into thinking that I did something, when in fact I didn't. Repetitive actions can have that sort of effect on your brain, but I'm telling you, that's not the case here.'

Webb ran his tongue against his top lip. 'So you really do think that someone broke into your house last night, walked into your room while you were asleep, took away your brace-let, already with the intention of doing this.' He jerked his chin in the direction of the note and the bracelet on the table. 'And maybe even smelled your hair.'

'I do, Detective, because I can't see any other explanation.'

'Did you notice any signs of a break-in?' Webb asked.

Dr. Barnes let go of a breath so heavy with frustration, the air inside the interrogation room seemed to thicken.

'I can't be sure because I didn't really check for any. I woke up this morning, I couldn't find my bracelet, obviously my first thought wasn't that someone had broken into my house.'

'Your first thought was that maybe you had lost it,' Webb pushed.

'Yes,' Dr. Barnes admitted in defeat.

Even Detective Webb had to take a deep breath. 'OK,' he

tried again. He really did want to help her. 'Before leaving the house this morning, can you remember if you found your door locked or unlocked?'

'The front door was locked.'

'Are you sure?'

'Yes. I'm sure. I remember unlocking it this morning. I didn't check the back door, but it's always locked.'

Webb was unsure of what else to say. Instead, it was Dr. Barnes who spoke again. Her next few words came out slowly and flooded with emotion.

'Detective, I don't really know what else I can tell you, but I know that I did not lose my bracelet.'

She folded her arms in front of her, as if all of a sudden the temperature inside the room had dropped a few degrees. That was the first time that Detective Webb saw Dr. Barnes display fear. Real fear.

'Someone was in my room, Detective. I'm telling you. Someone was in there, by my bed, watching me while I slept.'

Thirty-Nine

As the screen on his cellphone faded to black, Mr. J felt his whole world collapse around him. His legs buckled under his weight and he had to hold on to the wall so as not to fall down. His fingers lost their grip and his phone slipped from his hand, bouncing off the bed and on to the floor. Nothing made sense. He felt as if his entire existence had just been devoured by a black hole, leaving behind nothing but an empty human shell.

'What just happened?' he whispered under his breath, his crazed eyes searching for refuge in every corner of his hotel room. They found none. Instead, the walls seemed to be closing in on him. 'I must be losing my mind. This can't be real. It just can't be.'

Mr. J brought two shaking hands to his face and rubbed it as vigorously as he could.

The walls were still closing in on him.

He turned around and quickly made his way back into the bathroom, where he splashed more cold water on to his face.

'Cassandra,' he said, as he found his own eyes in the mirror, 'this isn't real.' He tried to convince his reflection. 'It isn't. And I will prove it to you. None of it was real.'

Mr. J rushed back into the bedroom, fetched his cellphone from the floor, returned to the bathroom, and paused before the mirror again.

'You'll see. I'll prove it to you right now,' he said, shaking a finger at his reflection, before speed-dialing his wife's number. 'I don't know what the hell this was, but it wasn't real. None of it was. You'll see.'

At the other end, instead of ringing, the call went straight into voicemail.

'Hello, you've reached the phone of Cassandra Jenkinson. Unfortunately, I can't—'

Mr. J disconnected and quickly redialed.

The reflection in the mirror waited.

'Hello, you've reached the phone of Cass—'

Disconnected. Redialed.

'Hello, you've reached—'

Disconnected.

Mr. J's eyes reverted back to the mirror. His reflection was still waiting.

The house, a voice inside his head whispered. *Call the house.*

Mr. J speed-dialed his home number.

Ring. Ring. Ring. Ring. The call finally connected.

'Hello ...'

Mr. J immediately recognized the voice at the other end of the line and it was as if his life had just been sucked out of him. It was his own. The answering machine had picked it up.

'... you've reached the house of ...' He waited for the beep at the end of the message.

'Cassandra, honey, it's me. If you're there, please pick it up.

Please.' His voice wavered. 'I need to talk to you, hon. I need to hear your voice. Please answer the phone. Please.'

There was no answer.

'FUUUUUUUUUCK!' His agony-filled scream echoed throughout the entire room.

Five minutes later, Mr. J was still sitting at the edge of the bathtub, his face buried in his palms, his cellphone on the tiled floor by his feet. His reflection in the mirror had grown tired of waiting.

Another five minutes went by before Mr. J finally moved his hands away from his face. His arms dropped by the side of his body aimlessly. He felt totally drained of energy. His eyelids flapped a couple of times, his pupils contracted, filtering away the excessive lighting as it reflected off the white tiles. It took him another minute to crash through the blur of confusion and regain focus, and as he did, everything seemed and felt different – the room, the air, his entire world. His blood had gone cold in his veins, his lungs breathed hate instead of oxygen, and he couldn't feel his heart beating in his chest anymore. Everything inside of him had died with his wife. Everything except his brain. He needed to keep it alive. He needed to think. And think he did. A few minutes later, he reached for his phone and made the first of three calls.

Forty

As Hunter's attention moved to the person standing before him he frowned, but the uncertainty in his stare lasted just a fraction of a second before it was substituted by a look of total surprise – a look that the woman standing there failed to recognize.

'Oh, I'm so sorry,' she said, unable to hide her embarrassment. 'You don't remember me, do you?' There was a touch of disappointment in her tone.

'Of course I do,' Hunter said, returning his drink to his table. 'The twenty-four-hour reading room at UCLA.' He searched his memory for her name. 'Tracy, right? Tracy Adams.'

Her disappointment gave way to a coy smile.

'Your hair looks a little different,' Hunter added. 'That's why it took me a second.'

Tracy's wavy red hair was pegged back over her ears by two small hairclips, revealing a pair of dainty skull earrings, with tiny black rocks for eyes. The rest of her hair fell loose past her shoulders, framing a very attractive heart-shaped face, where expressive green eyes sat behind old-fashioned, cat-eye glasses, but the real difference was in her fringe. This time, instead of looping above her forehead to form a pin-up-style victory roll, it simply fell naturally over her face, partially covering her left eye.

'Sorry about the intrusion,' Tracy said, her demeanor still showing a little embarrassment. 'I was sitting at the bar when I saw the hostess showing you to your table.' Her shoulders moved up in a delicate shrug. 'I thought I would come and say, "Hi."'

'No intrusion at all.' Hunter's gaze gravitated towards the bar for a quick second. 'I'm glad you did.'

Not wanting to sound too forward, he quickly assessed the scene. At the bar sitting area, no one was expectantly looking their way. Tracy also had her drink in her hand, which suggested that she hadn't left anyone waiting for her back at the bar or at a table. Hunter indicated the empty seat across the table from him.

'Would you like to have a seat?'

She hesitated for a moment before reinforcing her point. 'Are you sure? I really wouldn't like to intrude.'

'You're not,' Hunter reassured her. 'It would be a pleasure.'

The coy smile returned to Tracy's lips and she finally nodded in acceptance. 'In that case, sure. Thank you.'

She took the seat, placed her drink down on the table and nodded at Hunter's glass, making a reference to when they first met by the coffee vending machine.

'I must say, that looks a lot more appealing than a Caramel Frappuccino Deluxe.'

Hunter smiled. 'I agree. Probably healthier too.'

'So, what are you having?' she asked. 'The choice in here is overwhelming.'

'Yes, that's for sure,' Hunter replied as his eyes settled on his glass. 'Scotch. Kilchoman ... Caramel Barley Deluxe.'

Tracy laughed. 'Year?'

The question surprised Hunter.

'Twenty-ten.'

She made a face, impressed. 'Great choice. They're a very traditional distillery. If I'm not mistaken, I think that they are the only ones that complete all parts of their whisky-making process on site. Nothing gets outsourced.'

Hunter tried not to frown at her again, but he was sincerely intrigued. Women in general weren't very fond of Scotch whisky, which wasn't at all surprising. Whisky was undoubtedly an acquired taste, one that at first would certainly overpower anyone's palate and knock the air out of their lungs in the process. Hunter knew that only too well. The trick was to persist, to keep trying, to keep sipping it until one day it finally made sense. Women usually weren't that patient with drinks. They either liked it at first sip or they didn't.

'It sounds like you know quite a bit about whisky.' Hunter didn't ask the question, but it silently floated in the air, begging for an answer.

'My father was Scottish, from the Highlands,' Tracy explained, before having another sip of her drink. 'So I was introduced to it at a very early age, and I mean – *very early age*. He used to dip my pacifier in it when I was a baby to get me to go to sleep. After that, from when I was about four onwards, he would allow me a sip of his Scotch on special occasions, like Christmas and New Year. If my grandfather were around, he'd do the same. My mother didn't like it at all and she used to tell my father off all the time, but he didn't care. He'd just turn around and say, "Aye, let the lass have a wee snifter, hen. It's guid for her, aaricht."'

To Hunter's surprise, Tracy's Scottish accent was absolutely flawless, and terribly sensual.

'On my sixteenth birthday,' she continued, 'my father poured me my first full shot of Scotch.' She paused, feeling the need to clarify. 'Have you ever been to Scotland?'

Hunter shook his head. It was his turn to feel a little embarrassed. 'No, unfortunately not. Actually, I've never been out of the country.'

A new, surprised look from Tracy. 'You need to go sometime. It's an astounding place, especially the Highlands, but since you've never been there, you might not know this – by law, pubs, bars, and restaurants in Scotland have to use a measured shot. No free pouring like over here, so when I say a shot, I mean about this much.' She indicated on her glass. It was less than half the original measure Hunter had received.

'Wow.'

'But as I've said, from the age of four onwards, my father wouldn't just allow me a sip of his Scotch and that was that. He would always explain about the nose, the palate, and the finish, so by the time I started having my own when I was sixteen, I could already discern flavors and underlying tones. Scotch is my favorite drink.' She paused and made a half-pained face. 'And I have just bored you stiff, haven't I?'

'No, not at all,' Hunter shook his head. The truth was, he found Tracy very charismatic. Very easy to get comfortable with. 'That's a very interesting story.'

Tracy laughed. 'I can tell that you don't know many people with Scottish heritage then. They are very serious about their whisky over there, and they start training their young ones early.'

'And it works,' Hunter commented, 'because, as I've said, it sounds like you really know your stuff. So now I'm curious. Since you're a connoisseur, what are *you* drinking?' He nodded at her glass.

She paused for a moment.

Hunter couldn't tell if it was for effect or not.

She looked back at him as she replied. 'Same as you – Kilchoman, 2010.'

This time Hunter couldn't hide the frown. 'You're kidding.'

'No.' She pushed her glass in his direction. 'There, have a sip.'

Hunter regarded her for a second before reaching for the glass. He first brought it to his nose. As he inhaled the fumes the curious look on his face deepened.

Tracy waited.

Hunter had a small sip and his eyes shot in her direction.

Tracy had a whole new smile on her lips. 'I had you there for a second, didn't I? With over three hundred different types of whisky served here, it would've been an amazing coincidence.'

Hunter returned her glass to the table and pushed it back towards her. 'Yes, it would've been. And yes, you did have me for a second. So what is it, Balvenie?' Hunter shrugged. 'Maybe Caribbean Cask or Doublewood?'

The impressed look was back on Tracy's face. 'That's very good,' she confirmed. 'Fourteen, Caribbean Cask. You're talking about me? You sound like a connoisseur yourself.'

Hunter chuckled. 'Not quite. I have a bottle at home, so its palate is a little familiar to me.'

A tall waiter, carrying a round silver tray, approached Hunter's table. 'Here we go: cheeseburger and fries?'

'That would be mine. Thank you.' Hunter said.

The waiter placed the plate on the table in front of him. 'Could I get you anything else – ketchup, mustard, another drink . . .?'

'No, I'm fine, thank you. This will do.'

The waiter looked at Tracy.

'I'm still going here.' She lifted her glass. 'Thank you.'

'Enjoy.' He addressed Hunter again. 'If you need anything else just give me a shout. My name is Max.'

As the waiter walked away, Hunter looked at Tracy. 'Please help yourself to some fries. There's enough here to feed about four people.'

'That *is* a lot of fries,' Tracy agreed. 'But thank you, I've eaten already.'

'Please, have at least a couple.'

Tracy studied Hunter for an instant. He hadn't touched his food yet. Her next question came out cautiously. 'Are you fearful of eating in front of others?'

Hunter studied her in return. 'No,' he finally said. 'Not at all.' He reached for the salt and sprinkled some over the fries.

Tracy was still studying him. He still hadn't touched his food.

'It's OK to be, you know?' she said in a comforting tone. 'It's actually very OK to be. The condition is a lot more common than you'd expect. About ten to twelve percent of Americans are either fearful or embarrassed of eating in front of others. Did you know that?'

'Well,' Hunter said, 'you're the psychology professor, so I trust you're right, but I'm really not fearful or embarrassed of eating in front of others. I just thought that it would be a

waste because I certainly won't be able to eat all these fries.'
He finally reached for his cheeseburger and took a bite.

Silence.

Hunter pretended not to notice the confused look on
Tracy's face.

'And now we are back to our starting point,' she said at
last. 'Which was – you owe me an explanation.'

'Do I?' Hunter asked, once he was done chewing.

'Well, OK, no, you don't owe me anything, but I'd love to
understand how you knew.'

Hunter played dumb.

'C'mon. The first time we met back at UCLA we talked for
about two minutes outside the reading room. I gave you no
clues, but somehow you knew that I was a professor.'

Hunter had another bite of his cheeseburger.

'I know you didn't figure any of that out from the books
I had with me that night because none of them were on academia, or on the subject I teach. Nonetheless, just now you
revealed that you also knew that I'm a psychology professor.
How?'

Hunter had a few fries.

'Obviously, from the phone call you received that night, I
gathered that you were a detective with the Homicide Special
Section of the LAPD.'

Hunter looked back at Tracy.

'I had to check that online to find out what it was,' she
explained. 'So fine, your specialty is figuring things out. At
least I'm not that freaked out about you anymore.'

'Freaked out?'

'Well, you meet a complete stranger in the middle of the
night and within a couple of minutes he's telling you things

about you that he shouldn't really know. That could be a little unsettling, don't you think? Especially in a city like LA. You could've been a secret stalker for all I knew.'

The word 'stalker' triggered Hunter's brain to re-engage. He put his cheeseburger down.

'Are you having problems with a stalker?' Hunter's tone was so heavy with concern it caused Tracy to do a double-take.

'What . . .? No. It's not that. I was just giving an example.'

Hunter remained quiet.

'The truth is,' Tracy moved on, 'you're right. I'm a psychology professor, and as such I'd love to be able to understand the thought process behind your deduction. What gave it away? How did you piece it together?'

Hunter had a few more fries. 'Are you sure you don't want any?'

Tracy sighed. 'Will you answer my question if I have some?'

'Sure.'

Tracy grabbed a few fries and dipped them in the tomato relish that accompanied them.

'Like I told you before,' Hunter finally said, 'it's just observation.'

'That's what you've said, yes,' Tracy agreed. 'And that's also why I told you that I couldn't see it, despite replaying everything I could remember about the episode in my mind countless times. Like I said, none of the books I had with me that night were on academia, or on any subject related to psychology. I didn't have my badge on display, so how did you figure out that I am a psychology professor at UCLA?'

Hunter was about to reply when he felt his cellphone

vibrate inside his pocket. He reached for it and checked the display screen.

'Give me just a minute,' he said, getting to his feet and bringing the phone to his ear. 'Detective Hunter, Homicide Special.' Hunter listened in silence for several seconds. 'What?' Disbelief filled his entire body. 'Are you sure?' He consulted his watch – 11:03 p.m. 'OK. OK. I'm on my way.'

'You've got to be kidding me.' Tracy's comment came as a whisper. 'Again?'

'I'm terribly sorry,' Hunter said. The look on his face was somewhere between confused and incredulous. 'I have to go.'

Tracy didn't know what to say, so instead, she kept her surprised eyes on Hunter.

He reached for his wallet and placed a couple of bills on the table. As he took the first steps in the direction of the exit, he paused and looked back at Tracy.

'I know that this will sound odd but ... could I call you sometime?'

Tracy really wasn't expecting that. 'Umm ... yeah, sure. I'd like that.'

Hunter winked at her before setting off again.

'Wait,' Tracy said, quickly jotting down her number on a paper napkin and getting to her feet. 'It would help if you actually had my number, don't you think?'

'Yes, that *would* help,' Hunter replied as he took the napkin. A second later he was gone.

Forty-One

Detective Webb took the keys from Dr. Barnes' hands and unlocked the front door to her two-bedroom house in Mid-City, a very diverse and densely populated neighborhood in Central Los Angeles. The white door with a decorative beveled glass window opened with a slightly eerie creak.

At the end of their interview back at the police station, Webb had told Dr. Barnes that, given the circumstances, all he could really do was take the note and the bracelet to their forensic lab so they could be tested for fingerprints.

'No offense, Detective,' she had said, visibly disappointed, 'but we both know that chances are, they won't find any prints other than my own. Who goes through this kind of trouble and forgets to wear gloves?'

'You'd be surprised, Doctor.'

'Can't it be tested for DNA?' she had pushed.

Webb had to do a double-take. 'Why, Doctor? Do you think that the person who took the bracelet might've worn it for a few hours before leaving it on your car?'

He was unsure if his words had come out with a sarcastic tone or not. By the look Dr. Barnes gave him, they had.

'No, Detective.' Her tone had matched his. 'But what if

after it was taken from my house, he placed it in his pocket, or in a bag, or anywhere else where the bracelet could've come into contact with something else that contained his DNA?'

Webb had looked even more puzzled then. He sincerely doubted that Dr. Barnes had thought her words through properly.

'You mean DNA transference? Also known as DNA contamination? That's a defense argument, Doctor, not an incriminating one.'

Webb had been right. Dr. Barnes hadn't thought this through at all and right then her frustration had threatened to surpass her fear, but she still had one last angle to try.

'OK, how about my house? How about searching it for fingerprints or DNA? We'll have a better chance of finding something there, won't we?'

Webb had looked back at her with "sorry puppy" eyes.

'I can't justify putting in a request for a forensic team, Doctor, not even a forensic agent. There was no burglary. Nothing is actually missing because you have the bracelet with you, and you admitted that you haven't noticed any signs of a break-in. My captain would never sign the request because, technically, no crime has been committed.'

Frustration didn't surpass her fear, but it certainly equaled it. She had no idea of what to do next. She felt completely exhausted, but the thought of going back to her house alone filled her heart with dread.

Something about Dr. Barnes had struck a chord within Detective Webb. Maybe it had been her charisma. Maybe it had been the sincerity that came across in every word she spoke. He wasn't sure what it was, but he knew he wanted to help her.

Understandably, she felt too rattled and scared to go back to her empty house. Webb had asked her if there was anywhere else she could go and stay for the night – a friend or a family member's house, for instance.

The thought had already crossed Dr. Barnes' mind. She had actually considered calling her sister, Erica, who lived with her boyfriend on the opposite side of town. Maybe she could stay the night, but Dr. Barnes and Erica's boyfriend had never got along well. She had also thought about her best friend, Nancy Morgan, but in the end she'd decided against calling either of them. What she really wanted was to feel safe in her own home.

Webb could easily see her logic, so given the circumstances he did the best he could do – he offered to follow her home and carefully check her house for her.

The eerie creak that came from her front door would've given the dark room beyond it a very sinister feel, if not for the fact that the air inside it carried a delicate aroma of roses and summer berries.

'The light switch is on the wall to your right,' she said, standing on her porch just a few paces behind Webb.

For an instant, maybe to make the doctor feel a little more secure, Webb almost unholstered his weapon as he switched on the lights and stepped into Dr. Barnes' house. His hand did actually move towards his gun, but he paused mid-movement, feeling positively silly.

Dr. Barnes' living room was relatively spacious, and it had undoubtedly been decorated very much with a woman's touch. There were fluffy cushions on the sofa, scented candles in candleholders, rugs that made you want to lie down and fall asleep on them, vases filled with roses and sweet alyssum, and the walls ... the walls were peach.

Webb walked over to the center of the room and paused by the navy-blue armchair. Despite his skepticism, his eyes circled the room with the utmost attention.

Dr. Barnes stayed by the door.

The detective checked each and every one of the room's six windows. All locked. He walked back to the front door and checked its lock. No sign of forced entry. Satisfied, he nodded in the direction of the hallway that took them deeper into the house.

'Everything else is through there?' he asked.

'Everything but the kitchen,' the doctor replied, indicating a door to his right.

'I'll have a look in the kitchen first then,' Webb said, making his way towards it.

Dr. Barnes finally stepped into her living room and closed the door behind her.

The kitchen was compact, with no real hiding space, unless Webb considered the fridge or the cupboard under the sink. He checked them both. No one hiding anywhere.

'OK,' he said, 'let's have a look at the rest of the house.'

'Guest bedroom is the first bedroom on the right,' Dr. Barnes said as they crossed the living room in the direction of the corridor. 'First door on the left is the bathroom. The door at the end of the hallway is my bedroom.'

Webb checked every room as carefully as he could, including inside wardrobes and behind shower curtains. All clear.

'OK,' he said, getting back on to his feet after looking under Dr. Barnes' bed. That was the last place he had to check. 'The house is clear, Doctor. There's no one here.'

She finally stepped into her bedroom and looked back at him with a mixture of gratitude and embarrassment. She felt so mentally tired, she was beginning to doubt her own thoughts.

'Thank you,' she said, not knowing what else to say. She was sure that Detective Webb had considered all of this to be a huge waste of time, but she could tell that he was a caring and committed police officer. Back at the station, he could've ended their interview within five minutes, but he didn't and she was sure she knew why.

Webb had read the fear in her eyes. He had noticed the discomfort in her movements and despite what he believed and how busy he was, he still gave her all his attention. He gave her every benefit of the doubt. In a way, he did to her what she did to all her patients – he listened to whatever problem she brought him, regardless of it sounding crazy or not, and he tried his best to help her. The fact that he had accompanied her to her house just so she could feel a little more secure was a clear indication of that.

Webb walked over to the double glass doors that opened on to her backyard. They were securely locked. He then made his way to the large window on the east wall. Also locked. He turned to face Dr. Barnes.

'All locked, Doctor, but I've got to be honest with you. I don't want to scare you or anything, but your locks aren't great quality.' He lifted his hands, already aiming to calm her down. 'They are fine, please don't get me wrong, but they can be breached.'

'You don't want to scare me with a statement like that?'

Webb's hands stayed up. 'It sounds worse than it is. All I'm trying to say is that if you really are concerned for your safety and for the safety of your house, you could consider upgrading your locks.'

'You said that these could be breached?' she asked, anxiously.

'Not by just anyone.' Webb again tried to calm Dr. Barnes down. 'One would need the knowledge of how to and the correct tools.'

'But somebody could've done it, right? Somebody could've opened one of my windows from the outside, or even one of the doors?'

'Technically, yes, but then again, with the right knowledge and the correct tools, safes can be breached.'

Dr. Barnes considered Webb's statement. He was right, she could be overreacting; nonetheless she made a decision right then to upgrade all of her locks, and maybe even get the house alarmed. She nodded back at him.

'Could I maybe offer you a coffee?' she asked.

Webb checked his watch. It was late. Too late. He needed to get going.

'I'd love one, but I do need to get back to the station.'

'Are you sure?' she insisted. 'It will take me just a couple of minutes. I had the coffee at your station. It tasted like it's been filtered through a dirty diaper.'

Webb laughed. 'That's because it probably has. I don't think anyone really knows who makes that coffee. I don't think anyone really wants to know.'

Dr. Barnes smiled at him.

Webb checked his watch one more time.

'How about if I take a rain check on that coffee?' he asked. 'How about tomorrow? That way I can check on you again, make sure everything is fine.'

Dr. Barnes' smile widened as she nodded.

'Sure. Tomorrow sounds great.'

'Is six o'clock OK?'

The doctor had the whole day off.

'Yep. That works for me.'

'Great,' Webb said, walking towards the bedroom door. 'I'll see you tomorrow then.'

Detective Webb exited Dr. Barnes' house and jumped into his unmarked police car. As he turned on the engine, he smiled internally. This had been a lot easier than what he'd imagined.

Forty-Two

The two-story house was located at the end of a quiet street in Granada Hills – a somewhat rich neighborhood on the San Fernando Valley portion of Los Angeles. In a cab, even at that time of night and with traffic considerably reduced, it took Hunter about fifty-five minutes to cover the distance between where he was and the address he was given to Cassandra Jenkinson's house.

As the cab turned left on to Amestoy Avenue and approached Flanders Street on the right, the driver geared down and looked at Hunter through the rearview mirror.

'Damn, man, something big is going down where you're going. PD is all over the joint like flies on shit.'

Hunter nodded. 'Yeah, I know. That's why I'm here.'

The driver's stare left the mirror and he twisted his neck to look at Hunter. 'You a cop?'

Hunter didn't reply. In his head, this just didn't make any sense. The phone call he had received had come from Captain Blake herself. She had told him that their investigation had just escalated into a multiple homicide with a serial pattern, because they now had a second victim. If that was really the case, then they had to have been wrong in most of their assumptions so far.

A marginal number of stalkers reached what was known as the sixth phase of stalking – aggression and violence towards humans. Once that phase was reached, avoiding thoughts like 'if I can't have her/him then no one else can either' would become almost impossible, and fantasizing about killing the subject of their affection would begin to torment them. But even out of those who'd entertain such morbid thoughts, few would actually act on it. The ones who did, in the aftermath of their actions were nearly always overwhelmed by a feeling of such guilt and sadness they tended to isolate themselves for weeks, months, sometimes years. Some would also punish themselves in some way. But stalkers were people with obsessive personalities and, almost inevitably, after the guilt and sadness had finally dispelled, they would once again turn their obsessive attention on to a brand new subject and the chances of that murderous cycle repeating itself were high, very high.

But it had been just three days since Karen Ward had been murdered, not weeks, months, or years. Three days, which meant one of two things – either this killer was not Karen Ward's stalker, even though she did have one, or he stalked multiple subjects at once, which was extremely rare but not unheard of.

From the backseat of the taxi, Hunter quickly studied the scene.

Flanders Street had been completely cordoned off, but the yellow crime-scene tape that established the police perimeter extended at least another forty-five yards on either side of the street entrance. Black and white units seemed to be parked just about everywhere.

The media had also already received word of the murder and a couple of news vans, with TV cameras being set up on their roofs, had strategically claimed their spot on the sidewalk, directly across the road from the cordoned-off street. Three photographers, all armed with telescopic lenses, were tirelessly walking from one end of the perimeter line to the other, searching for a shot, but the distance and the position of the Jenkinsons' house made the task a virtual impossibility. Nonetheless, none of them seemed like they were about to give up any time soon.

A small crowd, who looked to be filming and photographing everything on their cellphones, ready for the 'obligatory' upload to the never-ending number of social media sites, had already gathered by the crime-scene tape.

At the south entrance to Amestoy Avenue, two policemen were busy coordinating traffic and signaling every curious driver who slowed down to keep on moving.

'I don't think I can go any further, man,' the cab driver said, pulling up behind a police cruiser.

Hunter paid the fare and jumped out.

The rain that had announced itself when he first got to the Seven Grand Bar still hadn't materialized, but the dark clouds that had now completely obscured the stars gave it the five-minute call. Water was coming, there was no doubt about that.

Hunter zipped up his jacket.

Five uniformed officers with sturdy expressions on their faces maintained the perimeter, keeping reporters and curious onlookers alike from getting any closer. Hunter zigzagged through the crowd, flashed his credentials at two of the officers and stooped under the tape.

From the top of Flanders Street to the Jenkinsons' house,

Hunter calculated it to be somewhere between one hundred and one hundred and fifteen yards. Officers were already going through protocol and running a door-to-door up and down the street. Every front window on every house was lined with shocked and frightened faces.

On the left, towards the end of the street, a white forensic van was parked next to Garcia's Honda Civic. As Hunter approached the house, he spotted his partner standing next to a black and white unit, talking to a senior officer.

'Robert,' Garcia called, waving his hand. 'Over here.'

Hunter approached the large house. It was painted a light shade of green, with white trimmings around the gable-styled roof. The front lawn was small but very well maintained, with colorful flowerbeds contouring its entirety. To the left of the house, a two-car garage sat at the end of a concrete driveway with black inlays, where a silver Cadillac SRX was parked. From the outside, one could easily tell that whoever lived in that house took pride in their home. This was the nicest house in a street of very nice houses.

'This is Sergeant Thomas Reed from the Valley Bureau,' Garcia said once Hunter reached them.

They shook hands.

Reed was about Garcia's height and in his mid-forties. His head was shaved, but he wouldn't have much hair had he let it grow. An old scar crossed his chin from the right edge of his lips to the left edge of his jaw.

'Sergeant Reed was first response,' Garcia revealed.

'I was just telling your partner here that the circumstances of the nine-one-one call were a little odd.' There was a certain smooth quality to Sergeant Reed's voice that made him sound like a children's story narrator.

'How so?' Hunter asked.

'For starters, the call didn't originate from here,' Reed said. 'And when I say here, I mean Los Angeles.'

Both detectives squinted at the sergeant.

'The call was made from Fresno.'

Confused looks all around.

'That's right,' Reed confirmed, noticing their intrigue and giving them a firm nod. 'The nine-one-one call came from about two hundred miles away.'

Forty-Three

A blue-and-white forensic tent had already been set up at the entrance to the Jenkinsons' house, completely covering the entire front porch. A CSI agent was busy checking the concrete driveway, searching for any tire tracks that differed from the ones left by the silver Cadillac SRX that was parked there. Two other CSI agents were carefully checking the front lawn, the flowerbeds and the window to the right of the porch.

'If we really are talking about the same perp here,' Garcia said, as he and Hunter left Sergeant Reed behind and began making their way towards the house, 'this doesn't make a lot of sense, does it?'

Garcia had noticed the overly concerned look on Hunter's face when he first saw him coming down the street. He figured it was for the same reasons he himself could hardly believe it when he got the call less than an hour ago: *Karen Ward's stalker has killed again?*

'No, it doesn't.' Hunter shook his head. 'What do we have on this victim?'

'Very little at the moment. Just the basics, really.' Garcia reached for his pocket notebook. 'Her name was Cassandra Jenkinson, forty-two years old, from Santa Ana in Orange County. Worked as an events organizer for a social club not that far from here in Porter Ranch.' Reflexively, he pointed west. 'Apparently she also volunteered once a week to help at a coalition for women with heart disease called "WomenHeart".'

Hunter's eyebrows arched. He had shopped at one of their charity shops before, he was sure of it.

'She was married to a John Jenkinson,' Garcia continued. 'Forty-eight years old, from Los Angeles. He runs his own business consultancy practice based downtown. As we've heard from Sergeant Reed, he's the one the killer video-called. John and Cassandra Jenkinson have a single child, a son, Patrick, twenty years old, who goes to college in Boston, Massachusetts. Ms. Jenkinson also had a complete clean record. No priors. No problems with the IRS. No outstanding debts. Not even an outstanding parking fine. From her records alone, she was a stand-up citizen.' Garcia flipped a page on his notebook. 'And that's about it for now.'

Hunter nodded as his gaze moved from CSI agent to CSI agent.

'They basically just started their operation,' Garcia clarified. 'They were just setting up when I got here about five minutes ago.' He returned his notebook to his pocket.

'Who's the lead agent, do you know?'

'Same one as last time,' Garcia replied. 'Dr. Susan Slater.' He gave Hunter a quirky smile.

'What was that?' Hunter asked.

'What was what?'

'That "I ate the last donut" smile. What was that for?'

'C'mon.'

Hunter paused and squinted at his partner.

Garcia made a face. 'C'mon, Robert, she's hot and you know it.'

'Who, Dr. Slater?'

'No, my grandma in a Brazilian bikini, doing the samba on Copacabana beach. Yes, Dr. Slater. Don't play dumb, Robert, it really doesn't suit you. I saw the way you were looking at her last time . . . and she at you. You should ask her out.'

'We were working a crime scene, Carlos.'

'So? Romance can blossom in the strangest of places.'

Hunter chuckled. 'You're sick.'

As they set off towards the house again, Hunter felt a drop hit the top of his head and looked up. Garcia did the same. Another one hit them both on the forehead.

On the driveway, the CSI agent searching for tire tracks seemed to have found something, but he too saw the first drops of rain hit the concrete and all of a sudden his movements became a lot more urgent.

'Shit!' they all heard him say as he frantically searched the bag he had with him for something he could use to cover the driveway patch directly in front of him.

Hunter and Garcia rushed over to help him, but one of the agents on the front lawn beat them to it.

'Have you got something?' Hunter asked as he towered over them, unzipped his jacket, and pulled it wide open like bat wings, to use it as an improvised umbrella.

The raindrops got thicker and more frequent.

'I think I've got a partial tire track here,' the agent replied, without looking up. 'If we manage to protect it from the rain, that is.'

Garcia unzipped his jacket and mimicked Hunter's movements.

'Crap!' the first agent said to the second. 'I didn't even have time to photograph it. If the rain washes this off, we've got nothing.'

The two agents were moving as fast as they could. A few seconds later, after using some tape to fix a piece of impermeable material to the concrete, the first agent finally looked up at Hunter and Garcia.

'This will hopefully do it,' he said. 'Even if the rain manages to wash some of it off, I'm sure we'll still get something. You guys with Homicide?'

Both detectives nodded, as the rain got a little heavier.

'As I've said,' the agent continued. 'I barely had time to analyze it, but one thing I can tell you is, this partial doesn't seem to belong to an SUV like the Cadillac.' He nodded at the car parked on the driveway.

Hunter and Garcia zipped their jackets back up and rushed towards the house.

The officer standing at the porch handed them two sealed plastic bags containing disposable forensic coveralls. The officer at the door got them to sign the crime-scene manifesto before stepping to one side.

Hunter and Garcia finished suiting up, pulled their hoods over their heads and finally stepped into a brand new horror show.

Forty-Four

Cassandra Jenkinson's house was no less gracious on the inside. The front door led Hunter and Garcia into a spacious anteroom with a striking crystal chandelier hanging from the ceiling. A large, gothic-framed round mirror occupied most of the wall to their left. To their right, a sculpture of twisted stainless steel sat atop a rectangular, double-pedestal console table. On the floor, directly in front of them, a circular, Turkish knot rug filled the room with color. At first glance, nothing seemed disturbed or out of place.

Nicholas Holden, the same forensic fingerprint expert who had worked the first crime scene, was carefully dusting the door lock and studying its keyhole.

'Any signs of a break-in?' Hunter asked, bending down to have a closer look.

Holden shook his head. 'Nothing apparent. Neither the door nor the lock look to have been forced in any way.'

'Picked?' Garcia questioned.

'Unlikely. That's what I was looking at right now, but this is a five-lever mortise lock. They are hard to find in the US, which is surprising because they're rock solid. Due to its five levers, picking it becomes a monstrous task. You'd need all the right tools and plenty of time to get through it.'

'How much time?' Garcia pushed.

Holden shrugged. 'Hard to say, but probably a lot more time than any assailant would be prepared to waste at the front porch of an exposed house.'

None of the houses on Flanders Street were sheltered by any sort of gate or fence. A person standing or kneeling by the Jenkinsons' front door would've been easily spotted by most of the neighboring houses.

'I've just started here,' Holden added. 'But I've already come across two sets of prints. One – female, probably belonging to the victim herself. The second one, undoubtedly male. Big hands.'

Both detectives thanked Holden, pulled open the next door, and moved on to the following room, which had been drenched by the brightness of two powerful forensic spotlights.

The split-level living room they entered was simply stunning, with a towering dark-granite fireplace and gleaming hardwood floors. It had been lavishly decorated with antique furniture, works of art, and a large Persian rug that gave the space a somewhat serene but exotic feel. If the chandelier they saw as they entered the house was striking, the one at the center of the living room ceiling was nothing less than impressive, with ten candle-shaped light bulbs surrounding hundreds of stringed crystal beads that dropped down like sparkling raindrops. But all that beauty, all that tranquility, had been completely shattered by the horror that now took center stage in the room.

From the dining table that sat across from the fireplace,

one of its six chairs had been dragged closer to a wall where several framed original paintings hung. On the chair, with her hair, face and torso drenched in blood, a woman sat naked, with her eyes wide open and her mouth contorted in a frozen scream that Hunter was sure had reached no one, except the monster who had mutilated her.

'Detectives,' Dr. Slater said in greeting, nodding at Hunter and Garcia. She was standing just behind the victim's chair.

Neither detective replied, their intrigued stares still battling against the terrorized one that had mummified in the victim's eyes. Dr. Slater didn't take offence.

'Not what you were expecting, is it?' she added.

Hunter looked deep in thought, like a chess player analyzing his opponent's unexpected move, trying to figure out what he was up against.

'I'm not really sure what I was expecting,' he finally replied, before returning the doctor's greeting gesture. 'Hi, Doc.'

Garcia followed suit.

Dr. Slater gave them a few more seconds. A lock of blonde hair escaped from under the hood of her Tyvek coverall. Calmly she moved it back into place.

'How certain are you that this is the same perp from three nights ago?' she asked.

Both detectives could clearly see why Dr. Slater had asked that question. Judging from the crime scene alone, anyone would be forgiven for thinking that the killer's MO and signature suggested otherwise.

'Right now,' Garcia replied, 'not that certain.'

'I figured as much,' the doctor came back. 'And that's why I asked, because I sure have my doubts. Linking both murders based solely on crime-scene evidence . . .' she allowed her eyes to quickly circle the living room, '. . . would be a hell of a stretch. Other than the fact that the victim was also left sitting on a dining chair.' She reinforced her point by indicating it. 'Most of the killer's MO differs greatly from the one we saw the first time we met.' She stepped away from behind the chair. 'Here, let me show you.'

Hunter and Garcia moved closer.

'As I'm sure you'll remember, the victim of three days ago was restrained to the chair by her ankles and torso, immobilizing her arms, but still allowing enough freedom of movement for the "bending forward, slamming" action.'

Both detectives nodded.

'OK, so first major diverging point – this victim wasn't restrained to the chair at all, at least not by ropes, or cords, or anything similar.' She called their attention to Cassandra's wrists, ankles and the patch of skin directly under her breasts. There were no binding or friction bruises. No marks, either. 'You'll need to wait for the toxicology results to find out if she was drugged or not, but I'd be seriously surprised if she wasn't.'

'A paralyzing agent?' Garcia suggested.

'That's what I would expect, yes, and that would be a second diverging point in the killer's MO. As I'm sure you'll remember, toxicology came back negative on all accounts for the first victim.'

The doctor interlaced her fingers together to readjust her latex gloves.

'Third major diverging point,' she continued, now indicating Cassandra's lips. 'There are no lacerations, scratches, or impressions of any kind to suggest that she was gagged prior to her demise, unlike the first victim.'

Hunter walked around and joined the doctor by the victim's left side. For several silent seconds, he regarded the victim's entire body. With the exception of a small cut to the right corner of her bottom lip, there were no other visible wounds, superficial or otherwise, anywhere on her torso, arms, legs or face. He bent forward to examine her mouth and the cut to her lip, but he found it hard to get past the look immortalized in her eyes – total and utter fear.

'Fourth,' Dr. Slater carried on with her assessment, 'and undoubtedly the most obvious conflicting point in both MOs, is the complete break away from the kill method.' She regarded the detectives before her. 'From the surprised look on your faces as you walked in here, I'm guessing that, just like me, you were expecting to find another facially mutilated victim.'

She took their silence as a 'yes'.

'It would've been understandable if the killer hadn't used broken glass this time, but I for one was expecting to find another grotesquely disfigured victim.' Dr. Slater paused and once again called their attention to the naked woman on the chair. 'As you can see, despite it being completely covered in blood, the only other injury to her face is this tiny cut to the right side of her bottom lip.' She indicated as she spoke. 'It's a brand new cut, so my guess is that it was probably inflicted upon her with a firm hand slap, either to shut her up or to prove his resolve.'

Even through all the blood, Cassandra's facial features were clearly identifiable – the petite nose, the high cheekbones, the full lips, the rounded chin. She no doubt had been a very attractive woman.

Hunter had already noticed that the victim's fair hair was

completely caked in blood, with the biggest concentration at the very top, which indicated that that was where the blood pour had originated from.

'She obviously bled from the head,' he said. 'But I can't see any major cuts or blunt-force trauma wounds.'

'That's also what puzzled me,' Dr. Slater agreed, 'because it doesn't look like she was bashed over the head with any sort of blunt or sharp instrument. As you've said, there are no visible cuts to her scalp. No depressions to her cranium either.'

Hunter regarded the top of Cassandra's head again, and, though he couldn't see past the thick cluster of blood and hair, an image began forming in his mind.

'Small breaches.' Hunter didn't phrase it as a question.

Dr. Slater's eyes followed Hunter's gaze as she nodded, looking a little impressed from his deduction. 'He killed her by puncturing small holes into her skull.'

Forty-Five

Less than two hours earlier

Suddenly, the demon's gloved hands appeared above Cassandra's head.

They weren't empty.

His right hand held a regular, household-type metal hammer. His left, a six-inch-long masonry chisel with a nail-sharp tip.

Cassandra couldn't see what was happening behind her. She couldn't move her neck. She couldn't turn around. All she could do was stare straight at her cellphone's screen and into her husband's eyes. This time, it was she who saw something that she had never, ever seen in them before – total and utter despair.

'Don't do this. Please don't do this,' reflexively, Mr. J pleaded, but his voice carried no conviction.

He had lost count of how many times he'd been in the demon's place before, his mark helpless before him. They all pleaded. They all begged. They all offered him money, excuses, promises. It had never worked. Mr. J was never there to negotiate or to forgive. He was the last stop. The ultimate consequence to whatever mistake the mark had made. And Mr. J had recognized the same determination he carried with him in the demon's words. In his actions. From his hotel room, miles away from his home, Mr. J knew that there was absolutely nothing he could do or say that would stop the demon from doing what he was about to do. He blinked at his wife again, and just before her vision was completely blurred by a new explosion of tears, she saw the anguish in his face. The sorrow. The helplessness.

Behind Cassandra, the demon placed the tip of the metal chisel on her head. He positioned it about three inches up from her forehead, and a little right from center.

Feeling the sharp tip touch her scalp, Cassandra's desperate eyes shot up as far as they would go, as if she was trying to look at her own eyebrows.

The demon lifted the hammer.

Cassandra's eyes came back down and she returned to doing the only thing she could do – look at her husband through her cellphone screen. His lips moved, but no sound came out of them. His diaphragm lacked the strength. All he could do was mouth the words: *I'm so sorry.*

BANG.

The demon brought the hammer down on to the chisel. As its tip ruptured through Cassandra's skull, fracturing her cranium, her eyes rolled up into her head and her whole body jerked violently. Despite the paralyzing drug she'd been given, her body was still responding to motor nerve impulses.

In silence, and shaking with rage, Mr. J jolted in place. He found himself lost in a void so deep inside of him, he could feel his soul being consumed.

Then came the surprise.

Forty-Six

Mr. J had expected to see the chisel driven into Cassandra's brain in its entirety, but instead, not much more than a centimeter had managed to penetrate. The demon had controlled the strength of the hammer strike with the perfect precision of a master sculptor – one single blow, nothing more, because nothing more was needed.

As the demon finally moved his hands away, thick, sticky blood dripped from Cassandra's head on to her face, creating an uneven red path past her temple, her cheek, and all the way down to her chin.

Mr. J held his breath, grinding his teeth with the wrath of a thousand gods.

Cassandra's eyelids fluttered erratically for seconds before they stabilized again. Her eyes came back from her head tortured and overflowing with pain.

'Ha, ha, ha, ha, ha.'

The distorted laugh caught Mr. J by surprise and he lurched in place once again.

'Did you think that I would just nail the chisel deep into her head with a single blow?' the demon asked.

No reply.

'You did, didn't you?'

Silence.

'That would've been no fun. No, John. We'll keep on going until you either get another correct answer, or your wife dies. Every wrong answer, I puncture a new hole into her cranium. I'm not really sure how many it will take before she's gone, but I don't think that it will take too many, do you?'

'You sonofa—'

'You know the rules,' Mr. J was interrupted again. 'We cannot move on until you give me a correct answer. So let's try it again. Your wedding date. You have five seconds.'

The gears inside Mr. J's brain didn't know which way to turn. Anger collided with fear, which collided with doubt and despondency, all of it wrapped up in a feeling of total emptiness.

On the screen, Cassandra blinked again, this time slowly. Behind her eyelids, her eyes seemed lost.

Blood dripped from her chin on to her shoulder.

'Four . . .' the demon counted down.

March seventh. The date returned to Mr. J, but he now knew that that was wrong, so how come the date was still hammering his thoughts? Had he gotten the whole thing wrong or only the day? The month?

'Three . . .'

On the mantelpiece, in Mr. J's living room, there were at least a couple of photographs from his wedding day. He and Cassandra were standing outside the church, sporting larger-than-life smiles. Was that how this psycho had gotten the idea for his question? From the photographs?

That's not what you're supposed to be thinking about, John. Think, goddamnit, think.

'Two ...'

For just an instant, Cassandra's eyes regained focus and she looked back at her husband with purpose. The despair she had seen in his face seconds earlier had intensified exponentially.

'One ...'

'April seventh?' Those words left Mr. J's lips totally lacking in conviction and sounding more like a question than a statement. All they were was a guess, nothing more. His psychological distress was so intense, it would probably take him a few tries to get his own birthdate right.

As those two words reached Cassandra's ears, she blinked and, even through her tears, Mr. J saw her eyes abandon hope once and for all.

'Wrong again,' the demon said, as calm as a priest giving his opening remarks on Sunday mass. He brought the chisel and hammer back to Cassandra's head. This time he positioned the chisel just a little left from center, and only about an inch up from her forehead.

Mr. J wanted to plead again. He wanted to beg, get on his knees, cry, but what good would any of that do? The demon wouldn't listen. He wouldn't stop.

Up went the hammer. Down it came.

BANG.

Another perfectly controlled blow, sending only the tip of the chisel into Cassandra's skull. Once again, she jerked on her seat viciously and her eyes disappeared into the unknown, but this time her head frighteningly convulsed for a full second, as if a large insect had somehow crawled up her nose and stung her brain.

Mr. J felt life lose its meaning. His wife, his rock, his

world, was dying in front of his eyes, and not only was there nothing he could do to protect her, but she was dying because of his stupidity. Because he couldn't remember his own wedding date.

Blood began oozing from her new wound, dripping over her temple, and running down her left cheek. Her eyelids moved, but this time they paused halfway. She had no strength left in her to fully open her eyes.

The soul-destroying pain of watching his wife being tortured in front of him, together with the suffocating guilt he felt inside, caused Mr. J to feel faint, and for the quickest of instants he took his eyes off the screen.

The demon saw it.

'You looked away,' he said.

Immediately, Mr. J looked back at his phone.

'NO,' he called out, shaking his head. 'NO.'

'You know the rules, John. You look away, she gets punished again.'

Once again, the demon repositioned the chisel, choosing to place it right at the center of Cassandra's skull this time.

Mr. J locked eyes with his wife one more time and, as he did, he went frighteningly quiet. Cassandra wasn't there anymore. Behind her tearful and wondering eyes he saw nothing but a dark void. Her pupils had dilated. The white of her eyes had gone the color of cheap red wine. Even if right now he managed to remember his wedding date, and hoping that the demon would stay true to his word and leave her alone, the Cassandra he knew was gone. From what he'd seen, the chisel had penetrated deep enough to crash through her cranium. Her brain had probably already sustained irreversible damage. After God knew how many operations, if her life could still be saved, who knew what she would be like? Would she still be able to talk? Walk? Move her arms? Recognize anyone? And Mr. J wasn't even factoring in the kind of psychological annihilation that the events of tonight would bring her. No matter what he did from now on, he had already lost Cassandra.

BANG.

The hammer came down again, but this time it sounded like the demon had used just a fraction more force in his blow than he had before, because Mr. J actually heard the bone fracture. A noise that sounded like someone stepping on crushed glass. A millisecond after that, he saw a fresh stream of blood surge from her new wound.

In her seat, Cassandra convulsed once. Twice. Three times. The demon let go of her head and, almost in slow motion, it collapsed forward clumsily.

Stillness before one more violent convulsion that seemed to have come out of nowhere. Cassandra's mouth fell half-open and she began drooling from the right corner of her lips. Muscle spasm caused her shoulders to heave back and forth a couple of times before her body finally came to a complete stop.

This time, Mr. J was the one paralyzed. His eyes were glued to the small screen. His breathing was heavy and labored.

Letting go of the hammer and chisel, the demon allowed the image of a lifeless Cassandra to grace the screen for several seconds before he brought two fingers to the right side of her neck. A moment later, he tried the other side.

From his hotel room, Mr. J did the same. He extended two fingers and gently placed them on his cellphone screen, moving them around delicately, as if he were really touching his wife's face.

'I'm ... so sorry.' The painful words came in a murmur. 'I'm so, so sorry, my love. I love you so much. Please forgive me.'

'Congratulations, John,' the demon said. He had already moved away from behind Cassandra. 'You succeeded in letting your wife die.'

A single tear rolled down Mr. J's face. He closed his eyes and breathed in hate. When he reopened them, they were as void of life as his wife's. His hand moved away from his cellphone screen.

All of a sudden, in one quick movement, the camera panned again, left and up, and Mr. J's screen was filled by something that he wasn't expecting – the demon's face – only it wasn't a face, it was a mask. But despite how real and grotesque it looked, with its lacerated and melted flesh, its deformed, devil-looking eyes, its ripped nose, and its blood-smeared sharp teeth, Mr. J didn't blink. He didn't move. He didn't look away.

'Now that your little game is over,' he said in a tone so calm and cold, he could've frosted the windows in his hotel room, 'you and I are going to play a new one. A game in which I'm the best there is. A game that I've been playing for years and I have never lost. Are you listening to me?'

The demon said nothing in return.

'Do you really think that hiding behind a camera,' Mr. J continued, 'hiding behind an ugly mask, will somehow keep you safe?' He paused, holding the demon's eyes. 'Every single mark I'm sent to deal with is a runaway. They all make the same mistake you are making right now. They believe that if they run away, if they move cities, or states, or countries ... if they change their names, their appearances ... if they obtain new documents ... whatever. They all believe that that somehow will keep them safe. They all believe that disappearing is the key to a whole new life and all their old problems will be left behind.' A new, pregnant pause. 'They are all wrong. Let me tell you something else you didn't know about me, whoever you are. The first part of the job I do is to track these runaways down, wherever they might be ...' Mr. J leaned forward, getting closer to his cellphone. 'And I am the absolute best at what I do. So know this. Wherever you go, wherever you hide, whoever you become after this. I *will* find you ... and I will rip your heart from your chest. Do you hear me, you sick freak?'

Surprisingly, the demon kept the call connected throughout Mr. J's entire speech.

'Ha, ha, ha, ha.' The demon laughed. At first it was a subdued laugh, as if he was trying to control it, but it soon got louder. Much louder.

'Ha, ha, ha, ha, ha, ha!'

The horror-clown mouth of the vile mask twisted awkwardly out of shape as the laugh became almost hysterical.

'Ha, ha, ha, ha, ha, ha, ha, ha, ha, ha, ha.'

As if hypnotized, Mr. J found it impossible to drag his eyes away from the small screen. He knew he'd seen things in his life that no one else had ever seen. Ugly, horrific things that would've unsettled the sturdiest of individuals, but he'd never seen anything like this before.

Suddenly, without any warning, the demon simply stopped laughing.

A split second later the call disconnected.

Forty-Seven

Mr. J was born John Louis Goodwin, the unplanned only child to the parents of Bruce and Sally Goodwin. He was born in Madison, Nebraska, under the sign of the Crab, which was intriguing, because according to recent research done by the FBI, Cancerians were by far the most dangerous and the most cunning criminals of all the zodiac signs. The really peculiar fact was that in second place came Taurus, followed by Sagittarius then Aries. Mr. J's father was Taurus, his mother, Aries.

The birth of a child was supposed to bring joy to a family, but in Mr. J's instance, it seemed to bring the exact opposite. His mother, a trivial drug user since her mid-teens, who at first truly believed that a baby would bring her salvation, was struck by a debilitating case of postnatal depression. Her answer to it, completely disregarding the wellbeing of her newborn, was to upgrade her drug use from mild to junkie. In one quick step, salvation became damnation.

His father, who had never really wanted a child, preferred the bottle to the needle and the fist to dialogue. As a result of such a volatile mix, John Louis Goodwin grew up the neglected child – the proverbial 'invisible boy' – of a complicated, love–hate relationship.

All of that lack of love and affection didn't go unnoticed by young John and from a very early age he realized that he just didn't fit into his parents' plans. The beatings he got became more and more frequent as he grew older, but to his mother's surprise and to his father's anger, instead of crying and running for cover, he would always stand his ground and take the beatings fearlessly and in silence.

But all of that came to an end one rainy summer night, just days before John's fifteenth birthday. That night, after another drunken beating from his father, John returned to his bedroom, packed the very few items of clothing he had into a small rucksack and sat on his bed, arms hugging his knees, eyes focused on the dirty wall in front of him. For hours he listened and waited, until total silence took over his house and he was certain that both of his parents had passed out drunk in their bedroom. Without an ounce of regret, John opened his bedroom door and tiptoed into the kitchen. He knew exactly where his mother kept her drug money. After collecting the whole stash, he forever left the 'living hell' he was never able to call home.

For John's plan to work, he needed to get out of that backwards town he lived in, pronto. At the city bus station, the only bus going anywhere that rainy night was heading to the city where angels were supposed to live – but instead of angels, all he found as he got there were demons.

At first, John roamed the streets in a fog, sleeping rough and eating out of garbage cans and back alley dumpsters, but the funny thing was that, in those dumpsters, he would usually find a better meal than any he ever had when he lived with his parents.

Life on the streets of LA was never easy, and though John

had seen first-hand the destructive effects that drugs and alcohol could have on a person, at fifteen and homeless, he was literally powerless to escape the pull of those two vices. Soon, John also discovered gangs, girls, money, parties and a life that was exciting, frightening and dangerous in more ways than one. It was then that John came face to face with his first internal demon – his addictive personality.

It was that demon that made him grab on to that life of vice like a parasite, and he fell into it like an anchor into the deep sea. For three years that life was all he had and he lived and breathed it with every atom in his body, but the madness of it all was destroying him inside, eating away his brain, obliterating his emotions. He needed to escape it before it was too late. At the age of eighteen, John Louis Goodwin joined the US Army.

During his first tour of duty he acquired the moniker Mr. J. Three tours later, and after two medals and several commendations, John finally returned to Los Angeles, deciding he'd had enough of the military life. John was twenty-five then and, upon his return, he found out that without his fatigues, his country, the country he fought for, killed for, and would've given his life for, had decided to treat him as if he were diseased, and for the second time in his life he became the 'invisible boy'. For the second time in his life he experienced neglect on a scale he never thought possible. No one would hire him, people looked at him as if he were scum, and his government did very little to help him out. Suddenly John found himself in the same situation he was in when he first arrived in the angel-less city, but this time he knew the streets and he knew whom to contact.

To John's surprise, some of his old friends had elevated

themselves to the very top of their 'street' organizations, and those organizations were stronger and more powerful than ever. Some had joined forces, forming a cartel. They had distanced themselves from their old 'street trade', acquiring several distinct businesses, including but not limited to casinos in California, Nevada, Louisiana and New Jersey. They were the ones who approached John.

'We could use someone like you,' he was told. 'Someone with the kind of knowledge and skills you acquired while you were away.'

John considered himself betrayed by his own government, and that played a major part in his decision to join the cartel.

'What we can offer you, if you make the right decision, no one else can. You know that, don't you?'

'If I take your offer,' Mr. J had replied, 'there will be a few conditions. One – I always work alone, not as part of an outfit.'

'Go on.'

'I want to lead as much of a normal life as I can, so I will need a front ... a legit business that will pass any sort of scrutiny.'

'That can be very easily arranged.'

'And I'll also need a new identity. The name I have is no good for me.'

'But of course.'

Two years after that, Mr. J met Cassandra.

Forty-Eight

Garcia stepped closer to have a better look at the victim's head but, just like Hunter and Dr. Slater, he couldn't see past the dense, sticky cluster of blood and hair.

'Perforations to her cranium?' he asked, his tone as skeptical as the look on his face. 'Using what? A small drill?' His gaze quickly moved around the room as if searching for the tool.

Hunter shook his head. 'No, not a drill,' he disagreed. 'A drill would've cause her hair to twist around in speed.' He made a circular motion with his index finger. 'That would've created thick knots at the base of the wound, bunching her hair together like dreadlocks. We've got nothing like that here.'

A quick silent second went by before Garcia contorted his face as if he could feel the pain. 'A hammer and nail.'

This time Hunter nodded. 'Or something very similar.'

Hunter's head movement was mirrored by Dr. Slater. 'And that conclusion, I'd say, brings us to the only other similarity in MO I could find so far between this victim and the one from three nights ago. The first one being, as you remember, the dining chair.'

'Torture,' Garcia said.

'Exactly,' the doctor confirmed. 'The first victim had her face lacerated little by little, this one had her skull punctured . . . a hole at a time.'

Hunter thought it was about time to give Dr. Slater a little more information. 'There *is* a third similarity between the two murders, doc.'

She turned to face him.

'The video-call,' Hunter explained. 'Just like with the first murder, the killer broadcasted the whole ordeal over a video-call. This time to the victim's husband.'

'Nothing is a hundred percent confirmed yet,' Garcia took over, 'as we're still to talk to Mr. Jenkinson.'

'Where is he?' Dr. Slater asked.

'Apparently on his way here right now, but he was in Fresno when he received the call.'

'Fresno?'

Garcia nodded. 'He's a business consultant. He was away on a job.'

'Another question game?' Dr. Slater asked.

Garcia's head tilted sideways slightly. 'Apparently yes, and if the rules were the same as the first time, with every wrong answer the killer was given . . .' He nodded at the victim. 'She got punished.'

'Another "face slam" into a glass container,' the doctor said in thought. 'Another hole hammered into her skull.'

'Once the game was over,' Hunter said, 'the husband made the nine-one-one call.'

'That would explain how come we all got here so fast,' the doctor said. 'Her blood is practically still warm. Rigor mortis hasn't even started yet. I'd say she's been dead for about two hours, maybe less.'

'How many would it take, Doc?' Garcia asked. 'How many punctures into her skull before the game was over?'

'Very hard to tell, Detective.' Dr. Slater's eyes, now full of pity, returned to the victim. 'Different factors would influence that number – diameter of the nail used, location of the perforation, how deep the nail was driven into her cranium, and if it hit brain matter or not. Depending on the killer's accuracy and how much torture he wanted to inflict, the game could've been over with one wrong answer or ten. The killer controlled everything here.'

Hunter took a couple of steps back as he finally managed to drag his attention away from the victim. Just like he'd noticed in the Jenkinsons' anteroom, nothing in their living room looked to have been either disturbed or moved out of place. He had already studied Cassandra's fingers, hands and arms. There were no bruises, no scratches, and no hints of any sort of defensive wounds. She was a reasonably tall woman – five-eight, maybe five-nine, slim and muscle-toned enough to suggest at least one weight-training session in the gym a week. Unless she had been taken completely by surprise, or subdued at gunpoint, she would've put up a fight, and a good one, Hunter was fairly certain of it, yet there were no signs of a struggle anywhere – not on her body, nor in her house.

'Has her cellphone been found?' Hunter asked.

'It has,' Doctor Slater answered. 'Would you like to have a guess as to where we found it?'

'Microwave,' Garcia said.

Doctor Slater confirmed it with a sideways head nod.

'Computer? Laptop? Tablet?'

'We haven't checked the whole house yet, but there's a

laptop on the kitchen counter.' With her index finger she pointed in the direction of it.

Something new for IT Forensics to have fun with, Hunter thought.

Dr. Slater had gone back to studying the victim's body. 'This doesn't make any sense,' she said, dragging Hunter's attention away from his thoughts.

'You mean the apparent fluctuation in MO?' he said.

She first nodded then paused, re-evaluating Hunter's words. 'Apparent? I thought I'd just described four major diverging points.'

'And they were all correct and very valid,' Hunter replied. 'But I think that we're maybe forgetting something here.'

'And what's that?' the doctor asked.

'If we are indeed talking about the same killer of three nights ago, this is his second offence. Right now, what really constitutes his MO, even his signature, is not totally clear because we have only one point of comparison.'

Dr. Slater thought about it for a quick second before accepting Hunter's argument with an eyebrow movement.

He walked over to the fireplace and picked up a framed wedding photograph from the mantelpiece. It showed the victim and her husband standing at the steps that led up to a church entrance. Hunter recognized it as being the Cathedral of Our Lady of Angels in downtown Los Angeles. The smile on both of their faces told its own story.

'Yes,' Hunter said. 'There are a lot of indications to what this killer's MO might be. There are a lot of diverging points as well, but the truth is that right now he might just be experimenting.'

The doctor kneeled down in front of Cassandra to study

her eyes. 'Wait a second,' she said, finally picking up the meaning in Hunter's words. 'If you're right and he's still experimenting, then we all know what this means, don't we? This won't end here. He's going to kill again.'

Neither Hunter nor Garcia replied.

They didn't need to.

Forty-Nine

As Mr. J joined the freeway heading towards Bakersfield and Los Angeles, he brought the speed on his Cadillac CTS-V up to seventy miles per hour, the maximum permitted by the California Department of Transport and the Highway Patrol. His head was still a mess. Thought processes would start at the back of his mind but, before developing into anything significant, they would be shattered into tiny pieces by flashback images of Cassandra being tortured in their own living room, by the hopeless look in her eyes, by the way she convulsed for the very last time. They would be drowned by the sound of that demonic voice, a sound he knew he would never forget.

Mr. J took a deep breath and the effort made his whole body shake with sadness once again. He began coughing as if he was about to throw up, but his empty stomach produced nothing.

Coughing frenzy over, he checked the dashboard clock and then the speedometer. He'd already been driving for over an hour and even if he kept to the maximum limit throughout the entire journey, it would still take him around two hours to get back to Los Angeles and his house in Granada Hills.

'Shit. *Shit. Shit!*' he screamed at nothing and at everything while punching the steering wheel.

He knew that LAPD Detectives and a forensic team would already be there, probing through his house, disturbing Cassandra's body. He knew it because he was the one who made the call. That had been the first of the three phone calls he'd made just before leaving his hotel room in Fresno. The second call was made to one of his contacts inside the LAPD. Someone who he paid well, but who also owed him a lot more than his own life. He owed Mr. J his wife's and his kid's life too.

'Hello!' Skeptically, the deep, rough voice answered the call after the second ring.

'Brian?' Mr. J asked out of courtesy. Besides being able to recognize Brian's very distinctive voice anywhere, Mr. J had called him on the usual number. A number no one else knew about. A number no one else used, except for the two of them.

There was a long pause where Mr. J heard muffled foot-steps, followed by the sound of a door opening and closing, then a few more muffled footsteps.

'Mr. J,' Brian said, letting out a heavy lung of air, his tone now a little anxious. Mr. J never called him at night. He never called him at home.

Brian Caldron wasn't an LAPD detective. He wasn't a police officer either. In fact, he could barely use a handgun. What he was, was a mega computer geek, a top analyst inside the LAPD's Scientific Investigation Division, with a very high clearance level. A clearance level that gave him direct and unrestricted access to most national and local law-enforcement databases, and with that he was able to provide Mr. J with the most valuable commodity of the modern age – information.

'I'm sorry for calling you at home,' Mr. J said, 'but I need a favor.' As soon as that last word left his lips, Mr. J regretted it. It was never a favor, it was always business. The word 'favor' implied weakness. It implied that Mr. J would now be in Brian's debt. He hoped Brian hadn't picked up on it.

He hadn't.

'Can't it wait until the morning?' Brian asked.

'No.'

Mr. J heard Brian take another deep breath. 'So how can I help?'

'A nine-one-one call was made to the LAPD not that long ago,' Mr. J explained. 'Probable homicide.'

Brian took down the address Mr. J gave him.

'The first thing I need from you is – I need you to find out if the call was a hoax or not.'

For some reason, Mr. J was still holding on to a sliver of hope that all this could've been nothing more than some sort of sick prank.

'OK,' Brian replied. 'And if it's not a hoax?'

'Then I need you to ghost this case twenty-four/seven. Everything, and I mean *everything* that gets logged regarding this investigation, I need to know.' A short pause. 'Is there any way you can get that confirmation from your place, or do you need to be back at headquarters?'

'If confirmation is all you need right now,' Brian said, 'I can do it from here.'

'OK. Let me know when you get it.'

*

Mr. J checked his speed again. He was still keeping to the speed limit.

Ring. Ring. Brian's secret number popped up on the large screen display on Mr. J's dashboard. He thumbed a button on his steering wheel and accepted the call.

'Brian. So what do you have for me?'

'The call was no hoax.'

Mr. J felt an invisible dagger penetrate his heart. His fingers began choking his steering wheel until his knuckles went white.

'Female victim,' Brian continued. 'Forty-two years old. Her name is Cassandra Jenkinson.'

'Any doubt about her identity?' Mr. J asked. His hope was now just fantasy.

'Not according to the team at the scene. Official identification is just a matter of protocol. The victim's driver's license was found inside her handbag.'

The invisible dagger dug deeper into Mr. J's heart. He could feel it lacerating everything inside of him.

'Have they found her cellphone?' Mr. J asked. Once again his voice was as cold and as emotionless as ever.

'Cellphone? That I won't know until a manifesto is logged into the system. Hopefully in the morning.'

'It doesn't matter,' Mr. J thought. He would find that out before Brian could anyway.

'She was married to . . .' Brian tried to move on, but Mr. J cut him short.

'It's OK. For now this was everything I needed.' A short pause. 'Now. As I've told you, I need everything about this investigation ghosted. Same format as always. Same untraceable email as always. Any new discoveries you deem important, call me on this number ASAP. If I need any other information, I'll be in touch.'

The call disconnected.

Mr. J peeked at the speedometer one more time. Seventy miles an hour just wouldn't do. His Cadillac CTS-V went from zero to sixty in 3.7 seconds. It packed a 6.2-liter super-charged V8 engine under the hood, with a top speed of two hundred miles an hour. It was also equipped with a state of the art radar detector that could pick up a speed gun or camera from a mile away. The car was, without a shadow of a doubt, a super sedan. It was time to put all that power into use.

Fifty

By 2:00 a.m., Hunter, Garcia and Dr. Slater were just finishing up at the crime scene. In accordance to protocol, after being photographed and documented from all possible angles in relation to the location and position in which she'd been found, Cassandra Jenkinson's body had finally been taken to the coroner's office. The heavy rain that had started falling as they arrived had continued for over an hour, washing away any potential clues, including footprints that the killer might've left behind as he either approached or left the grounds of the house. Thanks to his quick work, the agent in charge of the driveway had succeeded in preserving the partial tire track he had come across earlier. After the rain had stopped, he had managed to lift an impression of it using a gelatin lifter – a sheet of rubber with a low-adhesive gelatin layer on one side that can lift prints from almost anywhere, including porous, rough, curved and textured surfaces.

'Any luck?' Garcia asked Nicholas Holden, who for the past two hours had been dusting doors, windows, and all relevant indoor surfaces and objects.

'Depends on what you call luck,' he replied with a shrug, as he finished packing up his equipment.

Garcia enquired with a subtle eyebrow raise.

'How many people in this household?' Holden asked almost rhetorically, as he'd seen plenty of pictures throughout the house.

'The victim and her husband,' Garcia replied.

'No one else?' The question was dusted with a little surprise.

'Not according to the info we got.' Garcia paused, thought about it, then rephrased. 'Well, they've got a twenty-year-old son, but he doesn't live here anymore. He goes to college in Boston. Why?'

Holden nodded as if that information explained a lot.

'From a simple pattern comparison, I can tell you that I've retrieved three different sets of fingerprints,' he explained. 'One of them belongs to the victim herself. The other two are undoubtedly male. Of those, one reoccurs prominently all throughout the house – kitchen, bathrooms, bedrooms, living room, hallway ... it's everywhere. The second set doesn't show up as much as the first one, but it still reoccurs frequently enough to suggest that neither of them belong to a stranger to this household.'

Garcia scratched his chin. 'The husband and the son.'

Holden agreed with a head movement. He had just finished zipping up his bag when they all heard a loud commotion coming from outside the front door. Before anyone was able to react, a tall and well-built man with a shaved head pushed his way into the living room. The look on his face was a mixture of fear and bewilderment. Two angry officers followed him inside.

'Sir,' one of the officers said, hastily reaching for the man's arm. 'This is still an open crime scene and you're contaminating it. I'm going to have to ask you to step outside.'

The man jerked his arm away from the officer's grip.

'It's OK,' Hunter said, turning to face them and signaling the officers to let the man go. He didn't have to ask. He recognized the man from the pictures on the mantelpiece. 'We're all done here, right?' He looked at Dr. Slater.

She nodded in response. 'We've collected everything we needed. There's no more risk of contamination.'

The officers looked at each other before nodding back at Hunter and exiting the house.

'Where is she?' Mr. J asked in an unsteady voice, his crazed eyes searching the entire room.

Hunter stepped forward to meet him. 'Mr. Jenkinson, I'm Detective Robert Hunter with the LA—'

'Where's my wife?' Mr. J cut Hunter short. His gaze moved past the detective to first find the lone dining chair by the east wall then the pool of blood underneath it. His wife's blood. For a moment, he stopped breathing.

'Her body had to be transferred to the coroner's office,' Hunter replied in a conservative tone.

Mr. J didn't ask for an explanation because he didn't really need one. If there was something he understood very well, it was police protocol.

Catatonically, he walked past Hunter, Garcia and Dr. Slater in the direction of the chair. Everyone and the world around him disappeared and all of a sudden there she was, sitting directly in front of him, her eyes full of fear and sadness, imploring him to know the simplest of answers. An answer he should've known.

Slowly, his right arm extended in the direction of the chair, as if Cassandra was really still there. As if he could touch her face ... caress her hair ... wipe away her tears.

'I'm so, so sorry.' The words escaped his lips without him even noticing it.

In respect, no one said anything, giving Mr. J his moment alone.

Dr. Slater silently signaled her team to leave.

Mr. J felt his stomach pirouetting inside of him and his legs threatened to buckle under his weight. To steady himself, he closed his eyes and took a deep breath. When they reopened, just a couple of seconds later, Hunter saw something in them that no one else in that room did – tremendous anger, coated by unwavering focus and determination.

'OK,' he said, finally meeting Hunter's gaze. His tone of voice was arctic cold. 'I guess you want to ask me a few questions.'

Fifty-One

Back in his hotel room, with his face still buried in his hands, Mr. J had thought very hard about what to do next. He would've preferred to have left the LAPD completely out of it, and if he had seen any way around the problem, that was exactly what he would've done, but even with all his connections, he knew that there was no way he could pull that off.

His second thought was to maybe pretend that he had never received that damn video-call in the first place. That would've given him some much-needed advantage over the LAPD. He knew that he could've made it back to LA by 2:00 a.m. His car was certainly fast enough and his radar detector system would've kept him from being pulled over. Once home, and without the interference of the police or a forensic team, he could've studied the undisturbed crime scene for as long as he needed. He could've crawled through his living room looking for possible clues before anyone got there. Clues that, if they existed, he knew the LAPD would've never shared with him. But most of all, he could've touched Cassandra's face one last time before she was taken away from their home. He could've kneeled down in front of her and begged her for her forgiveness. Forgiveness he could never and would never give himself. Then and only then, he would've made the nine-one-one call and pretended that he'd just got back home from a business trip to find his wife murdered in their own living room. But that plan would've also collapsed at the first hurdle.

One of the reasons why Mr. J was the best at what he did was because he understood how law enforcement agencies worked. He knew their protocol, their investigative procedures, their tricks ... and the guidelines for such a case were simple – a married woman gets savagely tortured and murdered inside her own home without any apparent motive, and the 'people of interest' list would be headed by none other than the husband. Add to that the fact that the husband was conveniently away at the exact same time his wife was being murdered, and that he had no alibis to corroborate his story, and his life would be completely picked apart by the investigative team. They would easily obtain warrants to approach banks, Internet providers, phone and credit-card companies ... whatever and whoever they wanted. His old emails and text messages would be read. His phone calls would be listened to. His bank account, his business, his trips, his expenditures, his friends, his medical records, all of it would be dissected into tiny little pieces. But even if Mr. J had an alibi, real or forged – and he could easily get an airtight one if he so wanted – he knew that that plan still wouldn't work.

In a murder investigation, one of the first things to be examined by the homicide team was the victim's cellphone account. They would want to know with whom she'd been texting and speaking to recently, especially in the last few hours before her death. Mr. J's cellphone number would've flagged up as the last number Cassandra had ever called, and at around the exact same time she was being murdered. Mr. J had no way of circumventing that. And that had been where he'd gotten lucky.

The killer had used the video-call feature, instead of making a regular voice call. Though the dialed number would get logged in, no cellphone provider in the USA was allowed to store their clients' video-calls. The LAPD, the FBI, the CIA, the NSA, it didn't matter, no one would be able to obtain even a text transcript of the call, because none existed, and Mr. J was well aware of that. Everything Mr. J had told the killer during that call would stay between him and the killer.

With everything considered, Mr. J came to the conclusion that his best option was to tell the truth … or at least to a certain extent. After that, Brian Caldron would monitor the entire police investigation, while Mr. J ran his own.

Fifty-Two

Hunter peeked at the clock on the wall just behind Mr. J – 2:03 a.m.

'Mr. Jenkinson,' he said, his voice smooth and cordial. 'We don't need to do this right now. It's perfectly OK for us to wait until the morning. I understand you've been driving for hours—'

'And you think I'll be more rested in the morning?' Mr. J interrupted Hunter again. 'You think I'll be able to sleep?'

Hunter didn't reply. Mr. J had a point.

'I'm guessing you've either heard a recording of the nine-one-one call I made, or you were told how I came to know about what happened here. You know about the video-call I received.'

Hunter gave him a sympathetic nod.

'So if it's all the same to you,' Mr. J continued, his tone calm and rhythmically perfect. 'I'd rather talk about it while everything is still fresh in my head. Sleep, if I were to get any, would bring dreams ... nightmares ... visions ... images ... whatever. Some of them would be real memories of what happened, but some would no doubt be just my mind going crazy on me. Things that weren't really there. Things that I didn't really see. Things that I should've said, but didn't.' He paused for a second, as if his last few words pained him too much. 'The problem then is, in my head, there's no way I'll be able to discern between what really happened and what didn't. All of it will seem as real to me as the people in this room.' His gaze bounced from Hunter to Garcia to Dr. Slater and finally back to Hunter. 'The longer we wait, Detective, the greater the risk of reality and fantasy getting mixed up in my head.'

Though no one could ever say with total confidence how a person's brain would react after such a traumatic episode, the nightmares and the images that Mr. J had mentioned would come, of that Hunter had no doubt. As a psychologist, he just couldn't fault Mr. J's logic. At the same time, everyone in that room was astounded and intrigued by how composed Mr. J appeared to be.

'I understand,' Hunter said, allowing his eyes to quickly circle the room. 'Would you rather we talk down at the station?'

'Why?' Mr. J asked. 'Is that necessary?'

Everyone's intrigue intensified.

'No. Not at all. I just thought that maybe . . .' Hunter left the suggestion floating in the air.

'The room would pose a distraction?' Mr. J picked it up, his gaze repeating the same movement as Hunter's, except he chose not to look back at the chair and the pool of blood underneath it. 'You're right,' he admitted. His eyes focused on a random spot on the floor in front of him and his composure finally faltered. 'I don't think I could do it in here.'

Again, Hunter gave him a moment.

Mr. J at last looked back up.

'We don't have to go downtown, Mr. Jenkinson,' Hunter proposed. 'We could use a local police station, or even one of the police vans parked outside if you prefer.'

Mr. J considered the suggestion before throwing a new question back at Hunter.

'Has any other room in the house been disturbed?'

Hunter's reply came with a slight lift of the eyebrows. 'You're the only person who'd be able to tell us that with any degree of certainty, Mr. Jenkinson, but as far as we can tell, this seems to have been the only room used.'

Looking thoughtful, Mr. J nodded. His answer came several seconds later. 'We could use my office, if you don't mind.' He indicated with a hand gesture.

Seeing no reason why not, Hunter exchanged a quick look with Garcia.

'Yeah, sure,' Garcia said, padding his pockets over his Tyvek coverall. 'I've got my notepad with me and I can use my phone to record everything. We're set.'

As Mr. J turned to lead the way, his gaze brushed against the photographs resting on the mantelpiece and he froze in place. The bottomless pit inside of him that had threatened to swallow him whole came back with the fury of a tornado. Right there, staring at the photographs in those picture frames, he felt his soul abandon him. The question asked by the demonic voice roared inside his ears like a new thunder.

Your wedding anniversary, when is it?

For a long moment, no one moved.

'Mr. Jenkinson, is everything OK?' Hunter asked.

No reply.

He looked to be pondering something inside his head.

'Mr. Jenkinson?'

'There's something I need to ask. Something I need to know,' he finally said, his gaze struggling to meet anyone else's.

Everyone waited.

'My wife, I know that she was undressed.' A new long, emotional pause. 'I need to know. Was she ...' he stumbled on his next word and decided to start again. 'Did this psycho ...' Still he couldn't bring himself to say it.

'Mr. Jenkinson,' Dr. Slater said, taking a step forward and pulling down the hood of her white forensic coverall. Her blonde hair had been bunched up into a disheveled bun at the back of her head, but it didn't distract from how attractive she was. On the contrary, the messy look added a certain charm to it.

Mr. J's attention moved to her.

'I'm Dr. Susan Slater.' She kept her voice quiet and collected. 'I'm the lead forensic agent assigned to this crime scene. I'm the one who was in charge of thoroughly examining your wife's body before authorizing it to be transported to the coroner's office. All I can tell you is that her body showed absolutely no external signs of having been sexually assaulted.'

Mr. J breathed in that information. 'No offense, Doctor, but that's not exactly one hundred percent guaranteed, is it?' He pinned Dr. Slater down with a gaze that could cut diamonds. 'I'll need to wait for the autopsy report to be certain, won't I? Because technically speaking, this psycho could've still—'

'This killer is not a sexual predator, Mr. Jenkinson,' Hunter intervened, his voice firm and confident. 'He's not after sexual gratification.'

'And how can you be so certain, Detective?' Mr. J came back.

'Because I've encountered hundreds of them before,' Hunter said resolutely. 'Their incessant quest for sexual pleasure is always the ultimate driving force behind what they do. The sexual act is never subtle. Never hidden. Always violent. It's one of the first things that's noticeable as we enter a crime scene.' Once again, Hunter allowed his gaze to move about the room. 'We have nothing like that here, Mr. Jenkinson. Given the fact that this killer was alone with your wife for who knows how long, if sexual gratification was what he was after, there was nothing to stop him from gaining it.'

'That's precisely my point, Detective,' Mr. J countered. 'We won't know that for certain until we get the autopsy results.'

Hunter didn't want to reveal that now, with Cassandra Jenkinson, a non-sexual aggressor pattern had been established, because the 'video-call' killer had already claimed his first victim less than sixty hours ago. A victim he had also shown no sexual interest in whatsoever.

'Mr. Jenkinson.' Dr. Slater was the one who interposed this time. 'In over twelve years as a forensic agent, I know of no sexual assault case where the victim has shown no external physical signs of it. Not one. There would've been something – dermal abrasions, traumas, bruises, scratches … something. There was nothing. Not even a tiny scuff. I promise you, your wife was not touched in that way.'

Mr. J looked away as if he needed time on his own to go over every single word Hunter and Dr. Slater had said. His eyebrows lifted ever so slightly and that caused the light wrinkles on his forehead to deepen, forming a series of ridges that carried on halfway up his shaved head.

From the quick report Garcia had given him outside, Hunter knew that John Jenkinson was forty-eight years old, but at that particular moment, he looked at least twenty-five years older. His eyes looked tired, with dark circles and heavy bags under them. His skin, dull and yellowish, gave everyone the impression that he'd spent half of his life sitting inside a locked room under strong fluorescent lighting. And the worst of all was that from now on every year would count for two, maybe more. Hunter had seen it happen before count-less times to spouses, parents, siblings, partners, children, whoever. People who had lost someone dear to them in an overly violent way tended to lose their path in life easier than most, and the years were never kind to those. People who had unfortunately witnessed that violent death for whatever reason usually suffered a great deal more, but Hunter could barely even begin to imagine the sort of physical and psych-ological devastation that people in Mr. Jenkinson's shoes would have to endure for the rest of their lives. People like Tanya Kaitlin. People who were *forced* to watch a loved one being brutally murdered. The images they saw, Hunter was certain of it, would haunt their every living second until their last day.

Mr. J finally looked back at Hunter and Dr. Slater. Their words from just seconds back at last seemed to have their desired effect. Before guiding Hunter and Garcia into his office, his eyes glassed over and he was only able to utter two simple words, but they came out full of meaning.

'Thank you.'

Fifty-Three

Mr. J's house office was about twice the size of Hunter and Garcia's back at the PAB and a lot less cluttered. Its center-piece was undoubtedly the antique mahogany partners desk, which sat just a few feet in front of a boxed-out window. The curtains, heavy and dark, had been drawn shut. A brownish-red, winged Chesterfield armchair was positioned in front and a little to the left of the desk, while two hand-knotted Persian rugs covered most of the floor. The east wall was taken by a very large bookcase, with every shelf packed to its limit with a mixture of neatly arranged hardcovers and paperbacks.

'Let me get you another chair,' Mr. J said as they entered the room.

'That's not really necessary, Mr. Jenkinson,' Hunter replied. 'I can stand, it's not a problem.'

'Please, I insist. It will take me two seconds.'

Once Mr. J left the room, Hunter pulled down the hood of his forensic coverall, walked over to the bookcase and browsed some of the volumes. The majority of them were business and finance books, with a few scattered ones on law, accounting and architecture.

Garcia checked the opposite wall, which was adorned by framed photographs and achievement awards.

'Here we go.' Mr. J re-entered the room, carrying a high-back chair, which he placed by the Chesterfield, before finally taking a seat behind his desk.

'Thank you,' Hunter said, taking the chair. Garcia took the Chesterfield.

'We'll try to take as little of your time as possible, Mr. Jenkinson,' Garcia said, reaching for his smartphone. 'Do you mind if we record this interview?'

Mr. J shook his head. It was time to put his A-game forward.

Once Garcia hit 'record', Hunter began.

'Mr. Jenkinson, I know that what you've been put through will be hard to revisit, and I apologize for having to ask you to do so, but could you tell us as much as you can remember about the video-call you received. The more detailed you can be, the more it will help us.'

Mr. J looked down at his sun-beaten and wrinkled hands, which were tightly clasped and resting on the desk in front of him. After several silent seconds, he finally lifted his eyes to meet Hunter and Garcia's gaze. For the next twenty minutes, he recounted only what he wanted to recount of the video-call, but he did it all in tremendous detail. Hunter and Garcia interrupted him sporadically to clarify certain points, but for most of it they simply allowed him to tell his story in his own time. As Mr. J reached the part where the killer asked him for his wedding date, he paused and looked down at his hands again. They were shaking. Embarrassed, he moved them to his lap and went completely quiet.

Hunter and Garcia waited.

In a faltering voice, Mr. J told them that he tried, but he couldn't remember. He just couldn't remember. Then, without realizing it, he whispered the words, 'I'm so sorry'.

Neither Hunter nor Garcia said anything. They both knew that those words weren't meant for them. They were meant for Cassandra. Guilt had already settled in and spread itself on to every corner of Mr. J's body. Whatever psychological damage that video-call would cause him, the guilt that came from not knowing the answer to that *damn* question would make it a lot worse.

And that was when Mr. J finally realized what he had done – seventh of March was his son's birthday. That was why the date kept on flashing so intensely inside his head when he was asked for his wedding date.

PING.

And just like that, as if a dark veil had suddenly been lifted from his memory, his wedding date appeared before his eyes, clear as daylight.

April tenth. He and Cassandra had gotten married on April tenth.

Mr. J's eyes closed and he threw his head back as if he'd been stabbed in the stomach by a fire dagger.

Why? He silently cursed himself, his memory, his brain, his whole existence. *Why couldn't I remember that earlier?*

He finished his account without ever meeting the detectives' gaze again. He never told them about the demon's hysterical laugh.

'Could I ask you how long you were in Fresno for?' Hunter began once Mr. J was done.

'I left here on Thursday morning.'

'And before that, when was the last time you were away?'

Mr. J paused before deliberately but very delicately allowing his eyes to move up and to the right. He knew that both detectives would be monitoring everything about him, especially his facial expressions and eye movements. Textbook behavior psychology preached that if the eyes went up and to the left, the subject was trying to access his/her visual constructive cortex. In other words, trying to create a mental image that wasn't there to start with. If the eyes moved up and to the right, the subject was searching his/her memory for visually remembered images – memories that did exist.

'About three and a half weeks ago,' he replied truthfully, his voice tired and defeated. 'I had to fly to Chicago for a couple of days.'

'Business again?'

'That's right.'

Hunter wrote the information down in his notebook. 'Does anyone else, other than you and your wife, have a key to this house?'

Mr. J's reply came with a very slight lift of the shoulders. 'My son.'

'No one else? A cleaner perhaps?'

'No. Cassandra did all the cleaning herself, once a week,' Mr. J explained. 'She said it relaxed her. We use a pool cleaning company for the pool in the backyard, but they don't have a copy of the key.'

'Have you, your wife, or your son lost those keys recently?' Hunter insisted. 'Do you know?'

'Not that I'm aware of. I've never lost my keys. I don't think Cassandra ever did either. As for Patrick, if he has, he's never told me about it, but I can ask him when I talk to him.'

Hunter nodded. 'We'd appreciate it if you did.'

Mr. J didn't say anything because he didn't want the detectives in his office to become suspicious of how much he knew about police interrogations and interviews, but the line of questioning they were pursuing could mean only one thing – no signs of forced entry had been found all throughout the house. They had no idea of how his wife's killer had got in.

'You said that a hammer and chisel were used,' Hunter asked, finally moving the subject along. 'Are you sure it was a chisel, not a nail?'

'It was a masonry chisel with a pointy end,' Mr. J replied confidently. 'Not a nail. I'm sure of that. But the hammer was a regular claw hammer.'

'Did it belong to this house?' Hunter asked. 'Is that something he would've found inside a drawer, maybe?'

Once again, Mr. J shook his head. 'No, neither the hammer nor the chisel belong to this house. He must've brought them with him.' He regarded both detectives intensively. 'From your line of questioning, I take it that none have been found.'

'No,' Hunter admitted. 'The house and its grounds have been searched, but we've found nothing. In the morning we're widening the search to include neighboring streets.'

The look Mr. J gave Hunter and Garcia was totally lacking in confidence.

'How about Cassandra's phone?' he asked. 'This psycho used her phone to call me. Have you found it?'

'Yes,' Garcia this time. 'We found it inside the microwave in the kitchen.' He shook his head. 'It's worthless. Even Forensics won't be able to get anything out of it.'

Mr. J played dumb for a moment. 'Can't you contact

her cellphone company? Ask them for a digital copy of the call?'

'They won't have any,' Hunter replied.

'How come?'

Hunter gave Mr. J the explanation he already knew.

'We did find a black Asus laptop on the kitchen counter,' Garcia said. 'Did that belong to your wife?'

Mr. J nodded. 'It was Cassandra's, yes.'

'You said that the perpetrator was wearing a mask?' Garcia asked, taking the subject back to the killer's video call.

Mr. J nodded. 'The fucking coward. Man enough to break into my house and murder a defenseless woman. Man enough to place a goddamn video-call to me just so he could play God. But not man enough to show his face.'

A vein on Mr. J's forehead threatened to explode.

'Could you describe this mask for us?'

Mr. J's description of the killer's mask was identical to the one Tanya Kaitlin had given them three days ago.

Garcia looked at his partner but said nothing. 'And you also mentioned that the caller told you that calling the police would be a waste of time, is that right?'

'Yes. He said that the police would never make it in time.'

Another quick look exchange. They would have to check the nine-one-one records for bogus calls once again, but Hunter and Garcia were both sure that the killer had used the same tactics as before.

Hunter decided to bring the questioning a little closer to their first victim.

'Do you know if your wife knew someone by the name of Karen Ward?' he asked.

Mr. J's eyes narrowed for a beat, while he repeated the name to himself a couple of times.

Hunter observed him attentively.

'The name doesn't really ring any bells,' he replied. 'But Cassandra knew a lot of people who I never met. People from her gym. People from the charity shops she volunteered at. People from the support groups she attended. Her circle of friends was much bigger than mine.' He fixed Hunter down with a new serious stare. 'Why? Who is she?'

'We don't know yet,' Hunter lied. 'Her name was on a card we found outside on the street.'

'Outside on the street like what?' Mr. J asked, buying it. 'On my front yard? On the street in front of the house? Where?'

Hunter had to think fast. 'That's the reason I asked. It was found on the street a little further up the road. It's probably nothing, but we'll check with every house on the street anyway.'

Mr. J wasn't able to tell if that was a lie or not, but he immediately committed the name to memory. He would have to ask Brian Caldron to check on who she was.

Hunter quickly moved the subject away from Karen Ward. 'You mentioned your wife and support groups?'

'Cassandra lost her mother to an undiagnosed heart condition several years ago,' Mr. J explained. 'Support groups helped her a lot during that time, but she's the kind of person who likes helping others too.' He paused, realizing his mistake. His pain was almost palpable. '*Was* the kind of person who *liked* helping others,' he corrected himself. 'So every now and again she would attend support-group sessions for people who had lost loved ones to illnesses. Try to help them in some way. That's the kind of person she was.'

'Do you have any other details on these support groups?' Hunter asked. 'Names? Locations where they met? Anything?'

'No. Not really. But I can call a few of her friends and try to find out.'

'That would be very much appreciated,' Hunter said, though he would get a team on to it straight away as well.

'Did your wife use any type of social media network sites?' Garcia asked.

'Doesn't everyone nowadays?'

'Yes, that's very true,' Garcia accepted it. 'Did she ever mention anything to you about anyone trolling her, or sending her inappropriate messages, or anything?'

Mr. J brought a hand to his face and used his thumb and index finger to rub his exhausted eyes.

'No,' he said. 'Never. But she mainly used it just to keep in touch with some old friends from Santa Ana. Nothing like what most kids do nowadays, like my son, spending most of his time online.'

'How about you, Mr. Jenkinson,' Garcia asked. 'Do you have a social media page?'

'I do, yes. My company also has a business page.'

Hunter knew that his next question would sound a little strange. 'The question about your wedding date, Mr. Jenkinson . . .'

Mr. J locked eyes with Hunter and in them Hunter saw devastating pain.

'Can you remember if you've been asked that same question recently, maybe in the past year? Maybe while out with friends, at a dinner party, by anyone you have worked with, while having a few drinks at a bar . . . anywhere?'

Mr. J *did* find the detective's question somewhat strange.

'No, I don't recall ever being asked anything about my wedding date in ...' He shook his head. 'I don't even know how long.'

'Do you remember who it was? The person who asked you about it?'

Mr. J's look became distant for a moment, before switching to sadness. 'Cassandra. That's how she used to remind me of it because I used to forget it every year. She'd wait until late at night, just before we went to bed, and then she'd say something subtle like, "What's the date today, do you know?" And that was when I knew that I had screwed up big time and it was way too late to dig up an excuse. It didn't use to be like that, you know?' he said, as if he saw the need to defend himself before both detectives. The look in his eyes became even sadder, yearning for a time long gone. 'I used to remember it every year, buy her gifts, flowers, take her to dinner ... I don't really know what happened. I don't really know how or why I let all that go, but even she gave up on reminding me a few years back. I guess she thought that there was no point in doing it anymore.'

Hunter remained silent, waiting for Mr. J to push the memory all the way to the back of his mind.

'Can you think of anyone who for whatever reason would want to harm your wife?' he asked at last.

Mr. J sat back in his chair and rested his elbows on the chair's arms. His stare moved to the picture frame on his desk.

'Cassandra was the most gentle of souls,' he replied, his voice almost strangled by the knot in his throat. 'And I'm not just saying that because she was my wife. Ask anyone who knew her. She was a caring and loving person. Polite to everyone. Humble. Understanding. Generous. Helpful. I don't think that she has ever upset anyone in her life.'

'Can you think of anyone who could possibly want to harm your wife to ... maybe get back at you?'

Mr. J's acting was flawless, adding a perfect layer of shock to his words and expressions.

'Get back at me? For what? I'm a simple business consultant, Detective? I have no debts. I don't gamble. I have no grudges against anyone, and as far as I'm aware of, no one has any grudges against me. We were a simple family, living a simple life.'

'So you've never received any sort of threats of any nature?' Hunter asked.

'Threats?' Another award-winning surprised facial expression.

'Yes. Either via emails, phone calls, text messages, letters, whatever.'

'No. Never.'

'How about your wife? Did she ever mention anything about being threatened? Anything about ... letters or phone calls she'd received? Did she ever mention anything about a possible stalker?'

Once again, Hunter's question did truly surprise Mr. J, and this time there was no faking of his reaction.

'A stalker?' His mouth remained half open, while his eyes jumped from one detective to the other.

'Did she ever tell you about any letters she'd received from someone who could possibly be pestering her?'

'Letters from a stalker? No. Never. What are you talking about, Detective?'

Hunter looked at Garcia, who quietly stood up and made his way towards the door.

Mr. J's sincerely confused gaze followed his every step until he exited the room, before shooting back to Hunter.

'OK, what is going on, Detective?'

'Are you sure you can't recall your wife mentioning anything about being harassed by someone?' Hunter insisted. 'About receiving any sort of strange notes?'

'Harassed? Strange notes? No. Never.' Mr. J was adamant. 'I have no idea of what you're talking about, Detective.'

'Do you think she would've?'

'Would've what?'

'Mentioned it to you.'

Back came the head-creasing lift of the eyebrows. 'That she thought that someone was stalking her? That she had received some sort of threatening note, or message, or whatever?'

'Yes. Do you think that she would've mentioned it to you?'

'Yes, she would definitely have mentioned it to me,' Mr. J replied with the utmost confidence. 'Why wouldn't she?'

At that exact moment, Garcia re-entered the room.

Fifty-Four

Still with a sincerely puzzled look on his face, Mr. J turned to look at Garcia, who had just re-entered the room. The first thing that he noticed was that the detective was carrying a medium-sized, see-through plastic evidence bag in his right hand.

'Your wife's handbag was found in your living room, Mr. Jenkinson, just by the sofa,' Hunter explained. 'Inside it, we found this note.'

Garcia placed the evidence bag on Mr. J's desk.

His confusion lasted an extra couple of seconds before he managed to snap out of it and drag his attention to the note.

Have you ever felt like you're being watched, Cassandra?

Mr. J blinked a couple of times, as if his eyes were having trouble focusing. Then he read the note again. And again. And again.

'I don't understand,' he finally said, his tone almost robotic.

'There was also an envelope with her name across the front of it,' Garcia added. 'No address. No stamp. Which means that it was hand-delivered. Slid under the door, placed in the mailbox outside, left on her car, maybe at the place where she works … What we do know is that this note wasn't posted to her.'

'Was the name on the envelope a cut-out as well?' Mr. J asked.

'Letter by letter,' Garcia confirmed.

'She never mentioned this note to you?' Hunter this time.

Mr. J looked at him with a mixture of frustration and embarrassment. Just seconds ago, he had told Hunter with unflinching conviction that his wife would've certainly shared something like this with him.

'No,' he finally replied. His eyes, now heavy with anger, returned to the note. 'Maybe she got this while I was away,' he suggested. 'This morning, yesterday morning or the day before.'

'Maybe,' Garcia accepted it. 'But wouldn't she have called you?'

For an instant it looked like Mr. J hadn't heard the question.

'Mr. Jenkinson?'

'No, she wouldn't,' he replied thoughtfully. 'That was just the way Cassandra was. My business trips are usually very rushed, so when I'm away, she'd only call me if she considered whatever it is that she needs to talk to me about to be something very important.'

'And you think she wouldn't consider this to be?'

'Oh, c'mon, Detective.' Mr. J looked back at Garcia. 'Don't be naive. You find a note that looks like it came out of an old *Kojak* episode.' He nodded at it. 'Written by putting together a few cut-out letters and words from a magazine, with a cliché scary line like this one, and what do you do, freak the fuck out? Believe that your life is at risk?'

Garcia didn't reply.

'Well, I can tell you that Cassandra wouldn't. It would take a hell of a lot more than something like this to scare someone like her.' He paused and for a quick second looked like he was searching his memory. 'In fact, I don't think I've ever seen her scared. She was strong like that. She probably laughed at this when she got it. Dismissed it as a hoax or something, which is what I think most people would've done. She would've never called me on a business trip to tell me about a note that looks like it was put together by a four-year-old.'

'I'd have to agree,' Hunter cut in. 'Most people would've discarded this note as a hoax, a very bad practical joke, and that's why I would like to ask your permission to properly search the house, more specifically, your wife's belongings.'

Mr. J knew that the use of the word 'properly' meant that they had already searched the house and Cassandra's belongings. They just haven't done it meticulously enough.

'What for?' he asked.

'For other notes similar to this one. Notes she might've received previously.'

'What?' Mr. J studied both detectives' faces, but found nothing. 'You think she received other notes like this one?'

'I do,' Hunter admitted it.

Mr. J chuckled anxiously. 'And what makes you think that?'

'Because this note,' Hunter said, pointing at it, his tone firm and confident, 'unlike what you might think, Mr. Jenkinson, certainly scared your wife.'

Another intrigued frown. 'And you know that how?'

Hunter scratched his chin. 'Because she never threw it

away, Mr. Jenkinson. We didn't find it in a trashcan, tucked away in a drawer, or under a sofa. We found it inside her handbag, together with her car keys and her purse. If she had thought that this note was nothing more than a silly prank, why keep it? And better yet, why keep it in her handbag?'

Mr. J hadn't thought of that. He had actually forgotten that Hunter had told him that the note had been found inside Cassandra's handbag. And the detective had a point. Mr. J knew Cassandra better than anyone did. She would never have paid any attention to something like this, unless she had received enough of them to either test her patience or scare her.

It was while pondering that idea that the reason why she had kept the note in her handbag came to him – she wanted to show it to him, get his opinion on it, ask him if she should be worried about something like that.

Of course, he thought. *It must've been. She was waiting for me to get back from my 'business trip' so she could show it to me. Talk it over.*

That thought drove a new spike of guilt right through Mr. J's heart. His eyes closed instinctively and he pressed his lips tightly together, as if an unforeseen wave of pain had taken over him.

'Mr. Jenkinson?' Hunter said, legitimately concerned. 'Are you all right?'

He reopened his eyes and for a second lost grip of his cool. The anger in his voice painted the room red.

'My wife was tortured and murdered inside my own house while I was away, arguably by some psychopath who had been tormenting and stalking her with stupid notes like this one.' He stabbed his finger at the evidence bag. 'Which I knew nothing about. How "all right" would you like me to be, Detective?'

'I'm sorry, Mr. Jenkinson,' Hunter replied, his eyes low and apologetic. 'I didn't mean it that way.'

'Please,' Mr. J said, lifting a hand. His cool was back, and so was his perfect acting. 'If you have no more questions, could I be left alone now?'

Hunter exchanged another troubled look with Garcia.

'Unfortunately, we can't allow you to stay in the house, Mr. Jenkinson. Not tonight.'

Mr. J glared at Hunter. He knew fully well that he would never be allowed to stay, but he needed to play his 'oblivious citizen' part.

'What do you mean – you won't allow me to stay? This is my house.'

'We understand that, Mr. Jenkinson.' Once again, Hunter's voice was calm and composed. 'And the only thing I can do at the moment is apologize, but unfortunately your house is now also a crime scene, and for reasons I'm sure you can imagine, we need to keep it isolated until it's given the "all clear" by us and the forensic team. We'll be back here in the morning to go over everything again with fresh eyes, looking for anything we might've missed tonight.'

Retaining the angry look on his face, Mr. J remained silent, pretending to consider Hunter's words.

'I can promise you that we'll work as fast as we possibly can, Mr. Jenkinson. With a little luck, we'll be able to hand the house over to the crime and trauma scene decontamination team by tomorrow night. After that, the house is yours to do with as you please again.'

Still silence.

'I'm very sorry about that,' Hunter restated.

'Could I at least grab some fresh clothes?' Mr. J asked, being sure to keep some of the anger in his tone of voice.

'Of course. Take as long as you need. We'll wait outside.'

Fifty-Five

This feels all wrong, Mr. J thought as Hunter and Garcia exited his office.

Despite feeling exhausted and emotionally drained, his brain was still able to ponder basic facts, and four of the most basic ones, when it came to this investigation, simply weren't adding up.

One: He had been conveniently away at the time of his wife's murder. Two: No signs of forced entry had been found, which meant that the investigation would have to consider the possibility that the perpetrator had a key to the house to start with. Three: The video-call he claimed he had received could never be properly verified. Even the detectives had confirmed that. And four: The note that was found inside Cassandra's handbag could've easily been planted there to create the illusion that she was being stalked and to try to drag the investigation down a different path.

Considering those four facts alone, Mr. J knew that he was supposed to have been grilled like a rack of ribs at a fat men's barbecue, but that just didn't happen.

As he left his hotel late last night, he had begun thinking about what sort of questions would be coming his way. Questions about alibis to corroborate any of his stories. Questions about what sort of business or meetings he was supposed to have had back in Fresno. Names, phone numbers, schedules, addresses ... everything. As the interview started, with questions about his last two trips and who had keys to the property, he thought that he was well en route to the expected grilling but, to his surprise, the line of questioning quickly moved on to something he could never have predicted. Neither detective seemed too interested in digging any deeper into his business trip.

To Mr. J, that was problem number one. Problem number two was that Cassandra had been murdered inside their own home without an apparent motive. No burglary. No obvious sexual assault. When Mr. J added problem number one to problem number two, and he was sure that the detectives he met had already done so, the main result was a big and shiny 'crime of passion', blinking right at the top of the list, but the interview hadn't gone down that route either. They never asked him if he and Cassandra had been arguing a lot recently, or if he had any indications that she could've been involved in an extra-marital affair. They never asked him if he was involved in one himself, or even if any of them had talked about, or considered, a divorce. In fact, there had been no questions whatsoever concerning the state of their marriage after twenty-one years. What the detectives seemed really interested in was the video-call, and in as much detail as possible.

Why? he asked himself.

If they believed that the video-call had been fabricated,

maybe it was because they were trying to catch him on a lie, make him contradict himself, but still ...

Mr. J's breath hitched within his throat, because that was when he realized the mistake he had made.

Fifty-Six

By 8:30 a.m., Garcia was back at the Jenkinsons' house together with two uniformed officers. He was studying the photographs on the mantelpiece when Hunter finally got to the house, almost two hours after him.

'How are you guys doing?' asked Hunter. 'Anything?'

'*Nada*,' Garcia replied. 'We've been through everything in the bedroom, everything inside Ms. Jenkinson's wardrobe, every pocket, every pair of shoes, every box we could find, every drawer.' He shook his head Hunter's way. 'No other note, or anything else to indicate that she was being stalked.'

The honest truth was, Garcia was just going through the motions. After what Mr. J had told them in the early hours of the morning, neither detective was really expecting to find another stalker's note inside the house. They both had figured out the same thing that Mr. J had – the reason why Cassandra Jenkinson had kept the note they'd found inside her handbag was because she was waiting for her husband to come home so she could show it to him. That had been the note that had either scared her or tested her patience. The note that had made her decide that she'd had enough. Even if she had received other notes previously to the one they'd found, and neither Hunter or Garcia doubted she had, according to what Mr. J had told them about the kind of woman his wife was, she probably did discard them as a silly prank and threw them away.

Garcia reached for another picture from the mantelpiece. In the photograph, Mr. J was standing behind his wife with his arms wrapped around her waist. He seemed to be whispering something into her ear.

'Do you think that this was how the killer got the idea for his final question?' Garcia asked, putting the picture down and facing Hunter.

'I'm not sure,' Hunter replied. 'But if these pictures were what made him think of the wedding question in the first place, then the killer has been in this house before. And I mean, before last night.'

Garcia nodded. 'That was exactly what I was thinking when you got here. Just like he did with Tanya Kaitlin, the killer knew beforehand that Mr. Jenkinson wouldn't be able to answer the "big" question. This guy does nothing by chance.' He looked at the picture frames again. 'It would be naive of us to think that this prompted the wedding date question on the spot, just like that.' He snapped his fingers.

'Too great a risk for him to take,' Hunter agreed. 'If you put it all into perspective, this was an even easier question than the one he asked Tanya Kaitlin.'

In his head, Garcia ran through both questions using himself as a subject. If he were asked for his wedding date, he wouldn't hesitate half a second. If he were asked for Anna's cellphone number . . .

Right then, a guilty feeling punched him square in the face. In all the years they'd been married, he had never memorized his wife's number. Then guilt turned into shame because he realized that he had never even tried to. He had always relied on his cellphone memory not only for her number, but also for every number in his contact list, including Hunter's. The only number he knew by heart was his own. Silently and ashamed, Garcia made himself a promise right there and then.

'But I think that that is exactly what he wanted us to believe,' Hunter said, dragging his partner back from his thoughts.

'Believe that these pictures were what made him come up with the wedding date question?' Garcia asked.

Hunter nodded. 'Think about it, Carlos, the killer doesn't know that we've figured out that the questions he asks aren't simple or random at all, though they are designed to look that way, right?'

'Yes.'

'OK, so just for a moment let's pretend that we know nothing about this killer. We get the call. We work the crime scene as we always do. We notice the wedding pictures on the mantelpiece, but they don't jump out at us because there's no real reason for it. Then we interview Mr. Jenkinson and he tells us about the video-call and the questions he was asked. We might've made a connection then, but even if not, there's always the second look at the crime scene. Not to mention all the scene photographs that we'll be looking at, over and over again.'

Garcia jumped into Hunter's thread of thought. 'So unless we were either blind or stupid, we would've seriously considered the possibility that his second question had been a spur of the moment thing, triggered by these wedding photos.'

Hunter agreed again.

'And that,' Garcia continued, 'at least for a while, would've caused us to lose track of what to really look for, which is the fact that the killer already knew that Mr. Jenkinson would get the question wrong. The fact that, just like you've said, he has probably been in this house before.'

'Exactly. I'm thinking, maybe that's how he first picks his victims.'

'Very possible,' Garcia accepted it. Garcia was about to say something else when Hunter's phone rang.

'Detective Hunter, Homicide Special.'

It was Dr. Carolyn Hove, the Chief Medical Examiner for the Los Angeles County Department of Coroner. She had just finished the autopsy on Cassandra Jenkinson's body.

Fifty-Seven

After Mr. J left Hunter and Garcia, he checked himself into a cheap motel in Porter Ranch, not that far from his house in Granada Hills, but that had been just for show in case the LAPD came checking. He didn't even see the inside of the room. As soon as he got the keys from the stick-thin night attendant who smelled of grease and fried cheese, he jumped back into his car and drove straight to the apartment he kept down in Torrance, South Los Angeles. The apartment, which absolutely no one knew about, had been rented under a completely bogus name several years ago and it was paid for in cash at the beginning of every year – always a full year in advance.

Mr. J needed to make a few phone calls, but he knew that until the sun had once again recolored the LA sky, there was very little that he or anyone else would be able to do. He felt exhausted and his brain kept on telling him that his best option was to try to recharge and get some much-needed rest, even if only for an hour or two, but sleep never came. The turmoil inside his mind simply wouldn't allow it. Every time he closed his eyes, he was bombarded by images of Cassandra covered in blood.

In the living room, Mr. J poured himself a healthy measure

of bourbon – enough to take the edge off and slap his nerves back a few notches, but not enough to cloud his thoughts. Drink in hand, he switched off the lights and dumped himself into the compact sofa that faced the large window on the east wall. The view from it was nothing spectacular, but when the sun was up, it did manage to catch a sliver of Redondo Beach and the Pacific Ocean beyond it, and that alone had a tremendous calming effect.

Staring at the city lights, Mr. J had a sip of his drink and let the intense alcohol, which carried notes of sweet oak and caramel, linger in his taste buds until it started burning his tongue and the inside of his cheeks. Only then did he allow the golden liquid to finally flood his throat. Usually his body would immediately begin warming up from inside, but Mr. J doubted that could ever happen again. He felt as if his soul had frozen and all that was left inside of him was hatred, shadowed by an insatiable desire for revenge.

He got himself comfortable on the sofa and his mind took him right back to the moment he had re-entered his home and met the two detectives who were in charge of the investigation.

Mr. J had crossed paths with more cops and detectives in his lifetime than he had friends. To him, they were all potatoes from the same sack, but there was something about one of the two detectives that had intrigued him. Unlike every other detective he had ever met, who seemed to be always on edge and fighting a losing battle against his/her own demons, this one seemed to be right at the other end of the spectrum. There was something about the calm in his eyes, about his composure, about the degree of confidence with which he spoke, that made him stand out. Right then, Mr. J was unsure if that was a good sign or not.

He had another sip of his bourbon, pulled out his wallet and reached for the card the detective had given him:

Robert Hunter, LAPD Homicide Special Section.

Mr. J would have to ask Brian Caldron to send him a complete dossier on Detective Hunter.

By the time Mr. J had finished his second drink, cracks of blue light had begun sliding through the dark sky. He put his glass down and checked his watch. It was time to make his first call.

Mr. J made his way into the apartment's only bedroom, opened the wardrobe door and kneeled down by the heavy-duty, fingerprint biometric safe that sat where his shoes should've been. Thumb scanned and six-digit security code entered, the safe opened with a muffled thud. He grabbed one of the several brand new prepaid cellphones he kept locked in there, unwrapped it and dialed a number he knew by heart. The phone number belonged to someone else who worked for the same cartel as Mr. J. Someone at the very top of it and who he knew only as Razor.

The phone rang twice before it was answered by someone with a smooth crooner's voice.

'Razor, it's Mr. J.'

'Mr. J?' Razor replied, his tone intrigued and inquisitive. He certainly wasn't expecting to get a call from Mr. J, let alone at that time in the morning. 'Is everything all right? Have you run into any problems in Fresno?'

'No. Fresno went as smoothly as it could've gone. No glitches.'

'I'm glad to hear.'

'I do have another problem, though.'

'I'm listening.'

'I have to step back for a while.' Mr. J's tone was decisive but calm. 'I can't take any more contracts for the foreseeable future.'

There was a short, thoughtful pause.

'How long is "a while"?'

Mr. J had been expecting that question. 'At the moment – indefinitely.'

A much longer pause this time.

'What's this really about, Mr. J?' Razor's voice remained unaltered. 'Are you calling me to tell me you're retiring? You know better than anyone that, in this business, retirement comes in a very ugly and *final* manner.'

Mr. J stayed silent.

'Is this about Fresno? Did something happen that you're not telling me?'

'No, Razor, this is not about Fresno.'

'So talk to me straight, Mr. J, because right about now your request is sounding a lot like a getaway, like you're changing sides, and you know we don't take kindly to those.'

Mr. J had thought long and hard about this. There were very few people on this earth who he trusted completely. In the whole of California, Razor was the only one. He told him enough for Razor to appreciate his decision.

'Wait a second,' Razor said when Mr. J was done, this time sounding tremendously surprised. 'Are you ... punking me, Mr. J? At this hour of the morning?'

Mr. J could picture Razor shaking his shaved and shiny head like he always did when he found out that he had been tricked. The reason for Razor's huge surprise was because Mr. J never joked.

'I'd give anything for this to be a joke, Razor.' Those words were delivered calmly, but full of sadness.

The long pause returned to the call.

'So you mean to tell me that someone really did break into your house and not only murdered your wife, but he also made you watch it via a video-call?'

'Yes.'

Mr. J could practically hear Razor's thinking gears begin to spin faster.

'Well, that's just plain fucked up. No other way to put it. And you're telling me that this isn't payback for a job. This ... masked freak didn't somehow manage to track you down?'

'It's not payback,' Mr. J confirmed decisively. 'Whoever this guy is, on the phone, he had no idea of who I was. No idea of who I work for.'

'How can you be so sure of that?'

Right then, Mr. J's memory took him back to the thought he'd had just hours ago, when the interview with the LAPD detectives was finally over.

Yes, he now knew exactly what his mistake had been, or better yet, he knew exactly what the detectives' mistake had been. He now knew why that interview had sounded so wrong. Why he had not once got the impression that he was a suspect in his wife's murder, when he knew he should've been.

What had betrayed the two LAPD detectives hadn't been one of their questions or anything they'd said, on the contrary, it had been something left unsaid. A question left unasked.

Once Mr. J was done describing the killer's mask, one of

the detectives should've asked him if he minded talking to a police sketch artist so they could have a composite drawing of it. That was the only logical progression to the interview, but the request never came.

Why?

Had they not believed him?

They had no reason not to.

It was then that Mr. J had remembered the look Detective Garcia had given Detective Hunter. It had been a subtle shifting of the eye that had lasted a mere second. He had seen it, but his tired and fragmented brain had failed to interpret it properly. That had been *his* mistake.

The look shared between both detectives had been a confirmation look, not a doubtful one, as if his description of the mask had matched what the detectives were already expecting, and that could mean only one thing – that they already knew about the mask – and if they already knew about the mask, then they already knew about the killer, and the only way that that was possible was if he had killed before.

'Trust me, Razor, I'm sure. This wasn't about me or any job I've done.'

The confidence in Mr. J's words made Razor abstain from asking any more questions. For a moment, he put himself in Mr. J's shoes. He also had a wife and two daughters who he loved very much. Even the quick pretend scenario in his head made him shake with anger.

'I'm ... sincerely sorry for your loss, my friend.'

Mr. J stayed quiet.

Razor knew then that this wasn't a getaway. If the roles were inverted, he would be doing the exact same thing.

'Do you know how to find him?'

'Not yet, but I will.'

'Of that I have no doubt, my friend. Do what you need to do ... and Mr. J?'

'Yes.'

'You know you can count on me, right? If you need anything, and I mean *anything*, all you need to do is call. I have contacts all over this fucking country. This motherfucker isn't getting away with this.'

'Thank you.'

Mr. J disconnected from the call and smashed the pre-paid phone.

Fifty-Eight

The main facility of the Los Angeles County Department of Coroner was located on North Mission Road, number 1104. The building was an outstanding piece of architecture with hints of Renaissance. Old-fashioned lampposts flanked the extravagant entry stairway, with terracotta bricks and gray lintels fronting the stunning old hospital-turned-morgue.

Hunter and Garcia made their way up the steps that led to the building's main entrance and approached the reception counter.

'Hello, Detectives,' the attendant said. She was a petite woman, with deep-set eyes, a pointy nose, and gleaming white teeth behind a very gentle smile.

'Good morning, Audrey,' Hunter greeted her back.

'Morning, Audrey.' Garcia followed suit.

'Dr. Hove is in Autopsy Theater Two,' Audrey said. With her index finger she indicated the double swing doors to the right of the reception.

Hunter and Garcia pushed through them and moved on to a bright white corridor with shiny linoleum floors that smelled heavily of antiseptic detergent. An empty gurney was pushed up against one of its walls. They went through a new set of double doors at the end of the corridor before turning left into a shorter hallway. As soon as they cleared the doors, the antiseptic smell changed into something much, much punchier, an odor that seemed to claw at the back of the throat and slowly burn the inside of the nostrils.

Hunter immediately brought a hand up to his face, cupping his fingers over his nose. No matter how many times he'd been through those corridors, he had never gotten used to that smell. He didn't believe he ever would either.

A final right turn at the end of this second hallway and they were finally at the door to Autopsy Theater Two. Through the two rectangular windows on the stainless-steel plated doors, the detectives could see Dr. Hove inside. She was sitting on a tall stool, completely absorbed by something on her computer screen.

Hunter knocked three times.

Dr. Hove looked up and as she recognized the detectives she turned and hit the round green button on the wall behind her. The doors unlocked with a pressure-seal-like hiss. With a hand gesture, she motioned them inside.

Hunter and Garcia pushed the doors open and finally stepped into the large and uncomfortably cold room. Its walls were tiled in brilliant white. Its floor, just like the corridors outside, were done in shiny, squeaky-clean linoleum. Two stainless-steel autopsy tables sprang out of a long and wide drainage counter that hugged the west wall. At the end of each table sat an oversized sink equipped with a powerful water jet. Cassandra Jenkinson's body, half covered by a light-blue sheet, lay on the table closest to them. Her head had been clean-shaved. Her hair would now be at the forensics lab for analysis.

'Robert, Carlos.' The Chief Medical Examiner for the Los Angeles County greeted both detectives.

Dr. Carolyn Hove was tall and slim, with piercing green eyes and long chestnut hair that had been tied back into a ponytail. Her surgical mask hung loosely from her neck, revealing full lips, prominent cheekbones and a small Grecian nose. Her voice had the sort of velvety and calm tone usually associated with experience and knowledge.

'Not really how I'd like to spend my Saturday morning,' she said. 'But one can't always choose.'

'We're sorry about that, Doc,' Hunter said. 'I guess we would all rather be somewhere else.'

'No need to apologize, Robert,' the doctor replied. 'It's not your fault and I was scheduled to be here anyway. If not this case, I'd be working on a different one. The backlog is weeks long.'

Neither detective doubted that for a second. The LACDC was one of the busiest coroners in the country, and despite performing anywhere between twenty and forty postmortem examinations every day, the work would still sometimes accumulate.

'OK,' Dr. Hove said in a subdued tone, turning towards the body on the table. 'Let me show you what this monster has done.'

Something in her tone of voice worried both detectives.

Fifty-Nine

Dr. Hove pulled back the light-blue sheet to completely reveal Cassandra Jenkinson's naked body. The infamous Y-shaped incision, now closed and punctuated by thick black stiches, ran the entire length of her torso, starting at the top of each shoulder and terminating at the lower point of the sternum. A cranial incision, where a triangular cut is made across the top of the scalp to create a lid to the brain, had also been made.

Hunter and Garcia stepped a little closer.

The body on the table, with its shaved head, its eyes sunk deep into their sockets, and its rubbery-textured skin, appeared almost alien, but for some reason, the look on Cassandra's face seemed a lot more peaceful now than it had back in her house. It was as if she was glad that her nightmare was finally over and she could feel no more pain.

'Let me start with the basics,' Dr. Hove said, handing each detective a copy of her autopsy report. 'As I'm sure you both noticed back at the crime scene, with the exception of the fatal wounds inflicted to her skull and a small cut to the right side of her bottom lip, there are no other injuries to her body, defensive or otherwise. Her nails were also clean of any skin tissue. Unfortunately, she didn't scratch at her assailant.'

'So she really didn't put up a fight?' Garcia asked.

'Not even a tiny one,' the doctor confirmed. 'Do you know how the killer gained access to the property?'

'Not yet,' Garcia replied. 'There were no signs of forced entry anywhere, but we have reason to believe that he has possibly been in her house before.'

'So you think that he was known to her?'

A small shrug from Garcia. 'We're looking into it, Doc.'

Dr. Hove nodded before facing Hunter. 'I've put in an urgent request with the toxicology lab, so hopefully we'll have confirmation by tomorrow, but your report says that according to the witness statement, the killer told him that he had injected the victim with something that would numb most of her body, but it would not do the same to her brain or her nervous system.'

'Yes, that's correct,' Hunter confirmed.

Dr. Hove breathed out. 'OK, so here is where the evil starts.' She called their attention to the right side of Cassandra's neck.

Both detectives bent forward to have a better look at it. Now that her head, face and neck had been cleaned from all the blood, Hunter and Garcia were able to clearly notice a tiny needle-prick to her skin, just under her ear.

'In order for the killer to achieve that desired effect,' the doctor explained, 'he would've had to use a neuromuscular blocking agent and dose it absolutely perfectly, or else it would've also paralyzed the muscles needed for respiration and been lethal to her in minutes.'

Garcia flipped a page on the report. 'And how easy would it be to obtain something like that, Doc?'

Dr. Hove made a 'Who knows?' face. 'Go back fifteen years, maybe a little less, and any neuromuscular blocking agent would be pretty hard to come by, unless you were in a medical profession or had some very good contacts. Today? With the Internet and the thousands of illegal online drugstores? People can get it delivered to their door – gift-wrapped. No questions asked. No real record of purchase anywhere either.'

'Great,' Garcia said, shifting his weight from foot to foot.

'I'm sure that both of you must've had a pretty good idea back at the crime scene,' Dr. Hove continued, 'but I can confirm that, just like the first victim, this one wasn't sexually assaulted either, which solidifies the case for a non-sexual motive. Whatever this is about, it isn't about sexual pleasure.'

Following her accounts, both detectives flipped another page on the report.

'But whoever this killer is,' the doctor added, 'he's very skillful, and he's got at least some basic knowledge of neuro-anatomy and trauma.'

'Neuroanatomy?' Garcia asked.

'Let me explain.' She stepped left and this time directed their attention to the victim's head wounds. 'As I've said before, there are no other injuries to her body, with the exception of the three perforations to her scalp.'

Hunter and Garcia repositioned themselves by Dr. Hove's side. With Cassandra's head now completely shaved, even with the rubbery-like skin and its discoloration, three very small punctures to her scalp were clearly noticeable. None of them looked to be any larger than three millimeters in diameter.

'These perforations to her scalp caused a very particular type of fracture to her skull,' the doctor proceeded.

'Pyramid splinters,' Hunter said, studying the three small holes on Cassandra's head.

'Exactly,' the doctor confirmed.

'Pyramid what?' Garcia looked at his partner.

'Dr. Hove can explain them better,' Hunter said.

Garcia turned and faced her.

'It's all in the report,' she said. 'But I'll give you the quick version.'

'That works,' Garcia replied.

'OK,' she began. 'Every human bone has a certain elasticity to it. The skull is no different. So, with a forceful traumatic impact, the skull bone depresses in the shape of the striking instrument.' She brought her hands together, fingertips against fingertips, and slowly moved them downwards to simulate a bending effect. 'With that, two things happen. One: You get parallel break lines on the surface of the bone; these are called terraced fractures. Two: On the interior of the bone, you get a deep depression fracture. In other words, a dent. It can happen to any bone, but when it happens on the inside of the skull, this dent causes a fracture called a pyramid splinter. As the name suggests, this is simply a pyramid of splinters, moving from top to bottom. The top splinter moves down, creating another splinter, which in turn moves down, creating yet another one, and so on. Are you still with me?'

Garcia nodded.

'So, if the impact is forceful enough, these splinters will keep on projecting downward through the interior lining of the skull until they propel themselves deep into the brain tissue, like a bullet, causing instant termination of brain function and death.'

Garcia grinded his teeth as if he could feel the pain.

'That's what happened with the third and last puncture we have here.' She indicated the wound right at the center of Cassandra's skull. 'The splinter fracture from this particular wound ripped through the precentral gyrus and the central sulcus of her brain, ending its trajectory at the postcentral gyrus.' The doctor drew in a deep breath before locking eyes with both detectives. 'She never had a chance.'

'How about the other two wounds?' Garcia asked.

Hunter looked down at the floor with sad eyes, as if he already knew the answer.

'They both were forceful enough to also produce splinter fractures,' Dr. Hove confirmed. 'And though they did reach her brain, they didn't travel deep enough to cause instant death.' The tone in which Dr. Hove's next few words were delivered practically froze the air. 'But if she had lived, they would've produced irreversible brain damage.' She went quiet for a few seconds while her eyes rested on Cassandra's alien-looking face. 'Though it took three fractures for her to perish, her life as she knew it was over from the very first hit.'

Sixty

As soon as they got back to their office, Garcia went straight to his desk and fired up his computer. Something had begun nagging at his brain halfway through Dr. Hove's postmortem explanation. Something he desperately wanted to crosscheck.

Hunter left his partner to it, stepped outside, and placed a call to Cassandra Jenkinson's husband. The phone rang only once before Mr. J answered it.

'Hello!'

From his exhausted and full-of-gravel sounding voice, Hunter knew that he hadn't slept a single second.

'Mr. Jenkinson, this is Detective Robert Hunter with LAPD Homicide. We met at your house?'

Mr. J remained silent. At his request, Brian Caldron had already compiled a very comprehensive dossier on Detective Hunter. A dossier he had just finished reading, and he couldn't deny that he was impressed.

Robert Hunter grew up as an only child to working-class parents in Compton, an underprivileged neighborhood of South Los Angeles. His mother lost her battle with cancer when he was only seven. His father never remarried and had to take on two jobs to cope with the demands of bringing up a child on his own. A child who turned out to be a prodigy.

From a very early age it was obvious to everyone that Hunter was different. He could figure things out faster than most. School bored and frustrated him. He finished all of his sixth-grade work in less than two months and, just for something to do, sped through seventh, eighth and even ninth-grade books. After being put through a battery of tests and exams, Hunter was transferred to a special school for gifted children, but even a special school's curriculum wasn't enough to slow his progress. Four years of high school were condensed into two and, with recommendations from all of his teachers, Hunter was accepted as a 'special circumstances' student at Stanford University. By the age of nineteen, he had already graduated in psychology – *summa cum laude*. At the age of twenty-three, he had received a Ph.D. in Criminal Behavior Analyses and Biopsychology. His thesis paper – titled *An Advanced Psychological Study In Criminal Conduct* – had become mandatory reading at the FBI's National Center for the Analyses of Violent Crime (NCAVC) and it still was to this day.

The FBI had tried recruiting him several times, first as a profiler then as an agent, but for some reason, not mentioned in Brian's report, Detective Hunter had politely declined each and every offer, choosing to stay with the LAPD. The FBI's NCAVC Director had once said that Robert Hunter was the best criminal behavior profiler the FBI had never had.

After joining the police force, straight after his Ph.D., Hunter had moved through its ranks at lightning speed, becoming the youngest officer to have ever made detective with the Los Angeles Police Department. Since then, his track record had been second to none. He had closed almost every investigation he had ever led. The ones he was unable to were brought to as near completion as humanly possible.

Robert Hunter was now the lead detective for the Ultra Violent Crimes Unit of the LAPD Homicide Special Section. Inside the LAPD, the UVC Unit was also known as the Freakshow Unit, not because of its team of detectives, but because of the kind of criminals they chased. It was the type of unit most detectives would give their right arm not to be assigned to.

'I was wondering if I could maybe ask you a quick question over the phone,' Hunter said, seeing no point in trying to make any small talk.

'Yes, of course, Detective. Whatever I can help with.' Time to become the clueless Mr. Jenkinson again.

'Could I ask you,' Hunter began, 'have you had any work done to your house recently?'

'Work?'

'Yes,' Hunter clarified. 'Renovations, paint jobs, quick fixes, plumbing, installations, anything at all where a stranger had to visit your home?'

It took a couple of seconds for Mr. J's fatigued brain to fully engage. *The photos on the mantelpiece,* he realized. *Cassandra's killer didn't get the idea for that damn question right there and then ... he'd been to the house before. Not only that, but he knew I wouldn't know the answer to that question. That whole game was a farce.* The gears inside his mind started spinning faster. *Any work done to the house? Any installations? Anything at all where a stranger had to visit your home? Think, goddamnit, think.*

'Mr. Jenkinson?'

'Cassandra was the one who usually dealt with anything like that,' Mr. J finally replied. 'But she'd always let me know for budget purposes and all.' Another short pause. 'I can't recall anything, Detective. I'm sorry.'

'That's fine,' Hunter replied. 'At the moment we're just speculating around the little we have, really.'

'I understand, and I'm very sorry.'

'There's no need to be, Mr. Jenkinson.'

Hunter knew that in addition to being completely exhausted, Mr. Jenkinson's head would be a total mess of emotions, and memories, and images, and everything else, not to mention the overly destructive feeling of guilt that Hunter knew had already settled in. Right now, for anyone in Mr. Jenkinson's shoes, trying to recall simple memories – like a repairman coming to the house for whatever reason – would be a monstrous uphill battle.

'If anything comes to mind,' Hunter said, 'anything at all, please call me straight away, no matter the time of day or night.'

'Of course, Detective,' Mr. J replied. 'If I remember anything, I'll call you immediately.'

What Hunter didn't know was that Mr. J had lied.

Sixty-One

Garcia had just finished making a brand new pot of coffee when Hunter stepped back into their office. The mouthwatering smell of the strong Brazilian brew Garcia had used had completely intoxicated the air and Hunter found it impossible to resist. Not that he wanted to, anyway. He walked over to the machine and poured some into his mug. As he began stirring his coffee, Garcia chuckled, sat back in his chair and crossed his legs.

'Why do you do that?' he asked.

'Do what?'

'Stir your coffee? You drink it black. No sugar. No cream. No milk. There's nothing for you to stir into the coffee, so why do it?'

'I like the noise it makes,' Hunter replied with a shrug, deliberately hitting the metal spoon against the side of the porcelain mug.

'Yeah, I bet you do. You know, that's just like putting water inside a shaker, adding absolutely nothing to it, shaking it vigorously, then drinking it. It's still just water.'

'Yes,' Hunter replied. 'But that would be water shaken, not stirred.'

'Oh, hell, no,' Garcia said, half laughing. 'You didn't just make a double-oh-seven joke, did you? That was absolutely awful, Robert.'

'You laughed.'

'That wasn't a laugh.'

'Yes it was.'

'No it wasn't ... Anyway. Any luck?' Garcia asked, referring to Hunter's phone call to John Jenkinson.

'No,' Hunter replied, placing his mug on his desk. 'He can't remember any sort of work being done to their house recently. No technicians either, but he said that his wife was the one who took care of things like that.'

'Just like we thought,' Garcia agreed.

As they'd left Mr. Jenkinson's house that morning, before getting to the coroner's office, Hunter and Garcia had asked Operations to run a search, backtracking all of Cassandra Jenkinson's credit-card transactions in the past five years. The idea was to flag any sort of home improvement or home repair company she might've used, including electronic repairs, plumbers, gardeners, gutter cleaning, even delivery people who might've had to walk through her living room – a new sofa, new rug – anything. The same was also being done to Karen Ward's credit cards. The lists would then be cross-referenced. If Karen and Cassandra had used the same company, or even the same tradesman at any time, they knew that they were probably on to something.

'While on the phone,' Hunter said, sipping his coffee. 'I thought of something else. Let's add John Jenkinson's credit cards to our search. Maybe his wife used one of his to pay for something and forgot to tell him. If he's not tight with his finances, he could've easily missed it.'

'Good point,' Garcia agreed, reaching for the phone on his desk.

Hunter finished his coffee and consulted his watch. 'There's something I need to go check with the forensics lab, but can I ask you a favor?'

'Sure. By the way, this something you need to check doesn't happen to be called Dr. Susan Slater, does it?'

'What?'

'Just saying. Anyway, what's the favor?'

Hunter shook his head. 'Remember how you came across the probable way in which our killer found out about Tanya Kaitlin not knowing Karen Ward's cellphone number by heart?'

'Of course, the entry on their friend's social media page. Pete Harris. The brainlazy fun chart thing.'

'I was thinking,' Hunter said, 'if the killer really used social media to gain that sort of information on Tanya Kaitlin, why wouldn't he have tried the same thing to gain information on Cassandra Jenkinson's husband?'

'I've been thinking about that myself,' Garcia admitted. 'Don't worry. I'm on it.'

Sixty-Two

As soon as he disconnected from the call with Hunter, Mr. J urged his exhausted brain to pick up speed. Until then, he had to admit that he was sold on the assumption that the idea for the killer's wedding question had been something he had come up with on the spot, instigated by the photographs on the mantelpiece. The thought that maybe the killer had been to his home before had never crossed his mind. At least not yet, but it made sense. It made a hell of a lot of sense. When Hunter mentioned the possibility of a stranger entering the house – someone doing some sort of repair work, like a technician – then, and only then, the memory came back to him.

About two months ago, while he was away on another 'business trip', a major pipe had burst in their utility room, flooding most of the kitchen with it. Cassandra had called a plumber who had been recommended to her by a friend of hers. According to what she had told Mr. J, the plumber was a very skillful and friendly man. Not only did he fix the problem in a lot less time than she expected he would, but he also helped dry the kitchen floor and put everything back in place. She also told him that he was a very pleasant man to talk to. Very chatty. She even mentioned that he had paid her a very nice compliment, saying that her husband was a lucky man. Once in conversation, extracting the information about Cassandra's wedding anniversary would've been child's play.

On the phone, while speaking to Hunter, Mr. J made a split-second decision to keep that information to himself, at least for the time being. He wanted to talk to the plumber first before the police did. Even if the detectives found out about the repair work, and Mr. J had no doubt they would eventually, Mr. J could easily blame his forgetfulness on his exhausted brain.

Cassandra had paid the plumber in cash, he clearly remembered her telling him that, but, as always, she had obtained a receipt, which also served as a guarantee for the work done. The receipt would be with all the other house receipts – in a drawer in their kitchen – but, before getting back to his house, Mr. J had to make one more phone call.

Sixty-Three

Once Hunter had left, Garcia went back to his computer. He had two separate browsers and several applications open at the same time. Essentially, what he'd been trying to do was find some sort of link between the two victims – places they both could've been to in the past, activities they enjoyed, groups they could've belonged to ... anything.

Serial murderers rarely chose their victims at random. There was always something that would grab the killer's attention and attract him to them. It could be a physical attribute, a mannerism, a tone of voice, a belief ... the possibilities were almost endless and most of the time obscure, because in truth, they didn't have to make sense to anyone else but the killer. To the outside world, it could be something as silly and insignificant as wiping their mouth from right to left, instead of left to right, but to the killer, for some reason, that insignificant action made him mad. Mad enough to want to kill.

Garcia knew that he was clutching at straws, but straws were really all they had at the moment.

He spent another half an hour or so trying a few new combinations, but they all ended up at a brick wall. Frustrated, Garcia got to his feet. What he really needed was a break.

He refilled his coffee mug and placed it on his desk. After a quick trip to the bathroom, he began pacing the room. Just like Hunter, he liked walking when he was thinking. He spent five minutes punishing the office floor before he got back to his seat.

Think out of the box, Carlos, he told himself. *Think out of the box, because that's exactly what this killer is doing.* A few minutes later, he'd had a couple of very odd ideas. 'Oh, what the hell! What have I got to lose, anyway?'

For the next forty minutes he scrolled through pages and pages of information, some of it mind-numbing. His eyes were watering and a ghost of a headache began haunting him. He decided to take another break and try something completely different, but just as he closed the browser tab he was on, something at the bottom of the page caught his eye for a fraction of a second.

'Shit! What was that?' he said, blinking a couple of times. Immediately, Garcia right-clicked on the browser window and selected 'reopen closed tab'. The tab popped back up on his screen. He scrolled down and slowly read the entry.

'You've got to be kidding me.'

Sixty-Four

Michael Williams – that was the name of the plumber Cassandra had called to fix the burst pipe in her utility room two months earlier. Despite paying him cash instead of using one of her credit cards, Cassandra had demanded a receipt. She had always been very strict and organized when it came to those, especially when that receipt also doubled as a guarantee for the work done.

Williams was employed by a company called NoLeaks Plumbing, based in Sylmar, San Fernando Valley. It took Mr. J just one phone call to get a residential address on Williams. The drive there took him just over an hour.

The house was a small bungalow that sat halfway down a discreet dead-end street, just a couple of blocks away from the plumbing company itself. The entire property looked like it'd been neglected for years. Its front lawn was a mess, with overgrown patches of grass, dead leaves from nearby trees, and rubbish sprinkled all over the place. The house itself looked tired and in desperate need of some repairs. Its once vibrant yellow had lost its fight against the Californian sun years ago, fading into a pastel cream color that reminded Mr. J of sour milk. The front door, with an oval bevel glass window, was dirty and stained with what looked to be either oil marks or grease. The windowsills were peeling and riddled with dry rot. There was no driveway, but parked on the street, directly in front of the house, was a black Chevy Mark 2 van, with the plumbing company's logo, phone number and web address showing on both sides of it.

Mr. J walked up to the house, knocked on the door and waited. He looked nothing like what he did earlier that morning. The wig he had on was black, with the hair layered in waves. It made him look like an aging rock star from the 1990s. His cheeks and under-chin had gained half an inch in volume, making his face look unhealthily puffy. His peppery goatee was thick, but well trimmed. His eyes – light blue. His fake nose looked like it had been broken at least a couple of times.

Twenty seconds went by with no reply from the house. Mr. J stepped closer, bringing his right ear to an inch from the door. No sound from inside. He knocked again, a little firmer this time. Another twenty seconds went by before he saw some movement through the beveled glass window.

'Hold your fucking horses,' a thick male voice called from inside, 'I'm coming.'

Mr. J took a step back and cracked his knuckles.

The door was pulled open by a man who looked to be around the same age as Mr. J. He wore basketball shorts, an old pair of sneakers, and a blue tank top that seemed too small for his muscular physique. His strong arms were completely exposed.

'Can I help you?' the man asked, sizing Mr. J up. He didn't seem to be in a good mood.

With the open door, Mr. J picked up the scent of food cooking in the background. Something spicy and greasy.

'Mr. Williams? Michael Williams?' Mr. J asked.

There was a moment of hesitation.

'Who wants to know?'

Mr. J produced an almost perfect forgery of an LAPD's detective badge. Even an expert would struggle to tell the difference.

'I'm Detective Craig Lewis with the LAPD.' Mr. J's voice also sounded completely different. His tone had gone up about half an octave and the accent was typical of northern California.

In hearing those words and seeing the badge, Michael Williams' demeanor changed slightly.

Mr. J noticed it.

'I was wondering if I could ask you a few questions?'

For a second, Michael Williams looked like he was debating what his next move should be.

'What's this concerning?' he asked.

'I think we would be better if we could talk inside,' Mr. J replied.

Both men studied each other for a couple more seconds.

'Sure,' Michael Williams said, taking a step to the side.

Mr. J stepped forward, but as he was about to enter the house, Michael Williams lifted his right leg and delivered a front kick to Mr. J's abdomen so powerful, it lifted him off the ground and sent him stumbling back at least six or seven feet. As Mr. J crashed on to the messy front lawn, he heard the front door slam shut.

'Motherfu . . .' He coughed frantically, trying to breathe in. The kick had knocked the air out of Mr. J's lungs. He tried to get up, but pain forced him to sit back down for a couple more seconds. He brought his right hand to his stomach and squeezed his eyes tight. Finally. He was able to breathe life back into his limbs.

'You sonofabitch.' He got back on to his feet and ran towards the door.

Locked.

'Arghhhh ...' Mr. J let out a full-of-frustration cry. He stepped back and, using all the power he had in his muscles, threw his whole body, shoulder first, against the door. It rattled but that was about it.

'Shit!'

He stepped back again and this time used his right leg to deliver a kick into the door handle. The door shook again, but it still didn't open. He tried again. Nothing. One more time. Almost. Again, and this time Mr. J gave it everything he had. If this failed, he would use his gun.

SLAM!

The door finally flew open, cracking the doorframe and throwing splinters up in the air.

As he cautiously stepped into the house, Mr. J pulled out a Sig Sauer P226 Legion from his lower-back holster. The pistol was equipped with a silencer.

The front door took him straight into a sparsely furnished living room.

Empty.

Mr. J looked left, then right.

Nothing.

'Michael?' Mr. J called in a loud and angry voice, while taking in the room.

No reply.

'Michael? C'mon, let's talk.'

Silence.

Across the room from him there was a shut door. 'The kitchen,' he thought. To his right, a corridor would take him deeper into the house. There was no one there either.

Mr. J decided to go for the kitchen door. If he went for the corridor that would mean that he would have his back to the shut door. Never a good idea. He crossed the room and threw his back against the wall to the side of the door. He was about to try its handle when he heard the sound of a motorbike engine revving up. It hadn't come from the front of the house. It came from the back, through the kitchen.

'Motherfucker.' Mr. J reached for the door handle.

Locked.

There was no way that he would be taking the time to kick this one in. Instead, he took a step back and aimed his pistol at the door lock. One barely audible 'thuffft' was all it took. The lock exploded out of the door as it swung open.

The kitchen was tiny, and it smelled as if Michael Williams had been deep-frying lard in goose fat. The back door was wide open and Mr. J got to it just in time to see the motorbike vanish through a side passage on the backyard fence. He squeezed two shots from his pistol, but it was way too late. The shots hit the woodwork.

In a flash, Mr. J turned and ran back into the house. He got to the living room and was about to run out to his car when his mind let go of the anger and began thinking clearly again.

What's the point in trying to go after him now, he thought. *He's on a bike, cutting through small alleyways and backstreets. Right now he could be three, four, maybe even five streets over in any direction. Driving around in a car to try to find him is a pretty dumb idea.* He looked around the living room. *Your best chance to find him is in here, somewhere. Something in here will give him up.*

Mr. J walked to the front door and looked outside to see if anyone had seen what had happened. The street was as dead as it was when he got there. He calmly closed the door and began searching Michael Williams' house.

Sixty-Five

Garcia was just getting off the phone with the LAPD Cyber Crime Unit when Hunter got back to their office.

'Robert, you've got to come have a look at this.'

Garcia's tone filled Hunter with intrigue. He walked over to his partner's desk.

'I'll admit that I made a huge mistake,' Garcia explained. 'I spent a lot of time going over Cassandra and John Jenkinson's social media pages, searching through entries, looking at photos ... everything.'

'How's that a mistake?'

'It's the same mistake I made the first time around, Robert. I looked through everything in both Karen Ward and Tanya Kaitlin's personal pages, remember? But I found absolutely nothing there. The break came when I looked at their friend's page, Pete Harris, and that was when I remembered something very important about our second victim – she's got a son, Patrick Jenkinson, who is twenty years old and goes to college in Boston. To his generation, social media is like oxygen. They can barely function without it.'

'So you checked his page.'

'Pages,' Garcia corrected Hunter.

'He's got more than one?'

'Not exactly, but he's a member of several different groups,' Garcia explained. 'Each one with their own page, so I spent the whole morning bouncing from one page to another, reading entries, replies, basically everything I could find, until I came across this.' He loaded a page on to his browser and scrolled down until he found the entry he was after. 'Check it out,' he said, tapping his finger on the screen.

Hunter leaned forward by his partner's left shoulder.

'You only have to read up to the fourth reply to know what I'm talking about.'

The thread had been created on a group page, not by Patrick Jenkinson, but by another member. A woman named Isabel.

Isabel: *Oh, my father is in so much* 🪦 *with my mom after last night.* 💩 *He'll be sleeping in the living room for a month.*

The first question came from another female member named Martha:

Why? What happened? 😮. *Tell. Tell. Tell.* 😊

Isabel: *He forgot their wedding anniversary. Turned up after work with nothing - no* 🌹, 🍫, 🍷 *not even a shitty card from a gas station. Didn't mention a thing. My mom was* 😐, *but she also didn't say anything. This morning, at breakfast, she was all quiet. My dad asked - 'are you OK, hon?' That was when the shit hit the fan, and let me tell you, that fan is still spinning lol*

Martha: *Oh that's bad. That's real bad.* 😬. *My dad is awesome when it comes to that. Twenty-three years married, never forgot it once.*

The next comment came from Patrick Jenkinson:

I know exactly what you're talking about, Isabel. My dad

doesn't remember his and my mom's wedding anniversary anymore either. Hasn't for several years. My mom used to remind him, but not without getting into an argument at the same time. She gave up after a few years. If he couldn't remember it by himself, what was the point?

Hunter looked at Garcia.

'You were right again,' Garcia said. 'The killer knew beforehand that Mr. Jenkinson wouldn't know the answer to his question.'

Sixty-Six

Mr. J's ribs hurt as if they were broken. The kick Michael Williams had delivered to his abdomen had gotten him completely by surprise. At the time his body wasn't exactly relaxed, but it wasn't rigid or foreseeing an attack so soon either, so the kick had penetrated with maximum force.

'You should've expected that, J,' he whispered to himself, while opening another drawer inside Michael Williams' bedroom. 'What the fuck were you thinking? You turn up unannounced, pretending to be a cop, and you thought he would just invite you in for donuts and milk?' He lifted his shirt to take a look. Bruising was already starting to come through.

Mr. J had already gone through every drawer, every box, every hole he had found in Michael Williams' living room. So far, he'd found nothing that could give him a lead as to where he could've run to, but the search wasn't over yet. Inside a box that had been slid under an old display unit, he'd found receipts, house bills, and some documents regarding NoLeaks Plumbing. The company had been established two and a half years earlier, and it belonged to Michael Williams himself. As far as Mr. J could tell, he was also its only employee.

Once he was satisfied that he had looked absolutely everywhere in the living room, Mr. J moved his search operation to Michael Williams' bedroom. Just like the living room, the bedroom was small, lightly furnished, and it smelled of stale sweat and fried food.

Mr. J started with the chest of drawers that was pushed up against the east wall. His living room search had already told him that Michael Williams was an extremely organized man. Every object seemed to have its specific place, but the bedroom told him that Mr. Williams was undoubtedly OCD. Every item of clothing he'd found inside the drawers had been folded to perfection, completely maximizing the use of space, but the obsession didn't end there. The items had also been color- and type-coordinated.

Mr. J unfolded and looked through each and every single item, including pockets. He found nothing, not even a scrap of paper.

Next, he tried the small wooden wardrobe, where he found a gray suit that looked to have been purchased from a charity shop, two white button-up shirts, one striped tie, a pair of heavy-duty working boots, and a pair of black shoes, which had certainly seen better days.

He checked all the clothing before looking on top and under the wardrobe but, once again, Mr. J found nothing.

There was only one bedside table, set on the right side of the bed, closer to the door, and that was where things began getting exciting. In the drawer, Mr. J found a Beretta 96 A1 .40-caliber pistol. Next to it, two boxes of 180-grain full-metal-jacket ammunition.

'I don't suppose I'll find a permit for this anywhere,' Mr. J said, as he picked up the weapon and released its twelve-round magazine. None were missing. He brought the gun's chamber up to his nose. It didn't smell of gunpowder, but of oil and lubricants.

After securing the pistol between his trousers' waistband and his lower back, Mr. J got down on all fours and checked under the bed – nothing except for a dark-gray suitcase. He reached for it and dragged it towards him.

It was a polycarbonate suitcase, with a two-way zipper, held shut by a three-digit combination locking mechanism. It felt very light, as if it was empty, but if that was the case, why was it locked?

Mr. J reached for his pocketknife. The average commercial suitcase locking mechanism is there more as a deterrent, rather than as a security feature. All it really takes is a quick flick with the tip of a knife and the system comes apart. It took Mr. J less than three seconds to breach this one.

Zippers free, he flipped the suitcase top open and frowned. Inside it he found a second bag – this one a military-style, thick canvas duffle bag. Its zipper was secured shut by a high-grade, enclosed shackle padlock. There was no way Mr. J was breaching that lock with a pocketknife, but it was still only a zipper on a canvas bag, and that, a pocketknife could rip open in no time.

'OK,' Mr. J said to himself. 'I'm done playing games.' He stabbed the knife through the zipper, forced its jaws open, and looked inside.

'Motherfucker.'

Sixty-Seven

In seeing what Garcia had achieved from searching the social-media sites, an idea came to Hunter. He returned to his computer and called up his browser before reaching for the phone on his desk and dialing an internal extension.

'Dennis Baxter, Computer Crimes Unit.' A tired-sounding voice answered after the third ring.

'Dennis, it's Robert from the UVC Unit.'

Baxter coughed to clear his throat. He knew that when Hunter called him on his work line, something serious was either going down, or about to. 'Hey, man, what's up?'

'Listen,' Hunter said, 'does the LAPD have some kind of bogus social media account? Something I can use without having to create a whole bunch of accounts myself?'

Garcia's brow creased as he leaned sideways on his chair to look at Hunter past their computer screens.

'You mean a bogus *personal* account,' Baxter questioned back. 'Not a business one. Something with which you could send out friend requests, and messages, and join conversations and all that?'

'Exactly,' Hunter replied. 'Does the LAPD have anything like that?'

'Yeah, we've got a few of those. Why? Do you need one?'

'By yesterday.'

'Sure. No problem. What do you need, Facebook?'

'I need everything you can get – Facebook, Instagram, Twitter – whatever it is that people are using the most these days.'

'OK. Do you need the same email account to be the primary account across the board here? For legitimacy?'

'Not really necessary,' Hunter answered. 'All I want to be able to do is browse through a few pages, but I understand that I can't really do that without an account.'

'Yes, that's right. So you mean to tell me that you don't have a Facebook or a Twitter account?'

'I don't have any social media accounts.'

'You're a caveman,' Baxter laughed. 'OK, any particular look or gender you'd rather have or be? I can give you any sort of profile you need – hot chick, super nerd, naive little girl, badass motherfucker, old, young, black, white – when it comes to cyberspace profiles, I provide a God service.'

Hunter thought about it for a second or two. 'Can I get two identities? One male, one female. Just average people will do.'

'Sure,' Baxter replied. 'Give me a couple of minutes and I'll email you back.'

'What's going on, Robert?' Garcia asked once Hunter had put his phone down. 'What do you have in mind?'

'I'm not really sure, myself. But it looks like our killer spends a lot of time on social media sites. That could be how he got his insight into his victims' lives. If that really is how he does it, then I need to do the same.'

The phone on Hunter's desk rang twice before Hunter picked it up.

'Sending the email with your new identities to you now,' Baxter said.

Hunter called up his email application and his eyebrows arched – lolitasmokinghot@gruntmail.com and pipethe-piper@gruntmail.com? 'Nice,' he said. 'Swift.'

'Wait until you see their profile pictures I gave you,' Baxter said. 'The passwords to the accounts are in the email.'

'Thanks, Dennis.'

'No problem. Let me know if you need anything else.'

'Will do.'

Hunter ended the call and used his new cyber-identities to log into several different social media sites at the same time.

'OK,' he said to himself. 'Let's start digging.'

Sixty-Eight

Without knocking, Captain Blake pulled open the door to Hunter and Garcia's office and stepped inside. They were both sitting at their desks.

'OK,' she said in an already irritated tone, her eyes bouncing from one detective to the other. 'What have you guys got for me on this? And you better tell me you've got something good, because with this second victim, Cassandra Jenkinson, those freaks from the media have caught the smell of blood, and when it comes to anything that could possibly turn out to be a serial homicide story, they all become ravenous vampires. And the colony is starving.'

Hunter was amused by the comparison.

'Word on this killer broadcasting his murders live over a video-call hasn't got out yet,' the captain continued. 'But that's just a matter of time, we all know that. Since the new murder last night, the phones in our press office have been ringing off the hook. Right now, everyone is looking for some sort of statement from us.'

Both detectives knew that that was coming.

'Has one been issued yet?' Garcia asked.

'What?' Captain Blake glared at him. 'Is that a joke,

Carlos? How the hell could we issue anything if no one, other than the two of you, knows what's really going on with this case?'

Garcia sat back and clasped his hands together over his stomach. 'I thought bullshitting was our press office's specialty.'

'Oh, we've got jokes now, is that it?' Captain Blake said, her eyes about to flash fire. 'Because this seems like the ideal moment to crack one.'

'What would you like to know, Captain?' Hunter asked in a serene tone, bringing her attention to him.

'*Everything*, Robert,' she replied, checking her watch. 'I've got a meeting with Chief Bracco in two hours, and he'll be expecting to be fully briefed. Unless you'd like to go in my place?'

'No, I'm good. Thanks, Captain.'

'Yeah, I didn't think so.' The captain took a deep breath to steady herself. 'So, the last time I left this office we had one victim and the speculation seemed to be moving in the direction of a stalker. Is that still the case?'

'You better make yourself comfortable, Captain,' Garcia said.

Captain Blake grabbed a fold-up chair that was resting against a metal cabinet by the office door. Once she had a seat, Hunter and Garcia took turns explaining everything that had happened since her last update, including their new Internet discovery just moments ago.

'Wait a second,' the captain said, lifting a finger to pause Hunter as he explained the results to Cassandra Jenkinson's autopsy exam. He'd been detailing the bizarre way in which she'd been murdered. 'It says here, and I quote.' She read from the copy of the postmortem report they'd handed her: '"With a forceful traumatic impact, the skull bone depresses in the shape of the striking instrument" – I take it that that means any striking instrument?'

'That's right.'

'So to create a pyramid splinter fracture, the killer didn't have to use a pointy chisel?'

'Nope,' Hunter replied. 'He didn't even have to use a chisel at all, Captain. The hammer on its own would've been more than capable of doing that.'

'So why *did* he?' she asked, looking unsure.

'Because the problem with using any sort of blunt instrument on its own,' Hunter clarified, 'is that it would've been a lot harder to control and measure the impact, and there was no guarantee that the killer would've achieved the desired effect.'

'What desired effect, Robert, death? I'm sure that a hammer to the head would've done the job, no problem.'

'Not death, Captain,' Hunter said, sitting back on his chair, 'blood.'

Captain Blake didn't voice a question. All she did was look back at Hunter and shake her head ever so slightly.

'There's something you're forgetting, Captain.'

'And what might that be?'

'This killer is broadcasting his murders live over a video-call, so whichever way you look at this, you can't deny that what he's essentially doing is putting on a show. It doesn't matter if he's got an audience of one or a million. To him, it's still a show. And the game he plays requires two main things to happen in order for his show to work the way he wants it to.' Hunter lifted his right index finger. 'One: He needs the person on the other end of the line to panic, because that plays directly in his favor and he feeds off it. It empowers him.' Hunter paused for breath. 'If he had used a hammer on its own, that would've been a lot harder to achieve, if he'd managed to do it at all.'

'Are you saying that if the killer had decided to hammer Cassandra Jenkinson's head in, her husband wouldn't have panicked? Watching it live over a video-call?'

'Sure he would've, but that could've easily played against the killer's second requirement.'

'And what requirement is that?'

'For our killer to have his "fun".' Hunter used his fingers to draw quotation marks in the air. 'The killer also needs his victims to stay alive for at least two wrong answers, because that's how he gets his kicks, Captain. To him, torturing and murdering his victims isn't enough. He needs more because his sadism goes way beyond killing. He needs the total desperation from the person watching. He needs them to lose their minds. He needs to make them feel guilty.'

The captain paused and mulled over that thought for an instant. Hunter helped.

'This game he plays, though it may sound like it's a simple enough question-and-answer game, it's been very well thought of, Captain, and meticulously designed to unbalance the person answering the questions.'

This time, it was Captain Blake who sat back on her chair. 'You're going to have to give me a little bit more than that, Robert, if you want me to at least try to follow this surreal mind of yours. What the hell are you talking about?'

'OK,' Hunter accepted, getting up and walking over to the picture board. 'Hidden in this question game our killer plays are some simple, but very effective psychological elements.'

'Such as?' the captain asked, turning to face the board.

'Well,' Hunter began. 'The first thing he does, after taking a victim hostage, is call the person who will become the player in his game. Someone who is very close to that victim. Someone with a strong emotional connection to them – best friend – husband.' On the board, Hunter indicated Tanya Kaitlin and Mr. J's photographs, respectively. 'His first trick is that he uses the victim's phone to make that call, and that brings in the first psychological element – surprise.'

Captain Blake's eyes narrowed a fraction as she began considering Hunter's words.

'The person answers the phone,' Hunter continued, 'thinking that they'll be speaking to a best friend or a wife, and that is indeed the impression they get, because according to both witnesses, the first image they see is a zoomed-in shot of the eventual victim. Mainly their eyes, but as the shot pans out . . .'

'Surprise,' the captain agreed, seeing what Hunter was driving at.

'And as the shot continues to pan out,' Hunter added, 'that surprise is immediately followed by the next two psychological elements – confusion and shock.'

He gave his captain an extra moment. In her eyes, he saw that she had made the connection. He proceeded.

'Then comes the explanation about what is happening and the rules to his sick question game. And with that we've got two new elements. First, doubt – because that's when the mind starts going, "Is this for real? Am I dreaming this crap or what?" Second, an introduction to fear – because if this turns out to be real, then your best friend's life . . . your wife's life . . . is in your hands.'

Captain Blake crossed one leg over the other, the look in her eyes clearly indicating that things were just starting to make sense in her head.

'So even before the question game starts, Captain,' Hunter carried on, 'in the space of two minutes or less, the witnesses' brains have been bombarded by a shower of unbalancing elements – surprise, confusion, shock, doubt, and just enough fear to make them question everything. In the midst of all that, while the witnesses are still trying to figure out if they're dreaming or not, if they've been caught in the middle of an elaborate prank or not, the killer hits them with his first question. An extremely easy question. Something he knows they'll get right.'

Hunter indicated both questions on the board: 'How many Facebook friends do you have?'; 'Where was Cassandra born?'

'That first question is a very clever question because it essentially does two things, Captain. One: It brings back a combination of "confusion" and "doubt", because right then the witnesses can't believe that this *game* can be real. Not with such easy questions. So they start believing that whatever this is, it must be a prank. And, two: It gives them a false sense of security, because if these are the types of question they're going to be asked,' Hunter made a 'c'mon' gesture with both of his hands, 'then bring on this stupid game.' This time, Hunter paused for effect. 'And that false sense of security expands inside the witnesses because after all, they're now fifty percent there. Remember the rules of the game? Two correct answers and the game is over. Your friend is free. Your wife is free. And here's where this killer shows how clever he really is.'

Captain Blake pushed a lock of hair away from her face.

'By now, he's already unbalanced their thought processes without them realizing it and he's given them a false sense of security, but his trump card is still to come.'

'Trump card?' the captain asked.

'He's never told them what the consequence to a wrong answer is,' Garcia jumped in.

Hunter pointed at his partner as if he'd given the answer to the ultimate question.

'They have no real idea of what will happen if they get a question wrong, Captain,' Hunter said. 'And after that first easy question, the game is now sounding silly. So the killer hits them with his second question. *The* question.' Once again, Hunter indicated the questions on the board. 'Something he researched. Something he'd found out that they should get wrong, but it's still only a "should".'

'What do you mean – only a "should"?'

'Think about it, Captain. This killer didn't just decide to go on a killing spree from night to day. He's been planning his murders for some time. And he's very, very patient, because his is a lengthy process. He starts by choosing the victim, someone he taunts with messages, and, from what we gathered, he does it for months. Then he chooses the person to play his question game. Someone close to the victim. Finally, he researches what question to ask them, because the trick is – the question needs to *sound* easy, but *be* difficult.'

Captain Blake nodded. 'OK.'

'If we are right about this killer finding out which question to ask by scrutinizing social media websites –' Hunter continued, 'and I think we are – those posts have been up for months. But even if we're wrong about the social-media websites, how long do you think it's been between him finding out which question to ask and the murder itself, which is when he actually asks the question?'

The captain scratched the top of her forehead, considering it.

'Days, weeks, months ...?' Hunter suggested. 'In that time, both witnesses could've very well learned the answer to that *easy* question.'

Again, Hunter gave the captain a few seconds to think about it.

'On the morning of the murder,' he proceeded, 'Tanya Kaitlin could've decided to memorize her best friend's number for whatever reason. John Jenkinson could've decided that this year he would go back to being a romantic husband and surprise his wife by remembering their wedding anniversary, bring her flowers, take her on a holiday ... whatever. The killer had no real guarantees that they *would* actually get it wrong, Captain. The best he could do is go for a question that they *should* get wrong.'

Captain Blake stayed silent.

'So he strengthens his chances with yet another clever trick,' Garcia said, taking over. 'Both of his second questions carried either a number sequence, or a date. It's a proven fact that number sequences, formulas and dates are the hardest things for the average human brain to memorize.'

The captain couldn't argue with that. She always had trouble remembering dates and phone numbers. Formulas? That was a definite no-no.

'So,' Garcia continued, 'going back to where we were: The killer hits them with his second question immediately after he gave them a false sense of security. Both witnesses have told us that with that second question, the first thing they did wasn't to search their memory for the answer.' Garcia shook his head. 'No. They question the question: "What? What do you mean? Wait a second . . ." and so on.'

'Big mistake.' Hunter again. 'By the time they actually start searching their memory for an answer, three maybe even four out of the five seconds the killer gives them are gone. And they know this, because he counts them down, which adds to the pressure. Now we have one more element. One that even if the numbers and dates are there . . .' Hunter pointed to his own head, '. . . it could cause them to mix them up.'

'Panic,' Captain Blake said.

'Almost, but not yet,' Hunter disagreed. 'What we've got is anxiety, nerves kicking in, maybe even a little fear. So just before the killer counts them down to zero, they blurt out the wrong answer, either because they don't really know it – Tanya Kaitlin's case – or their time is up and anxiety causes them to mix up the dates – John Jenkinson's case.' Hunter stepped away from the picture board. 'With that, the killer finally shows them his trump card – the punishment for their wrong answer.' He nodded at the captain. '*Now* we've got panic. And that's why he used a pointy chisel instead of the hammer on its own.'

'Too soft an impact,' Captain Blake said, the puzzle finally solved in her head. 'And all he would've had would've been a victim with a bump on the head. No pyramid splinter fracture. Too hard an impact and the victim would've either been dead too soon or have been knocked out with a concussion.'

'Correct,' Hunter agreed. 'Neither case would've worked for our killer because with the first strike he needed two things to happen. One: He needed Cassandra Jenkinson to be in pain but stay conscious. Two: He needed to drive panic deep into her husband's heart and consequently his brain. And what better way to do that than to make him watch his wife bleed?'

Captain Blake closed her eyes for an instant while shaking her head.

'A light hit with a blunt instrument wouldn't have caused her scalp to rupture,' Hunter added. 'For that, he would've needed a much more powerful strike, and controlling that would've been a problem.'

'As soon as he's got blood pouring down his victim's face,' Garcia took over again, 'it's game over, Captain. Even if the answer was right at the tip of his tongue, he wouldn't be able to get it out because the final psychological element is the most destructive of all.'

Captain Blake had thought that 'panic' would've been the last of those elements. She frowned at both detectives.

'Guilt,' Hunter explained. 'John Jenkinson now knows that whatever is happening is not a prank, and the reason why his wife is bleeding, the reason why his wife is in pain, the reason why his wife is dying ... is him. It's because he can't remember their anniversary date. As the five-second count starts again, his brain is mush. In less than five minutes it's been through surprise, confusion, shock, doubt, panic, terrifying fear, and now soul-destroying guilt. Add to that the fact that he's watching his wife being tortured inside his own home and there's nothing he can physically do to stop it, and any dates or numbers won't make any sense in his mind anymore. It's not a fail-proof plan, by any means, but it's very clever because it tips the odds heavily in the killer's favor.'

'And that guilt will sit with him for the rest of his life,' Captain Blake said.

Her confirmation came in the form of silence from both detectives.

Sixty-Nine

'Wow! You look stunning,' Detective Julian Webb said as Dr. Gwen Barnes pulled open her front door. She wore a white knee-length cocktail dress with spaghetti straps, revealing well-toned arms and legs. Her clutch bag, decorated with rhinestones, matched her platform evening sandals. Her hair sparkled under the dying rays of the late afternoon sunlight.

'Thank you so much,' she replied, giving him a smile that was as inviting as it was mysterious. 'You look very nice yourself.'

Dr. Barnes didn't know this, but Webb was pretty much wearing his everyday work attire – a dark suit with a white button-up shirt and a striped tie. The shoes were black, comfortable and shiny.

Dr. Barnes checked her watch: 6:00 p.m. sharp. 'You are ... exactly on time. I'm impressed.'

'If at all possible, I try to be,' Webb replied. 'But in my line of work, it gets hard sometimes. Things don't really happen by appointment, if you know what I mean.'

Her smile widened. 'Yes, I can imagine.'

'So, how have you been?' he asked, looking past her

shoulder and into the house. 'Everything OK? Did you manage to get any sleep during the day?'

As he had promised, Webb had called Dr. Barnes in the morning to check on her. She had told him that other than having almost no sleep overnight, everything else was fine.

She shook her head. 'No, no sleep at all, hence the heavy makeup under my eyes, but . . .' she turned her head to look over her own shoulder, 'everything seems to be all right. Thank you.'

The look in her eyes as she delivered her last few words made Detective Webb wonder if she was now debating what she seemed so confident about before – that her bracelet had really been taken from inside her bedroom. He decided to leave the subject alone, at least for now.

'Look,' he said, renewing his smile, hoping to cheer her up a little. 'I know that we sort of agreed on having coffee, but I was thinking, what do you say if we grab some dinner?'

'I was about to suggest the same thing,' Dr. Barnes said. 'But with one condition.'

'And what is that?'

'That you take me to a place where you and your detective friends usually go to.'

'Excuse me?'

'You know, during your regular day, where do you usually stop to eat?'

'During a regular day I barely have time to breathe, never mind eat.'

'Yes, I understand that, but you do eat, don't you?'

'Yeeeeees?'

'And I bet you have a couple of favorite places you like dropping by, don't you?'

Webb tilted his head from side to side two or three times, accepting it.

'Great, because it's to one of those that I would like you to take me.'

'Oh no, you *really* don't want to go to any of those places.'

'But I do. I really do.'

Webb looked at Dr. Barnes from head to toes. 'But you're dressed so nicely, and those places are proper dumps. Believe me.'

'I can change. It's not a problem.' She began swerving her body around.

'No. Please don't.' He stopped her. They locked eyes. 'That really *is* where you'd like me to take you?'

'Yes.'

Webb chuckled to himself. 'OK, but don't say I didn't warn you.'

Just over thirty minutes later, Webb parked his car on Hollywood Boulevard, just in front of a tiny pizza place called Joe's Pizza.

'Here we are,' he said.

Dr. Barnes looked at it from the passenger seat and smiled.

'I told you that the places we go on the job are dumps.'

'Is the food good?'

'The food is awesome. Best pizza pie in Hollywood Boulevard. It's just not the place where anyone brings a date to.'

'Did you say pizza pie?'

A short pause.

'I did. Do you like them?'

'I love pizza pies.'

Webb's face lit up. 'Oh, in that case, get ready for this

then,' he said, with a proud twist to his tone, 'because this will change your life.'

Dr. Barnes was unsure if she could call it a life-changing experience, but it certainly was a habit-changing one. The special Grandma Pie they shared was the best pizza pie she had ever tasted, and she hadn't laughed so hard in years. As it turned out, Detective Webb was a very amusing person.

As she finished her last slice, she looked at Webb and smiled again.

'What?' he asked, looking back at her sideways. 'Do I have cheese on my chin?' He grabbed a paper napkin and dabbed it against his chin.

'No. It's not that.'

'Oh!' He put the napkin down.

'It's just that ... I was worried that we would struggle with conversation.'

Webb found the statement strange. 'I'm not sure I follow.'

'Well, because of the line of work we're in,' Dr. Barnes explained, 'neither of us can really talk about our jobs, am I right? I mean, you probably can't tell me anything about any of the investigations you are involved in at the moment, and I can't really talk about any of my patients.'

Webb had a sip of his Dr Pepper before agreeing.

'I for one spend most of my days involved in something to do with my work,' she said, 'including weekends, and I have a feeling that so do you.'

'Yeah, that's an understatement.'

'So,' she said, 'I just thought that since neither of us could talk about what keeps us busy for most of our days, conversation would die a death, but I have been proven wrong.' She toyed with her can of root beer. 'So far, I've had the best time

I've had in a very long time.' The inviting smile was back. This time, the mysterious part of it wasn't there anymore.

Webb lifted his drink, proposing a toast. 'Me too. And I'll drink to that.'

They touched cans before a moment of awkward silence took over.

'I'll tell you what,' Dr. Barnes said. 'I know you're not drinking because you're driving, right? But how about we go back to my place, you park your car there, we call a cab, and go have some real fun – tequila style.'

Webb regarded his date for a few seconds. He liked her more and more as the night went on.

'That sounds great,' he said. 'But you're forgetting that I still have to drive home when we get back from wherever we go.'

The look Dr. Barnes gave Detective Webb put a definite end to that theory.

He smiled at her. 'OK. You're on.'

'Why don't you come in?' she said as Webb pulled up in front of her house, around forty minutes after they left Joe's Pizza. 'We could have a glass of wine while we wait for the cab.'

'That sounds great to me.'

As they approached the doctor's front door, they both heard Webb's phone go off in his pocket.

'Just a second,' he told her, bringing the phone to his ear. 'Detective Webb.' As he listened to the person at the other end of the line, his facial expression shifted. 'When?' He listened for a little longer before drawing an extra deep breath. 'Motherfu ...' His eyes found Dr. Barnes' and he paused mid-word. 'OK. OK,' he said into his phone, breaking eye contact. 'I'm on my way.' He disconnected and returned the phone to his pocket.

'Gwen, I'm so sorry about this, but . . .'

For a second she looked upset, but Dr. Barnes knew better than most what a call like that meant.

'It's OK, Julian,' she stopped him. 'I understand.' She stepped closer and gave him a peck on the lips. 'How about you drop by whenever you're done.' She winked at him. 'I'll keep the wine and the tequila chilled.'

'That's a deal.' He smiled before kissing her again, this time for a lot longer.

'I'll be waiting.'

Once Webb was gone, Dr. Barnes unlocked her front door and stepped into her living room. Even if she tried to, she wouldn't be able to get rid of the smile on her face.

She hadn't dated anyone in nearly two years, and she had almost forgotten how exciting it could be. How a single kiss could make a person feel. And right then, she felt good. So good that the note and bracelet incident had completely slipped her mind. So good that for an instant, she kept the lights switched off, leaned back against her front door, closed her eyes and savored the moment. So good that she failed to notice the dark shadow now standing just outside her window, his eyes staring straight at her.

Seventy

Erica Barnes placed the popcorn bag inside the microwave, set the time to two and a half minutes and hit the start button. While waiting for the 'pops' to begin, she poured herself a large glass of wine.

Popcorn and red wine, that was how Erica fought off her Sunday night blues. Not that she suffered badly from it. She didn't hate her job and the people she worked with were ... well ... 'bearable' would be the word she'd use. She also didn't fear Monday mornings. She never had a problem getting up early, and she rarely started her week in a 'grumpy' mood, but still, there was just something about Sunday evenings that always made her feel a little sad.

Sunday nights were also *poker nights*, the nights when Trevor, her boyfriend of two years and who Erica shared her small one-bedroom apartment with, would usually lose one hundred and fifty dollars (maximum stakes allowed) to his friends. True, every now and then he would win a little, but those Sunday nights were rare, to say the least.

But there was one thing about this particular Sunday evening that did excite Erica. Her sister, Dr. Gwen Barnes, was going out on a date. That thought alone brought a smile to Erica's lips. Gwen hadn't dated anyone in a very long time and, in Erica's view, it was about time her sister got back in the game.

They had spoken briefly on the phone earlier in the day. In the conversation, Gwen mentioned that she'd met someone ... someone who seemed to be a nice person. She also mentioned that they were supposed to go out for coffee later today. Erica's immediate reaction was to shower her sister with questions: 'Who is he? Where did you meet? How did you meet?' But Gwen smoothly dodged the questions by telling her that she was running late for something and that she would call Erica again later, after the date.

Erica heard the first popcorn pop after thirty-three seconds. She placed her wine glass on the counter and leaned forward, getting closer to the microwave. The instructions on the packet said two and a half minutes but, just like most people, she preferred to listen to the time gap between pops. As soon as it got to any longer than two seconds, it was time to stop it.

Erica poured the popcorn into a large bowl, grabbed her wine glass and walked over to her living room. There, she switched on the TV, and dumped herself on to the sofa.

'OK,' she said, in conversation with the popcorn. 'Let's find something to watch, shall we?'

Before she began flicking through the channels, she reached for her cellphone, took a picture of her wine glass and the popcorn bowl, and quickly uploaded it to her social media page. That done, she swopped the phone for the TV remote.

Flick – *Rerun on and old show*. Flick – *Rerun on and old show*. Flick – *Rerun on and old show*.

'Are you kidding me?'

Flick – *The Real Wives of Somewhere*. Flick – *The Real Husbands of Somewhere*. Flick – *Big Brother*.

'No way. This crap is still going on? Do people still watch this?'

Flick – some romantic comedy was just starting.

'I guess this will do.'

Erica placed the remote down next to her and had a sip of her wine followed by a mouthful of the friends she was just talking to. She had just gotten comfortable, with the popcorn bowl resting on top of her crossed legs, when her cellphone rang.

'Typical,' she whispered, reaching for it.

A video-call from her sister.

'That's weird,' she thought. Erica and Gwen didn't video-call that often. Erica checked her watch: 10:12 p.m. She accepted the call.

'Hey, Sis,' she said as the image began materializing on her screen. 'That was a quick date. Did everything go OK?'

All Erica could see were her sister's eyes.

'Sis, you're too close to the phone. What are you doing? Have you gone blind? Move back a bit.' She stuffed another handful of popcorn into her mouth.

'Hello, Erica.'

The voice Erica heard from her phone speakers was scarily deep and time-delayed. Immediately, she frowned at her screen.

'Sis, you're too close to the phone. Your voice is distorting. Move back, woman. What's wrong with you?'

Only then did Erica notice how red her sister's eyes were. It looked like she'd been crying.

'Gwen, is everything all right?' Erica's tone of voice became ominously serious. 'What's going on? What's wrong?'

Her sister blinked, but there was no reply.

'Gwen, what the hell? You're starting to scare me now. Will you say something, please?'

Finally, the image began panning out, but strangely enough it stopped before Gwen's face came into full view. Erica frowned. She couldn't see her sister's ears. In fact, she couldn't see past the outside edge of her eyes. She was now certain that her sister had been crying.

'Gwen? What the fuck is going on? Why were you crying? And why is the sound all fucked up?'

. . .

'Talk to me, Sis.'

'There's nothing wrong with the sound,' the distorted voice came again. To Erica, it sounded like some sort of B-horror film demon's voice. 'And your sister can't answer you because she's not allowed to speak,' it continued. 'If she does, she dies.'

Gwen had an unusual sense of humor. Erica knew that well, but this wasn't it. She was a psychiatrist, and one thing that she would never do was play with people's emotions in this sort of way.

'What?' Erica's voice wavered. 'Who is this?'

'I'm nobody. But *you* can be somebody. You can be a hero for your sister. All you have to do is give me two correct answers and all this is over.'

Erica shook her head. 'What? What questions? What are you talking about?'

'You'll see.'

'No, I won't.' Erica sounded angry. 'What I'm doing is calling the cops.'

'Do you really think that the cops can get to your sister's house before I slice her up?' the demon asked.

Suddenly, a gloved hand appeared on the screen, holding a kitchen knife, its tip just millimeters away from Dr. Barnes' left eye.

'I'll start by gouging her eyes out,' the demon continued. 'Then I'll slice her nose off.' The tip of the knife moved to it. 'Then I'll rip the sides of her mouth open all the way to her ears and leave her here, bleeding to death for the cops to find her. How would you like that, Erica?'

Dr. Barnes' eyes were filled with desperate panic, as they tried to focus on the knife. Her mouth opened, readying a scream, but fear silenced her voice.

'Oh, my God!' Erica's heart began crawling up to her throat. Tears welled up in her eyes. 'Gwen.'

'You better listen carefully, Erica, because I'm only going to explain this once. Are you ready?' Without waiting for a reply the demon explained the rules to his game. 'That's it,' he said when he was done. 'Simple, isn't it? All you have to do is answer me. So ... shall we begin?'

Erica was shaking so much she had to hold the phone with both hands.

'Here we go. First question.' To heighten the suspense, the demon added a long, stagnant pause. When he spoke again, his words came out slowly and syncopated. 'What was the last post you uploaded to your social media page?'

Instinctively, Erica's head moved back a couple of inches. She doubted her ears.

'What? *My* last post? What is this? Are you serious?'

On the screen, Gwen's lips began trembling.

'Yes,' the demon replied. 'I'm very serious. You update

your page several times a day with the kind of needless information about your life that no one really cares to know, don't you, Erica?'

Erica looked lost.

'So I want to know what your last totally unnecessary post was about. That was less than five minutes ago, remember? You added a picture to it.' Another pause, this time a lot shorter than the previous one. 'You have five seconds.'

Erica blinked once. Twice. Three times. To her, this made absolutely no sense.

'Four ... three ...'

'Umm ... I posted a picture of my popcorn and my wine, saying that I was just getting comfortable to watch some Sunday night TV.'

The demon stopped counting.

Silence.

Erica waited.

Still silence.

For a moment, Erica doubted her answer. 'Isn't that right?'

'Ha, ha, ha, ha, ha.' The demon laughed such a guttural laugh, Erica felt her blood run cold inside her veins. 'Yes.' He finally accepted it. 'Of course it is, but you doubted yourself for a second there, didn't you?'

Erica felt so relieved, she almost wet herself.

On the screen, Gwen's terrified eyes moved right and stayed there for several seconds. A couple of tears rolled out of them, but Erica was so confused, so lost, she failed to notice something very odd. The tears didn't roll down her cheeks. They rolled to the side of her face.

'Question two. Answer this one right, and this exercise is

over. You and your sister win. Answer it wrong and . . .' The demon didn't finish his sentence.

Erica sucked in a difficult breath of air.

'Your mother's death anniversary, Erica, when is it?'

'What?' Fear exploded inside Erica's mind and heart. 'My mother's?'

This time the demon gave no explanation. He didn't repeat the question. He simply began counting down. 'Five . . . four . . .'

Dr. Barnes' trembling shifted from her lips to her entire face. A second later, she began sobbing violently.

Every year, on the anniversary of their mother's death, Gwen would take flowers to their mother's grave. Erica had tried joining her on her very first visit. At the time, Gwen was fourteen years old and Erica thirteen, but Erica never made it. At the entrance to the Home of Peace Memorial Park, on Whittier Boulevard, Erica froze.

'C'mon, Erica,' Gwen had said. 'Let's go.'

Erica couldn't speak. All she could do was shake her head.

'Erica, c'mon.' Gwen had reached for her arm to lead her sister in with her, but Erica was as rigid as a statue. Her muscles had literally stiffened in place. That was when Gwen noticed how much her sister was shaking, and how sweaty and clammy her face was. Seconds later, she had started hyperventilating.

'Erica, what's wrong?'

Still, Erica couldn't speak. Her eyes had started moving from left to right frantically, focusing on nothing at all, as if she was about to have a seizure.

Erica never made it through the gates. She had to wait on the other side of the road while Gwen said a couple of prayers and placed the flowers they had brought with them on their mother's grave. It was only much later that they found out that their mother's funeral had been such a traumatic experience for Erica that she had developed coimetrophobia – fear of cemeteries. She remembered her mother, but her condition had caused her to push everything related to her death to the absolute edge of her mind.

'Three . . .'

Erica's breathing became labored.

'Two . . .'

She tried to think.

'One . . .'

Nothing.

'Time's up, Erica.'

'No . . . please . . . I . . . I don't know the answer. I have this condition . . .'

'I told you the rules,' the demon cut her short. 'No answer – your sister gets punished.'

'No . . . please . . .'

'And remember, if you look away, she gets punished again. You have to watch it. Now let's have fun.'

Finally, the image on Erica's smartphone widened horizontally, allowing her to see past the edge of her sister's eyes . . .

. . . And what she saw filled her heart with horrifying fear and panic.

Seventy-One

As Hunter parked in front of his six-story apartment block in Huntington Park, he peeked at his watch – it was coming up to 11:00 p.m. He leaned his head back on to the seat's headrest and looked up at the aging building for a moment. By one of the windows on the second floor, an old man sat chain-smoking cigarettes. With every third drag he had, he would cough two or three times before spitting down on to the sidewalk below. On the fourth floor, Margaret Dixon, a very sweet lady in her early fifties, was staring out the window of apartment 416, teary-eyed. Every night, without fail, she would stare out of her window at the road below for several long hours, waiting for her husband to come back from his night shift. Her husband, Philip, had been involved in a work-related accident several years ago. He had died that same night.

A far-away siren dragged Hunter's attention away from the building and he wondered if going home right now was really the best idea. Sleep, if it came at all, wouldn't be until the very early hours of the morning. His brain was still wide awake and he wasn't looking forward to another night either tossing and turning in bed, or pacing the length of his small apartment.

He began contemplating taking a drive down to Santa Monica or Venice Beach when a completely new idea entered his mind. He considered it for just a few seconds.

'Oh, what the hell. Why not?' he said, staring into his own eyes in the rearview mirror. He shrugged and reached for his cellphone.

'Hello,' a female voice replied.

'Hi, is this Tracy?'

'This is she, yes.'

'Hi, Tracy. It's Robert. Robert Hunter?' He thought that he would have to help her out with a little bit more information than just his name, but he was pleasantly proven wrong.

'Oh, the mysterious detective. What a surprise.'

Hunter took that as a good sign.

'Is this a bad time?' Out of habit, he consulted his watch again.

'No. Not at all. I was just about to ... do nothing, really.'

Hunter smiled. 'Funny, me too. Listen, I know it's quite late on a Sunday night, not really the best night for going out, and you probably have lectures in the morning, but I was wondering if you would like to go grab a coffee somewhere.'

'You mean ... somewhere that's not the UCLA library?'

'Preferably not.'

Hunter heard Tracy laugh. The laugh was followed by a short pause.

'I'll tell you what,' she replied at last, 'I have a better idea. Why don't we go somewhere where they serve something a little stronger than coffee? There's a great bar not that far from me. How long will it take you to get to West Hollywood?'

'At this time ... about an hour.'

'OK, so how about I meet you there in an hour?'

'That sounds great.'

Seventy-Two

'Oh, my God, Gwen, what's happening?' Erica Barnes cried out in a voice choking with emotion. 'I . . . don't understand.'

The image on her cellphone screen had stopped zooming out and, though her eyes could now see a more complete picture, her fragile brain struggled to make any sense of it.

Her sister seemed to be lying down on some sort of wooden surface. It was hard to tell because in width, the picture on Erica's cellphone screen didn't show past her sister's shoulders. In length, it didn't show past her breasts, which were fully exposed, and that was where Erica's confusion began. Her sister's phone, the one broadcasting the images, didn't seem to be positioned in front of her. It looked like it had been positioned above her, as if it was somehow hanging from the ceiling, but what really made the scene look absurd was the fact that Gwen's face lay between two huge, serrated iron jaws. That was why, at first, the image didn't pan any wider than the edge of her eyes. The demon didn't want to reveal his murderous device too soon.

'Do you know what this is, Erica?' the demonic voice asked, referring to the strange device.

Erica didn't speak, didn't blink, didn't move. Never in her

whole life, not even on the day that her muscles froze at the entrance to the cemetery, had she experienced fear like that before. It was like her brain had disconnected from the rest of her body.

'This is something I created myself,' the demon continued. 'And I decided to call it ... *The Skull Crusher.* Good name, don't you think?' He laughed the same sickening, throaty laugh from moments ago. 'I guess it can be compared to ... an industrial-size vise, only better.'

'Please ... please ... please ...'

This time, the desperate cries came from Gwen herself. Her sobbing was so intense, Erica could see her entire body shake from the effort.

'Why are you doing this to me? Why?'

'Shush ...' A gloved finger was pressed against Dr. Barnes' lips. 'You're not supposed to speak, remember?'

Dr. Barnes was struggling to breathe, which was something that she could now only do through her mouth. Her nose had completely clogged up.

'Apparently,' the demon said, once again addressing Erica, 'an average human skull can withstand anywhere up to twenty-one hundred pounds of pressure, did you know that, Erica?'

'Please ... don't do this.' Tears and fear had caused Erica's voice to go up almost a whole octave.

'But I must add,' the demon continued, disregarding her pleas. 'I did find that information on the Internet, so there's a chance that it could all be just bullshit.' He paused for effect. 'But let me tell you what's not bullshit, Erica. Every full turn of the crank on this device adds about five hundred pounds of pressure to the jaws. Isn't that beautiful? Can you imagine what these serrated jaws would do to somebody's face?'

In hearing those words, panic, in a way she never knew it could exist, exploded inside Dr. Barnes, spreading like lightning to every atom of her body. As a result, she summoned all the strength she had left in her and tried to free her head from between the jaws, but the demon held her back by powerfully placing the palm of his hand against her forehead.

'This . . .' he said, 'will hurt . . . a lot.'

'Noooooooorghhhh.' The scream that came out of her throat was gurgling in spit and tears.

Erica was watching everything semi-paralyzed. Even her breathing seemed to have stopped.

'Let's have fun, shall we?' the demon said. His right hand reached for the Skull Crusher's crank and he rotated it around – one full turn.

The iron jaws, which were already in contact with the sides of Dr. Barnes' head, began closing in on each other. As they compressed her skull with five hundred pounds of pure pressure, the jagged-edged jaws ripped through her skin. Unimaginable pain caused her eyeballs to stop moving, but her eyes widened as if they were about to explode out of their sockets. The scream she had in her throat died suddenly, as the air was viciously sucked out of her lungs. Her mouth, still wide open, seemed to stutter, with her lower jaw trembling awkwardly in place. The rest of her body began wriggling like a sea snake trying to get away from danger.

With her head now completely immobile, held in place by the powerful iron jaws, the demon moved his palm away from her forehead.

'Annnnnnnnnnnnnnnnnd . . . we're back to the game, Erica.' If not for the digitally altered voice, he would've sounded like a game-show host.

Starved of oxygen, Erica's brain forced her to breathe again. As she sucked in a lungful of air through her mouth and nose, she almost heaved.

'Your mother's death anniversary, Erica,' he asked again, losing no more time. 'When is it?'

Through her tears, Erica could barely see the small screen on her cellphone. She brought a hand to her face to try to wipe them away. It made no difference.

'Five ...'

'I ... don't ... know ...' A heart-melting sob strangled her throat between words.

'Four ...'

'You ... don't ... understand ...'

'Three ...'

'I ... have ... a condition ...'

'Two ...'

'It ... hinders ... my ... memory ...'

'One ...'

'Oh, Gwen ...'

'Time's up.'

On the screen, the demon's hand reached for the crank one more time.

'Nooooooo.'

Another full turn.

Once again, the jaws closed in on each other, but this time, as they started moving, Erica heard a 'pop'. It was a very similar sound to the first 'pop' she heard coming from her microwave less than ten minutes earlier. The main difference was that this 'pop' was followed by a heavy crushing sound.

On the screen, all of a sudden, as tens of blood vessels ruptured beneath the tissue covering the white of Gwen's eyes, they began hemorrhaging and changing color. Her face contorted out of shape – a consequence of both of her cheekbones fracturing.

Another muffled 'pop'.

Gwen's jaw dislocated out of place, distorting her mouth, which was now also filled with blood.

'Oh ... my God.' Erica couldn't look anymore. She closed her eyes and allowed her body to jolt forward violently before vomiting on to the coffee table.

On her small screen, Gwen's body stopped wriggling. Her eyes, now completely bloodshot, twitched one last time before the final breath of life left them.

It was done. Dr. Barnes was no more.

'Sorry, Erica. You lose. I win.'

Erica lifted her head again. Bile dripped from her chin on to the floor between her bare feet. Slowly, her eyes moved back to her cellphone screen. Her sister's face was unrecognizable, crushed between the two large, serrated metal jaws.

'Why?' the question came midway through a sob.

The demon didn't reply, but the camera began moving again. Then, suddenly, the ugliest face Erica had ever seen appeared on the screen. Her head jerked back in shock as she held her phone with both hands.

It wasn't a face. It was a mask.

For some reason that Erica would probably never be able to explain, her brain went into automatic mode and she reacted in a way the demon could never have foreseen.

Seventy-Three

As soon as Mr. J got back into his car, he got on the phone to Brian Caldron.

'Brian, I need you to check something for me.'

There was a labored pause from Brian's side.

'Who is this?' he asked. 'How did you get this number?'

Only then did Mr. J realize that he was still speaking with a heavy northern California accent, and his tone of voice was still half an octave higher than usual.

'Brian, it's me, Mr. J. No one else has this number, you know that.'

'Umm ... sorry, Mr. J. For a moment you sounded completely different there.'

Not wanting to lose any time, Mr. J told Brian about what he had found out in Michael Williams' bedroom. He also sent him a digital picture of Mr. Williams, something he had snapped from a picture frame in Williams' living room.

'I need this ASAP, do you hear me, Brian?'

'Yeah.' Brian's voice was full of hesitation. 'I'll do my best.'

Mr. J didn't like that answer. 'What does that mean, Brian?'

'It means that obtaining information about this case might prove to be a problem.'

'And why is that?'

'Because the LAPD Homicide UVC Unit is running this investigation, and though I've never met them, there's one thing everybody knows about them – those guys trust no one.'

'And how is that my problem?'

'Well,' Brian replied, 'I'm an IT geek. I deal in cyberspace. Yes, I can get you pretty much any information you need, as long as that information exists in cyberspace … and that's where the problem lies with the Ultra Violent Crimes Unit – *they don't trust anyone.* Until they close a case, they keep about ninety-five percent of their investigation off-line. Everything they find out, every lead, every interview, every deduction, all of it, is either kept on paper only, locked inside their office, or worst yet, kept nowhere but inside their own heads. Those guys aren't like normal detectives, Mr. J. They aren't even like normal people.'

Mr. J ran a hand over his mouth and chin a couple of times.

'On an open UVC Unit investigation,' Brian continued, 'all the information that's flying around in cyberspace is only there because it was uploaded by a different department – forensics lab, coroner's, toxicology lab – you know what I'm talking about, right?'

'Yeah.'

'So,' Brian carried on, 'if they run any sort of search from their computers, or a result comes back from any lab, or a photo is sent to them … anything like that, I can easily grab it and send it your way. But whatever they deduce from the results, or the photos, or whatever it is that they get, that will be in UVC Unit-land only and there's no way I can get to it.'

Despite the bad news, Mr. J smiled to himself. Detective Hunter was still surprising him.

'So, do you have anything at all for me?' he asked.

'I do. The woman you asked me to find out about – Karen Ward – she was murdered on Wednesday night, four days ago.'

Another victim, Mr. J thought. *That was why Detective Hunter asked me if I knew her – if Cassandra knew her. He was trying to establish a link between the killer's victims.* 'How? What was the cause of death?'

'Perforation of the temporal lobe, achieved through the left ocular globe cavity.'

'What?'

'She was stabbed through the left eye with a glass shank long enough to reach her brain,' Brian explained. 'Her face was completely mutilated by glass, as if she'd flown, face first, through several windows. I've just emailed you the official autopsy report and all the photographs, together with a file on Ms. Ward. A word of warning, the photographs are shocking.'

'OK. Anything else?'

'Yes, earlier today they began a credit-card transaction check on Cassandra Jenkinson, her husband John Jenkinson, and Karen Ward.'

Mr. J thought about it for an instant. *Detective Hunter is checking for that 'house visit',* he concluded. *Any tradesmen who have been to my house or Karen Ward's house for whatever reason. Whichever names he gets from one credit card, he'll cross-check with the other. Smart. Unlucky for him that Cassandra had paid Michael Williams in cash.*

'OK, Brian, I'll need all the results from this search. Whatever they get, I get. Is that clear?'

'Sure. I'll ghost the search.'

Mr. J jotted down some notes. 'OK, now get started on this Michael Williams. Pull whatever stops you need to pull and find me this sonofabitch.'

The call disconnected.

Mr. J's phone didn't ring again until 9:52 p.m. that night.

Seventy-Four

It took Hunter fifty-three minutes to get to West Hollywood from Huntington Park. As he pulled up in front of the place Tracy had told him about – a cocktail bar called the Next Door Lounge – he saw her at the traffic lights, just about to cross the road.

Tracy looked even more attractive than Hunter remembered. Her bright red hair was loose, falling in beautiful waves past her shoulders. Her fringe once again looped over and above her forehead, this time forming two very gracious victory rolls. She wore black jeans, a white T-shirt under a cropped leather jacket, black Mary Jane shoes and the same old-fashioned, cat-eye glasses she'd worn the first twice they'd met. Her delicate makeup made her look like a pin-up model.

'You walked here?' Hunter asked, meeting her by the lounge's front door.

'I told you, I don't live that far from here.' She pointed west. 'Just a quick fifteen-minute walk.'

'It's a nice area,' Hunter commented.

'It can be,' Tracy agreed.

'Shall we?' Hunter asked, pulling open the door for Tracy.

The Next Door Lounge wouldn't have looked out of place in a film about the prohibition era in America. Its interior carried all the glamour and forbidden excitement of a speakeasy of the 1920s, with shiny floors, Chesterfield leather seats, and a small stage with an old-fashioned piano where artists would perform jazz and ragtime classics. Even the air carried a very gentle scent that seemed to belong somewhere in the past.

On that Sunday evening, the place wasn't very busy, which suited Hunter just fine.

'Would you prefer to sit at the bar or at a table?' he asked.

'I don't mind. You choose.'

'Table,' Hunter said confidently, indicating two high-back winged armchairs by a crude brick wall. As they sat down, a waitress walked over and placed two menus on the table in front of them.

'You're a whisky man, right?' Tracy asked.

'Single malt Scotch,' Hunter replied. 'But do you know what? I feel like having something different tonight.'

'Really?'

'Yeah. Maybe I'll go for a cocktail. Why not?'

Tracy replied with a smile that Hunter found hard to read. 'You're in good hands. They make some great cocktails in here.' She paused and pinned Hunter down with a serious stare. 'But before we order anything.' She took the menu from his hands. 'Before your phone rings on you and you dash out the door like you do, I need answers.'

Hunter sat back, crossed his legs and placed his hands on his lap. 'What answers?'

'Don't play dumb,' she said, with a shake of the head. 'It doesn't fit with your image.'

'You're talking about you being a psychology professor?'

'That's right,' Tracy confirmed. 'How did you know? And how did you know it so fast? As I said last night, I know you didn't figure any of it out from the books I had with me in the reading room that night because none of them were on academia, or on psychology. So how?'

'I think I've answered that question already, haven't I?'

'Ha, ha' Tracy chuckled. 'Your reply was ... "It's just observation".'

Hunter nodded. 'Yes, that's correct.'

'Well, I'm listening. What *did* you observe? Please feel free to be very specific.'

Hunter regarded Tracy for a moment before he began.

'OK, I've seen you at the UCLA library a couple of times before.'

'Yes, I've noticed you there before too,' she came back. 'Always at night. Always at the twenty-four-hour reading room, but I didn't manage to figure out that you were a detective with the LAPD. And, let me add, I never have any psychology reference books with me when I go there. I prepare my lectures in the afternoons or early evenings, never that late at night. And I never prepare them in the library, anyway. I prefer to do it at home. So I know that it wasn't the books that gave it away.'

'Not *your* books.'

Tracy looked puzzled. 'I'm not sure I get it.'

'In the library,' Hunter clarified, 'you're always sitting at a table by yourself, while all the other tables usually have groups of students sitting together. In a public library, sitting by yourself is expected, but in a university library, students sit together.'

'UCLA is a very big university, Robert, with over forty thousand students. And furthermore, when *you* are there, you sit by yourself too.'

'True,' Hunter accepted it. 'And that's where the second observation comes in.'

Tracy looked intrigued.

'I'll admit that the first time I saw you at the reading room, sitting by yourself, I thought that you went to UCLA, but within a couple of minutes, a group of three, maybe four students, walked past your table, said "hello" and carried on to the next available table. They didn't ask if you wanted to join them. They didn't ask if they could join you. That meant that they knew you, but not as a fellow student.'

Tracy finally began catching on.

'The night we met by the coffee machine,' Hunter continued, 'the same thing happened again, but this time one of the students showed you something on her textbook. You looked at it, then smiled and nodded at her. A teacher's confirmation nod, as if you were saying, "Yes, that's right."'

For Tracy it was as if a light had finally been shone on a dark secret. 'And the book she showed me was on psychology,' Tracy said.

'Forensic psychology,' Hunter confirmed.

She smiled. 'That *is* my main field, yes – forensic psychology, hence why I was so intrigued by your powers of observation and deduction.' She paused and looked at Hunter in a peculiar way. 'Thanks for finally clarifying it for me.'

'Am I in the clear now?' Hunter asked, extending his hand. 'Shall we order?'

Tracy handed the drinks menu back to him. 'Yes, I think that would be a good idea.'

Hunter didn't stray that far from home, ordering a Scotch-based cocktail; Tracy went for a rum-based one.

'I guess it's my turn to come clean,' Tracy said, as the waitress walked away with their order. 'I did check you out a little bit.'

'Did you?'

'I was intrigued,' she confessed. 'I wanted to at least find out which LAPD department you were with.'

'And how would you have done that?'

Tracy shrugged. 'I have a few good friends in high places within the LAPD.'

Hunter laughed.

'The Ultra Violent Crimes Unit?' From the way Tracy had phrased her words, Hunter wasn't sure if it had been a question or a statement. He said nothing.

'I must get you to come and talk to my students some day.'

'I'm no teacher,' Hunter replied.

'You don't need to be.'

The waitress came back with their drinks and, for the next fifteen minutes, they talked and laughed about different subjects, none of them related to their jobs. They were just about to order a second round when Hunter's phone rang.

Tracy looked at him dumbfounded, failing to stop the disbelieving smile that came to her lips. She could barely believe that it was happening again.

Hunter took the call and listened for a moment.

'I'm on my way,' he said as he locked eyes with Tracy. The look in them explained more than words could ever do.

'I'm so sorry,' he said, getting up.

Tracy stood up with him, took a step closer and kissed his lips.

'Call me, OK?'

Seventy-Five

Garcia had just arrived at the address he'd been given when he saw Hunter's car appear at the top of the road. He waited for his partner to park before meeting him by the police perimeter.

'Is this guy trying to break a record, or what?' he said, lifting the yellow crime-scene tape for Hunter to stoop under it. 'Three victims in five days?'

Garcia's anger didn't reflect off the killer's actions. It reflected off their failure to advance their investigation. Hunter knew this because he felt the same anger inside him. While they barely had anything worth pursuing, the 'video-call' killer was claiming victims at the speed of light.

Suddenly, Garcia paused and frowned at Hunter.

'What?' Hunter asked.

'Is that red lipstick on your lips?'

'What?' He wiped his lips with the back of his right hand. It came back red.

'It is lipstick.' Garcia gave his partner a cheeky smile. 'Were you on a date?' The surprise in Garcia's voice was real. 'You never told me you were going on a date.'

'It wasn't exactly a date.' Hunter used a paper tissue to

wipe his lips clean and quickly moved the subject away from him and Tracy. 'So, what info do we have on the new victim?'

'Her name was Gwen Barnes,' Garcia said, reading from his cellphone. '*Dr.* Gwen Barnes – thirty-eight years old. Born and raised right here in Los Angeles – Hawthorne.'

'Married?'

'Divorced. No kids. Ex-husband, Kevin Malloy, lives in Pomona. We don't have much on him yet.'

'How long were they married for?' Hunter asked.

'Umm . . .' Garcia thumb-scrolled the information on his cellphone screen. 'Four and a half years. They got divorced just over two years ago.' He thumb-scrolled back up before continuing. 'Dr. Barnes ran her own small psychotherapy practice in downtown LA – West Ninth Street.'

'How long had she been living at this address?'

'Practically since her divorce.' Garcia paused, made a face and shrugged at Hunter. 'That's it. That's pretty much all we've got on her at the moment. Operations hadn't had much time to dig things up. We'll have a more comprehensive file on her by tomorrow afternoon.

'Who did the killer call this time?'

'The victim's only sister,' Garcia replied. 'Erica Barnes.'

'Is she local?'

'Not that far. She lives in Carson.'

'Are you guys with the UVC Unit?' an LAPD sergeant asked, coming up to them. He was about five-foot-ten, with bony shoulders and skinny arms. His dark hair was cut short and neat. His eyes, which were just as dark as his hair, were shaped like sideways teardrops.

'That's us, yes,' Garcia said, facing him and displaying his credentials. Hunter did the same.

'I'm Sergeant Prado from the West Bureau, Wilshire Area Division.' He spoke with a light Puerto Rican accent.

They all shook hands and began making their way towards the single-story, green-fronted house at the end of the street.

'Two of my men were first response here tonight,' the sergeant explained, pointing at two young and pallid-looking uniformed officers by a black and white unit. 'I've got to tell you, this isn't the quietest of neighborhoods, meaning that we get our fair share of violent homicides, but somebody did a job on that poor woman in there in a way I've never seen before. And I take it you've heard about the crazy nine-one-one call that came in, right? Apparently whoever did this called the victim's sister and made her watch over a video-call. Is that sick enough for you guys at UV, or what?'

As they got to the front porch, two media vans rounded the corner at the top of the road.

'The wolves are here,' Sergeant Prado said, jerking his chin at the vans.

Brian Caldron wasn't lying when he told Mr. J that Hunter and Garcia trusted no one when it came to the UVC Unit's investigations. The press paid people inside the LAPD for information, and they paid well. That was the main reason why they keep their investigations off line. When it came to crimes, nothing sold more papers or increased the number of viewers nationwide like a serial-killer story, not even crimes involving Hollywood celebrities. But with the killer now claiming his third victim, keeping the story from leaking to the press had become a virtual impossibility, despite the UVC Unit's efforts. It was now all just a matter of time. The best they could was to try to keep the story under control. The LAPD press office would probably issue an official statement soon. Their key concern now was to keep the details from being exposed.

'Other than you and the two first-response officers,' Hunter asked Sergeant Prado, 'who else has walked the scene?'

'Forensics. That's it. No one else.'

'And who else here knows about the nine-one-one call.'

'No one except myself,' he replied. 'None of the details were passed on by dispatch.'

Hunter fixed the sergeant with a firm stare, but before he was able to say anything, Sergeant Prado nodded, lifting both hands.

'Yeah, yeah, Detective, not a word to the press. I know the drill. This isn't my first time, you know.'

They got to the front of the house and an agent handed both detectives the customary sealed bags containing a disposable white coverall each. In solemn silence, Hunter and Garcia suited up, signed the manifesto, and stepped into the house.

Seventy-Six

As the door closed behind Hunter and Garcia, Dr. Susan Slater, who was standing at the far end of the living room, turned to face them. A couple of feet behind her, the same photographer who had attended the previous two crime scenes was snapping away at something they couldn't yet see. Two other forensic agents were busy dusting surfaces at opposite ends of the room.

'Detectives,' the doctor said in greeting, her head tilting forward slightly. She kept her voice quiet and subdued. 'Over here.' She motioned them closer with a hand gesture, while at the same time signaling the photographer to take a break.

Just like the previous two crime scenes, nothing really seemed to have been disturbed. Nothing looked to be out of place either. If there had been any sort of struggle between the victim and the killer, there was no visible sign of it anywhere.

'No dining chair this time,' Dr. Slater said, taking a step to her left and finally allowing Hunter and Garcia to see what the photographer had been snapping at.

Both detectives stopped dead.

The victim lay naked on top of a six-seater wooden table

in a crucifixion position. Her arms were wide open, pulled at the wrists by two pieces of nylon rope that had been firmly secured under the table. Her legs were also fully extended, with her ankles shackled together by a third piece of rope, but the entire scene was overshadowed by the grotesque disfiguration to her face and skull.

They didn't need an autopsy examination to work out that several of her facial bones had been shattered. Her eyes, wide open and still full of terror, were completely bloodshot and skewed out of line, clearly indicating that her eye sockets and her cheekbones had been fractured. Her jawbone had been broken in at least three places, fissuring her lower and upper gum line and distorting her mouth completely out of place. Her ears, together with the skin on both of her cheeks, had been practically scrapped off, leaving behind a mess of dried blood and flesh. The sides of her skull had sunk in, as if someone had brought a hammer to it, with extreme prejudice.

'You were right, Robert,' Dr. Slater said, breaking the silence and bringing the detectives' attention back to her. 'Once again, the killer has changed several aspects of what at first appeared to be his MO.'

Hunter and Garcia joined Dr. Slater by the left side of the table.

'At least a couple of his signatures are now also becoming very clear,' the doctor continued. 'He microwaves his victims' cellphones and he likes to strip them naked.'

'No sexual assault again?' Garcia asked.

'I haven't checked it yet. We haven't been here that long, but for that I'll need to untie her legs. I was waiting for you guys to arrive because I knew you'd want to see the body *in situ*. But there's no visible bruising to her thighs or groin area.' She indicated as she spoke. 'No scratches either, so chances are that, just like his previous two victims, he hasn't touched her in that way.'

'So why strip them naked?' The question came from the photographer, who was standing across the table from them.

Everyone looked back at him.

'Robert, Carlos,' Dr. Slater said, nodding at the photographer, 'this is Curtis Norton. You might remember him from the previous two scenes. He joined the team a few months ago. Transferred from Anaheim.'

'Pardon the intrusion,' Norton said a little timidly. He was about six feet tall, with a strong frame, a squared jaw and thick eyebrows shaped in a way that made him look like he was constantly sad. 'I'm just curious. We never really got this sort of stuff back in Anaheim, but if the killer's attacks have no sexual motive in them, why strip them naked?'

'Humiliation,' Hunter replied. He had repositioned himself at the head of the table and was carefully studying the injuries to the victim's face and skull. 'The technique was widely used in concentration camps during the Second World War. It's still used today. It makes the victims feel even more vulnerable. More helpless. More frightened.'

'Hard to imagine them feeling any more frightened than what they probably did,' Norton commented.

'This killer's sadism is as psychologically brutal as it is physical,' Hunter clarified. 'He doesn't only torture and murder his victims. He gets into their heads. He nurtures their fear. He toys with their emotions. That's why he stalks them with notes beforehand. But, as we know, he doesn't stop there either because he also likes to get into the heads of others.'

'The people he calls,' Dr. Slater said.

Hunter agreed in silence, as he began studying the table surface.

For a moment, Norton looked like he was about to say or ask something else, but instead he simply stepped away from the table, giving Hunter and Garcia some more space.

'This is insane,' Garcia commented, studying the victim's injuries as he tried to visualize what had happened. 'What did he do this time, put her head in a vise?'

'That would be a pretty good guess,' Dr. Slater confirmed, before explaining: 'The types of fractures inflicted to her facial bones,' she said, indicating the victim's eye sockets, jawline and cheekbones, 'couldn't have been caused by an impact instrument, or by hand, or by smashing her face against a harder surface. All of those methods would've also caused lacerations, of which we have none. These fractures were caused by slowly applying hundreds upon hundreds of pounds of pressure to her skull until the bones cracked inside her. That's why we have these injuries right here on the sides of her face. That's why her skin was practically scrapped off. The jaws of whatever device was used were probably serrated.'

'The table is clean of scratches,' Hunter said. 'No marks at all around where her head is located. A commercial table, bench, or drill-press vise, the type you can easily buy from a hardware store, would've left grooves, marks, scratches . . . something on the table surface, but we've got nothing. Whatever he used, he either created himself, or had it made.'

Through the corner of his eyes, Hunter saw Norton scratch the back of his neck and look away.

Suddenly, the front door was pushed open again and a man

who looked to be in his mid-forties stepped into the house. To everyone's surprise, he wasn't wearing the mandatory Tyvek coverall, which gave away the fact that he wasn't part of Dr. Slater's team. His hair was short, dull and uncombed, and the expression in his eyes, as they circled the room and paused on the body on the table, was one of pure shock.

Hunter immediately realized that he was someone known to the victim, but what he couldn't figure out was how the man had been able to get through the wall of cops outside. He quickly moved towards him, blocking his path and his line of vision.

'Sir, this is an LAPD crime scene. You can't be in here.'

Disregarding Hunter's words, the man lifted his head, trying to look over the detective's shoulders. Hunter moved with him.

'Sir? Did you hear what I said? Who are you?'

The man reached for something that was clipped on to his belt – an LAPD detective's badge.

'I'm Detective Julian Webb with the Central Bureau, Rampart Area Division.'

With over ten thousand officers and more than three thousand civilian staff, the LAPD was the third-largest municipal police department in the United States, just behind the cities of New York and Chicago. Linked to the LAPD, which officially was the police department that served only the city of Los Angeles, were over forty-five other municipal law-enforcement agencies, each with their own hierarchy of command, including officers, detectives, sergeants and captains. In total, the aggregated municipal law-enforcement agencies that formed the LAPD served an area of 498 square miles, and a population of over three and a half-million people. With such a large police department, it was no surprise that neither Hunter nor Garcia had ever crossed paths with Detective Webb.

Hunter and Garcia frowned at the badge. The Central Bureau, Rampart Area Division served the areas of Echo Park, Pico-Union and Westlake. Gwen Barnes' house was located in Mid-City, which fell under the jurisdiction of the West Bureau, Wilshire Area Division.

'Mid-City is way out of your jurisdiction, Detective,' Hunter said. 'How come you're here and so quickly? Did you know the victim?'

Detective Webb was still trying to look past Hunter.

Hunter locked eyes with him. 'Detective?'

'Gwen and I were out on a date earlier this evening,' Webb finally replied. 'I was forced to cut the date short, but I promised her I would come back when I was done. That's why I'm here.' His eyes left Hunter's and moved first to Garcia, then to Dr. Slater. 'This can't be true. I dropped Gwen back here less than three hours ago. I walked her to her door. How can this have happened? I should've listened to her. I should've believed her.'

Webb's last few words made everyone pause.

'What do you mean by that?' Hunter asked.

Silence.

'Detective?' Hunter's voice was commanding. 'What do you mean by – you should've listened to her ... you should've believed her?'

Once again, Webb matched his stare. 'The note ... the bracelet ...'

All of a sudden, before anyone could question Webb further, everyone's attention was grabbed by a loud female voice that was fast becoming hysterical. The voice was coming from just outside the front door.

Hunter immediately realized what was happening.

'The victim's sister,' he said as he signaled Garcia to handle Detective Webb. A second later he was rushing out of the house.

Seventy-Seven

'Erica?' Hunter called, pulling down the hood of his Tyvek coverall. 'Erica Barnes?'

At the house's front lawn, a woman who looked to be in her mid-thirties was frantically fighting being dragged away by two police officers. Her long and straight dark hair was bunched up into a messy bun above her head. Her dark-brown eyes were overflowing with tears, and her small, upturned nose had gone a light shade of pink from all the crying. In hearing her name, the distraught woman hastily jerked her arm away from one of the officer's grip and looked back at Hunter. The expression on her face was a combination of desperation and anguish.

'Let me go,' she screamed at the officers, trying to free her other arm. 'She's my sister.' Her voice was full of pain.

Hunter got to them in no time.

'Sorry, Detective,' Sergeant Prado said, looking a little embarrassed. 'I don't know how she managed to get through the tape.'

'It's OK, Sergeant.' Hunter placed a hand on his shoulder and firmly but tactfully pushed him away from the fragile woman. 'I'll take it from here.'

Sergeant Prado let go of Erica. The officer with him followed suit.

'Are you sure, Detective?'

'Yes, I'm sure.' Hunter had never sounded so confident.

'My sister . . . where's my sister?' Erica cried out, trying to look past Hunter.

He placed a hand on each of Erica's arms, delicately holding her in place. 'Erica, I'm Detective Robert Hunter of the LAPD.' He kept his voice calm and quiet.

Erica wiggled her body away from Hunter's hold. 'Gwen . . . where's Gwen?' She tried to push past him in the direction of the house.

Hunter stepped with her, blocking her path. Their eyes met and all Hunter could do was give her a subtle, but very meaningful shake of the head. 'I'm so sorry, Erica.'

She kept her eyes on his.

'No . . . no . . . no . . . no . . .'

With each new word, Erica punched Hunter's chest with a closed fist. He kept his arms down, offering no defense, allowing all of her emotions to be taken out on him. As her arms finally lost the strength in them, Hunter gently hugged her, bringing her head to his shoulder and turning her around, so she wouldn't be facing the house. She fought him for all of two seconds, before giving in to his embrace.

'It can't be true. It can't.' She exploded into a brand new barrage of tears.

Hunter held her in his arms for a full minute. 'Erica,' he finally said. 'Do you mind if I call you by your first name?'

Erica moved back from his grip and brought a hand to her face, wiping her runny nose with her palm.

Hunter unzipped his coverall and reached inside his pocket for a paper tissue. He always carried them with him.

'Here,' he said.

She hesitated for an instant before finally taking the tissue and blowing her nose. 'Thank you.'

Hunter handed her the whole packet. 'Why don't you keep these? I have more in the car.'

Erica looked lost, her eyes unable to focus on anything.

'How about we go have a seat somewhere?' Hunter said, his head tilting in the direction of the road.

Erica allowed Hunter to guide her towards his car. As he walked past a uniformed officer, he asked him to get them a large glass of sugary water.

They sat inside Hunter's Buick for several long minutes in complete silence. Erica couldn't stop shaking or crying. Hunter gave her all the time she needed. He knew that nothing he could say would lessen the pain she was going through at that moment. Sometimes silence was the best conversation.

The officer finally returned with the glass of sugary water.

'Here, Erica, drink this,' Hunter said. 'It will make you feel a little better. I promise you.'

Erica drank almost the entire glass of water in just a few large gulps.

'I don't understand,' she finally said, looking back at Hunter. Her voice was still unsteady, but not as much as minutes earlier. 'How can that phone call be true? How can that monster be real?'

'Would you like to tell me about what happened? About the monster?'

Erica finished the rest of the water. 'I don't know. I don't know what to say. I'm not sure what is real and what isn't anymore.'

Hunter waited, allowing Erica to dictate the pace.

'I was home alone,' she began, 'just making some pop-corn ...'

For the next twenty minutes, Erica proceeded to tell Hunter everything her memory threw back at her. When she told him about the questions she was asked and about her phobia of cemeteries, panic took hold of her one more time.

Hunter asked the officer for a new glass of sugary water.

It took Erica another five minutes to recompose herself.

Then she told Hunter what she had done.

Seventy-Eight

As Hunter left the crime scene and exited the house, Detective Webb was finally able to focus his stare back on to Dr. Gwen Barnes' body on the dining table. He knew it was her, but her facial disfiguration had been so severe, he just couldn't recognize her.

'This can't be true,' he said again.

'Detective?' This time the imposing call came from Dr. Slater. She walked over to meet him.

Webb blinked once before meeting her stern gaze.

'I can't have you contaminating my crime scene, do you understand me?' She paused and took a breath. Her voice softened a little. 'I am terribly sorry for your loss. I really am. No one should find out about the death of a loved one, or a friend, or anyone this way, but you are an LAPD detective, you should know better than to enter an unprocessed crime scene unprepared and unsuited. I can't have you here. You are compromising not only this crime scene, but this entire investigation.'

'Detective Webb,' Garcia took over, approaching him. 'Why don't we talk outside, and allow forensics to process the scene?' He gestured towards the door. 'They have a lot to do in here.

Maybe you can give me a little more insight on Dr. Barnes. We need all the information we can get on her. You can also tell me about the note and the bracelet you've mentioned.'

Webb's professional side finally took over.

'Yeah, sure,' he said at last. 'I'm sorry I've acted so impulsively.'

'You were just being human, Detective,' Garcia said, his tone friendly and understanding. 'That's what we all are.'

Webb allowed his eyes to rest upon the body on the table one last time, before exiting the house. As they stepped outside, Garcia unzipped his coverall and freed his arms, allowing the top half of the white jumpsuit to hang loosely from his waist. Once they reached the edge of the house's front lawn, Webb reached inside his jacket pocket for his notepad, scribbled something down, tore off the page and handed it to Garcia.

'What's this?' Garcia asked as he read the note.

'My partner's name and badge number. He's the person who I went to meet after I dropped Gwen back here.' Webb reached inside his pocket again, this time for a pack of cigarettes. He tapped one out and brought it to his lips before offering Garcia one.

He declined.

Webb lit his up and took a long drag. 'There's no reason for bullshitting here, Detective . . .?'

'Garcia, but you can call me Carlos.'

'There's no reason for bullshitting here, Detective Garcia. I know how this works. I was the last person to see the victim alive. I was out with her on the night she was murdered and I was the one who drove her home. In short, right now, I *am* the suspect list.' Webb had another drag of his cigarette.

Garcia regarded the man in front of him for a second. Webb did fit the basic description they had of the masked killer – tall, with broad shoulders – but then again, half of the male population of Los Angeles fitted that description.

'This investigation goes a lot deeper than this murder alone, Detective Webb,' Garcia said.

Webb looked back at Garcia, measuring his words before his eyebrows shot up his rugged forehead. 'This guy has killed before.' His intonation didn't make it clear if it had been a question or a statement.

Garcia didn't address it either way.

'Why don't you tell me about this note and bracelet you've mentioned?'

Seventy-Nine

Mr. J snatched the cellphone from the tabletop a millisecond after it started ringing.

'Brian, you sure as hell took your time.' He did nothing to disguise the irritation in his voice.

'Sorry, Mr. J,' Brian replied. *His* voice, on the other hand, sounded fatigued. 'But you managed to pick one slick sonofabitch here. Gathering any sort of info on this guy hasn't been easy ... but we got lucky. *Twice.*'

'So what have you got?'

'You were right in your suspicions. Michael Williams isn't his real name, but the name was picked for a reason.'

'I'm listening.'

'There are over half a million men called Michael Williams in the USA,' Brian revealed. 'Around five hundred and fifty of them live right here, in Los Angeles. It's a common enough name to "escape him out", but ...'

'Hold on, Brian,' Mr. J cut him short. '*Escape him out? What the hell does that mean?*'

'Sorry, it's just a term we use. It means that with nothing else other than just a name to go by, and with approximately five hundred and fifty of them living in this city alone, it would take any law enforcement agency – LAPD, FBI, Sheriff's Department ... it doesn't matter – days, maybe even weeks to track the correct individual down, if at all. That time frame would be more than enough for him to disappear ... escape.'

'OK, so you were saying that Michael Williams is a common enough name to "escape him out", but—'

'But not common enough to raise suspicion if he applies for false documentation.' Brian decided to explain it better. 'Certain names are flagged by our government for being way too common – John or James Smith, Robert Jones, Michael Williams – basically, any name that totals over one million in the country gets flagged. Those are the names that top the "escape out" list because they're also the ones criminals use the most, for obvious reasons.'

'OK, so getting back to our Michael Williams,' Mr. J urged Brian.

'Yeah, OK, as I've said, we've got lucky twice here. One – if you hadn't sent me that photograph of him, we wouldn't be having this conversation. Not now, probably not ever. But with a picture, I was able to run a face-recognition program against some of our databases, and that was where we got lucky for the second time.'

'He's got a record,' Mr. J said.

'He did four years for sexual assault,' Brian confirmed. 'Quite a violent case too.'

Mr. J closed his eyes, trying to keep his calm, but he could feel his blood starting to boil inside his veins. Back at Michael Williams' house, inside the suitcase he had retrieved from under his bed, Mr. J had found a varied collection of women's underwear. Panties, to be more precise. The sizes ranged from six to sixteen. Michael Williams wasn't only a sexual predator. He was a trophy collector too, and that was when it dawned on him. Cassandra had been stripped naked, but her clothes hadn't been found.

'So who the fuck is he, really?' Mr. J asked.

'His real name's Cory Russo. I'm just about to send you his whole file. The guy is a scumbag, no doubt about that, but he's quite a clever scumbag.'

'And why is that?'

'While inside, he acquired three diplomas – plumbing engineering, mechanical engineering, and Internet security.'

'Yeah, well, that won't save him. Do you have an address on him?'

'That's the problem,' Brian said. 'Mr. Russo hasn't used his real name since his release, three years ago. I've got nothing showing under that name. The only address under the false name of Michael Williams is the one you gave me, together with his business one, the plumbing company.'

Mr. J knew that Michael Williams, Cory Russo, whoever he was, wouldn't be going back to either of those two addresses. He now believed that the police were after him, and the first thing that the police would do would be to stake out both of those addresses.

'Whoever this guy is,' Mr. J said, 'he's hiding somewhere, and I need you to find him, Brian. I need you to find him now.'

Eighty

'She managed to take a photo of the killer?' Garcia's tone of voice matched the stunned expression on his face. 'How?'

'No, not a photo,' Hunter clarified, handing his partner Erica Barnes' cellphone. Displayed on its screen was an image of the killer's masked face. 'She captured a screenshot at the end of the call.'

Erica was still sitting inside Hunter's car, just a few feet from where they were standing. Her eyes were puffy and red, with the skin around them raw from all the tears.

'Erica is a graphic designer,' Hunter explained. 'She works for a company that designs and develops applications for mobile devices. Capturing cellphone screenshots is something she does tens of times a day. It's part of her job.'

'So her brain is conditioned to do it,' Garcia said.

'Exactly. It was a reflexive movement, not a conscious one. Erica didn't even realize she had done it until she got off the phone with the emergency operator.'

Garcia's gaze moved to Erica for a split second before returning to the grotesque mask on her cellphone screen.

From Tanya Kaitlin and Mr. J's description, Garcia already

knew what to expect. He knew what the killer's mask looked like – the deformed, red-colored eyes, the lacerated mouth, the blood-smeared teeth, the lumpy and leathery skin, the mutilated nose ... all of it. Their sketch artist had created a very accurate composite image of it, but still, looking at the actual mask on that screenshot sent a nauseating taste down to his stomach.

'Is this the only image she managed to capture?' he asked.

'No,' Hunter replied. The look in his eyes changed. 'She got one more, about halfway through the call. Swipe back.'

As Garcia did, his heart seemed to shrink inside of him.

On the captured screenshot, Dr. Gwen Barnes was still alive, but the white of her eyes were already dusted with blood, with most of her face fractured and twisted out of shape. Death had already closed its ugly fingers around her. All that was left was one final squeeze.

Garcia studied the image for a very long moment.

'You were right,' he finally said, rubbing the skin between his eyebrows with one of his knuckles, his voice solemn. 'The vise-like device he used looks handmade. He didn't get this from any hardware store. He created it himself.'

'Just like he created the mask,' Hunter agreed as he watched another news van pull up at the top of the road.

'So what's happening with her?' Garcia nodded at Erica before handing the cellphone back to Hunter.

'We can't get hold of her boyfriend for him to come pick her up, so I'm going to drive her home.'

'Then what?'

'Then I'm taking these screenshots to Dennis Baxter from the cybercrime unit. If needs be, we'll break them down pixel by pixel.'

'What for?' The intrigue in Garcia's voice was real. 'There's nothing to be found in them, Robert.'

Hunter looked down at the cellphone in his hands, then at Erica sitting inside his car. When he spoke again, his voice lacked confidence. 'We don't know that yet.'

'Yes, we do,' Garcia countered. 'This killer is too clever, Robert, we both know that. He kills his victims inside their own homes, which means that there is no detail you can isolate in any of those two images that can lead us to a location, because we're already here.'

Hunter stayed silent.

Garcia pointed at the phone in Hunter's hand. 'That living room ... that dining table ...' he then pointed at Dr. Barnes' house, '... is the living room in there. The dining table in there. We already know where those images originated from. This killer also creates his own mask. He creates his own murderous devices, which again means that nothing in those images can lead us to a place where he has purchased anything. And to finish it all off he uses his victims' cellphones to make his video-calls, which means that there's nothing to trace, Robert. Nothing to listen to.'

'Yes, I know,' Hunter admitted, his tone half defeated. 'But what else am I supposed to do, Carlos?'

'Go home, Robert. Get some rest. You've barely slept in four days. We'll pick everything up again tomorrow. Even if only a few hours, you need the break. Your brain needs the break, and we all need you to be sharp and on your toes. Exhausting yourself, chasing something that isn't there, won't help.'

Hunter looked like he was considering his options. 'What are *you* going to do?' he asked.

Garcia jerked his chin in the direction of the house. 'I'll stay with the scene until everything here is done. Then I'll go home and I'll get some rest as well.'

Hunter noticed that Erica was starting to get fidgety again.

'Go on, Robert,' Garcia said, 'take her home then go home and get some rest. I'll wrap up here.'

Hunter watched his partner zip up his coverall and make his way back to the crime scene.

Eighty-One

His wristwatch read 11:23 p.m., when Mr. J's cellphone rang again.

'Brian, tell me you've got something.'

'I'm not really sure.' The fatigue in Brian's voice was evident. 'It could be something, or absolutely nothing.'

'Give me whatever you have.'

Mr. J heard fast keyboard clicks coming from the other end of the line.

'OK,' Brian began, 'what you told me got me thinking. Cory Russo, Michael Williams, whatever name this guy is using, he's now probably on the run, right? And in America, you can't run without money.'

'You flagged his credit cards.'

'I flagged everything under both names,' Brian confirmed. 'Credit cards, bank transactions, money withdrawals, the lot, so unless he has some hard cash stashed away somewhere, this guy won't be able to buy a pack of gum without my computer screen turning into a Christmas tree here.'

'And did you get a hit?' Mr. J asked.

Brian breathed out heavily. 'I did, but not on any of his cards.'

Mr. J made a face at his phone. 'What the hell does that mean?'

'Well, I didn't put a flag only on *his* credit cards and bank transactions ...'

'You extended it to family and known friends too,' Mr. J said, catching up with Brian's line of thought.

'Well, that was the idea,' Brian admitted. 'But unfortunately all we've got on Cory Russo are two distant relatives, both living in Oregon, and no known friends, but then I thought of something else.'

'And what was that?'

'Three years ago, when Cory Russo was released from prison, he didn't take the prison bus. He was picked up.'

A smile threatened to appear on Mr. J's lips. 'And you have the name of the person who picked him up.'

'That I do.' Brian's voice sounded triumphant.

'And who is he?'

'His name is Toby Bishop. He lives in Monrovia in San Gabriel Valley, and here is where it gets good. About twenty minutes ago, he withdrew twenty-five hundred dollars from his account. I've checked his withdrawal history going back two years. He has never withdrawn anywhere close to that amount, so unless he decided to buy a car this late at night ...'

'Do you have an address?'

'You should be getting an email right about now.'

Mr. J heard a bell coming from his laptop. He killed the call.

Eighty-Two

Hunter had every intention of following Garcia's advice. After dropping Erica Barnes back at her place, the idea really was to drive home and try to get some sleep, but the two screenshots Erica had captured on her cellphone were playing havoc with his mind, so Hunter decided to do a quick detour and stop by his office.

He had emailed himself the two screenshots from Erica's cellphone as he dropped her off, being sure to also delete them from her phone's 'Image Gallery'. The media had now definitely caught the scent of blood, and if they ever got word that those two screenshots existed, they would do just about *anything* to get their hands on them.

Once Hunter's computer finished booting up, he quickly found Erica's email and double-clicked on the first of the two attached images – the killer's horror mask.

Despite how terrifying, how sickening the mask looked, it was practically a work of art, crafted out of silicone rubber. The facial laceration that ran from the right corner of his lips, across his cheek and all the way to his right ear looked fresh, as if it'd been made into real flesh just moments earlier. Hunter almost expected blood to come pouring out of it.

The mask's sharp, blood-smeared teeth looked half-human, half-animal, but very real. The exposed lower jawbone and nose were incredibly detailed, with the eyes, covered by two blood-red sclera contact lenses, indeed looking like they belonged to a dem—

Hunter's heart picked up speed, as adrenaline flooded his veins with such intensity it made his whole body shiver, because that was when he saw it.

Eighty-Three

The address Mr. J was given by Brian Caldron took him to the edge of Monrovia, on the foothills of the San Gabriel Mountains. The road, a hilly street on a residential area where California oaks shaded the sidewalks, was desert quiet, which suited Mr. J just fine. He paused under a tree at the entrance to the road and spent five minutes taking everything in. At that time of night, most of the houses had all their lights switched off, with the exception of two. One of them was the house he was looking for.

Mr. J pulled the hood of his black jacket over his head, cracked his knuckles and began making his way to number 915. He walked at a normal pace. Not too fast. Not too slow. His shoes, black and with anti-squeak soles, made absolutely no noise. His gloved hands were firmly tucked into his pockets, where he carried the same weapon he had with him earlier, a Sig Sauer P226 Legion, and a small hunting knife for good measure.

As he approached the house, Mr. J quickly turned around, making sure that the road was still deserted. Satisfied, he finally crossed the front lawn in the direction of the side wooden door that led to its backyard. The lock on the door was old, the wood not too sturdy. One firm kick and the door would fly open, but Mr. J wanted to avoid the noise. It took him less than five seconds to climb over it to the other side.

The house's backyard was nothing more than a rectangular patch of green grass – no swimming pool, no garden, no flowers, no shed, nothing. Mr. J quietly stepped on to the back porch, avoided the squared window that looked into the kitchen, and flattened his back against the wall to the left of the back door. No lights were on inside or outside, which placed the entire porch in a dark shadow. On the floor, by the two short steps that led down from the porch, an ashtray was overflowing with cigarette butts and joint tips. Mr. J was about to try the handle on the door, when the lights in the kitchen came on. His back returned to the wall and he waited.

He heard the fridge door open and close.

He heard a screw top twist.

Then the back door was pulled open.

Mr. J waited.

The porch lights didn't come on.

The man who stepped outside wasn't Cory Russo, but he was tall and carried enough gym muscle mass to look like he would put up a good fight, but Mr. J had no intentions of getting into one. Still cloaked by dark shadows, he pulled his silenced weapon out of his right pocket.

The man walked over to where the ashtray was and sat down at the edge of the porch. He reeked of marijuana. His arms were the hairiest Mr. J had ever seen. From his shirt pocket, the man took out an already rolled-up joint that was as thick as his index finger. He lit it up and sucked in a drag that seemed interminable. When the man began exhaling, Mr. J made his move.

The man never saw him coming.

He never heard a thing.

As he was about to take a sip of his beer, Mr. J placed the barrel of his gun against the man's nape.

'I'm going to ask you a few questions,' he whispered by the man's left ear, his voice calm as a priest's, but firm as a drill sergeant's. 'You either nod or shake your head. You make any other movement other than that and you won't have a head to shake or nod with anymore, is that clear?'

With the huge joint still held between his thumb and index finger, the man nodded once.

'Is Russo in the house?' Mr. J asked.

The man hesitated.

Mr. J cocked his gun. 'Is Russo in the house?'

The man nodded once.

'Is he alone?'

The man nodded once.

'Is he awake?'

The man nodded once.

'Is he in the living room?'

The man shook his head.

'Is he in the bedroom?'

The man shook his head.

'Is he in the bathroom?'

The man nodded once.

Mr. J smiled. There was nothing easier than sneaking up on someone when they were in the bathroom.

'Thank you, and good night,' Mr. J said.

Before the man was even able to frown, Mr. J hit him

across the back of the head with the butt of his gun. He had done that so many times before, he knew exactly where to hit and how much strength to put into it.

With a painful 'urghh', the man slumped forward – unconscious.

Mr. J put out the man's joint, cracked his knuckles and, like a silent rat, entered the house.

Eighty-Four

Hunter squinted at the image on his computer screen before blinking once, twice, three times.

'What the hell is that?' He sounded confused within himself, but he wasn't imagining it. There was something there. Something in the killer's eyes that sent goose bumps up and down his spine.

Many people believed that a person's eyes were 'the windows to their soul'. Hunter wasn't sure if he believed that or not. He wasn't sure if this killer even had a soul. What he believed – what he knew – was that a person's eyes could reveal a lot about that person's personality. It could reveal their identity.

Hunter leaned forward on his desk and brought his face to just a couple of inches from his screen.

'Is that a smudge?' The loud question was thrown at an empty office.

Whatever it was, it was still too small for him to be able to tell.

Like a rocket, Hunter's hand shot to the computer's mouse. With two clicks he enlarged the image to ten times its original size, until all he had on his screen were the killer's eyes.

He blinked one more time, feeling something flip inside his stomach.

What he was looking at wasn't a smudge.

'I'll be damned!'

The picture had pixelated, which was expected after enlarging it tenfold, but he didn't even need to alter the color saturation on the image. He didn't need to call Dennis Baxter at cybercrime, or hurry the picture to IT forensics, because there it was, on the inside corner of the killer's left eye, sitting halfway between the tear duct and the iris – a small, but very distinctive, blood clot, shaped almost perfectly like an upside-down heart.

Still, just to be sure he wasn't seeing things, Hunter called up the filtering palette on the image application he was using. He was no expert, but he knew enough to be able to smooth out a pixelated image. It took him less than a minute to get it to the point of no doubt.

Hunter sat staring at his computer monitor, completely transfixed by a small blood splatter that in real life wouldn't be any larger than three millimeters, if that.

But what knotted his throat, what made Hunter's heart thump erratically against the inside of him, was the fact that that wasn't the first time his eyes had rested on that upside-down, heart-shaped blood clot.

Hunter had seen it before.

Eighty-Five

The odds of two people having identically shaped blood clots at the exact same spot on the sclera of their eyes were one in sixty million. Hunter had to look that up.

He pushed his chair away from his desk, stood up, took a couple of steps back and stared at his screen again.

He could feel his legs shivering under him.

'Where? Where have I seen it before? Where?' He urged his brain to remember, but that was something that Hunter had never been able to control. He had always been highly perceptive, even as a kid. His eyes would notice the smallest of details on people, objects, locations, images, whatever, but his brain, fearing an overload, would automatically push what it considered to be 'excess information' into his subconscious mind. Once there, retrieving it wasn't a fun game. That aside, Hunter also faced a second challenge – the number of faces he had seen in the past few days, even in the past few hours, had been overwhelming.

Once Dennis Baxter sent him the two bogus social-media identities he'd requested earlier, Hunter had spent the rest of the day browsing through social media sites. He had started with the victims' pages. He looked through all their photos, and scanned through all their posts going back two years. That done, he moved on to the people who the killer had called and did the same. More photos. More posts. After that he began cross-referencing the victims' friends.

Hunter wasn't really sure what he was looking for, but he was certain that the killer had been using social media sites to acquire information on his victims, so maybe, if he was lucky, something would catch his eye. The result had been an image overload but, in one of them, he had seen that same upside-down, heart-shaped blood clot. In one of them, he had seen the killer. He was sure of it.

Hunter knew that there was no easy way of doing this. He would have to start browsing through everything again. He took a deep breath, stretched his six-foot frame to try to get rid of the muscle stiffness, and got back to his computer.

As he dumped himself on to his chair and began typing, his right elbow brushed against some files that were at the edge of his desk, sending everything to the floor. Pages and photographs scattered by his feet in all directions. Hunter reached for them, but as he picked up an old report, the entire room span around him.

'I'll be damned,' he whispered almost catatonically, because that was when he realized that he had been wrong. He had been very wrong.

Hunter hadn't seen that upside-down, heart-shaped blood clot on a photograph over the Internet.

He had seen it face to face.

Eighty-Six

With his silenced Sig Sauer in hand, Mr. J crossed the empty kitchen and paused by the door that led into the living room. No lights were on. He listened for an instant, but the only sound polluting the air around him was the incessant low humming of the old refrigerator pushed up against one of the corners in the kitchen. He peeked around the door, studying his next move.

The living room was small and uncluttered, which made things easier, because he needed to get to the short corridor on the other side of it. Five quick and silent steps got him there. Still no signs of Cory Russo.

Mr. J regarded the hallway before him. It offered four doors – two on the right, one on the left, and one at the far end of it. The one at the far end was wide open, with the lights switched off, as was the first door on the right. The other two were shut, but a sliver of bright light escaped from under the door on the left.

Mr. J stepped into the hallway and flattened his back against the left wall, before sidestepping four paces until he reached the door. He held his breath, placed his ear against it and listened carefully. Someone was definitely in there.

Mr. J stepped forward, away from the wall, and positioned himself directly in front of the door. Out of habit, he looked left, then right, before taking a deep breath and holding it in his lungs for a couple of seconds. With his left leg firmly grounded, he sent a kick to the door's handle so powerful, the entire frame cracked.

Cory Russo, who was sitting on the toilet, flipping through a porn magazine, jumped back from the fright so hard, he smashed his head against the wall behind him, almost knocking himself out. The magazine fell to the floor. Russo came crashing back down against the toilet seat with a horrified look on his face.

'Hey, big guy,' Mr. J said, his gun pointed directly at Russo's forehead. 'So what do you say, want to try that kick to my chest again?'

Mr. J was wearing the exact same disguise he'd worn earlier when he'd knocked at Russo's door.

Russo looked back at Mr. J, still a little groggy from the head slam. 'Fuck, man.' His eyes moved down to his bare legs for a quick second. 'This is undignifying.'

'You think?' Only then did Mr. J catch a whiff of the smell in the room. His face screwed up. 'Goddamn, man, did you just crap a rotten animal carcass?'

'What?' Russo couldn't see the moment as a time for jokes.

'I told you I would find you, didn't I?' Mr. J said.

Russo frowned at him.

'Not that tough without that fucking mask, are you?'

The look inside Russo's eyes hardened. He still hadn't recognized him over his disguise, but he finally knew what Mr. J was talking about.

Eighty-Seven

A subconscious memory could be triggered back into the conscious mind by just about anything – an image, a sound, a smell, a place, a name ... there really was no telling, and that was what had happened inside Hunter's head. As he bent down and reached for the scattered files on the floor, his eyes settled on a lab report sheet, and something that was right at the top of the page opened a direct pathway to the memory he was searching for. It had indeed been a detail his eyes had noticed, but his brain had discarded as unessential, sending it straight into his subconscious, but he now knew that he hadn't noticed that detail on a photograph.

The memory Hunter was searching for didn't trickle back into his mind like he'd hoped it would. It smashed against it like an ugly train wreck. One second he had nothing, the next ... there it was, the eyes, the blood clot, the face.

'No way,' Hunter whispered, fighting the memory inside his head, because what it was telling him was that he had been that close to the killer, that he had looked into his eyes, that they had shared the same breathing space.

Hunter disregarded the files and photographs on the floor and reached for a blue folder that was sitting to the left of his computer screen. It didn't take him long to find what he was after.

He looked back at the enlarged image on his monitor and studied the killer's eyes again. Inside his head, the memory began colliding with reason, but if there was one thing that Hunter knew well, it was that reason and violent murder rarely crossed paths. Still, a memory wasn't enough. He needed more information, and he needed more information now.

Hunter minimized the image-viewing program and called up a different application. As it loaded up, he typed in the name he got from the blue folder and hit 'enter'. A few seconds later, he had that person's basic personal file on his screen, including a portrait photograph.

The first thing Hunter did was enlarge the photo and look into that person's eyes.

No blood clot.

He enlarged the picture further.

It wasn't there, but Hunter knew that a blood clot could appear in someone's eye at any time and for a number of reasons. All that was needed was for that person to suffer any sort of trauma that would cause the delicate blood vessels beneath the tissue covering the white of the eye to break.

The picture Hunter was looking at had been taken seven years ago. The blood clot could have appeared in his eye any time after that.

Despite knowing all that, doubts had started coming at Hunter from all angles. Was he really that desperate for a lead that his brain had given him a fantasy dressed up as a memory?

It was very possible, he knew that much, but why that person? And why did the memory feel so vivid in his mind?

Hunter minimized the portrait photo, went back to the person's personal file and began scanning through the information on the pages – name, address, place of birth, marital status and so on, but it wasn't until he got to the third page that something made him pause. Something about an accident.

'Wait a second ... What?'

He went back to the top of the page and read it again, slower this time. The information was flimsy at best, but it did provide him with a couple of important details he could use to run a more refined search. Intrigued, Hunter did exactly that.

The file the search returned wasn't very long, but the information and the photographs it contained shocked Hunter for two reasons. One: The devastating sadness of it all was life-changing. Two: If Hunter was right about the killer, this had to have been the trigger.

Suddenly, as he read the file for the second time, Hunter remembered a couple of photographs he'd seen while browsing through one of the social media sites that afternoon.

A lump lodged itself in his throat.

'You've got to be joking,' he whispered, already doubting the crazy theory that had just begun taking shape inside his head.

He quickly reloaded his browser and logged back into that same social media website. This time, he knew exactly whose pages to look for. There was no blind searching.

It took him about five minutes to find the first photo, and as he did, he felt as if his office walls had begun closing in on him.

'This can't be it.'

Stunned, Hunter moved on to somebody else's profile page and their 'photos' tab. He scrolled through the images until he found the one he was looking for.

'Oh, my God!'

Both pictures, despite coming from two different pages and belonging to two different people who didn't know each other, shared the same theme.

'This is nuts.'

His heart began sounding like a kick drum, but he wasn't done yet. They now had three victims. Three different people. Three different social media pages to check.

'Be wrong, Robert,' he said to himself, as he typed the third and last name into the search box. 'Be wrong.'

The page loaded and Hunter moved straight on to the 'photos' tab. His eyes began scanning the thumbnails like a lion searching for prey – forty, sixty, one hundred pictures – nothing. It wasn't there. One hundred and ten, one hundred and twenty – no. His crazy theory was just that, a crazy theo—

'No way.' The walls closed in further. His finger moved off the scrolling ball on his mouse as his eyes locked on to a specific thumbnail.

'No, no, no.'

He maximized it.

There it was, a photograph with the exact same theme of the two previous ones he'd just seen.

Hunter stepped away from his computer and started pacing the room. He could feel his muscles tensing up on him. He could feel a headache starting to grab the base of his skull.

The clock on the wall read 01:54 a.m.

His mind felt tired. Exhausted, actually. There was

nothing that Hunter wanted more right then than to go home and be able to fall asleep, but the key words were 'be able to'.

He paused before the picture board and stared at all the photos for a long while. The victims, the video-call witnesses, the savagery of the crime-scene shots. There were pieces missing everywhere and he knew he wouldn't find them by pacing the length of his office, or sitting behind his desk.

He considered what to do next.

Improvise, Robert, a voice said from deep inside his head. *Improvise.*

Eighty-Eight

Hunter had no problem finding the house, a brick-fronted, two-story, family home with a well-cared-for front lawn and perfectly shaped hedges. The house was in total darkness, with the exception of a dim light that bathed the porch in a weak yellow glow.

A note by the doorbell read 'not working'. Hunter gave the door three firm knocks and waited. No reply. He tried again, the knocks a little firmer this time. Still no reply. He stepped back from the porch and looked up at the house. No lights. No movement. No sound.

What are you doing here, Robert? You should go home. The 'sensible' half of his brain decided to engage in conversation. He paid it very little attention and skipped over the hedge fence that surrounded the front garden before trying the window on the left – locked, and the closed curtains kept him from seeing inside. He had no better luck with the window on the right.

It's a sign, Robert. Go home. Sensible half was back.

Hunter walked around to the right side of the house, where he found a door with a large frosted-glass window. Through the frosted glass he couldn't see much, except that the door looked to lead into the kitchen.

Hunter paused and considered his options for a short instant, before taking off his jacket and rolling it around his right fist. He looked left, then right. All quiet. He held his breath, steadied his legs and sent a firm punch through the frosted window. It smashed with a muffled crash. Instinctively, Hunter looked around again. Still all quiet.

'Awesome,' he said to himself. 'Breaking and entering, followed by an illegal house search. The captain is going to love this.'

Hunter retrieved a latex glove from his pocket, gloved up, slipped his hand through the broken glass and unlocked the door. After pulling his pen flashlight from his gun holster, Hunter stepped into the house.

He quickly cleared the dark kitchen, surfacing in a spacious living room decorated with a combination of antiques and modern furniture. A staircase at the south end of it led to the house's second floor. Hunter decided to check upstairs later.

Now that you're in here, Robert, he asked himself. *What the hell are you actually looking for? Do you have any idea?* He got to the door at the other side of the living room. It led him into a den with leather seats, plush white rugs and a tall bookcase. The east wall was framed entirely by full-length windows, looking out into the house's backyard. Hunter checked some of the titles on the bookcase and a pit started forming inside his stomach. There were books on medicine, electronics, mechanical engineering, information technology, law, forensic psychology, forensic investigation and police procedure.

'It looks like he likes to research,' Hunter said. He was about to go back on himself and check the rooms upstairs, when he noticed a wooden door by the other end of the bookcase. Faint spots of light were coming from underneath it. Cautiously, he walked over, flattened his ear against the door and listened for a moment – some sort of low droning noise was coming from the other side.

Hunter tried the door – unlocked. As he twisted its handle, he felt his heart pick up speed inside his chest. An uncomfortable tingling sensation began rubbing the back of his neck, as if trying to warn him about something. This time he tried to listen, but the sensible voice inside of him had said its piece and was now long gone.

Hunter reached for his gun.

The door opened without a single squeak, revealing a narrow flight of concrete stairs going down into some sort of basement. The stairs were lit by a single light bulb that hung from a wire above Hunter's head. The air was damp and soiled with a musty smell. At the bottom of the stairs, another closed door.

Hunter took the steps down one at a time, being extremely cautious not to misplace a foot and slip. His grip tightened around the handle of his semi-automatic, and as he got to the bottom, his eyes ping-ponged from one door to the other several times. He stood still for a while, listening for any sort of sound. Still, all he could hear was the low droning noise coming from somewhere on the other side of the new door.

Hunter wiped his forehead with the back of his gun hand and tried the door handle – unlocked. He pushed the door open just enough for him to be able to take a peek inside. He didn't need his flashlight anymore. At the other side of the door, a large basement room sprawled out before his eyes. There were several shelving units lining the walls to his right and left, with different-sized boxes occupying every inch of space on them.

Without twitching a muscle, and keeping his breathing as steady as he could, Hunter observed from the door for two full minutes. Nothing. No movement. He took a deep breath, steadied his trigger finger and stepped inside.

The large basement was lit by two fluorescent tube lights, parallel to each other on the ceiling. The droning sound seemed to be coming from somewhere behind one of the shelving units at the other end of the room.

Hunter took tiny steps forward. With each step, his eyes scanned and re-scanned his surroundings as if he was point in a Delta team, but with so many units and boxes, he might as well be walking into a minefield.

The tingling sensation at the back of his neck intensified.

After his tenth step, something to Hunter's left caught his eyes and he stopped moving. His gaze shot in that direction and towards the large board that had been fixed to the wall.

As he realized what he was actually staring at, his blood froze in his veins.

'Oh ... fuck ...'

Eighty-Nine

Cory Russo was still looking at Mr. J with firm steady eyes.

Mr. J stared back at him calmly, his gun still aimed at his forehead. He didn't mind the defiant look in Russo's eyes or the challenging smirk on his lips. He'd seen it before so many times, he actually enjoyed it, because he knew that soon, very soon, that defiance, that smirk, the entire 'badass' attitude, would vanish. In its place would come petrifying fear, and a hell of a lot of begging and crying.

Mr. J reached into his pocket and took out a small, wallet-sized photograph.

'Remember her?'

Russo's eyes settled on the picture for no longer than three seconds. 'Nope. Never seen the bitch before.'

Mr. J had been staring straight at Russo's eyes. He saw the recognition in them. He saw the lie coming.

'Is that right?'

Russo matched his stare.

Mr. J didn't ask again. He simply squeezed the trigger on his pistol. The nine-millimeter round missed Russo's left ear by a mere fraction, exploding against the white tiles behind him and sending shards and dust flying in the air. Mr. J had missed on purpose.

Russo's hand shot up to his ear like a rocket.

There it was, the vanishing of the defiant grin. The crumbling of the badass attitude. The crying would come soon.

'What the fuck, man?' Russo yelled. 'Are you fucking nuts?'

Another squeeze of the trigger. This time, the bullet missed Russo's right ear. More shards. More dust.

Up came the other hand. 'Fuuuuuuuck. What are you doing? Stop, man. Stop.'

Mr. J said nothing. He simply tapped his finger on the photograph.

'OK, man, OK,' Russo said. 'You've got the wrong guy, though. She wasn't one of mine.'

Mr. J found the answer a little odd. 'One of yours? You better start talking plain English.' He nodded with the barrel of his gun.

'Yeah, man, she wasn't one of mine,' Russo said again. 'She was supposed to be one of Toby's.' His chin jerked up slightly.

'No. That still makes no sense,' Mr. J said.

Russo saw the determination in Mr. J's eyes and knew that he was about to squeeze the trigger again.

'Wait, wait!' he yelled, lifting his hands in surrender. 'That's how we did it, man,' Russo began, his voice a lot less steady. 'I scouted the ones for him, he scouted the ones for me, then we'd swop info. We live across town from each other and we thought that there was no way anyone could link the women back to us. On his nights, I made sure that I was in a place full of people, and I made sure that they remembered me, you know what I'm saying? On my nights, he did the same.' Russo paused and nodded at the photograph. 'But Toby never got to her, man. I did scout her out for him, yes. Gave him her picture and all, but he never did her, man. Not yet. She was ... still to come.'

Mr. J was stunned. He now realized that he had the wrong guy. Cory Russo was a scumbag, but not the scumbag who had murdered Cassandra. He and his pothead friend, Toby, were two sack-of-shit rapists, who had devised a cunning plan so as not to be caught. In his job as a plumber, Russo would no doubt visit several homes a week. Toby would have a similar kind of job and did the same. They would then pick victims out for each other, probably based on some sick criteria. They would swop information, then choose a day. When Russo was out raping some poor woman that Toby had chosen for him, Toby would be at a bar, or at a park ... somewhere with lots of people, and he would make sure that he was noticed. If the victim reported the crime, and Mr. J knew that the sad reality in the USA was that less than 50 percent of rape victims would report the attack, there was a chance that the investigating team would come knocking on Toby's door, but Toby would have a number of witnesses who could vouch for his whereabouts on the day or night of the crime. The process would work the other way around when Toby was out raping.

A brand-new pit of hate began digging its way through Mr. J's heart.

'What was the time frame?' Mr. J asked. Despite his anger, his voice remained unaltered.

'What?'

'The time frame. How long between the picking of the victims and the attack?'

Russo stayed quiet.

Big mistake. Mr. J squeezed the trigger for the third time. This one exploded against Russo's right hand, splattering blood and flesh against the wall, fracturing several bones, and severing two fingers. They bounced against the cold tiled floor.

Russo went flying back, crashing against the wall, his face contorted in pain. Blood flowed from his mutilated hand.

'Fuck, fuck, fuck.' Russo's left hand moved to what was left of his right one. 'Are you fucking insane? You're a fucking cop, man. You can't do this.'

'The time frame.'

'We waited six to eight months, man. Six to eight months.' Spit flew from Russo's mouth. 'I'm going to fucking sue your ass, you motherfucker. I'm going to fucking sue the whole police department for this shit. You can say goodbye to your fucking badge, do you hear me?'

'You're as stupid as you look, do you know that?' Mr. J said. 'Let me ask you something. Do you know what this tube, this extension to the barrel of my gun is?'

The pain in Russo's face was blurred by confusion.

'Well, do you?'

'Yeah, it's a fucking muffler, a silencer, so what?'

The smirk was now on Mr. J's lips. 'How many cops do you know walk around with a silenced gun?'

Russo's eyes widened.

The bullet hit him inch-perfect right between them.

As Mr. J exited the house through the kitchen door, he stopped by Toby, still unconscious on the floor.

Calmly, Mr. J grabbed Toby's head with both hands and, in one swift but firm move, snapped his neck from left to right.

Ninety

Hunter stood before a large organizational board divided into twelve columns. Each column started with a photograph of the person it represented. There were eight women and four men. Underneath each image, a printed sheet carried all sorts of information about the subject on the picture – name, address, age, phone number and so on. The very last item on every sheet read: 'Question to be asked'. A red 'X' had been drawn over the faces of three of the twelve subjects. Three faces which were now very familiar to Hunter, but the twist was, they didn't belong to the three victims of the 'video-call killer'.

As Hunter's eyes studied the subject pictures, he felt sick, his stomach twisting inside of him, because he had been right.

The photographs on the board had all been downloaded from social media websites. They were the exact same photographs Hunter had been looking at back in his office.

'How could I have failed to notice this before?'

Click.

The sound of a round being chambered into a semi-automatic pistol came from just a few feet behind Hunter.

'If I were you, I'd put that gun down, Detective.'

As Hunter recognized the male voice, his muscles tensed and his finger curved itself firmly over the trigger of his H&K Mark 23.

'Do you really think you're fast enough?' the killer asked, as if reading Hunter's thoughts.

Hunter was a great marksman and a very fast mover, he knew that, but being able to spin around and squeeze a shot before the killer's bullet got to him first was a trick he didn't think he could pull off.

'Drop the gun, Detective,' the killer said one more time, his voice unaltered, 'or I'll blow your head off, and since the weapon I'm holding is a three fifty-seven Magnum, which I'm sure you're familiar with, it *will blow* your head clean off your shoulders. The only way that they will be able to identify you, after scooping your brains off that wall, will be through fingerprints or DNA.'

'You should know that well enough, Nick,' Hunter replied. 'After all, that's where your expertise lies, isn't it? Fingerprints.'

Nicholas Holden, the fingerprint expert forensic agent from Dr. Slater's team, smiled. 'Well, since you are in my basement uninvited, it's obvious that you figured out who I was. I'm intrigued by how you did it, because I know I've made no mistakes, but we'll get to that soon enough. Now, drop your weapon, or this conversation is about to end very badly, at least for you.'

Hunter closed his eyes and cursed himself. Walking into that basement alone had been a mistake. He should've trusted the tingling sensation he'd got moments earlier. He should've called for backup. There were too many shelving units down in that basement. Too many places one could hide behind.

There was no way that he could've secured that whole area single-handed. What he should've done was have a SWAT team with him.

All a little too late now.

'Arms wide open, Detective. Weapon dangling from your *left* index finger.'

Too many shelving units down in that basement. Too many places one could hide behind – that worked both ways. If Holden could hide behind them, so could Hunter ... or so he thought.

Without turning his head, Hunter's eyes quickly moved left then right. The closest shelving unit to him was on the left, but it was about seven feet away – way too far for him to get to before a bullet either blew his head off or added a hole the size of a grapefruit to his back.

'Still wondering if you're quick enough, Detective?' Holden asked. 'Why don't you give it a go and we'll find out. My money is on me. Want to take that bet?'

No reply.

'Arms wide open, Detective,' Holden repeated. 'Weapon dangling from your left index finger. Do it now.'

Hunter knew he had no other option but to comply. He took a deep breath and did as he was told.

'Now, toss it to your left. Don't drop it, *toss it*, and make me believe you mean it.'

Hunter didn't move.

'*Now*, Detective.'

Angering a man holding a three fifty-seven Magnum was a mistake in any imaginable scenario. Angering a serial killer holding a three fifty-seven Magnum was just plain stupid.

Hunter flicked his wrist firmly and his weapon flew across

the room. As it hit the floor several feet away, it slid up to a cardboard box by a shelving unit. Hunter followed it with his eyes.

'Keep your arms wide open, Detective,' Holden said. 'They come down, you go down, minus a head, is that clear?'

'Crystal.'

There was a long silent pause and Hunter couldn't help but wonder if he was about to get shot in the back anyway. What did the killer have to lose? He'd already killed three people, and according to his 'death board', there were nine more still to come. Adding Hunter to that list wouldn't make a difference.

'Admit it, Detective ...' Holden finally broke the silence. Hunter could tell he had moved a little to his left. 'You're impressed by my work, aren't you?'

Hunter hadn't seen it, but Holden had nodded at the board.

'I'm not sure "impressed" is the word I'd use, Nick.' Despite how fast Hunter's heart was beating, he still managed to keep his voice composed and its pace steady. 'More like ... sickened by it.'

The new pause that followed felt heavy and Hunter wondered if he had just sealed his fate with his poor choice of words.

'That's because you don't understand it, Detective.'

This time Hunter put more thought into his reply. 'What is there to understand, Nick?'

Hunter kept using Holden's first name for a very simple reason – he was trying to insert a subliminal message into his sentences. Trying to make Holden's subconscious mind perceive him as a friend, not an enemy. As he spoke, Hunter's eyes stayed on the board in front of him. The more he looked at it, the more dots he connected.

'You were ... *punishing* innocent people by killing someone they were close to. Someone they loved.'

The three familiar faces with the red 'X' over them didn't belong to the killer's three victims. They belonged to the people who the killer had called – Tanya Kaitlin, John Jenkinson and Erica Barnes. They had been the *real* targets of the 'video-call killer'.

'Innocent?' Holden asked, his tone almost sarcastic. 'Have you looked at the pictures at the top of each column?'

'I have,' Hunter confessed.

'And can't you see what they're doing?' Holden's voice was still calm, but Hunter could tell that anger was starting to creep into it.

'Yes, I can.'

The accident Hunter had read about back in his office was the connecting link between Holden and his targets ... his victims. It was the reason behind all his torturing. The reason behind all his murders.

The accident had happened three and a half years ago in Lancaster, Northern Los Angeles. At around two in the morning, on Sierra Highway – a single-carriageway road that links Los Angeles to Mojave – a blue Ford Fusion driving south crossed over on to the north-heading traffic and collided head-on with a white Saturn S. Both occupants of the Ford Fusion, a couple in their early twenties, died instantly. The Saturn S was carrying a family of four: Nicholas Holden; his wife of ten years, Dora; and both of their daughters, nine-year-old Julie and Megan, seven and a half. Nicholas Holden was the only survivor of that tragic collision.

Back in his office, Hunter had had no trouble accessing the report by the Collision Investigation Unit. The conclusion reached by the investigating detective had been that the accident took place because the driver of the Ford Fusion had diverted her attention off the road. The reason for that, as witnessed by the driver of another car, was that she had been using her cellphone to take a selfie with her boyfriend while the vehicle was moving at speed.

That was the recurring theme on all the photographs on Holden's board – a selfie taken with either friends or family while the subject was driving.

In Tanya Kaitlin's photo, which was the same photo Hunter had come across back in his office, she and Karen Ward had big bright smiles on their faces while Tanya held her cellphone at arm's length. The motion blur that could be seen through the passenger's window left no doubt that the car was moving.

A similar photo had been taken by Mr. J. His wife Cassandra was sitting on the passenger seat, smiling. Their son Patrick was giving them both bunny ears with his fingers from the back seat.

Erica Barnes and her sister, Dr. Gwen Barnes, were both making silly faces at the camera while Erica, the driver, took the shot.

'Did you know that one in every four traffic accidents in the USA is caused as a consequence of a driver using a cellphone?' Holden's voice got angrier. 'One in every four, Detective.'

Hunter knew the statistic, but he remained silent. His arms were starting to tire.

'I lost my entire family that night,' Holden continued.

'My wife, who was thirty-six, and my two daughters. The oldest was nine years old. The youngest, seven. They all died because some stupid woman decided to snap a selfie while driving down a highway, so she could upload it to her god-damn Facebook page. Now is that fair?'

Another piece of the puzzle just slotted into place – social-media websites. That was the reason he searched them.

'I too lost my life that night, Detective,' Holden said. The anger was gone from his voice. 'One moment I had everything to live for – a beautiful wife and two gorgeous daughters – the next ... all gone. My life was left without meaning. My heart had nothing to beat for anymore.'

Another heavy pause.

'After the accident,' Holden continued, 'I spent six months in hospital then another year just ... existing ... vegetating in this world, really. Everything I did, I did robotically, without any meaning. For me, life became nothing more than a vacuum.'

Hunter noticed that Holden's voice had moved again. This time, slightly to the right.

'Despite all the counseling I was given, nothing seemed able to stop the destructive thoughts that tormented me almost daily. Not towards others, but towards myself. Without my family, it didn't seem like I belonged in this world anymore. But isn't life ironic, Detective? When I was finally about to succumb to those destructive thoughts, when I had finally decided that I just couldn't vegetate any longer, I witnessed something that changed my life. As I was sitting at a coffee shop, wondering about the best way to go, I saw a car take out a mother holding a child at a crosswalk. The accident happened because the driver was distracted. Want to have a guess why?'

Hunter didn't need to reply.

'That's right. He was on his fucking cellphone.'

Holden delivered his last sentence with so much anger, Hunter thought he was about to pull the trigger.

'The mother survived. The child didn't. The driver never stopped to help.'

The pause that followed was long.

'What I saw that day, the way it made me feel, ignited something new inside of me.' Holden's voice was back to sounding emotionless. 'That was when it dawned on me that I indeed needed to stop vegetating. Not because I needed to end it all, but because I needed to start living again and I had finally found something to live for.'

'So you started planning,' Hunter said, filling in the blanks.

'So I started planning,' Holden confirmed. 'Getting back to work was easy. My counselor had been pushing me to do it for months. As she had always said – the best thing for me would be to keep busy, to keep my brain occupied. Sitting at home all day would undoubtedly force my mind to wander and, in the state I was in, that wasn't a good thing. I'd probably be digging through memories of the accident or, even worse, harvesting destructive thoughts, which, without her knowledge, I'd been doing since my family's funeral. So when I finally agreed, saying that she was right, that keeping busy and returning to work would be good for me, she signed on to the idea with a wide smile. After that, the real work started.'

'Finding your victims,' Hunter said, his eyes still on the board in front of him.

'That's right. I began browsing through social-media sites,

looking for anyone who had, at any time, posted a selfie taken inside a moving vehicle.' Holden laughed. 'You'd be surprised by what people post on their pages, Detective, by the pictures they upload. You can find out all sorts of personal information on them, on their friends, on their families, you name it. You can find out about their likes, dislikes, their preferences, where they're going to be on a certain day and at what time, what they know, what they don't know, what they *should* know, but don't.' Another animated laugh. 'Social media sites are like a free market of information on people. Information that they, themselves, freely put out there for others to find.'

'So your real target was the person taking the selfie,' Hunter said. 'The people you called, not the people you killed.'

'Of course,' Holden admitted. 'Killing them would've been too easy. That wasn't the point of the exercise.'

An exercise, Hunter thought. *Was that how Holden saw his murders?*

'You know, Detective, I really wish I had died in that car crash, but instead, I got trapped. Did you know that?'

Hunter didn't. It wasn't mentioned in any of the reports he'd read.

'I couldn't free myself from my seat.' Holden paused again, long and heavy. When he spoke, his voice was full of grief. 'My wife and my older daughter didn't die instantly. It took them almost five minutes to go. I had to watch them die right in front of my eyes without being able to do a thing. I was right there, so close, but I couldn't move. I couldn't reach them.'

Hunter breathed in another piece of the puzzle. That had been the reason for the video-calls. Holden wanted his targets to watch the ones they cared for suffer. He wanted them to watch them die, just like he had to watch his family die. He wanted them to feel powerless, just like he had felt that night.

'I hear my daughter's voice every night, Detective: "Please help me, Daddy ... Please help Mommy."' Holden's voice croaked. 'I see their faces every time I close my eyes. Do you understand what sort of destructive feeling comes from being so helpless, Detective?'

Silence.

'DO YOU?'

Hunter nodded. 'Guilt.'

One more piece of the puzzle – the reason for the question game. Holden didn't only want to make his targets watch their loved ones suffer in pain before dying, like he'd had to watch his wife and daughter. He also wanted to give them the false sense of power, the belief that they could save their lives, just so they could experience helplessness in the same way he had. That was where the real pain, the real soul destruction, came from – guilt. It came from the knowledge that they could've made all the difference, if only they'd known the answer to a simple question – an answer that they should've known. Holden wanted *guilt* to be a constant part of his targets' lives, just like it was in his.

Hunter wasn't sure how much longer he would be able to keep his arms up. The pain in his shoulders was starting to blind him. He needed a plan. He needed to think of something and he needed to do it fast.

'Would you like to know how they died, Detective?' Holden asked. 'My family?'

Keep him talking, Hunter thought. *Keep him talking.*

'How?'

'Julie,' Holden said, 'my older daughter, was sitting behind my wife. With the impact, she was catapulted forward like a bullet and, despite being strapped in, her head smashed against the passenger's seat in front of her.' There was a short pause. 'Do you know what a splinter fracture is, Detective?'

Hunter closed his eyes as the last piece of the puzzle slotted into place. Holden's killing methods.

'Yes ... I do.'

'Her little tiny skull was riddled with them. Her brain got punctured thirteen times.' Holden coughed as if he had something lodged in his throat.

Hunter's attention sharpened.

'Megan,' Holden continued, 'my youngest, who was sitting directly behind me, had her face and skull crushed by my seat – like a vise. The crash impact was so violent, my seat broke off its rails and flew back into her. She never had a chance.'

Hunter's shoulder muscles were now in complete agony, too fatigued to keep his arms up for much longer, but logic told him that if his arms were tired, so were Holden's.

They'd been talking for around eight minutes now. A three fifty-seven Magnum semi-automatic pistol weighed around two and a half pounds, which, after eight minutes, would add considerably to the effort his arm muscles had to go through to keep Hunter under aim.

'My wife, Dora, she suffered the worst.' Holden paused again, as if he had to breathe in the strength to explain it. 'The impact caused the windshield to explode into the car and on to the two of us, but because my seat broke off its rails and flew back, she took the bulk of the impact. Her face was completely lacerated by glass. It took her around five minutes to bleed to death. All I could do was look at her ... and scream ... and cry ... but I couldn't get to her. I just couldn't get to her. I couldn't get to my babies.'

Holden's last few words were delivered with a lot of pain and in an almost strangled voice. Hunter couldn't see it, but he had no doubt that tears had come to his eyes.

Teary eyes, tired arms. It was now or never.

Ninety-One

Without being able to turn around to face Holden, Hunter knew that his only chance was to play the odds ... and he had to play them blind.

For the past five minutes he'd been listening attentively to Holden's voice, searching for any sort of oscillation in it, waiting and hoping that the odds would tip his way, even if only for a split second.

Teary eyes, tired arms.

Once again, keeping his head completely still, Hunter's eyes moved left. Seven feet to the nearest shelving unit – way too far for him to make it ... or was it?

From that distance, with his full attention on his target and his gun aimed and ready, Holden just couldn't miss. Hunter was well aware of that, but teary eyes and tired arms would never add up to *full attention* and *aimed and ready*. If Hunter was playing the odds, he had to do it now.

Holden hadn't noticed it, but Hunter had already repositioned his feet. Both of them were now slightly facing left, with his right heel about an inch off the ground, ready for the explosive movement. In the blink of an eye, his right leg pushed forward with all its strength and Hunter's body shot left; but instead of running, he threw himself on to the floor and rolled away as fast as he could.

BOOM.

BOOM.

Inside a confined space like Holden's basement, a three fifty-seven Magnum sounded like an amplified cannon, the defining sound reverberating off the walls in all directions, but Hunter had read the odds like a pro. Revisiting the accident in the way Holden had just done had overwhelmed him with emotions. Tears had indeed come to his eyes, blurring his vision. To compensate for the weight of his gun and to release some of the muscle tension, his weapon arm and his trigger finger had also relaxed a couple of notches. The result had been an attention-lacking, poorly aimed first shot. By the time Holden's mind got back to business and he squeezed the second round, Hunter had almost disappeared behind the shelving unit.

The second bullet missed Hunter by just a fraction, exploding against the concrete floor and sending dust and cement pieces flying up in the air.

As Hunter made it to the temporary safety of the shelving unit, he immediately got to his feet; but, as he looked up, desolation hit him. All he seemed to have done was delay the inevitable. Without being able to turn his head to have a proper look, Hunter's assessment of his escape route had been limited by what he could see from rotating his eyeballs as far left as they would go. Now that he could see clearly, there was no escape route.

Hunter had thrown himself into a makeshift corridor. To one side he had a brick wall, to the other, solid shelving units with no break in between them. The only way Hunter could get out of that corridor was if he ran all the way to the end of it and ducked behind the last unit again, but that was way too far. There was no way he could make it there before Holden rounded the first unit and fired another shot at him, and this time, Hunter wasn't so sure Holden would miss.

Think, damnit, think.

Hunter did the only thing he could do. He played the odds again.

Holden had done exactly what Hunter had expected him to do – he had run forward, towards the shelving unit that Hunter had ducked behind, gun poised, ready to blast another shot at him. Hunter, on the other hand, didn't do the expected. He didn't run down the makeshift corridor towards the last unit. He did the exact opposite. He ran back to where he had just come from.

Hunter's timing couldn't have been more perfect. As Holden began rounding the shelving unit, expecting Hunter to be running scared towards the other end of the room, Hunter collided with Holden's six-foot-one frame with maximum force. The difference was, Holden wasn't expecting it – Hunter was.

Hunter had thrown himself forward headfirst, which hit Holden square in the chest. Reflexively, Holden's finger squeezed the trigger on his weapon, but the impact had been so brutal that he was hurled back several feet. His gun hand moved up and the shot went astray, hitting the ceiling. As he fell backwards, he lost his grip on his gun, which hit the floor and disappeared under a shelving unit. Gasping for air and with pain already burning through his ribs, Holden landed on his back awkwardly, crashing hard against the concrete floor. At that exact moment, Hunter and Holden's eyes met and for a heartbeat everything switched to slow motion. Hunter saw the ugly scar on Holden's chin contort out of shape and he paused. He hadn't seen it before. How could he never have seen it before? The thick scar traversed Holden's entire chin, from the left edge of his lip, across his jaw and cheek, disappearing just under his right ear.

It was then that Hunter realized why the image of Holden's eyes had come back to him so vividly back in his office – Hunter had never seen Nicholas Holden's face in full. They had only met a few times, all of them at crime scenes. With a nose mask always covering the bottom half of his face and the hood of his Tyvek coverall always pulled tight over his head, all Hunter had ever seen of Holden's face were his eyes.

By the time Holden realized what had happened, it was too late ... for him at least.

With one giant step, Hunter was already over him. All it took was one well-placed hit to Holden's left temple.

Lights out.

Ninety-Two

Twelve hours later

Police Administration Building

Hunter and Garcia were both at their desks, filling in paperwork, when Captain Blake stepped into their office.

'OK,' she said in a half surprised, half confused tone. 'How did this happen? Somebody please explain it to me.'

Both detectives paused and looked back at her.

'Yesterday when I left my office,' the captain began. 'We had two victims and nothing else. No clues, no links between victims, no suspects, nothing. Our press office was getting ready to release a short, but expertly bullshit-filled statement.'

Garcia curbed a smile.

'Don't you start,' the captain said, pointing a finger at him.

'I didn't say anything.' Garcia surrendered with his hands up.

'That was yesterday,' Captain Blake continued. 'I get in here today and I find out that not only did we have a brand new victim overnight, but the whole case has been wrapped up. Done and dusted. The "video-call killer" is sitting in a goddamn cell downstairs. And, as I understand it, he was one of the forensic agents who had been working the scenes?' Her eyebrows lifted as the palms of her hands flipped upwards. 'How did we move from "nothing" to "done" in just a few hours? What the hell happened overnight?'

Garcia pointed at Hunter. 'Robert happened, Captain. What else? I was still wrapping things up at the crime scene.' The look he gave Hunter could silence a small crowd. 'He didn't even give me a courtesy call to let me know what was going on. And I'm his *partner.*'

'I didn't really know what was going on.' Hunter's gaze moved first to Garcia then to Captain Blake. He then proceeded to tell her how the events of last night had unfolded. He showed her the screenshot Erica Barnes had captured on her cellphone and the upside-down heart-shaped blood clot in the killer's left eye. He told her how he was certain he had seen that same blood clot before, but he just couldn't remember where, or in whose eyes, until he knocked a file from his desk on to the floor. As he picked up the scattered pieces of paper, his eyes settled on a fingerprint sheet.

Fingerprints ... fingerprints ... fingerprints.

That was when his brain finally engaged. Nicholas Holden was a forensic fingerprint expert.

Hunter told Captain Blake about pulling Holden's file, finding out about the accident, then pulling the report from the LAPD Collision Investigation Unit.

'So the blood clot in his left eye had been a consequence of the accident,' Captain Blake said. 'That's why you didn't see it in his file picture.'

'That's right,' Hunter confirmed. 'Scar tissue left from the trauma and hemorrhage in his eye. The photo in his file was taken a few years before that.'

'So how long had he been a forensic agent for?'

'Seven years. The accident happened three and a half years into his career. He spent about five months in hospital and almost a year in counseling therapy, before he asked to be allowed back into work.'

'Seven years? And you've never met him before?' The captain's stare bounced between both detectives.

'Just a couple of times, Captain,' Garcia jumped in. 'Always at crime scenes, always with his nose mask on and the hood of his Tyvek pulled over his head.'

'How come only a couple of times?'

'He used to be a lab technician,' Hunter explained. 'And a very good one at that, apparently. He was also very clever, because he played his cards just right. He spent a year and seven months gathering information on his victims. During that time, he stayed as a lab technician. When he finally decided that he was ready to put his plan into action, he requested to be transferred to the crime-scene field team. That was five months ago.'

'Convenient,' the captain commented.

Hunter then explained that when he read the conclusion reached by the Collision Investigation Unit – that the accident that had claimed Holden's entire family had been caused because the driver of the other vehicle was using her cellphone to take a selfie – something clicked inside Hunter's brain and he remembered the driving selfies he had seen in Tanya Kaitlin and John Jenkinson's social media pages. He remembered them because he had seen them that same day.

He showed Captain Blake both pictures.

'You've got to be kidding,' she said, things finally starting to connect for her.

'That's not all,' Hunter said. 'We got a third victim last night, remember?' He loaded one last picture to his computer screen: another driving selfie – Erica Barnes and her sister, Dr. Gwen Barnes.

For a moment, Captain Blake was lost for words. Just like Hunter and Garcia, she didn't subscribe to the 'coincidence' fan club.

'So if you knew Nicholas Holden was your man,' she said at last, 'why didn't you get a SWAT team to storm his place? Why didn't you call Garcia? Why the hell did you go down there by yourself?'

Garcia looked at Hunter with the same crowd-silencing look from before. 'Yes, why didn't you call your *partner*?'

'Because my whole theory was based on a memory, Captain. No matter how certain I believed I was, I had no real proof that Holden was the "video-call" killer. For that I needed confirmation that he really did have that same heart-shaped blood clot in his left eye, because that was the only *real* piece of evidence we had that could identify the killer.'

'Ha,' Garcia laughed. 'Now tell her about your plan on how to get that confirmation.'

Captain Blake looked at Hunter questioningly.

'I didn't really have a plan,' Hunter began. 'I didn't really know what to do, but I knew that I had come across all of this new mind-boggling information in the space of an hour. Information that had potentially given us the killer's iden-tity, and I didn't want to sit on it until the morning to get confirmation.'

'So he grabbed a fingerprint sheet from a case.' Garcia took over. 'Any case, it didn't matter, and drove to Holden's house.'

Captain Blake began to understand Garcia's amusement. 'Oh, please don't tell me that your plan was to knock on his door with the excuse of asking him for his expert opinion on something ... at around two in the morning.'

Garcia's smile brightened. 'Got it in one, Captain. That *was* his plan. Foolproof, don't you think?'

The captain laughed.

'OK, I agree, it was a crap plan,' Hunter said. 'But it somehow worked out in the end.'

He then told Captain Blake about everything that had happened from the time he got into Holden's house, until the time he called it in.

'Twelve people on the board?' the captain asked, the amusement gone from her voice, her eyes full of shock.

'The daunting thing is,' Hunter said. 'That was supposed to be just the beginning. He wasn't going to stop after those twelve.'

Shock morphed into bewilderment. 'What?'

'Nicholas Holden's mind is ... broken,' Hunter said. 'The anger, the pain, the guilt, the never-ending heartache ... it had all become way too much for him to take. It was destroying him from inside. The only way his mind could cope was by finding some sort of escape valve. A release from everything – the pain, the guilt, the anger. In his own words: something that could give his life a new purpose – a new meaning.'

'So he decided to blame every driver in the world for his family's death?' Anger accented her words.

'No, not every driver,' Hunter said. 'Only the ones on whom he could find evidence that they had taken a selfie while driving. In his mind, because ultimately that had been the action that had caused the demise of his entire family, they were all as guilty as the driver of that blue Ford Fusion.'

'That's just ridiculous.' The captain shook her head.

'It happens every day and all around the world, Captain,' Hunter commented. 'Racism, sexism, homophobia ... it's all stereotyping. That's what Holden was doing – stereotyping down to a very personal level.'

Captain Blake hadn't thought about it in that way. 'Is he talking?' she asked. 'Have you interviewed him yet?'

'We've tried,' Garcia confirmed, 'but he lawyered up from the get-go. He isn't saying a word.'

'I would expect nothing else,' the captain said.

'We just got back from Holden's house about an hour ago,' Garcia informed her. 'Our team is still there, searching it for more evidence, but one thing that we already know for sure is that the twelve people on his "death board" were really just the beginning. The few he had found since he started trolling social-media sites, the ones he already had everything planned for, including which questions to ask. IT forensics have just started working on the two laptops we've found down in his basement, so God knows what else we might find, but on paper notes alone we've found evidence that he was already collecting data on at least five new people. Five new victims.'

'Ten,' Hunter corrected him.

'What?' Captain Blake seemed unsure.

'Every one of Holden's victims counts for two,' Hunter clarified. 'The person he kills and the person he psychologic-ally destroys, remember? The one who he considers his real target. The one he calls.'

'OK,' Captain Blake said, shattering the silence that had

ruled the room for almost half a minute. 'I can just about understand how his sick mind managed to blame all these innocent people for his family's death. I can just about understand the reason for the video-calls, the question game, the guilt, the helplessness, all of that, but why the notes? Why the stalker MO?'

Hunter called her attention to the picture board. 'Have a look at our investigation, Captain. Where do you think we were going with it?'

The penny finally dropped for Captain Blake. 'Down the wrong path.'

'His mind may be broken, but he's not stupid,' Garcia commented. 'He's a forensic agent. He has internal and detailed knowledge of how we work. He understands investigative procedures better than any criminal out there. He gives us something as real as a physical note found inside the victims' houses and he's got us chasing ghosts for years.'

'Maybe forever,' Hunter said. 'Without Erica Barnes' screenshot, I'm not sure how long it would've taken us to get to him. If we ever did. Holden didn't make a mistake, Captain. We just got lucky.'

'The worst of it all is,' Garcia said, 'I'm sure that they're going to use the "broken mind" defense when the time comes. They're going to say that his pain, his heartache, all of it, warped his perception of the world and of everyone around him. That he was acting with diminished mental capacity. That he was – and here's that word we all love so much – "insane", and with all that, he'll probably be sent to a psychiatric institution.'

Captain Blake made her way to the door. 'That's up to a judge and a jury, Carlos, you know that. It's not our concern.

Our job was to catch him and stop him from killing again and we did exactly that, so congratulations on a job well done.' She paused as she pulled the door open. 'Once all that paperwork is done I want the both of you to take a break, do you understand? Take the next couple of days off. That's an order. I see any of your faces in this building in the next two days and you'll be issuing parking tickets in Compton.'

'That's an order that I won't contest,' Garcia said as the captain exited their office.

'Neither will I,' Hunter agreed.

'Since we have a couple of days off, why don't you come over for dinner tonight, Robert? Anna would love to see you.' Garcia followed those words with a cheeky smile. 'You can even bring your date, if you like.'

Hunter locked eyes with his partner.

'You know, the one whose lipstick you were wearing last night.'

Hunter smiled back.

'Who knows, maybe I will.'

Ninety-Three

One month later

A psychiatric facility in California

The corridor was long and wide, brightly lit by a single row of fluorescent lights that ran down the center of the ceiling. The scent that lingered in the air was ... complicated. It started with a heavy antiseptic smell, as if the entire place had just been deep-cleaned by someone with a severe phobia of germs, but with every couple of steps, he would get hints of different odors – sometimes vomit, sometimes blood, sometimes something he just couldn't identify. The smell seemed to emanate from the squeaky-clean floor and bounce against the insanely white walls before hitting his nose. Despite how repugnant it was, the smell didn't really bother him.

He walked calmly, with neutral steps. He hadn't been there long, but he already hated the place. The good news for him was – he would be leaving soon.

He turned the corner and pushed through a heavy set of double doors. There it was again, the smell of vomit, as if it'd been hiding behind the door, waiting for him to come through before slapping him in the face. He ignored it, turned another corner and finally stopped before a thick metal door with a small window at eye level. He didn't look through the window. He didn't need to. He simply unlocked the door and stepped inside.

Nicholas Holden, who was lying on his bed, flipping through a magazine, looked up.

The man placed the square box he had with him on the floor and the two of them regarded each other in silence for a moment.

'Who the hell are you?' Holden asked.

'I'm the one you called,' the man replied, closing the door behind him.

'Wrong cell, buddy. I didn't call anyone.'

From his pocket, Mr. J retrieved a picture of Cassandra and showed it to Holden.

'Are you sure about that?'

Ninety-Four

The next day, 8:24 a.m.

The small, nondescript café was located in Chatsworth Street, sandwiched between an auto brokers and a Chinese restaurant. It wasn't a large place, but the coffee was decent, the service was good and their blueberry pancakes were literally something to write home about. Mr. J had just finished the last of his three pancakes, which had been covered in maple syrup, when he sensed someone approaching from behind and pausing about two paces from his table. He twisted his neck and looked up to find Hunter standing there.

'Detective?' he said with a quizzical look.

'Mr. Jenkinson,' Hunter said in reply. 'I'm sorry for interrupting your breakfast.'

'Oh no, not at all. I'm all done here.' Mr. J pushed his plate away from him. 'Please have a seat.' He indicated the empty chair across the table from him.

'Thank you.' Hunter accepted it, taking the seat.

They locked eyes for several silent seconds.

'Could I get you a cup of coffee, Detective? The coffee here is excellent.'

'No, I'm fine, thank you.'

Mr. J searched Hunter's expression but the detective was giving nothing away.

'Is something the matter?' he asked.

Hunter paused before nodding. 'I'm actually here on official business.'

'OK.' Once again, Mr. J's acting was impeccable. The concern he inflected into his voice was perfectly balanced. 'What ... sort of official business?'

'I'm here to inform you of a new development in your wife's murder investigation.'

Mr. J frowned. 'A new development? How so?' His concern intensified.

'As you know,' Hunter began, 'Nicholas Holden has been confined to a psychiatric hospital while awaiting trial.'

'Yeah.' Mr. J placed his elbows on the table and interlaced his fingers. 'Please tell me you're not here to say that that sack o' shit has escaped.'

'No, he hasn't.'

Mr. J breathed out.

'But he also won't be facing trial anymore.'

'What? What the fuck do you mean, Detective – he won't be facing trial anymore?' The anger, the voice intonation, the wide eyes, all of it was delivered flawlessly.

Hunter was still studying Mr. J's face. 'He won't be facing trial anymore because he was murdered in his cell late last night.'

'Murdered?'

'That's correct.'

Mr. J pretended to take a moment to think about it. 'How can you be sure, Detective? How can you be sure that that scumbag didn't take the easy way out himself? That fucking coward.'

'It wasn't suicide,' Hunter assured him.

'And how could you know that?'

'Because the skin was ripped from his face and his heart was cut out from his chest and left on the floor,' Hunter explained. 'Rats were feasting on it when they found him in the early hours of this morning.'

'Rats?'

Hunter nodded. 'No one has any idea where they came from or how they got into his cell. The hospital never had a problem with rats. The speculation is that whoever killed him, brought them with him.'

'Brought the rats with him?'

Hunter nodded.

Mr. J sat back on his chair with a shocked look on his face, his eyes wandering aimlessly.

Hunter regarded Mr. J for several long silent seconds before standing up. 'I thought you'd like to know,' he said. 'I figured that it would be better if you heard it from me than if you found out through the papers or the morning news.'

Hunter turned to leave.

'Detective,' Mr. J called.

Hunter faced him again.

'What's going to happen now? Are *you* going to chase his killer?'

'No.' Hunter shook his head. 'He was already a guest of an official institution of the California Penal System. The crime occurred inside their own estate facility. They have their own internal investigators for that sort of crime.'

'One last thing before you go.' Mr. J stopped Hunter again.

'How did you find him in the first place? You never told me that. How did you figure out who the killer was?'

Hunter locked eyes with Mr. J for the last time. For several seconds, neither of them blinked.

'His eyes,' he finally replied. 'There's always something in a killer's eyes that gives it away.' Hunter gave Mr. J a subtle wink. 'You take care ... *Mr. J.*' He turned and exited the café.

Acknowledgements

I am tremendously grateful to several people without whom this novel would've never been possible.

My agent, Darley Anderson, who's not only the best agent an author could ever hope for, but also a true friend. Everyone at the Darley Anderson Literary Agency for their never-ending strive to promote my work anywhere and everywhere possible.

Jo Dickinson, my amazing editor at Simon & Schuster and my literary Guardian Angel, whose comments, suggestions, knowledge and friendship I could never do without.

Everyone at Simon & Schuster for their tremendous support and belief and for working their socks off on every aspect of the publishing process.

My incredible partner, Kara Louise – my rock and at the same time my cushion – who was always there for me, listening to so many of my terrible ideas, chapters, paragraphs and tantrums. Thank you for putting up with me.

My most sincere thanks goes to all of my readers around the world for the most incredible support over so many years. From the bottom of my heart, I thank you all.

Love Robert Hunter?
Read on to find out where it all began . . .

THE HUNTER

Available now in eBook

**SIMON &
SCHUSTER**

London · New York · Sydney · Toronto · New Delhi

A CBS COMPANY

Chapter 1

'You have got to be kidding me,' Detective Scott Wilson of the LAPD Robbery Homicide Division said, as if he'd just heard the world's unfunniest joke.

Wilson was standing inside Captain William Bolter's office, staring at the piece of paper the captain had just handed him.

'You're dumping a suicide case on me, captain?' Wilson asked, still looking dumbfounded.

Captain Bolter was in his mid-fifties, but looked at least ten years younger. Tall, strong, and sporting a full head of peppery hair together with a thick mustache, the man was a menacing figure, respected by everyone in the force. He looked at his detective and shrugged matter-of-factly.

'What are you complaining about?' he said, returning to his seat behind his large and very messy desk. 'I thought you all liked easy cases.' He nodded at the piece of paper in Wilson's hands. 'They don't come much easier than that. The woman sliced her wrists and bled to death in her bed. It's an open-and-shut case.'

The law in the state of California stipulated that suicides had to be initially treated as homicides; therefore, a homicide detective would have to attend the site and commence investigative procedures to rule out foul play. Once that was done, the investigation, as far as the LAPD Robbery Homicide Division was concerned, could be closed and archived. It would be the work of twenty-four to forty-eight hours.

'Yeah,' Wilson said, placing the piece of paper back on the captain's desk. 'I love open-and-shut cases, but suicides are a hell of a lot of paperwork, captain, and you know it. Paperwork that needs to be done and filed ASAP.' He pointed to the main detectives' floor. 'I've got fourteen open homicide investigations sitting on my desk right now, captain. I'm up to my eyeballs in crap. I barely have time to take a piss, and you want me to throw one, maybe two days away because some rich bitch topped herself?'

'Well, somebody's got to do it.'

'Give it to Perez,' Wilson suggested. 'He loves paperwork.'

'Perez is in hospital. He took a bullet last week, remember?' Captain Bolter shook his head. 'Sorry, buddy. You're it. I've got no one else.'

A knock came to the captain's door.

'Come in,' the captain called out.

The door was pushed open by a young man in his mid-twenties, wearing a dark suit that looked rather uncomfortable on him. He was about six-feet tall with broad shoulders and a very powerful-looking physique. His youthful face had a certain serenity to it, the kind that suggested trustworthiness and determination. His eyes possessed a penetrating quality easily associated with self-confidence, but not the cocky kind.

'And who the hell might you be?' Captain Bolter asked, narrowing his eyes.

The young man stepped inside, closed the door behind him, and approached the captain's desk. 'My name is Robert Hunter, sir, I'm your new detective.' He handed over several signed forms he had brought with him.

'Wrong floor, kid,' Wilson said, pointing at the door again. 'This is the Robbery Homicide Division – the big boys. You're probably looking for Commercial Crimes or Support. Both of those are two floors below.'

Hunter nodded. 'Yes, I know, thank you, but I'm on the right floor, and in the right division.'

Wilson chuckled. 'You're joking right? You don't even look old enough to shave.'

Hunter wasn't surprised by Wilson's skepticism. In average it took a LAPD officer at least six years of street-crime-fighting before he was allowed to put in a request for a detective's position. If successful, it would then take a detective another four to five years, together with an impressive track record and a captain's recommendation, before he'd even be considered for a position with the Robbery Homicide Division's elite. And even then, very few were accepted into the RHD. The division was considered to be the top of the ladder when it came to being a LAPD Detective. Wilson had never heard of anyone younger than thirty-something reaching that position.

Hunter was also well aware of that fact. His main goal, once he'd joined the LAPD, was always to make Detective for the Robbery Homicide Division. Deep inside he had to admit that he was very proud of having scorched through the ranks at record speed.

Captain Bolter had forgotten all about the new detective who was supposed to be starting today. Some sort of prodigy kid with a PhD in Criminal Behavior Psychology, who, according to what the captain had been told, had turned down a position with the FBI to join the LAPD.

The captain quickly flipped through the forms. The young detective's records sure looked impressive, and all the documentation seemed in order.

'Is this for real, captain?' Wilson asked, pointing at Hunter. 'Baby-faced, pretty-boy, bible-salesman-looking kid-in-a-cheap-suit here is joining the division?'

Hunter frowned and looked at his suit. He liked that suit. It was his best suit. His only suit.

'That's what the paperwork says,' the captain agreed, placing the forms down on his desk.

Hunter turned and faced Wilson. 'Robert Hunter,' he said, extending his hand. 'It's a pleasure to meet you, detective . . . ?'

Wilson ignored the newbie's hand. 'Yeah, I'm sure it is.' He was still looking at Captain Bolter. 'Damn, are we recruiting out of kindergarten now, captain? Is the department that despera . . .' He paused, his eyes settling on the piece of paper he had placed on the captain's desk just moments ago. 'Problem solved,' he said, shrugging at Captain Bolter and reaching for the note.

The captain hesitated for a split second and then shrugged back as if saying 'why not?'.

Wilson turned towards Hunter. 'I'm Detective Wilson, but you can call me "Sir",' he said, handing the note to Hunter. 'Welcome to the Robbery Homicide Division, pretty boy. Enjoy your first easy case, because it will only get worse.' He paused before reaching the door. 'Oh, and do me a favor – get rid of that cheap suit, will you? You look like an idiot.'

Chapter 2

The apartment was on the twenty-eighth floor of a towering block in Cypress Park, a working-class neighborhood in Northeast Los Angeles.

Hunter exited the claustrophobic elevator and found himself at the end of a long corridor with brick walls, lined with doors on both sides – twenty-four in total. A strip of tube lights that ran down the center of the ceiling kept the hallway bright. The apartment he was looking for was number 2813, located about halfway down the corridor on the right-hand side. A uniformed officer was standing just outside the door. He looked bored. Hunter proudly flashed his new and shiny Detective's badge at him and pushed the door open.

The first thing he noticed was that the safety chain hung from the door, its wall mounting dangling from the chain's end. The doorframe had cracked and splintered where the four screws had once secured the metal mounting to the wood.

'We had to kick it open,' a senior police officer standing in the living room explained.

Hunter turned and looked at him.

'I'm Officer Travis,' the policeman said. 'My partner and I were patrolling just a block from here when we received a call from Central Bureau's dispatch to come knock on the victim's door. Her mother, who is confined to a wheelchair, had been unable to get in touch with her for three days, which I know, isn't that unusual, except for the fact that the daughter visited her mother every Monday without fail. Had done so for the past two years. According to the mother, if the daughter were going to be even a little late, she would always let her mother know in advance. If her car had broken down or something, she would've called. This afternoon the mother called the station worried sick. The daughter is bipolar, which can sometimes complicate things.'

Hunter's eyebrows arched.

'Anyway,' Travis moved on. 'We came by, knocked, but got no response. We called the building's superintendent, who unlocked the door for us, but the safety chain was on, and there was this faint smell of putrid meat coming from somewhere inside. Obviously something was wrong. That was when we rammed the door and broke in. We found the daughter in the bedroom.' He threw his thumb over his shoulder, pulling an 'I'm sorry' face.

'Had she attempted suicide before?' Hunter asked.

'If she had, it wasn't mentioned.'

Hunter nodded and allowed his eyes to circle the living room for an instant. It was spacious enough, decorated on a budget but with plenty of style. A black leatherette sofa, positioned at the edge of a fluffy black and red rug, faced a shiny black and white TV module. There was also a glass and chrome four-seater dinner table, a chest of drawers that matched the TV module, a stylish black console by the window, and a very elegant bookcase with no books, just decorative artifacts like vases, glass bowls and candle holders.

Crossing to the other side of the room, Hunter slipped on a couple of blue, plastic shoe-covers, a pair of latex gloves, a mouth and nose mask, and pushed the bedroom door open. Officer Travis followed him in.

The air inside the bedroom was hot, stuffy, and heavy with the sickening smell of dead flesh as it entered rotting stage.

Hunter's attention was immediately drawn to the queen-size bed with its headboard pushed up against the north wall. Lying on the blood-soaked bed sheets was the naked body of a five-feet-six brunette woman. From the note Detective Wilson had handed him, Hunter knew that she was only thirty-three years old. Her name was Helen Webster, and she was a self-employed interior designer.

A Medical Examiner was standing by a dresser unit near the window, quietly speaking on his cellphone. He quickly terminated the call as he saw Hunter and the officer enter the room.

'Are you from Homicide?' he asked, looking a little dubious.

Hunter nodded and quickly introduced himself.

The doctor looked surprised but he refrained from asking the detective how old he was.

Hunter approached the bed, being careful to avoid the large pools of dried blood that had formed on the floor. The curtains on the window to the left of the bed were speckled with blood, and so were both bedside tables. Hunter noted the pattern, before his attention reverted back to the woman.

Blisters, caused by the release of gases from body tissues, had already started to form all over the woman's body. Her skin had taken on a greenish-blue color, but body bloating was still in its very early stages. That, together with a few blowflies buzzing around the bed, told Hunter that she'd been dead for at least thirty-six hours. She was lying on her back. Her legs were close together and stretched out. Her arms were wide open, as if she was ready to hug a long-lost relative, but her wrists had both been cut horizontally. Two large and deep incisions that had clearly severed the main blood vessels in the forearms.

'Rigor mortis has come and gone,' the ME said. 'From the state of the body I can tell you that she's been dead for no less than thirty-six hours, and no longer than seventy-two. We'll be able to get a better time frame after the autopsy.'

Hunter nodded, still studying the body. 'What did she use on her wrists?'

'This.' The doctor showed Hunter a clear plastic evidence bag. Inside it was a blood-covered utility knife. 'It was on the floor by the right side of the bed,' the doctor clarified.

Hunter bent down to get a better look at the woman's hands, wrists, and arms. 'She's been photographed, right?' he asked. 'Is it OK if I disturb the body a little, Doc?'

The doctor nodded before shrugging. 'Suit yourself. My work here is pretty much done.'

Hunter used his index finger to clear some of the dried blood from the woman's wrists, and took his time examining the cuts.

'The incisions were deep and precise,' the doctor offered. 'Even before the autopsy I can tell you that they have severed both the radial and the ulnar arteries. Blood loss was intense and fast. Over fifty percent, I'd say.' He indicated the pools of blood on the floor. 'Which would have caused her to go into hypovolemic shock, leading to heart failure.'

'Was there a suicide note?' Hunter asked.

'None that we have found,' Officer Travis replied.

Hunter found that peculiar but carried on studying the woman's hands and fingers.

'Now,' the doctor said, approaching the body. 'Let me show you something interesting.' From his coat pocket he produced a pen-sized Maglite and a small magnifying glass before using his thumb and index finger to pull open her eyelids. 'Have a look,' he said.

Hunter moved closer.

Travis followed.

Her corneas were cloudy and opaque, which was expected, but the eyes and their lids were dotted with tiny red specks.

Hunter frowned. 'Petechiae?'

The doctor looked back at him, impressed. He wasn't expecting a detective to recognize the condition he was looking at, especially such a young detective.

'Pâté ... what?' Travis asked, trying to look over Hunter's shoulders.

'Petechiae,' the doctor repeated. 'They are tiny hemorrhages in blood vessels. They can occur anywhere in the body, and for a number of reasons, but when they occur on the eyes and eyelids like we have here, it is usually due to blockage of the respiratory system. In other words – suffocation.'

Hunter stood up again and started looking around the room.

'What?' The officer's gaze moved from the doctor to Hunter, and then back to the ME. 'But you just said that she died from severe loss of blood and heart failure. Are now you telling me she was strangled?'

'Not to death,' the doctor clarified. 'She did die from blood loss from her wrist wounds, which led to heart failure, but this indicates that she suffered some sort of severe blockage of the respiratory system prior to death.'

Travis chewed on his bottom lip and looked at Hunter once again, who was now having a look inside a shoebox on the floor by the dresser unit.

'So what are you saying?' Travis asked with a slight head-shake. 'That she first tried strangling herself or something, gave up halfway through, and then went for "plan B" – slicing her wrists?'

'No,' Hunter replied, checking some drawers. 'Someone else knocked her unconscious by suffocating or strangling her, before slicing her wrists and staging the suicide scene. This . . .' He indicated the body on the bed. 'Was a homicide.'

The officer's eyes widened in disbelief. 'A homicide? But the only way in or out of this apartment is through the front door.' He threw his thumb over his shoulder again. 'It was locked from the inside, remember? The safety chain was securely in place. We had to kick the door in. The windows in here don't open due to safety regulations. This is the twenty-eighth floor, way too windy. If somebody killed her, how did he or she get out?'

'That's the part I still need to figure out,' Hunter said.

Travis rolled his eyes. 'Of course you do.'

Hunter could easily tell what Officer Travis was thinking: why did they have to send a rookie?

But Travis wasn't finished yet. 'And you are basing this homicide theory of yours simply on that pâté-whatever thing? Little blood dots on her eyes and eyelids due to oxygen restriction? Maybe it's a sexual thing- erotic asphyxiation. Have you heard of it? Some people are into that. It's supposed to heighten the ecstasy. Look, I'm sure that you would love to impress your captain, but I don't think this is the case . . . *sir.*' Travis put a lot of emphasis on that last word.

Hunter knew he didn't have to explain himself to anyone in that room. He was the lead detective in the investigation, and that gave him the right to call the shots as he saw fit, but since this was his first ever investigation as a RHD Detective he decided, just for the sake of clarity, to better explain his reasons.

'You said that there was no suicide note, right?' he said.

'That's right,' Travis confirmed.

'Well, that's problem number one – in ninety-nine percent of suicide cases, there's a note. It follows an overwhelming feeling of guilt that comes with every suicide act. Victims will, inevitably, feel the need to explain their decision to go down such a drastic road. That note is their last ever statement in this world and, believe me, they all want to make it, even if it's only an 'I love you mom, and I'm sorry' line. You said that the victim visited her wheelchair-bound mother every Monday. Had done so for the past two years. Trust me, she would've at least wanted her mother to know the reason why she decided to end her life.'

Travis stayed silent, considering Hunter's words.

'Problem number two is her fingernails and toenails,' Hunter said.

Both the officer and the Medical Examiner's gaze moved to the victim's hands and feet.

'What about them?' Travis asked after a couple of seconds.

'They've been recently manicured ... professionally,' Hunter said, still looking around the room. 'Probably no more than three or four days ago. If she was depressed enough to consider suicide, I don't think she would bother grooming herself for it ... or buying a new pair of shoes, do you?' He pointed to the shoebox by the dresser.

The officer and the doctor's gaze shifted again.

'There's a receipt in the box. She bought them three days ago.'

Silence.

'Now,' Hunter turned and faced Officer Travis. 'I need you and your partner to do a door-to-door on this floor. Get statements from everyone. Check if any of the neighbors were friendly with the victim, if anybody saw or heard anything ... you know how it goes. Also, get the building's superintendent up here again.'

Travis scratched his chin, nodded, and left the apartment.

'You will still have to explain how the perp managed to escape through a locked and safety-chained door,' the Medical Examiner said, looking intrigued now.

'I know,' Hunter replied, reaching for his cellphone and requesting a forensics team to come to the scene. Maybe they could help.

Because of the skin discoloration, the blisters, and the initial rotting state of the body, Hunter knew that there was no way the Medical Examiner could tell if the victim had been sexually assaulted without the proper examination and a lab swab test. For now, that would have to wait.

Hunter returned to the living room to re-examine the door and the safety-chain lock. There was no gimmick. The chain and the wall mounting were made of strong metal, and the chain was still securely locked in place. The door's regular key lock hadn't been tampered with, neither had the door hinges, which were tarnished with age. Somebody had really locked that door from the inside.

Time to look around.

THE
DARK
PAGES

Visit The Dark Pages to discover a community of like-minded readers and crime fiction fans.

If you would like more news, exclusive content and the chance to receive advance reading copies of our books before they are published, find us on Facebook, Twitter (**@dark_pages**) or at **www.thedarkpages.co.uk**